EXILES OF TABAT

BOOK 3 OF THE TABAT QUARTET

CAT RAMBO

WFP
WORDFIRE PRESS

EBook ISBN: 978-1-68057-183-7
Trade Paperback ISBN: 978-1-68057-182-0
Hardcover ISBN: 978-1-68057-184-4
Library of Congress Control Number: 2020951456

Cover design by Janet McDonald
Cover artwork images by Shutterstock
Kevin J. Anderson, Art Director

Published by
WordFire Press, LLC
PO Box 1840
Monument CO 80132
Kevin J. Anderson & Rebecca Moesta, Publishers
WordFire Press eBook Edition 2021
WordFire Press Trade Paperback Edition 2021
WordFire Press Hardcover Edition 2021
Printed in the USA

Join our WordFire Press Readers Group for
sneak previews, updates, new projects, and giveaways.
Sign up at wordfirepress.com

BOOK DESCRIPTION

Former Gladiator Bella Kanto has been exiled from her beloved city of Tabat, finding herself aboard a hostile ship bound for a frontier town, her only friend a puppy. She's lost the magic that kept her young and vital, and for the first time is suffering the depredations of age. When she encounters an old lover along the way, she has a chance to escape—but does she really want to take it? And who is the mysterious woman Selene, who keeps appearing to Bella?

Meanwhile, former printer's apprentice Lucy and her friend Maz, a student from the College of Mages, have been kidnapped from Tabat and are being taken to the Southern Isles in search of ancient magic in a place called the Coral Tower. They fear what will happen when they get there, particularly when their kidnapper realizes he's wrong about Lucy's identity.

Dragons, oracular turtles, steam dirigibles, magical artifacts, and more combine in a kaleidoscopic tale that continues the saga of the city of Tabat and its inhabitants.

Return to a beautifully wrought and immersive world where intelligent magical creatures fight for their right to be free in a system that makes use of their work—and sometimes their very bodies—in a city full of revolution and riot, ready for the return of its lost Champion: the reluctant Bella Kanto.

DEDICATION

For my father, whose exile ended in December 2019.

THUS FAR

*T*abat is a city inhabited by both Humans and Beasts. The latter group are intelligent magical creatures, such as Centaurs, Dryads, Minotaurs, and the like. The city's economy is driven by the labor of the enslaved Beasts, as well as by its trade in their body parts, which are used to fuel magical spells and engines, such as the furnaces beneath the city, which burn Dryad logs. Humans have long justified the servitude of Beasts in one way or another, but as the series begins, for the first time, a substantial number of Humans, the political group known as Abolitionists, are arguing that they should be freed.

The boy Teo has been raised in a village of Shapeshifters: beings capable of taking on animal as well as Human form. Especially feared for their abilities, the Shapeshifters must hide their identity from the Humans in order to avoid being exterminated. When Teo's ability to change his shape does not manifest in adolescence as it should, his parents decide to save his terminally ill sister's life by dedicating Teo to the Temples of the Moon Gods in return for a cure, thinking he will be safe enough there.

Teo begins the trip southward to the city of Tabat, where the major Temples are located, with the priest Grave. When Grave is attacked and put out of commission by a sting from a Fairy, Teo is sent by himself on a riverboat, under the eye of a Moon Temple lay member, the river pilot Eloquence Seaborn. The Moon Temples, which worship the world's three moons, are one of two major religious groups in the city, the other being the Trade Gods followed by the upper classes.

Teo arrives in the city of Tabat and escapes his fate of Temple servitude when a fight breaks out at the docks between the ship's cargo and the man who has come to take that cargo to the College of Mages, Sebastiano Silvercloth. Sebastiano is in an odd position—while he studies at the College and they use him to manipulate their money, they also scorn him for the Merchant ties that allow him to do so.

Adrift in the city of Tabat, Teo goes in search of the single person he knows of,, the Gladiator Bella Kanto. Bella Kanto is a charismatic woman who, for the past 30 years, has been determining the outcome of a ritual that controls the yearly weather of Tabat: the annual fight between a Gladiator representing Spring and a Gladiator representing Winter. Bella has won this battle every year for three decades, ensuring that the city has an extra six weeks of winter every year, and people are growing tired of the pattern.

Charismatic and alluring, Bella's romances have become notorious and sometimes complicate her life, as when she breaks things off with a relative of the Duke of Tabat (Marta), who is driven by revenge to conspire with forces working against the Gladiator. When a student, Skye, on the brink of graduating falls in love with Bella, Bella yields to temptation and is soon embroiled in scandal. At the same time, she encounters Teo on the street and takes him in as a servant.

A major source of Bella's fame is the books about her written by her best friend and former lover, Adelina Nittlescent, whose publishing house is funded by the proceeds from the incredibly popular serials about her that Adelina writes for the newssheets known as the penny-wides. Since publishing is considered a disreputable employment, Adelina has kept her ownership and management of the press a secret from most, including her own dictatorial mother, Emiliana.

Emiliana pressures Adelina to run for public office. The city is about to move from being ruled by the Duke of Tabat, a structure established when the city was first settled, to an elected council, in fulfillment of a promise made long ago by the duke's ancestors. Adelina does her best to duck the responsibility, but finally is pressured into making a speech—and fails in a humiliating way. Wanting to succeed, she is tempted by and succumbs to a magical drug supplied to her by a woman she's met, a photographer named Jilly Clearsight.

At the same time, she finds herself encountering Sebastiano, whose father has directed him to find a bride and presented him with three candidates: Lilia, Marta, and Adelina. She is torn between the romantic attraction she feels for Sebastiano and that which she feels for Eloquence Seaborn, who has come to her to see if she will publish his book.

Bella is tricked into killing Skye in gladiatorial combat and withdraws from society, even from her favorite cousin, the artist Leonoa Kanto. Leonoa's paintings have been stirring civil unrest, including riots, due to their abolitionist content, and her own lover Glyndia, while not a Beast, is often mistaken for one due to the curse she is under.

Adelina is unable to comfort Bella; her own life has become increasingly complicated, including taking Eloquence's sister Obedience in as an apprentice, despite his disapproval. The increasingly independent Obedience renounces the Moon Temples and takes on the name Lucy, but when she inadvertently gives away Adelina's greatest secret to her mother, Adelina ousts her. Adelina is torn between Eloquence and Sebastiano, going back and forth before finally confessing her attraction to Sebastiano when she finds him talking with a potential rival, the Duke's huntswoman, Ruhua.

Confused and adrift, Bella is betrayed and drawn into a smuggling scheme of illicit magical supplies that pits her against the strictest laws of Tabat. She is imprisoned, tortured, and sent away from the city before this book begins. She is joined by Teo, although she does not realize it. Transformed into a dog by the Sorcerer Murga, the boy has been given to the Duke of Tabat and breaks free just as Bella's ship is leaving, leaping aboard it at the last minute, driven to join her.

As the book begins, Bella has been exiled from the city she loves with all her heart, knowing that those she leaves behind face riots, political upheaval, and worst of all, the unknown forces that have been working against her. Teo is condemned to doggish form. And Lucy, after trying to find shelter with her friend Maz, a student at the College of Mages, has been kidnapped.

CHAPTER 1

JOURNEY OF THE STOOPING HAWK (BELLA)

*T*hey have killed Bella Kanto; she is dead and gone. What's left is a husk, hollowed out, nothing inside it but air. If someone pushed at it, she would collapse, this ghost. This facsimile of Bella Kanto.

I walk to the cabin's porthole and look out over the ocean that surrounds us. Bella Kanto looks out. Would have looked out. If she were not gone.

I am Bella Kanto, but I am not. It's as though I never knew who I was.

The boat's creak and sway surrounds me, always, always reminding me that I am somewhere other than Tabat. This tiny vessel is not a city, isn't anything like it. The same handful of people every day.

Not that I talk to any of them, or they to me.

Ruhua, the Duke's Huntswoman, wishes to talk, perhaps. She was there at my elbow as we came on board. Hovered near me, watched the sailors bring my boxes aboard.

Perhaps she does not really want to talk. Perhaps she only wants to make sure that I do not jump overboard, that Bella Kanto does not commit suicide even though she is already dead.

I am nothing without my city, without Tabat. It was part of me,

5

it beat in my heart and breathed in my lungs. Now there is wave noise and wood plaint instead of the street bustle, the tumbling of wheels, the calling of vendors. This is nothing like Tabat.

Tabat, which I will never see again.

The thought, which I have tried to ward off, slips through my defenses, hits me like a dagger, like it has every time before. I thought I had gotten away from it. That I could slide my mind sideways and avoid its contemplation, but it comes at unexpected turns, and it is all the more painful when I am unprepared like this.

I miss Tabat. I miss waking in the morning to the mewing of gulls, the whisper and rustle of pines outside my bedroom window, the shrill buzz of the Fairies waiting for me to feed them. They will have forgotten me by now, if Abernia has not summoned someone to put them down, as she was ever threatening to do.

A scratch at the door. If it were a person, I would not answer. But I do. I go to the door and open it just enough for the puppy to slide inside. He snuffles against me, rubbing his head against my shins. Not really a pup, almost full-grown.

Alberic must be angry to have lost this dog. I'd seen him leading it about by the gilt leash that it still trailed when it jumped on board at the last minute. Ruhua confiscated that. She was not happy about the addition, but what could she do, order the ship to turn around for the sake of a mere dog?

The sailors do not mind him, but it is me the dog follows. My door that he slept outside last night since I will not allow him the comfort of my cabin. He wants attention; he wants love. I have nothing to give him, but he follows me still, so I sit now and pet him. I let him rest his head on my knee as I stroke his fuzzy ears. His eyes watch my face with that soulful gaze that only dogs can muster, as though his heart lies open before me, tender and beating.

Bella Kanto deserved such love. I do not.

We sit like that, the dog and I. I have no prescribed regimen for my day. Adelina sent me a box that I think holds books from the press, but I do not like to read. And worse, nowadays it makes my eyes and head hurt as they never have before.

And that is the worst of Bella Kanto being dead. She never felt the aches and twinges of age, never had a cold or sore throat, was always at her peak. I can feel all that age crawling over me, settling into my bones, making my knees ache in the cold mornings, making my back hurt when I have sat too long in one position.

I had grown unaccustomed to making accommodations for my body. Now it demands them as though angered by all those years of neglect.

I threw the little mirror that used to hang on the wall here out the porthole after the first time I looked in it.

Adelina would tell me I am still beautiful, but it's not Bella Kanto's beauty but someone else's. The face of an older, grimmer— so much grimmer—woman with no smile in her eyes.

Not Tabat's Bella Kanto. Whose Bella Kanto am I now? Not Adelina's. We will write back and forth, for a few years perhaps, but she will forget me soon enough.

This cabin stinks of melancholy and stale air. It's where I belong. As good a place as any, at any rate. Bella Kanto doesn't belong anywhere anymore.

The dog noses my hand because I have stopped petting him. I ignore his little whine. There is no point to petting him, there is no point to anything, because there is no point to being Bella Kanto.

What does Ruhua think of Bella Kanto, I wonder? Before all this, we had met, but I never thought much of her. If anything, I thought she might be a little jealous of me, but I always assumed that in those days. Who would be jealous of me now?

She is the Duke's Huntswoman, the one who organizes many of his outings. Not a hereditary position but one appointed. Someone he trusts implicitly. So implicitly that he's willing to lose her services for half a year, so she can do whatever is to be done with me. They say it is exile. Maybe it is, maybe it isn't.

Maybe I'll die mysteriously along the way.

The door swings open and a shadow falls across me. Ruhua stands there in the doorway, prim and neat as always. I cannot imagine her disheveled, but her outfit is not elegant or overly fussy, simply trim of line, the cloth immaculate and unwrinkled. It makes me wonder if there is some magic laid upon her wardrobe, but that's a pricey magic for vanity's sake.

No, it is simply that she is one of those people who is never taken at a loss.

As I used to be.

Now just her presence sends me into a blank abyss. What does she want? There is always a secret terror in me that she is here only to let me get close to escape before she takes me back to that cell. That would be a cruel thing, and Alberic can be cruel.

I swallow and stare at her.

She says, "Come and walk on deck before dinner. You will grow unhealthy sitting and brooding and breathing your own stink. There will be a storm this evening and no chance for fresh air."

Is it an order or a request? I am unsure, but I do not want to find out by denying it and having her force the issue.

Her eyes flit behind me. "You can bring the dog," she says.

Her tone makes me say something I had not planned to. "What is its name?"

"I beg pardon?" she says, politely but as though I had said something absurd.

"The dog. Surely Alberic named him. He seemed to dote on it."

She shakes her head. "I never heard him refer to it. In my next letter I will inquire."

WE WALK ON THE DECK, Ruhua and I. The dog trails me. He keeps to my right, on the opposite side from her, as though he does not trust her. I do not think he would have fallen under her care at any time —he is a healthy young animal, and still intact—so where would he have acquired this dislike?

It makes me not trust her as well. Animals have a way of knowing such things, are able to sniff out the corruption in a heart, or so I was always taught.

It is more likely that they know who is capable of cruelty by the way they smell and move, though. Not that they have some organ that can divine what lies within a Human heart.

Is there something about my own heart that pulls this dog? Is it that I am broken? Dogs are loyal, they say, but I never interacted with this one much. I remember yesterday, watching him racing towards the dock, the only thing moving while everyone held their breath.

I cannot help but love an animal that loves me so much. Even broken, I must be capable of that, surely? He is my fellow exile.

This ship, the *Stooping Hawk,* is one of Alberic's proudest possessions—what does it mean that he has chosen it to take me away? That he cares whether or not I make it to my destination? That he seeks to do me honor for my long service to the city?

That he wishes me gone as quickly as I can be?

Is there anything else about the ship? It is new, works both by sail and by the engine hidden in its hull, magic-powered and rarely used. The captain took Ruhua and me on a tour when we arrived, showed us the tiny room that holds the engine, and the shelf laden with the orbs that power it.

My mind circles that again, because I had never realized the source of that power: Dragon eggs. Each holding enough potential magic to take us hundreds of leagues before it is drained. No wonder the Duke's menagerie is always in search of Dragons, despite the danger and the fact that such Beasts must be crippled, their wings removed.

I have never considered until now of all the things that Tabat depends on, not until now, when I am no longer one of those things. The trees once housing Dryads burn in its furnaces; Dragons power its transportation. Minotaurs and Centaurs work its docks, and the smaller creatures are its servants. Others entertain it, like the great cage of Fairies in the College of Mages or the poet Melusine, beloved but still a slave.

They make me uneasy, these new thoughts.

Ruhua says, "Do you have any questions about Fort Plentitude?" That is my ultimate destination, the place where my exile will begin.

"I am sure my friend Adelina has sent along an armload of books about it," I say. I don't say that I have no intent of reading any of them.

"I have visited there and can tell you something of it," Ruhua presses. Is she merely entertaining herself or is there some purpose to this, a threat perhaps, or a warning? She is Alberic's creature and when I am not too tired and sunk in grayness to care about trust, I do not trust her and her immaculate persona. No one is that smooth, that perfect, I have found. And sometimes when such people crack and let you see what lies beneath, it is something frightening.

"Very well," I say. "Tell me of its culture."

She laughs, a dainty, amused chuckle. A laugh that makes me feel as though I have clumsily put my foot in a snare. "Culture! Well, little enough of that. It is the frontier, after all. I hope you are not expecting theaters and arenas and tailors and such."

She is scolding me for a presumption I have not made. That stings enough to get me past the grayness rolling over me at the thought of a city that is not Tabat. "I meant," I say, making patience evident in my tone, the way I might have done to rebuke a student without directly calling them out, "the people. Are they friendly sorts? Or all aloof, solitary-minded explorers?"

"Ah," she says. "Friendly enough to those they feel contribute something to their society."

Her tone leaves no doubt that she does not think that they will feel this way about me.

I try to see myself through her eyes. Does she really believe a Gladiator is good for nothing but showy arena fights? In my prime, I fought hand to hand on Alberic's missions a score of times, maybe more, particularly in the difficult Rose Kingdom, where it is so easy to step awry and offend someone in a way that can only be avenged with blood. No, I can fight, and more than that, I can teach people how to fight.

But I don't say this, don't really feel that I want to argue the point or assert my value to a society. When I get there, if I choose to, I can prove myself. Will they let me fight, even? Given the false charges, I may be in disgrace there, may be shunned because of rumors of sorcery.

But who cares what a bunch of provincials think? It might be easiest if they avoid my company entirely.

I imagine myself not just an exile but a hermit, living in a snug cabin in the hills, refusing all Human interaction, seeking only the dog's company. That seems very unlike Bella Kanto, but perhaps it is what I have become. The antithesis of that woman who always had friends and lovers—and enemies, I remind myself—at hand.

I rest my hands on the railing and watch the horizon as I pretend to contemplate Ruhua's words. I don't care about them, don't care what the new city will be like. It will not be Tabat, and that alone is enough to drive me to despair.

"Are you having nightmares?" Ruhua asks.

The unexpected question drives into me like a nail, makes me flinch, although I know that it is not her intention. Probably. "I am growing accustomed to them," I say.

"When someone has been through a deep trauma …" Ruhua pauses and, I am grateful to find, does not elaborate on the cause of such trauma before continuing, "they find themselves reacting differently than they used to."

That is certainly a word for it. How *different* could I be? But I keep my mouth shut.

She says into that silence, "Do you think that's true, Bella Kanto?"

I cannot tell if she is curious or mocks me. I say, "I do not know anymore what is true or not, Ruhua. I am told what is the truth, and that is my truth now, the Duke's truth. Is that what you wish to hear, at the heart of it all?"

My words do what I had hoped: silence her. I do not want to talk to her because I do not want to understand her. If I do, I might agree with her judgment of me.

The days of this journey will be very long.

The dog nuzzles closer to my side, perhaps seeking warmth, perhaps sensing the tension that thrums in the air like a taut rope. I can see the storm Ruhua predicted, darkening the blue of the horizon, smudging it like one of Leonoa's oil paintings, looking nothing like life and yet nothing so real as that.

I will never see my cousin Leonoa again. There is no way she could survive the rigors of a trip to the frontier. She gave me a painting, rolled up in my trunk.

I have not unrolled it to see what it is. I cannot bear to think she might have given me a canvas showing me as I once was: dressed in Winter's armor, cold and chilly as a steel blade, and so unbearably confident and proud. That was all Bella Kanto was, confidence and pride, and now that it is gone, what face will I show the world?

The dog licks my hand. His awkward, ungainly affection reminds me of the boy I took in, what seems like years, rather than a few weeks ago. I rest my fingertips on his head. "What will I call you?" I say to him, rather than speaking to Ruhua.

"You could name him after one of the expeditions that paved the path to Fort Plentitude," Ruhua says. "I am sure your books are full of such names." She sounds as though she is well aware I rarely crack a spine, even on the books about me that Adelina has written.

What does she want of me? I want to turn and confront her, demand an answer. Instead I keep silent, although my fingers twitch against the dog's skull, feeling the bone beneath the soft, loose skin.

She stands there as though she cannot believe my silence.

I stare into the distance. Her attention is a goad, poking at me, poking at me. It reminds me of when I was newly come to the Brides of Steel, and all the other girls picked on me, because they were so outraged that Myrila had allowed me in, despite the fact that I was too old and had not suffered through the years of training they had.

They tried all sorts of mean tricks and things that were more than tricks. I had so little experience with my peers, even at fifteen. I had been in Piper Hill, being trained by Jolietta, for the seven years before then, and there had been no other Human children there.

But I survived them.

I ignore Ruhua and think about the fact that, since Alberic

confiscated all my holdings, he now owns half of the school. Myrila must hate that.

After a time, Ruhua turns away and walks by herself up and down the deck. The sailors avoid her as though she is ill-omened in some way, I am pleased to note, but it is more likely her manner that is so off-putting to them. The dog stays with me, pressed against my leg, and the warmth and solidity are welcome.

"We need a name for you," I tell him again, and he looks at me as if to say, *Well, then, do something about that*, and I shrug at him before we go inside.

CHAPTER 2

*T*his ship has been newly outfitted; everything is fresh and clean and stiff. When they unwind the ropes, they come coiled as though long accustomed to that position, and they smell of fresh hemp. Gilt and inlaid wood gaud the interior of Ruhua's cabin, where we eat dinner together. The lamp has an expensive magical core, what the College of Mages call "Fairy-hearts," rather than being powered by oil, like the one in my own cabin.

The food was excellent last night and tonight as well: boiled beef and root vegetables, along with fresh biscuits and a pudding made from milk and dried fruit. Who knows what meals will be like once the fresh supplies the cook has brought with her have been used up? But this is an excellent cook, and that gives me pause.

The Duke would not bother to send us off in good style and order and, more than that, with the creature comforts that the cook represents, if he was not fond of someone on this vessel. I doubt that it is me—that is a deeper game than Alberic is capable of playing, in my opinion. His disgust at the thought that I might be associated with Sorcerers was surely genuine. Looking to *my* comfort would not have occurred to him.

But Ruhua's? He has seemed fond of her before. Not in the way that I associate with mutual bed play, but with respect and a sense that he can rely on her. So yes, perhaps he is coddling Ruhua, which means she is someone to be treated carefully, if she has earned the Duke's favor.

And why would she not have? She has brought him plenty of creatures for his menagerie, over the years, and most of them not ones that she traded for or bought with the city's funds, but prizes that she captured herself. Few other cities could boast of more than one Dragon or a Sphinx such as the one that walks the College of Mages grounds, but Tabat can, because of her, and that is definitely a source of pride for Alberic.

She butters her bread with small, precise movements, like flaying a songbird. Lamplight shutters and reveals her face, moving across it as the lantern swings on its brass chain.

What does it mean that Ruhua has been the one sent with me? There must be some ulterior motive. There always is with Alberic. Sometimes he has plans within plans, even if often those are executed badly. He is a ruthless man and a greedy one.

Is it because he sees me as a threat? Does he worry that I might come back to Tabat and challenge his power somehow? But no, his power is, in all probability, about to pass away with the upcoming elections.

Unless ...

Unless he has some plan to keep himself in power. A scheme that I—or my presence—might somehow put in disarray. Adelina said I was deeply tied to the city's magic, that because I fought its ritual battle every spring and represented it, became a stand-in for it, that magic ran through me. That magic kept me hale and hearty and unageing, while deluding myself that it was all natural and simply because I was the best Gladiator to ever fight.

It is very easy to fool yourself into things that you find flattering. Who would not want to be the chosen one, the ultimate, the person that the Gods selected?

Knowing that I am not, that has been the hardest lesson to learn. But I have learned it, more thoroughly than most.

Ruhua stares at me across the table and I realize she has been speaking to me while I worried away at all of this in my head.

"I beg pardon," I say and touch my brow as though headache brews there. "It is a long time since I have been aboard a ship, and it will take a while for me to become re-accustomed to it."

"I was asking what you thought of the pudding. It is a favorite of mine."

"It is excellent," I tell her and take a spoonful to demonstrate enthusiasm. It is indeed excellent and worthy of enthusiasm. Most ships do not carry much sugar, or they save it for rare occasions usually. Another sign of the Duke's favor, if they're carrying sweeteners to coddle to Ruhua's sweet tooth.

I excuse myself as soon as I gracefully can and, despite the threat of storm, take a turn around the deck, breathing in fresh air, before I go down to my cabin.

I pull myself into my bunk. The dog is already asleep and snoring outside the door, a happy, hapless sound that almost makes me smile. The bed is warm, and I do not have to stir from it.

Outside, the wind is cold and has a wet edge to it that makes it seem even colder, but I can hear the sailor who is night watch calling at intervals to reassure that the ship is safe, that it continues on, and that—*for the moment, oh this brief moment, can I just live in it forever*—all is well.

I DON'T KNOW why I hadn't anticipated the storm that comes a few hours later. I'd seen the clouds roiling on the horizon and thought nothing of them. Back in Tabat, snug upstairs in my bed, listening to the furnace's grumble and the whining wind fingering futilely at my windows, something like this would have been unremarkable.

Not so when we are at sea.

The ship shudders and moans aloud like it is dying. It slams one way then another. Every few minutes lightning flashes through my palm-sized porthole. It is terrifying and vast. I clench myself, too afraid to move and welcome this terror. At least it keeps me from sleeping and falling into nightmares.

I lie awake for what seems like hours. I think of what I once was and how it was taken from me. Did Alberic spin this plot, or someone else? If I knew who did it, I could plot revenge. Perhaps I would care about revenge in the first place. But nowadays I am always wrapped in grayness when I am not alive with terror.

Every time the thunder booms, it's as though it strikes me. I find myself full of rage at where I am, futile rage that cannot change a thing about my circumstances.

Finally, I creep from my bed and open the door to let the dog in. He crawls into the bed and we curl together. He flinches at the thunderclaps too, and in petting him to reassure him, I find myself growing calmer.

I wake screaming that night, as with every night. I was back in the cell with the torturers, who went on and on, past any answering, past any sound I could make. Sweat drenches me; deep, shuddering gasps shake my body.

The dog licks my face anxiously. The stink of his breath makes me start to push him away, but instead I gather him close, hold his doggy weight against me as we listen to the ship complaining, all through the night.

I fall asleep trying to think of names for him. Nothing seems worthy.

CHAPTER 3

THE STOOPING HAWK (TEO)

*T*eo awoke with a sense that everything was wonderful. Bella had never let him sleep in her bed before, and this warm, soft nest smelled of her, a lap of sunlight coming in through the window, even the ship's noises a gentle lulling song rather than the discordant complaint it had made all night.

Bella was asleep, though. That would not do! Now she was no longer sad, and they would do all sorts of things, and discover all sorts of wonderful smells. A happy Bella was what he wanted, and surely the Bella that had let him in last night had done so because she realized how important happiness was, he thought, losing track of his train of thought halfway through and wandering off into the sensation of licking Bella's face despite her best attempts to shove him away.

But she was not so happy, after all. Maybe a lick or two less sad than she had been, surely? Maybe it would grow on her, happiness, little by little. He would do his best to make it so.

Teo whined again and nudged Bella's hand, hoping she'd wake and take him up on deck. It was hard to think in this shape, hard to squeeze the Human-shaped thoughts through the channels that dog thought raced so swiftly in and out of, full of *smell smell sound smell air pressure motion smell oh what was that in the corner,* the come-play motion of a towel's sway where it lay draped over the chair.

He gave up on Bella and slunk over to stalk the towel, but the unworthy prey didn't fight back as he methodically ripped it to shreds, worrying it with his teeth, playing with it over his head and back like a puppy. It felt good to move.

Bella should move, he thought. Then she wouldn't be so sad. He bounded over with a swath of towel in his mouth and nudged her again, this time with determination.

She had been lying in bed, with the smell of sadness roiling off her thick as fog. Now she stirred and said, her tone a little less flat than her stare had been. "My towel!"

She rose enough to reach out a hand. He backed away, lowering his head while his tail wagged so hard his whole back half vibrated.

"You are a scoundrel," she told him sternly. "Why should I reward such bad behavior?"

But she was paying attention to him rather than her hands at least. He danced forward, just enough so she could snatch at the towel, then scrambled back as she did, dropping the towel as a happy bark escaped him.

"Fool," she said, but picked up the towel and held it out so he could grab hold and give it a good hard yank the way he wanted to. It tore in half and he fell backwards on his rear.

Bella laughed.

She had laughed! A whirlwind of delight, he spun around her, tail swinging in a wide sweep, doggy grin hovering on his face in answer. Everything was wonderful!

"I thought of your name," she said to him. "I'm naming you after a boy. I don't know what happened to him. I hope no ill came to him from association with me. Surely my old landlady Abernia would not have let that happen. She was fond of Teo, after all."

At the sound of his name, he stopped dead still.

"Do you like that name?" she asked. "Teo?"

He barked with joy, three sharp excited yips that somehow made her laugh. He whirled in place, barely able to contain himself. She knew somehow, even if she didn't know that she knew, and that meant there was a chance. A chance she could help him walk in Human form once again, in the form that she had known.

In his happiness, he'd paid no attention to the footsteps outside the door. But the knock came now, and Bella's smile fell away, and did not return as she put the piece of cloth on the table and went to answer it.

CHAPTER 4

THE STOOPING HAWK (BELLA)

*W*ater is always moving, or it looks as though it is, at any rate. It is all around us on the ship, it carries us along and we forget that there's a world underneath it.

I do not forget. I swim in it when I can, which is only every other day, because of the demands it poses for fresh water with which to sluice myself off afterward. Lucky for me the shipmaster grows roses in the aft garden and my bath does not contaminate the water allotted for them.

We travel out of sight of land most of the time, but we are still near the coast. Sometimes the wind carries smells from the lands, usually unremarkable ones like dust or greenery, but, every once in a while, something less pleasant. I had noted the scent of carrion earlier, as though we passed someplace where death lay heavy. So it does not surprise me quite as much as it might have, one early morning, when the first sailor spots the Dragon.

It is so far up among the clouds, thin mackerel clouds like fish scales on the sky's belly, that a careless eye might have thought it a bird. At least at first. But then, watching it, one would have seen the long, snakelike form, unlike any bird's.

When the sailors realize what it is, the newer ones among them panic and run about demanding to know what they should do in order to prepare. Their older fellows reassure them, although they do it by teasing them, telling them how many prayers they can get in before the Dragon swoops, and where they might leave a note for a loved one.

"Cap'n keeps a big box in his cabin," I hear the first mate say earnestly. "It'll float, and it's painted bright red, so as they'll see it a-floating in the waves. Ain't you never heard of such?"

The young sailor looks to me in question and I shake my head. She looks relieved.

The other hapless new sailor runs off in search of the captain, and the others double over, silently laughing, although they do glance up at the sky every now and again. I stay where I am, with Teo, having come up to let him run the deck a bit. He is all flop and ears and energy. He'd be no more than a dot of food to a Dragon, the sort of crumb I might let fall from my dinner napkin.

I watch the sky. The shape gleams when the sunlight hits it, moves in and out of the cloud shade as though enjoying the temperature shift, almost playing.

Dragons are not unusual when you are outside the settled lands, the ones where there is a village every ten miles or so. Of all the kinds of Beasts I have known, they are the most intelligent, and so they know better, usually, than to hunt Humans. They understand that to do so brings attention and retribution, and that while a Dragon can easily kill a single Human, or a handful of them, a larger group, armed with weapons and magic, is a very different story.

There once was a Dragon in the Duke's menagerie, the first since the two captured for the founding of the College of Mages, that died of mismanagement by their handler.

All were caught when they were very young and very foolish. Like its fellows, the one in the menagerie had its wings removed, along with the ducts that let it breathe fire, and its teeth and talons kept blunted. But it remained the most dangerous creature there, and only rarely did I speak with it, because there is one thing a Dragon does better than anything else, and that is twisting truth and telling lies.

The one in the menagerie escaped five years back; they said Abolitionists freed it, but I had my doubts. Dragons are dangerous, even without wings and fire and teeth.

I do not think that this one will come down and attack. This is a regular route for ships, and we would be much more trouble than we were worth, on the water. No, this is a Dragon out fishing, looking for its breakfast.

We watch as it hovers, staying between the land and us. Along much of the coast there is a place where the water drops off abruptly, and that is where many of the larger fish lurk, grazing along that edge. This Dragon is looking for something like a colossal shark or small whale, something substantial enough to make it worth the effort of catching it.

I can tell when it spots its prey. Its silhouette changes, more alert. By now, a small crowd is watching, including the captain and Ruhua. I do not see the sailor who was sent in search of the box in which to put letters, but I overhear the mate retelling the jest several times. It seems destined to become one of the jokes of the journey.

The Dragon shoots down from the sky almost faster than the eye can follow, hitting the water perhaps a quarter mile away. A splash of foam catches the air as it snatches something from the water's surface and ascends again, this time its powerful wings flapping, the first flap smacking one tip against the water, then working to pull it upward even while the long snakelike head tears at the enormous fish that still struggles in its talons.

I have traveled all over the world, but I have never seen this before. It makes me hold my breath. It makes joy stir in my heart because it is so beautiful. The dog's cold wet nose touches my fingers, urging me to pet him, and I kneel to do so, still watching the Dragon moving upward in the sky.

I expect that to be the last that we see of it, but the Dragon is not done with us. It circles.

"It is looking to see what weapons we have aboard," Ruhua says to the captain.

Some hunting ships have harpoon guns and or great darts

created by the College of Mages. We have twelve little brass cannons, etched with frosty runes, six along either side of the front. They would certainly hurt a Dragon if they shot one, but they are also fixed in place, and would be difficult to maneuver with the speed that would be necessary to repel one.

They also do not face inward. If it came straight down and landed on our deck, it could tear us all to pieces.

Her tone is cool and unafraid. Like me, she knows that the Dragon is smart enough to understand what would happen if it made a practice of killing ships. Humans would come hunting it, and they would be tireless in their pursuit, because ship routes are a matter of economic interest, and economic interest is money, and Money drives everything in this world, or so the Merchants tell us.

Beasts act according to their nature. We are taught that this is one thing that makes a Beast a Beast: their nature is always predictable. Unlike Humans, who have free will and can act against their natures, Beasts do not and cannot.

According to this theory there is no way the Dragon would come and attack us. But everyone on the ship knows that there is still a chance. There are always rogues.

What does that say about whether or not we really believe Beasts are Beasts?

This time when the Dragon descends, it is not a swoop for a strike. It is a much more leisurely approach, and the creature's attitude is curiosity rather than menace. Still, it approaches from the back of the boat, where the cannons cannot reach it. It does not land, but it flows along so close to the sails that it seems barely a cat whisker separates them. Teo whines at my side, ears and tail flattened, pressing himself to the deck, and pisses himself in his terror.

He is not alone in this. Several of the sailors do the same.

The Dragon's scales are like gems, colored in greens and dark blues. It is a young one, after all, despite its size, and its skin is glossy, its eyes bright and inquisitive. It glides through the air as though something were holding it up, as though it were a snake winding through unseen obstacles, and the wings are still, half-extended, half-folded. The sunlight shines through them as though they were colored glass.

The Dragon's shadow follows it, pouring over the decking in its wake as it blocks the sunlight from us for a moment, and then moves away, the sudden wash of sunlight slap-dazzling us all.

Maybe this is where I die. Maybe this is where my story ends, ignominiously, as part of the tale of the expedition that will end up slaying this Dragon, someday. It will not be anyone on this ship, that is clear. The creature could kill us if it wanted.

It returns and this time a few sailors fall to the deck on their knees. Most of us stay upright. Ruhua has her arms folded, watching the Dragon. I see it looking at her, specifically picking her out of the group of all of us.

Do Dragons speak with each other? Do they communicate in ways that we do not know, even when they are far apart, as some other Beasts are rumored to do? I think of the Dragon in the Duke's menagerie, with which Ruhua would have interacted, more than once. After all, she had led the hunt that had taken it.

I think of the Dragon eggs racked and ready to be used as fuel, far below us in the hold.

It comes to me that we are in very great danger indeed if this Dragon decides it will eliminate any chance that this woman will hunt more Dragons. That would be a reasoned decision of the sort that Dragons are known for.

Or it might also make another decision, one of anger. Because I know that just like Humans, Beasts can make decisions that are rash or hasty or against their own interests. That's the truth of things, no matter how anyone likes to pretend otherwise.

Ruhua stands there, perfectly calm, looking at it, every inch of her assured. It cannot be an act, that confidence. There is something up her sleeve that makes her think she is more than capable of taking on this Dragon.

She shifts an inch. Something about her body says, *Go ahead, I dare you.* Or maybe even, *The voyage was growing boring. Perhaps you'll liven it up.*

I hear the Dragon rumble something as it passes, but I cannot make out the words, if they are words. I don't look at it this time. I watch Ruhua, because somehow, she is pivotal to all of this.

I wonder what she would have been like to face in the ring if she had also studied at the Brides of Steel. I had not thought her the sort who might be much of an opponent—not particularly tall or muscular, or particularly graceful—but the way she is standing is making me rethink all of my assumptions.

Or perhaps it's me. Perhaps I'm scared of things—of people—in a way now that I never would have been before. Could Bella Kanto, the old one, have been as terrified as I was when I realized what was happening in the Duke's cells and that there was no escape? No, she was fearless, reckless, because she knew she was invincible.

She would have taken on a Dragon and she probably would have won, too.

Not so anymore.

This time the Dragon rises and glides away north and eastward, back towards the waft of carrion that must have signaled its lair. I let out my breath. The dog is pressed against the back of my knees now, so hard he makes balance difficult. Several sailors are vanishing to change their clothing, jeered by their comrades. The captain is looking at Ruhua as though she were some sort of goddess.

Once everyone in an entire city looked at me like that. I turn my face away to watch the water. Over where the Dragon swooped to grab its fish, the gulls are diving in the water; there is a school of smaller fish there that the larger fish must have been feeding on.

What did that fish think, one moment happily eating, the next soaring into the sky in a rush of pain? How sudden and savage it must have thought its life.

I look over at Ruhua again, talking with the captain. She catches my notice and inclines her head. I have no idea what she is thinking or how to read her expression and so I go downstairs again and eat my breakfast and remember how beautiful it was, that first strike of the Dragon, like the motion of the wind itself, drawing its name on the sky.

CHAPTER 5

*T*he white moon and the purple are high in the evening sky, both thin arcs, glittering scythe-knives facing each other in opposition. Clouds gauzy as lace scarves armor the lower stars here and there, and the air is cold and cutting to the point where I expect to see ice glitter on the ropework above me.

I have no gloves, and goose pimples glance up and down my arms, but I am Bella Kanto and will not shiver or hug myself for warmth.

A sailor watches me. I have caught her at it more than once.

One of the younger among them. Slim, dark-haired, dark-skinned. In truth she resembles no one so much as Skye.

She is a new sailor. I have heard the others teasing her about this being her first voyage. Some of them do not like her and I wonder if she got her berth through family connections or knowing someone, but she doesn't seem to be the bedmate or friend of any of the ship's officers.

She keeps to herself. That is why I catch her watching me the first time, because I notice her sitting off by herself in the rigging. It is a good perch to watch the water from. On other voyages I have climbed up there myself, many a time. But now, the way my hands ache with the cold, I do not trust them to not betray me and slip on a rope. Even if I avoid falling on the deck, I would render myself something worse than hurt: ridiculous.

How petty of me, to still have pride in such things when I am going off to a place where people will only know me as a disgraced exile.

Her name is Sofia. She has not earned a surname yet, but after this it will be Sailor, and she will be able to establish a house, by Merchant law, although that is something very few do, and only after they have worked a lifetime to build a fortune to do it with.

Journeys on a Ducal mission like this one do not even include the chance of some prize, of taking pirates or bandits, or more likely, taking Beasts in what would be claimed a preemptive raid before they attacked, no matter how peaceable the species. That was how Tabat grew to be such a motley gathering place, all the different creatures brought back to it by the explorers, all coming to become part of Tabat.

For a second something dances across my head as though … what? It's something about Beasts and Tabat and magic and it's almost complete for a moment … then scatters as I focus on it.

I almost knew something there. Almost understood something. I stand very still, trying to gather my thoughts, but then a shadow falls across me and I look up. Sofia, who started me on this train of thought and now drives it from its rails.

Oh, she looks so very much like Skye and nothing like her at all. They do not hold themselves the same way, do not breathe the same way.

And yet it is Skye's shy smile she gives me, tentative as a bird thinking of landing.

She says, "I do not mean to bother you …" and pauses, trailing off as though not sure what to say next.

If I were cruel, I would let her falter into that silence, but instead I say, as courteously as any trade negotiation, "You do not bother me. Is there something that you wish?"

It's clear her thoughts have never reached this far in the conversation when she planned it. She blinks, startled, then wets her lips.

"They are telling stories, the watch is. I mean, they do every night, but Bea is telling one tonight, and she is particularly fine at it."

The sweet, shy invitation tempts me. But what if the sailors ask me for a story, or expect me to venture one? I cannot tell stories of Bella Kanto the Brave because I am no longer that person and to speak of her—to brag as though I were still her—is inconceivable.

I shake my head and say, "You honor me with the offer, but I am tired and headachy this evening and will sleep early."

I regret the words as I speak them. I had, in fact, meant to stay on deck and watch the stars gathering tonight, because the skies will be clear after last night's storm. When the full red moon rises, the ship will sail in and out of clouds of phosphorescent plankton as though moving through the sky itself. That is why they will be up here, telling tales.

Disappointment blossoms in her face and regret surges in me even further. It is not sharp enough to prod me into action, and so I should let the grayness carry me below to my cabin instead of staying to watch the sky.

But.

I have never loved to read the way Adelina does. To her it is better than meat and drink and sleep and sometimes, I think, sex. Books are dry as dust, no matter what they promise. Teo noses at my palm, and I cup my hand over his snout for a second, letting his tongue lick at it, before I say, "Very well."

Though I do wish I had brought my thicker cloak.

I have always loved a good story, but the ones tonight seem thin and badly told. The sailors gathered around the firestone for warmth are too aware of my company. They do not joke with each other the way that they normally would, and after only a few tales have been told, they disperse.

"Gotta get on with it," one of the sailors on watch says to Sofia and claps her on the shoulder before nodding again at me and moving towards the fore. Moving this quickly in relatively safe waters, their job is not too hard, but the captain would not like to find them shirking it and not watching the water—and air for that matter, since there are more Dragons and others along the southern coast—for unexpected peril.

Sofia says, "The storytelling has been much better on other nights."

She stands bundled in on herself for warmth, looking dismayed. She is young and does not understand the shyness that fell upon her fellows. And I myself, I do not know if any of them believe what has been said of me, that I consorted with Sorcerers, and abetted their evil. I would like to think no citizen of Tabat would believe such a thing of their Champion, but back in the city, its citizens were ready—so ready—to think it of me.

I say, "Maybe you will tell me the best of the ones you heard." I lean on the railing near the firestone—the contrast between the warmth of the side facing it and the cold of the side that is not facing it is pleasant, but only if I turn myself around every once in a while, to remind my backside what warmth feels like.

"I'm not a storyteller," she says. "I could not do it justice. You'll have to come again when they are feeling more inspired."

She brushes against me as she leans forward to warm herself. Invitation in that touch. Question in her look.

If I were still myself, if I were the old Bella, I'd answer that question without hesitation. Adelina's books are full of my erotic encounters, all the beings I've loved and who have loved me, because I have never been shy with my body or the sharing of it.

But the answer to that question, the one that rises in my body, is not the one that I am used to giving. Something in me shrinks away from that opening, does not want to expose itself again. Some piece scraped raw, unrelentingly and unendingly so, in the torture cells.

Just thinking of what I have left behind shakes me to the core, makes my heart thud in a way that she mistakes. Who wouldn't, seeing that flutter in my throat, the way I work to take in air for a moment? She steps closer.

Only to encounter my hand, palm forward, between us. Her motion stops. She looks surprised.

"You will pardon me," I say. I cannot think of how to explain or even what it is, exactly, that I am explaining and so I stammer apologies and incoherencies—the once fluent and eloquent Bella Kanto, capable of charm and diplomacy at levels most Humans could never hope to achieve without magic. Then I flee, actually move clumsy and fast in my haste to retreat down the stairs.

I go back to my stuffy cabin and fling myself on the bed, to lie there, staring up at the back-and-forth sway of the lamp, at the light crawling over the wood's grain, making it look like worms, like puddles, like oceans and clouds and half-chewed beans, and in all of that, nothing of Bella Kanto.

ON DECK: JOURNEY OF THE STOOPING HAWK, A DAY (TEO)

Teo followed at Bella's heels as she and the other woman went up the stairs, his tail drooping. For a moment ... but now she smelled of sadness again.

If only he could tell her who he was! But every time he thought about that, it was as though his head was full of bees, angry and buzzing, driving thought away.

Life on board ship was infinitely better than the Duke's palace with one exception: Anba and Enba, the ship's cats, named for the Trade Gods of Supply and Demand. The pair were there to keep down ship pests, and they knew every corner of the vessel, including all the best places in which to lurk in order to catch him unawares, delivering a smarting claw rake across his tender nose or muzzle, and then leap away, blending into the shadows with their black fur.

He hated them as much as he'd ever hated anything in his life, including Bjort, the bully back home in his village, or Canumbra and Legio, who'd tried to kidnap him and sell him to Granny Beeswax, or even Murga, who'd turned him into a dog and given him to Alberic. Most of those people—perhaps not Bjort, who had just been mean—had at least had some purpose in doing what they did, while the cats simply did it because it was their nature.

And worst of all, Bella tolerated them! The day before, she had let Enba curl up in her lap, despite his growls, while she was sitting out in the sunlight on the deck, and if he came too close, she'd gently swat him away, all the while the cat smirked at him from her lap. It was the only thing he didn't like about Bella, that she actually seemed to like those cats, because who could like cats, the sneaky things, but every time he thought about that, there were flocks of geese honking in his head and then he would sneeze, over and over, because the air smelled like lightning and old feathers.

The ship had a thousand smells: tar and wood and cinders and people and spices and fish and more fish. At times like this he felt as though he were nothing but nose, smelling everything around him, the world shouting information at him. But not in an overpowering way, in a way, rather, like a wave that he could ride, until he felt as though the whole world was in his head, or at least everything that smelled.

Even magic had its own smells, sometimes bitter and electric, other times almost cloyingly sweet. Some smells made him feel like he couldn't help but do things, and when it was one of those magic smells that was worst of all, it was like it crept into his body until he could not help but bite at it.

That was the kind of magic the woman walking with Bella smelled of. It was a bad smell, and he kept watching her to make sure she wasn't looking at him.

But she wasn't. All of her attention was on Bella, and she was pretending to be calm, but underneath she was angry, oh how angry she was! As though she was made of it, was nothing but anger walking. He didn't like being so close to her, but he stayed there for Bella's sake, because he was there to protect Bella, he knew that with every inch of his being.

She made him remember what it had been to be Human. Or at least as Human as he had been since he had been a Shifter as well. All that time he had been in the Duke's palace he hadn't remembered. And then, at the Duke's heels, he'd caught the smell of her, the smell of Bella Kanto, and he could not help but give chase, to go after her, because to find her was like finding a part of himself.

ADELINA'S FIRST LETTER

Dear Bel—

I'm starting this the day before you're leaving, as much to say that I will keep writing as to tell you anything that's happened. I'll tuck it in with the bundle of books I'm sending—knowing you, you won't find it until a week out into the journey. Maybe more.

I met with your cousin just this morning and Leonoa sends her love. I actually went down to her studio since it's so hard to coax her out lately. She said that she'd wanted to come see you but she'd been sick lately and the Doctor forbade her to stand out in the cold.

Her friend Glyndia said she'd been there when they announced your sentence, but I didn't remember seeing her, and I would have noticed that one, I think. You know what I mean. What a strange pairing, Bel, little Leonoa and that great, glorious woman with those golden wings.

Do you believe her that she's not a Beast, Bel, that she actually is someone touched by sorcery the way she claims? You would have thought we would have heard something about that before. I know that Tabat's a big city, but sometimes its circles are very small. I asked around and she's not from any Merchant family that I know.

I'm not convinced she wishes Leonoa well, Bella, though they seem fond enough of each other.

I went by your boarding house and talked with Abernia to ask after Teo. She said he's been missing a while now, and she checked with the Moon Temples, but they said they didn't have him. I'll keep watching for him, Bel, and if I find him, I'll take care of him for you. I know that must be worrying at you a little.

Or is it? Have you forgotten Tabat already? That's a foolish question, I know, but maybe you would be best off to stop remembering it, because when you come back, you'll find it very changed.

Even now, during the days you've been in jail, there have been riots on the part of the Beasts and the police are more present than they ever have been. It's a tricky thing—the city depends on the Beasts to make it go, and so if they refuse—what happens? It's not as though they can be replaced, in many cases. The College of

Mages claims to be able to create all sorts of things, but even there the magic is dependent on supplies—which come from Beasts.

The elections are in another month. No one knows what will happen still. I've taken on some work printing political tracts, not particularly profitably, but it makes a little and keeps the press alive. A friend of mine has helped me find some other work, printing for the College of Mages, but they are hard to get to pay the bills, sometimes. He warned me about that—I think you know him, Bel, Sebastiano Silvercloth. I think—(here a passage is scratched out and illegible).

I won't bother you with inconsequential things from my life. I hope that you are well, and I miss you, Bella Kanto, and hope that you are finding your journey entertaining and instructive, as you always do, and full of stories that you will tell me in person someday.

Your friend ever,
Adelina Nittlescent

CHAPTER 6

THE STOOPING HAWK (BELLA)

*A*fter yet another unpleasant dinner with Ruhua, I go to my cabin. Teo is dutifully at my heels, though I can tell that, like me, he would rather be on deck. His claws click click in my wake along the cramped wooden staircase and the three steps of equally squeezed hallway, redolent of tar and pine and a whiff of urine, that leads to my cabin door.

On another ship, this would be the cabin the mates share, and I know neither of them are particularly happy to be ousted. But they can say little, since the captain himself has given up his cabin to Ruhua, decreeing that all of the officers be squeezed into the second room of his suite.

This ship is ill-adapted for an exile's journey. In one of Adelina's books all of these details would have been glossed over so the reader could glide along easy as a boat being carried by the current, requiring no labor of oar or trimming sail or poling.

And in one of Adelina's books, the cabin would not have been so cramped that my luggage could not all be stored in it, not the four large trunks of seasonable clothing Alberic—or someone, I cannot think who would have bothered—had commissioned for me. I have only delved into one so far—marked with early autumn sigils—but every garment is made in the Duke's colors, clothing me in his livery. His servant. His possession. The thing he has sent away and out of the city, discarded but marked large, "Still mine. Do not touch."

I enter my cabin to sort through the box of parting gifts that Adelina has sent with me. The sailor who'd brought my things had put the crate here, shoved it in a corner, stacking other boxes atop it, but I manage to redistribute the layers and uncover the box, a simple wood crate with an overlay of wooden reeds to hold it closed.

Now, as the lamplight flickers over the contents and I listen to the creak and sway of the ship, Teo's head warm across my sock-clad toes, I use a dagger to slice away the covering and examine what my best friend in all the world has given me, what may be the last real trace of her presence. Perhaps she will write to me—or rather, surely she will, and the question is whether or not Alberic— or even Ruhua, who does not seem favorably inclined my way— will decide to deliver the letters to me.

The thought catches in my throat, surprising me out of the dullness that has wrapped me. But its removal is not welcome, because in its wake is pain. To lose my friend ...

My fingers tremble as I run them over the contents.

Atop it all is practicality. A toiletry kit: ivory-handled wooden vanities, boar-bristled brushes, and a scallop-shell mirror. I recognize the set as one of hers. The thought touches me sweetly at first until I think that perhaps her purse is so lean as a result of my fallen fortunes that she cannot afford something else.

That worry nags at me as I look at the rest, but then amusement drives it away. What else might Adelina have sent, what luxuries and touches of home to comfort me in my exile, beyond the crate of books that accompanied this package?

A journal in case I want to keep notes, and a pen set. I laugh and turn to the crate, taking out each book to examine it, still smiling.

The first three are a fine, leather-clad set, bound with the embossed pattern that marks one of the press's scholarly works, the historical works that Adelina loves but which she has confessed bring in no money at all.

Flipping through it, I find it's an account of the early exploratory expedition that founded Fort Plentitude, although less about their adventures and more an exhaustive listing and analysis of the trade goods that they carried and what they brought back, all carefully mapped according to the Trade God that oversaw that type of merchandise, including the three new ones invented just to cover new things, like Anfranbo, God of Sellable Intoxication and his partner, Profit from Addiction.

I set those aside. The next is a bound set of maps, which is more useful and more entertaining. I page through them; this is an expensive and high-quality book, surely from her personal library. I check the frontispiece: her name, neatly written in a schoolgirl's hand.

Very well, more books. The inventory confirms my suspicions: these are her books, most of them marked with her sigil, Spinner Press's distaff and thread, on the frontispiece. A history of Fort Plentitude with a note tucked in regarding Adelina's opinion of the author's tendency "to get carried away by sensationalist elements." That sounds promising; I set it to one side.

Another book, a manuscript really, the bound proofs that I'm used to seeing my own books in, but this time not one of those but something else, *How Dogs Came to the New Continent*.

Accompanying it, another note from Adelina: "I am thinking of publishing this, but I thought you would be interested in it." "Dogs" sounds interesting, and it turns out to be written by my former downstairs neighbor at Abernia's boarding house, Scholar Reinart.

But opening its pages shows thick paragraphs of prose about the history of dog-breeding in Tabat, the sort of intricate chart and notes one keeps for breeding animals or Beasts, and I quickly put that one back on the pile.

Two personal accounts from explorers of the region around Fort Plentitude, this time with no note. Presumably Adelina felt no need to provide a disapproving gloss for those authors. A bestiary of the region. An account of the fish and medicinal herbs compiled by an early expedition.

And best of all, down at the bottom, three green-bound books.

Adventures, not Adelina's press, and having nothing at all to do with Gladiators or Tabat, but accounts of pirate romances in the Southern Isles. I carry one of those over to the bunk and settle in. Teo rises from his spot near the door and hops up onto the bed, looking at me.

"Good dogs," I tell him, "do not sleep in beds."

He wags his tail.

"You are a terrible dog," I tell him. He lets out a happy bark and climbs over to nestle under my arm, a warm and comfortable weight as I lose myself in a pirate tale.

CHAPTER 7

FROM BELLA KANTO AND THE BRIDES OF STEEL: AN ACCOUNT OF THE EARLY DAYS OF TABAT'S MOST FAMOUS GLADIATOR

From day one, Bella's classmates knew they had a Champion in their midst. Bella worked hard, practicing blade and footwork, training in the morning, and studying with her fellows in the afternoons, all of them striving to outdo each other in friendly competition.

WELL, now. That is just plain not true, what Adelina has written, and wrong enough to turn my stomach. Bad enough that she insists on the old conventions, such as using the family trade names rather than the common ones, making the reader pick their way through Nittlescents rather than Nettlepurses, Dellaroses rather than Coinblossoms, as though such conventions didn't muddle things up hopelessly.

I lay the book down and take a breath, roll my shoulders to stretch them, although I have not been sitting long enough to justify it. I do not like the cabin. It is cramped in a way that I have not endured since the days of the dormitories at the Brides of Steel, and the cubbies that the oldest girls got, hard-earned, hard-won, and needing to be defended in a way the open cots and chests of the junior girls did not. There was no way to protect those and so by mutual accord they were off-limits.

Not so with our cubbies, although I'm not sure what the rationale for that was since they seemed on the same level of defensibility.

You learned not to keep precious things in there. Lucky for me I was already wary. Life with Jolietta had taught me that at least, to keep things well hidden in places that were not the normal. I kept mine in the stable, in a wall crack behind a cluster of feed barrels.

The air here feels the same as it did in that tiny cubby the first night I lay down in it, aching from practice and bruised in places Jolietta's beatings had never found. But I had known I was there in the Brides of Steel, that I was on the path that I had chosen for once, rather than one than had been chosen for me, and that made all the difference.

And continued to do so, even in the face of all my hostile classmates.

All my time at school, I felt—no, knew, really, down to the very core of my bones—that I was different than the other girls. And they knew it too. Closed ranks against me.

Had I come from outside the family system that had spawned us all, I might have understood it better, if I'd been a transplant from elsewhere like Dina, the little brown Horserider, and the girl Chaissa, who had lasted for only three years before war with the Rose Kingdom drove her back to those shores. But those girls had been readily enough taken into the fold and admitted to all the whispering and giggling and secret celebrations and catchphrases and all the other ways that the girls pecked at the outsider, worse than any bird flock I ever saw at Piper Hill.

Little consolation that I knew the source of my difference, which was that I was capable of harder work and more focus than any of them. I'd been tested in the crucible of torment that had been life with Jolietta. Nothing there would ever match up to those days of privation and pain, when whether or not I had supper depended on my aunt's assessment of how hard I had worked that day and if I had lived up to her exacting, but never precisely defined, standards. They could not have survived a week in my place at Piper Hill, I told myself with a certain sense of superiority, even while I knew that it gave me a smugness to my demeanor that further alienated those around me.

A few of the teachers welcomed me, celebrated a student who listened so earnestly and practiced so hard. Most found me unnerving or uncanny, or found in my silent diligent presence a reproach that I myself did not intend, or even understand in those days. If anything, I envied those who could be less serious than I, and later on in life, I know, I reacted to those days lacking in comradeship by seeking it out more eagerly than most. It comes to me now that I've always craved and rejected, all at once, the approval that has been withheld, first by Jolietta and then by the school.

CHAPTER 8

That first day ... they sent me to the school stores, where I traded in almost everything I owned for three tunics, three trews, three sets of underclothing, three pairs of stockings, a single pair of dress boots and another of leather soled slippers. A cloak in school colors. They let me keep my little kit with toiletries, the penknife my mother gave me, and a piece of coral, strung on leather, that I'd picked up once on a trip gathering sea wrack to feed one of Jolietta's experiments.

Next, I was directed to the school's apothecary, who examined me and asked questions about anything that I might have been exposed to, mostly, and looked in my eyes and ears and mouth.

When I stepped out of her office, a girl my age was waiting for me. A big, brawny girl who towered over me, her skin and hair as fashionably dark as my own, as well bred as any Noble from the Old Continent. Pretty, but her expression was an ugly scowl as she looked at me.

"The new student," she said, with an emphasis on the last word that made it seem as though I were anything but. "I'm supposed to take you to the dormitory." She turned without saying anything else or even gesturing at me. I followed in her wake, rather than walking beside her.

I was just as glad of that, because at the next hall junction, two other girls fell in step with her, neither of them looking back at me. They were speaking softly in a language I didn't know, an odd buzzy half-familiar set of words that I'd later find was the secret language the oldest girls used, which supposedly the instructors did not understand. Of course they did, but I'd find that out later. Listening to them, I learned the girl's name was Neffa, but not much else.

I trailed behind them, feeling awkward and out of place and very sore from all the fighting that I'd had to do in order to convince them to let me in.

I had not been around many girls my own age. It was not something possible when I was with my aunt Jolietta at Piper Hill, and even before then, while my parents were still alive, the only child my age I spent time with was my cousin Leonoa, who had been crippled by a Mandrake attack as a baby.

And then we turned another corner and I found myself surrounded.

I had endured so much by that point that you wouldn't have thought there was anything that I feared. Not after Jolietta's beatings, or all her "training." But these girls, and their high shrill voices, so constantly talking, gabbling, and laughing, moons above, all the giggles and snickers and amused little sounds that they made! I had been much used to silence at Piper Hill and had not realized what a treasure it was.

There were perhaps two dozen altogether, I realized later, which was the entirety of the class in which I'd be placed for sleeping, my cohort. But while I matched them in a few things, primarily age, in others I did not and was forced to study with the smaller girls. It was an odd position to be in, and later on I'd find the littles liked me well enough, but they were never company.

The three girls that had led me there, the first one and her two companions, were used to being the leaders of our cohort, the Eagles.

This is how the cohorts worked. Normally girls were taken into the Brides of Steel when they had their first decade. When they came, those of their class were given a name: Kestrels, Peregrines, Eagles, Owls, Goshawks, Blue-tails, and Gulls.

Their cohort would be known by that name and their group would be distinct, in all but one thing: the oldest year and the youngest shared their name and were separated by being the Old and the New. This was so those new ones would have, in theory at least, mentors and role models, older students who would help them find their path that first bewildering year in the school.

There were three dozen in a cohort at first, but usually that number was well-trimmed by the time it came to graduation. A few students did not live there at the school but went home every day and were not there to become Gladiators, but rather to learn something of their training, one piece or another that their family or House thought would be useful to them later. Adelina told me once that her mother Emiliana had often threatened to send her to the school in order to learn how to defend herself.

I do not think it would have been a terrible punishment. Adelina is tall and graceful and would have done well at the lessons. Too many of the Merchants and Nobles see these things as beneath them, though.

Hyacinth and Pezi and Glim, those were Neffa's friends' names. Hyacinth's parents were mysterious but apparently quite rich; they rarely appeared at the school. Rumor had it that they had won their money somehow and that if you tried to press for their antecedents, they were mysteriously lacking.

This was not, however, a rumor that anyone ever mentioned around Hyacinth, who was, in many ways, the most class-and-status-conscious girl in the school, able to reckon others' estates and social stature with knife blade accuracy, and who never hesitated to look down on someone if she could find an angle from which to do so. She was tall and willowy, and of mixed Old and New Continent blood, so her skin was the color of the North-stretch river in the spring, when it is full of soil washed down from the highlands. She'd decided to be a Gladiator and her family had indulged her.

Pezi was fashionably dark-skinned, small and neat in appearance. Her family were Nobles who had been disgraced for some scandal (there were many variants on this story) three generations ago, and she was the youngest of four siblings, so she was intent on winning her way as a Gladiator and took her training more seriously than most.

I could almost always find her working on techniques or conditioning in the early mornings when I went. Of the three, I liked her the best, but she was also the most passive and inclined to let the other two lead her along, or at least not object as they went along.

Glim was also dark-skinned, but her family was newer to Tabat, having originally settled in the Southern Isles and established estates there before coming to the city two generations later. She had even been born in those Isles and sometimes affected their twang when speaking carelessly, but she was as capable as anyone in the school of speaking with the proper diction and grammar of Tabat's upper crust.

At first, they seemed to me obsessed with these matters: whose family was connected where and how close they were in gradations of blood or layers of service to the Duke. It took me longer than it should have to figure out that was because it gave them a way to sort each other.

It was not the only way, however. I chose to work at another, even though when push came to shove, the blood of my departed parents was just as good as the blood of anyone else there, even if I was linked to a scandalous figure, Jolietta.

Surely Hyacinth was the one who first spread and then fostered the rumors about Jolietta. She varied them with great inventiveness. I heard versions that included Jolietta fucking Beasts and inducting me in the same, Jolietta seeking solitude at Piper Hill in order to blaspheme against the Trade Gods, Jolietta having conducted treason against the Duke and being given the choice of Piper Hill or imprisonment, and worse.

Cruel stories, designed to hurt me when I heard them and to make others trust me less, or to treat me differently—never more kindly—than they would have otherwise. She was good with words, Hyacinth.

Luckily for me, I was good with a blade. Because that was the most important way to sort people at the school.

I would love to think that it was innate talent that made that happen and certainly I cannot discount that. But it was also considerable effort, and a willingness to try to catch up by working harder than the others, who had been there years, learning and conditioning themselves.

So I arose in the mornings when I heard first bell outside in the dark streets, despite the fact that we were not required to rise till second bell and even then could laze until one had to scramble to make it to breakfast at third. I went down the darkened stairways carrying my clothes and gear under my arm and changed down in the gymnasium's outer chamber before I went to practice.

At first, I worked with the stick, the way they had taught me, one foot pointing forward, the other sideways, the long stick an extension of my arm, reaching out to tap and retreat, tap and retreat, until my arms and upper thighs ached.

Later, I added other things, practicing them over and over until they became second nature, until without thinking my body enacted them as needed: parries and dodges, fallbacks and lunges.

I learned to use knives and arrows and sharp little throwing stars, the kind that assassins coat with poison and which Gladiators attached colored ribbons to, so you can throw them as a spectacle and then have your opponent tangled in them, slowed and distracted. Those are cruel little objects, which the Rose Kingdom that created them call *thorn blossoms*, and Hyacinth was very good with them.

I kept out of the way of Neffa and her pack because they weren't important. I didn't care whether or not they liked me. I was much more worried about proving myself to the instructors and staying in the Brides of Steel. Myrila and the rest of the staff had made it clear that if I flagged or disappointed, I would be let loose. There were other schools I could have trained with if that happened, but they were inferior ones, and I was bent on learning from the very best.

Because that was what the school was known for, and why I had chosen them. Myrila hired teachers who could show the students things they would learn nowhere else, tricky strategies and flashy maneuvers. The Duke's bodyguards at the time all came from the Brides of Steel. Nowadays Alberic has his own, which he trains himself, he claims for reasons of security. At the time the school had Janiver, who wrote three books on military strategy and taught us all to apply it to our bouts in the ring. That was useful stuff, and sometimes, when I find myself perplexed still, I think about what they might have done when faced with the same situation and follow the path that I imagine they would have taken.

I do not think any of those teachers thought much of me at first. Particularly since my initial swordplay lessons were with a woman used to teaching ten-year-olds, who felt that I had learned bad habits, and that it was my duty to break them before she could supply me with a better way. She was gruff and not unkind, though. To someone who had been raised in the shadow of Jolietta's cruelty, that lack of unkindness was the greatest kindness I had known, and so I would have died for that woman by the time, a few months later, that she passed me up to the next teacher, grudgingly admitting that I "had done all right."

How much of my life have I lived like that, shaped by the things that Jolietta did to me, while telling myself that I had moved past them and would never be affected by them again? And it happened again, when people repeated the stories to me, watching my face to see how I reacted.

Neffa and the others kept shadowing my footsteps and making fun of my mistakes. I let it go on for so much longer than I should have.

It wasn't because of fear, even though Neffa outstripped me in height and breadth of shoulder. Rumor held that there was Giant blood somewhere in her background, but it was a rumor that no one dared voice around her. And not just that she was big, but that it was clear: attack her and you'd have her cronies to deal with as well. And she did not move against me herself. When I failed to react, Neffa tried more brutal methods, getting several of the other girls to ambush me.

But by the time she thought to do that, it was too late. I had already absorbed as much as I could, enough to become an effective fighter in my own right, and I'd learned enough from Jolietta that no one took me unaware, even when I was sleeping.

I will not pretend it was a comfortable existence. But it was better than Piper Hill and, more than that, it had a future to it.

Jolietta had prepared me well for the unrelenting hostility.

They backed me into corners, elbowed me in passing so black bruises covered my ribs, tripped me from behind. They spit in my food while I was watching, tore pages from my books, smeared shit and menses on my equipment. On and on, a daily grind of it intended to wear me down.

After years of Jolietta's beatings and starvation, I just laughed at them.

And I kept fighting back. They'd leave me bloody and the school's nurse would sew up the gashes while she and Myrila both pressed me for the names that I refused to give up.

You might have thought that my refusal would have won me friends, but it didn't. People attack those among them who hold out a higher model, as though the presence of it were a criticism that they could not bear. Not that I think my model was that admirable. It was more born of stubbornness than anything else, and a refusal to give in.

When I'd finally had enough, I put a stop to it. I used some of what Jolietta had given me.

I never told Adelina this story. I don't know if she guessed at it in the cracks of things. She is often uncannily good at ferreting things out that I had not meant to reference. Still.

Jolietta taught me harshly, but she taught me well. With Beast-keeping comes medicines for them, and there is overlap between their cures and the cures for Humans, particularly among those whose forms have Human qualities to them, such as Centaurs or Mers. So when I was sent to the nurse again, I told her that I thought my earring had been dropped during the beating and begged her to go look for it, as piteously as I could.

After she scuttled out the door, I waited three breaths, then riffled through her apothecary's chest, extracting what I needed. Easy enough to find, kept in the drawer for sleeping draughts and calmatives.

When the group came across me next, they only roughed me up, for they were pleased to find me carrying a bag of fruit pastries from Figgis. They never thought to ask why I might have been carrying too many for me, but just enough for them to share among themselves.

I was not the only girl who'd suffered at their hands. It took all of us together to carry them out to the yard-sized orchard that lay beside the school at that time, long since made into more student barracks. We stripped them and put them into the treetops, considerately making sure they were well secured with ropes in order to make sure that none fell.

They slept so deep. I don't know how long it would have lasted if the gardeners had not arrived to discover them and made noise enough to summon the whole school, staff, and masters and all the sundry students, laughing.

Myrila had them cut down and cold water poured on them to waken them. They gasped like fishes and gawped as though they could not catch their breath.

Neffa was furious and red-faced, scanning the courtyard. I caught her eye and looked at her straight, letting her know exactly who was responsible. She stared back. Silence fell over the chattering mob as everyone, one by one, saw our wordless duel and looked to our stares.

Then her eyes fell beneath mine, and I had won a victory sweeter than Winter's blade ever gained me.

After that I had no more trouble with her, and I let her alone as well. Who knows what she thinks of me now, or how she remembers that moment that seemed to stretch for miles and weeks and endless corridors. I should have told this story to Adelina. Why did I never do so?

The thing was that, although the girls took a while to realize it, they could not do anything against me that I truly feared. Most of the teachers were already somewhat set against me, thinking that I was stubborn and spoiled, rather than persistent. None of the other students showed me any kindness and so I did not solicit it of them.

Perhaps Jolietta was the best training for the wilderness that was a girls' school that could have been bestowed on me. At any rate, I did not care at all for anything they could say. Jolietta had withheld all approbation or affection, and I no longer expected it from those around me. Even today, when someone is overly effusive about their affection, it wakes a distaste in me, a catlike part of my spirit that immediately wants to move away from any petting hand.

How much of my life did I spend wanting the love that Jolietta had denied me? Because my situation with the city now spells it out for me. I assumed it was mine by right, that I deserved all that love and adulation, that it was, indeed, my *due*.

When all the while the truth was that it did not matter who occupied the role. Any peg in that hole would have fitted and would have been admired for the way it managed to carry off that act, filling a space as though there were some credit or struggle for it.

I wonder what all those women who were my classmates thought of the news when they heard it. How many of them thought, "Oh, sorcery, of course. That's how she got all her success and I'm not surprised, knowing Bella Kanto." Hyacinth, perhaps, and she'd be quick to speculate and gossip and spread poison as freely as she did in the old days.

A knock of the door calls me away from remembering my days at the Brides of Steel. It is the pretty sailor, Sofia, carrying a tray of food. Ruhua plans to keep me entirely here, it seems, and not even let me above to watch the approach of the ship to the raft city.

Sofia is silent as she unburdens the tray and sets down the dishes on the desk/table that is the only suitable surface. Her look is sympathetic, and as she sets out the food, her fingers brush over mine, linger for a second before they move away, leaving a trail of sensation in their wake.

Once there would have been no hesitation in me. I'd have reached up, wound my fingers in her hair, pulled her mouth to mine without a thought, rose and danced her back into my bed for mutual delight.

But all of that seems so much more complicated than it used to be. What if she is a spy or assassin? Is that not the more likely thing, more likely than the thought that she wants to play at kissing games with a failed Gladiator? With a woman exiled from the city for one of the greatest crimes that city—or anywhere on this continent—has known, for abetting sorcery, sorcery of the kind that despoiled and destroyed the old continent, left it the wasteland that it is now? And so I watch the food as she lays it out, and ignore the warmth and smell of sunlight and tobacco that linger in her wake.

And after she is gone, the food sits there, and every time I try to take a bite, the gorge rises in my stomach, until finally I push the plate away.

When I first heard I was to be sent away from Tabat, I was angry. I had thought I had died and been rinsed of all emotion, but when they told me I would still be alive, but that I would be sent away from the city whose heart I had been, that was a torch. A bonfire of anger, and I could voice none of it because if I dared speak, if I dared protest, there would be some reason found to send me back into the room where the torturers ply their trade.

Alberic had not said that aloud, but he spoke it with every possessive look, every arrogant motion of pity and consolation. He always wanted to have me—not simply to be his lover, that was not enough—but to have me, own me. Be able to predict and direct what I should do.

If he had not sent me away from Tabat, I might have killed him for that, eventually. I have seen others smolder under burdens until they burst into flame.

But thinking of any of that tires me, pushes me back into the grey exhaustion that has ridden me ever since we left Tabat. I curl back into my bed, pull the blankets around me, even though their warmth seems oppressive in this small cabin that I cannot leave.

Resentment at Ruhua stirs in me again, creeps through my dreams. In them she and Hyacinth are walking hand in hand, talking about me, deadly little tangles of thorn blossoms, with ribbons of flame attached to them, setting the city of Tabat afire.

CHAPTER 9

EXITING TABAT (LUCY)

Of all the various terrible and unfair things Lucy had known in her lifetime—beyond the fact of being the youngest of seven sisters and one brother in a family that could scarcely have supported one child, beyond the death of her mother in a riot and her sisters (unfairly) blaming her for it, beyond being thrust out of a promising apprenticeship with Adelina Nettlepurse because of factors over which Lucy had absolutely no control—this, the most recent, was beyond question the worst.

She was being jostled along, her head in a burlap sack that kept rasping against her face, the bony shoulder she was slung over uncomfortably poking into her belly.

She was being kidnapped.

She was not sure what the kidnappers intended. You always heard about slavers, but that was other cities, not Tabat, where you got abducted and sold to ships and then sold somewhere else where you didn't speak the language and never laid eyes on your family (not that she cared about that) again.

At least it gave her somewhere to be going, she thought between the jostles. She'd gone to the College of Mages to ask her friend Maz for help. Enough money for dinner and a place to sleep, at least. If he had not had enough money for that, surely he would have been able to find her space somewhere on the large campus where he was a student. So she had found him, and when she had explained her situation he had tried to find her a corner to stay, and in return she had gotten him kidnapped along with her.

At least, she presumed that he was still, like her, being carried along but she did not dare ask or make any sort of sound. Her earlier shouts for help had only gotten her head buffeted by two quick and dizzying blows along with the hissed promise that there would be more to come if she didn't keep her mouth shut.

Suddenly she was slung off the shoulder and thrown forward to collide with a splintery wooden surface. Something thudded beside her, and then rolled into her, and the warmth and solidity made her whisper, "Maz?"

He whispered back, "Lucy! Where are we going? Who are these people?"

The surface under them jolted into motion. She realized they were in a cart, rumbling forward over the cobblestones. She pushed into him, trying to brace herself while vainly trying to grab purchase on the surface beneath her with her bound hands.

"I don't know. They said something about knowing who one of us was, but I didn't catch it all. I don't know any reason why anyone would know who I was. Is there any that you can think of, that would explain why someone would seek you out and think you were important enough to kidnap?"

He was still for a moment before he said, "No, there isn't any reason."

"That's not good," she said.

"Why?"

"Because if they were taking us for a particular reason, then it's probably to get a ransom and we will be returned safely. If that's not the case, then they've taken us in order to sell us as slaves." She'd heard the stories. She even thought that perhaps her mother's friends, Canumbra and Legio, might have sold a few people in their time. There was always a need for labor in the Southern Isles, or on the trade ships, and not all sailors went willingly.

"They will take us far away to a place where no one knows us in order to do so," she finished. No one in her family would hunt her down or come looking for her. They would think that she had run away and met some suitable end, no doubt.

Well, that was all right. She wouldn't be missing any of them either. And it wasn't as though she had any sort of future in the city. Maybe this was for the best.

Except she didn't see how it could be, unless this were like a Fairy tale and she'd do something so valuable and noble that she was freed, like saving her owner's life or maybe one of their children. Or something. At fourteen, life had made her pragmatic.

She could feel when they moved from cobblestone to brick and back again, as well as the long slant that meant they were headed down to the harbor, which was another bad sign. She rolled over and said, "Bring your hands up to mine, let's see if we can untie each other's ropes."

She realized her error when an unexpected presence cuffed her and said, "Let's see if we can't, girlie. Just you lie still and don't make no more noise and there won't be no more smacking your head. Otherwise, there'll be plenty of it and more." He smacked her again in illustration and she was silent.

Instead, she focused all her senses on the city as they moved downward, trying to record all the sensations: a whiff of rolls from a bakery, a waft of ozone from some aetheric light's broken bulb, a tang of salt and dried fish. The cart's rumbles changed in tone as they moved through dirt-floored alleyways. The twang of gulls, a cat mewing, and then the sound of the waves lapping the docks, the creak and grumble of moored boats. Someone shouting at someone else in the far distant, voice thin and drunken and indecipherable.

The cart rolled to a stop. Before she could gather her wits, hands grabbed her with casual ferocity, pulling her off the surface so fast her hands collected splinters from the wood as they slid along them. She cried out at the pain and was slapped again.

They dragged her along so fast it was difficult to keep her feet. A voice said, "Almost there," its tone cheerful. "An' a nice night's work of it, in my opinion. Keep them 'ween ya so they don't slip going up the plank."

Underfoot, a wobbly gangplank, the smell of fish and salt pronounced now. Her hands burned where the splinters throbbed, their intrusion, the sense of wrongness about them almost as bad as the pain. But not quite.

On a boat now. Shoved along and then down steps, colliding several times as she tried to walk against the boat's sway. She'd never been on one before; the feeling of unsteadiness underfoot made her nauseous and dizzy. The burlap was still over her face, making it difficult to breathe, but she could see dazzles of light now and again, a lantern carried in front of her.

Yanked to a halt, then shoved through a doorway without warning, unable to stop herself from falling onto the flooring, catching more splinters. The thud nearby of the same happening to Maz.

The door's slam, and silence.

Her legs almost buckled as she was set on her feet and the bag pulled away with a rasp of rough cloth. A knife flashed and the gag fell away. She licked her dry lips and swallowed.

She found herself in a small cabin lit by guttering gilt lanterns set in pairs beside the doorway and reflected in the rounded mirrors on the opposite wall. The plushy carpet's color was peacock-feather brilliant.

Space was at a premium here, but every inch had been used. A desktop folded down from the wall on brass chains, its shelf rimmed to prevent objects from rolling off in rough seas, and a bookcase had been set into one wall, jammed with worn volumes in motley assemblage beside a map holder whose round holes were filled with paper and parchment rolls.

The only excess was the bed, which was wide enough for two and spilled with bead-bright, lozenge-shaped cushions. Like the desk and shelves, it had a railing edging it, presumably to keep the occupants contained during storms.

Two sailors stood on either side of the door. A carved wooden chair sat in the middle, a man perched on it. He leaned forward to glare at her, arms folded.

"This," he said in dubious tones, "is the Pot King's son, the College of Mages' prize?"

"He's in disguise, we thinks, Cap'n," one man said. "At the taverns we asked at, they said he was likely to disguise hisself. Amulet pointed at him, and the magic was so strong it fell to pieces. An' he was coming from the College of Mages, just like you said. We didn't see the other one till afterwards."

Lucy stole a glance over her shoulder. Her captors stood on either side of the door. Movement drew her eye downward. Legs in unremarkable grey trousers and worn boots that twitched as though her stare had awakened them lay protruding from another burlap bag. Maz. Her thoughts were tangled. Why had they believed *her* their prey, instead of him?

A cough returned her attention to the man before her.

"I am Captain Jusuf Miryam, of the ship *Fancy Bliss*," he said.

He was small in stature, perhaps a shade shorter than Lucy, who was used to having everyone tower over her. His beard and hair were a bristling black, combed and well-groomed. His skin was leathery and bronzed, and his eyes were a perilous poet's green. When he flexed his hands impatiently, she noted their well-kept nails and the bright red stone framed in gold on his left hand. His clothes were gaudy although wrinkled and not much washed.

"Well?"

"I don't know why I'm here."

He frowned. "Let me cut right to the bone, lad. I will not put up with prevarication and the tongue-twisting that wizards are known for." He nodded down at the bundle of burlap and legs. "You said this one came along later, my fine fellows?"

"Tried to stop us from nicking her … er, him," one said. He jerked the sack away and Maz's pale, freckled boy-face blinked upwards from the floor. "Figgered we always needed canaries, our line of work."

There was a knock on the door. "Cap'n, 'at finger-wiggler ya wanted tah speak to is 'ere."

"Throw them both in the hold for now," Captain Jusuf said. "Give him a taste of what no cooperation would be like." He smiled faintly at Lucy. "Not that your present form isn't charming enough, but you might consider releasing it."

"Put them in cold iron chains," he said to the men. "Keep the candles I gave you burning in there, that'll keep him woozy enough to cast no spells. Check on them every turn of the glass."

They were hauled away.

THE HOLD, Lucy found, was deep in the ship's belly, damp and cold. The timbers creaked and groaned around them and every time a wave slammed into the ship, Lucy felt the blow through the wall to which she had been chained.

The older of the two sailors brought out a fat black candle and stooped to set it in a brass holder bolted to the floor. The younger stood staring at Lucy. He was a scrawny, scowling boy, his head shaved to gray-brown fuzz.

The other was old enough to be his grandfather. She nicknamed them Scowl and Kindly in her head. After setting the wick a-kindle, Kindly took the boy by the shoulder with an admonitory shake and jerked him from the room.

The door slammed behind them and there was a clunk as it was barred. Lucy raised her head to look across at her companion.

"*Are* you the one they're looking for? The Pot and Kettle King's son?" She'd heard the name before, a Sorcerer who ruled the northern part of the Old Continent. She'd never heard of him having a son. And Maz had never talked about his family. She'd assumed him an orphan from his demeanor.

"Oh, no," he said hurriedly. "No, I'm not. But listen, I'm thinking that if they think you're him, that's the only thing keeping you from being used as a canary. And while I don't know what being a canary means, I'm willing to bet that since they have to kidnap people to be them, it's not a great thing."

Lucy mulled this over. The air in the chamber was thick and close, making thought difficult. It seemed reasonable enough. "You're probably right."

"You can at least find out what they want," Maz said.

"What if he asks me again to drop the disguise?"

"Tell him it was a shape-shifting spell that went awry and you were heading back to the College to have a Master Mage remove it. That happens all the time."

"It does?"

"You'd be surprised how often."

"I can't do it," she said, turning back to the question. "He'll glare at me, and I'll start crying."

He frowned over at her. "Just put your chin up. Think about him naked."

She blushed, even more frightened. She still couldn't figure out how she, once Obedience the Mouse, had ended up on a boat with pirates. It was like something from a ballad but much less glamorous somehow. She hadn't realized how frightening adventures could be.

They heard footsteps and the door being unbarred. Scowl stuck his head in and looked between them, then at the candle. Before either could react, he withdrew his head with a rapid snakelike motion and slammed the door.

"Not much chance for conversation," Maz said.

"How long do you think they'll keep us here?"

"Your guess is as good as mine. Look, Lucy, you've got to bluff your way through this. Pretend you're someone else. Perhaps some character from a play you've seen?"

"I haven't seen any plays since I was very little," she said, dismayed.

"Well, what about one that you liked as a child?"

She thought. She remembered the stories that she loved listening to. In the bedroom, all four children crouched around her mother's skirts. Lucy had been so small she could barely remember the stories, but they came back to her now: The Rabbit that Stole the Moon, and Mary Silverhands and Sister Wind and the Golden Bridle, Whitepetal and Blackleaf, and the Princess with the Copper Scales.

There had been a street puppet theater, a cloth screen stretched over a wooden framework, so different on one side from the other. In front, the puppets moved, but past the curtains had been the dancing puppeteers, pitching their voices upward, avoiding each other as they maneuvered the wooden sticks manipulating the forms above them.

She remembered Mary Silverhands, her glowing hands held before her, turning everything she touched to metal: the food on her plate, the drink in her glass. And the blonde-haired puppet's dignity, its upright stance, the patient grace conveyed by its inanimate face.

She closed her eyes and envisioned herself something other than Lucy, the youngest, the clumsiest, the least listened to and the most overlooked. She was Mary, her life a constant struggle to look out for those around her, to avoid unleashing the deadly power that would, unless contained, turn the whole world to silver.

"All right," she said. It was Mary's voice, not a quaver, not a quiver.

"You'll do it?"

"Yes," Lucy/Mary said.

CHAPTER 10

THE STOOPING HAWK (BELLA)

I have never written a fine hand, although my tutors tried to teach such a thing to me when I was a child. At Piper Hill, I wrote little and read less; Jolietta's work was not something that she recorded. Indeed, most Beast Masters prefer to keep their secret lore to themselves, as though to mark down their superstitions might make them realize their flimsiness.

Because that is one of their marks, that flimsiness, that belief in luck. People talk of Gladiators as though chasing luck was our particular plague, but every job has it, to the point where Rupru, one of the most popular Trade Gods, is devoted to the tending of customs and luck rituals.

But the Trade Gods are funny things—you can see what they do in this world, and yet it is as though they were not people at all, no matter how many little dolls of them one's house holds.

I have been postponing taking up pen to write to Adelina, though I am sure she has written an abundance to me by now. I am not sure what I would say to her if she were here, let alone on paper, which can play one false in such encounters, misrepresent tone through an accident of spelling or grammar.

She came to see me at my worst point, after the torturers had stolen all the fire in my veins and replaced it with milk, so all I could do was sit and shiver and remember, remember so clearly, all that they had done.

Not as though I will not have plenty of time to reply. All this long journey stretches in front of me and then at its end? Exile. A frontier city, filled with those who have left the larger cities for reasons of their own. Perhaps not disgrace like mine but some other prompting, like love of exploration or thoughts of some financial opportunity or—what? Love of the lands outside Tabat, inconceivable as that may seem?

I have traveled all over the world at Alberic's behest. Three times to the Rose Kingdom, more than any other ambassador. To the Southern Isles and the land far north, all snow and tundra and enormous bears.

I could take another nap. I could drill, here in the cabin's privacy, or else up on deck, but every time I play at that, I seem to find new ways my body can betray me.

How did I amuse myself back in Tabat, where there were hardly enough hours in the day to do all that I wanted? I can scarcely think of it at all, it seems so distant now, that busy life, now replaced by grey days aboard a ship.

But Teo is already scratching at the door. He is never bored, never glum. Every day is a new adventure to him, with no idea what it might bring.

I follow him up on deck. The sailors grumbled at his presence at first, saying he would chase the ship's cats. But those cats, an enormous yellow and gray tom Enba and his long-suffering son Anba of the same color, have shown themselves well capable of handling any eager puppy and the three reached an accord early on, although not before Teo's inquisitive and sensitive nose acquired a few scratches.

"We are two days out from the Silent Sea," one sailor tells me.

It takes me aback. I had not thought our route could go that way. To do so requires magic.

The Silent Sea receives its name from a lack. Winds reach its edges and turn away. It is calm and steady, and no sails work there; all are unbellied and becalmed. To cross it, the captain will have to empower the engine in the ship's belly and that is pricey magic of the sort Alberic is usually unwilling to spend. Ruhua must be undertaking some mission for him.

To enter the Silent Sea means we are going to the Long Slow City, the great raft settlement in the middle.

Clouds hang low in the sky, barely illuminated in the pre-sunrise light that seems to come from nowhere. This low, they are not clouds but fog, suspended in the air, thick and heavy, as though the world were trying to hide itself. Fuzzy as wool, but much damper.

It is cheering to watch the sailors at their work. Certainly there have some leisure—they play at cards and spillikins, carve bits of wood or embroider. They sing songs, some that I've never heard in Tabat. But the captain keeps them busy, keeps the ship neat and clean.

I've seen the engine on our tour of the ship, the captain displaying it to Ruhua, while I trailed along after her. It lies in the hold, a covered thing made of metal and something else. Its labor is not fast. Such an engine can never match the speed of sail, surely. But it will move us slowly but surely, across the Silent Sea, and to the city that floats there.

I was there once, in my youth. Do the people remember me? I hope at least one still does, if she is still alive. But there is no guarantee of that, and she is yet another person who I have not written to, over the years.

Everyone used to concern themselves with connecting to me. I never used to worry about these threads. And now they all are torn asunder, or most of them.

And the few frayed ones that do remain—Leonoa, Adelina—I am no longer sure I am capable of maintaining.

The old me would not have worried about such things. She trusted the world not to give her any challenges she could not master.

But I, I have learned that the world is different than that. That its obstacles can smash you to pieces, that there can be disasters past comprehension. That wanting something is not, in the end, sufficient.

You would think Piper Hill would have taught me that. But it only made me want something so much that I would have told myself anything in order to achieve it. I am hollowed out by all this thinking and wondering and worrying.

Teo brings me the knotted rope the sailors have made for him as a toy. He holds it hopefully in his mouth, drops it at my feet. Retreats a few steps, front legs bent a little to show him ready to play, tail wagging frantically in anticipation of joy.

"I don't feel like it," I tell him, but he is not dissuaded. He drops it at my feet over and over again until I give in.

A sailor, sent to fetch me to Ruhua, interrupts our game.

"I will show you something now that we have left Tabat," she says to me when I enter her cabin. "The Duke gave it to me. They created it for him, the ones who … questioned you."

That sly pause, that careful hesitation before the solemn intonation, are almost my undoing. The thought of that "questioning," the methodical and unceasing tortures that had been part of it, I will hold those memories all my life. I hope that someday their pull will fade, will not hold me frozen and motionless, unable to react, the way that they do now.

Strung on the silver chain around her neck is a pierced coin, of the sort that Moon Worshippers wear, showing which moon they were born under, white Selene or purple Toj or sullen red Hijae.

"I do not worship the Moons," I point out, trying to steady myself. I am pleased my voice does not tremble. Ruhua's eyes sharpen just a trifle, a last lick of the whetstone before she plunges in the knife.

"You do not need to, for this to work," she says. "This coin holds your death. Break it, and it will be released. You cannot steal it from around my neck, either, for when it no longer touches my skin, that death will be freed. I hold your life in my hand, Kanto, and can snap it like that if I wish. The Duke has given me that authority."

"Then why not do it here and now?" I challenge. "You don't

want the task of nursemaiding me until I reach the place of my exile. Do it now and return quickly."

I feel weary to the bone. If she snapped the coin, at least I could lie down and sleep and be done with all this.

She holds it between forefinger and thumb. I can see how it has been filed, a silver line across its midsection, so it could be snapped in half with ease. But she tucks it back away into the neckline and smiles pleasantly.

"I will return soon enough," she says softly. "Sooner, by far, than you."

THE DAY SLIDES by as so many have, one after another, grey and cold granite. This far out, the wind always has a chilly edge, no matter how the sun shines. At least Alberic thought enough of me to send me on one of his finest ships.

Was it simply that he wanted to make sure I got there? Or at any rate, out of Tabat?

Why exile me? This question has occurred to me every once in a while, nudging up against my thoughts, but I have not cared enough to pay it much attention so far. Now it occurs to me again, and I walk the deck with Teo at my heels, contemplating it.

Alberic does nothing for love, and less for honor, so long as he maintains the appearance of honor. He is the sort of man who cheats at cards, but everyone is well paid enough to not breathe a word of it. His butler stands outside the evening dice games and reimburses the losers as they come out, and that is the price they are paid in return for not complaining too loudly about his ways. He is motivated by power and by profit, the latter only so much because it gives him power, particularly in a city so ruled by Merchants.

Because make no mistake of it, Adelina has told me more than once, Merchant power has come to wax much greater than the Duke's. That is the only reason Tabat is having elections, regardless of anything said about the ancient promise. If he could, Alberic would break it, and stay in power forever, or at least his family. There are two children, but he pays them little mind other than thinking them ornaments. No, I do not think he cares much what comes about after his death. But while he draws breath, he wants to be in charge.

What does he gain by sending me away, rather than choosing imprisonment or, worse, some public execution? Why does it matter that I am not in Tabat? Is it something to do with Tabat's magic, the magic that made me Winter's Champion so long?

I rub at my aching head. I wish that Adelina were here. This is her sort of puzzle, the kind of thing she tracks down in history through bills of lading and old notes and maps, and ordinary papers of the day. She might be able to understand this.

All I know is that he does not care about my welfare. What matters to him is that I am out of the city, and not likely to return. Or does he have some purpose for me in Fort Plentitude? Surely Ruhua would have hinted at it already, if only to rub my nose in the fact that even so far away, I am expected to obey his wishes.

The waves roll on and on, and silver fish swim among them, small ones no longer than my hand. We are being pulled along by the wind fast enough that I can feel the motion, as though the boat were a living thing, enjoying itself, leaping into the waves like a Mer or dolphin, racing along for the sheer fun of it.

This far out, we have seen both, and whales, and a great Kraken once, the reason that the masts and rails have wards laid on them, to be activated if one should try to pull us down. I have been told they are only curious when they come exploring, but no one has ever succeeded in communicating with them, and there is always argument whether they are Beast or animal, with most favoring the latter.

The city we are coming to is one I have visited before. How long ago was that, perhaps a decade? There will still be people there that I know and that itches at me. Ruhua will tell them I am in disgrace, and why, and then none of them will wish to speak to me.

An irrational terror seizes me. Although I was freed from the Ducal dungeons, perhaps here again I will be taken to a cell and questioned, tortured. Who knows what sort of justice rules here? I focus on my breathing, feel it go in and out despite the thudding of my heart.

Teo whines at my heel. The anger that always sweeps me after these moments of terror sweeps hold, and I kick at him, connecting harder than I mean to. He yelps and scrambles back.

Remorse strikes me.

His tail is held low, as though he thinks he has done something wrong. I kneel down beside him, pull him into my arms. He is trembling from nose to toe. I had seen Alberic kick him more than once, but he has never known such treatment from me.

No creature has known such treatment from me.

What have I become, to strike without thinking like that? I am a Gladiator. If I did that to a Human, I might kill them without realizing.

His nose is wet against my cheek. He snuffs once. He smells of dog, the smell that my old dog Gelert used to bring to my room. Anger falls away from me like rain, washed away by a sorrow so strong I can barely move lest I begin to weep.

Are the sailors looking at me, watching me? They do it when they think I am not looking and they murmur among themselves, to see Bella Kanto brought so low. Once they would have all pressed around me, sought conversation and favors and stories, wooing me like the celebrity I was.

But no longer. Never again.

I don't look around as I rise to my feet. I could not bear to find Sofia looking, could not bear to see the pity in their eyes. That is all anyone has for me, other than the ones that hate me.

I do not force Teo to sleep outside the door any longer, and so he comes in with me. It is time for dinner, but they will not notice if I do not come to it. It will not be the first meal I've skipped. I hold up my wrist and look at it, so much thinner now, as though the muscle were ebbing away every day.

Well, perhaps that is melodramatic, I hear Adelina say in my head. For some reason, this memory hurts worst of all. I gather Teo to me and weep into his fur, crying for the first time, a storm of tears, as though I were emptying myself out, crying myself into just a husk.

He whines low in his throat, distressed, and licks my face as fast as the tears roll down it. Finally he throws his head back and howls, a long dolorous sound that I have never heard him make before. The strangeness of the noise stops me, and I stare at him.

His anxious brown eyes stare back. It's been so long since I had a dog. And Gelert was smart, smarter than most. But still, sometimes, Teo acts so undoglike, like a dog that has been raised around some other type of creature and thinks itself one of them.

I hug him to me and rest my chin atop his head. He doesn't howl again, just whines low in his throat.

"I won't cry anymore," I promise him. I cannot think of the last time I have done so. Not since Phillip's death, perhaps. It has always hurt me in my pride to think that another might see me cry, might know me not so indestructible. Something to fear, crying.

But in its aftermath, I feel better. Cleansed, even here in this stale room that I have made so dirty.

CHAPTER 11

*Y*ou will not be allowed to go onto the city," Ruhua says in leaving breakfast the next day. Stung, I say that I hadn't planned on going, but the truth was that I had found myself not so much looking forward to it as anticipating it, the thought of something fresh, something other than daily shipboard existence. New textures, new smells, new sounds. That had always been my favorite part of traveling.

I ask why I will not be allowed to talk to anyone. Ruhua shrugs. "I don't care about the rationale behind it," she says, "Alberic's order and thus to be obeyed."

"Why don't you like me?" I ask. The question has been haunting me all this while.

"What, not like the famous Bella Kanto?" she sneers. "The toast of the town, strewn with honors and accolades? Which it turns out were the result of magic, not skill. All those girls you taught, 'Work hard and you can be just like me.' What do you think they think of your lessons now? Do they follow them still? Or do they try their best to forget anything ever taught them by that cheat, Bella Kanto? I rather think the latter, myself."

Teo barks indignantly. Her gaze travels to him.

"Alberic might write and tell me to kill that dog," she says. "He can be petty when it pleases him. It would be a shame to deprive you of your faithful companion. Your only friend, so to speak."

Her gaze measures my reaction, storing the information away. I try to keep my face as stolid and still as I can; I cannot tell from her expression whether or not I have succeeded in doing so.

I remember these games, from early days at the Brides of Steel. Every student my age had years of experience against my lack, plus I was still settling out Jolietta's estate, which made them all envy me for supposed wealth, while the legalities and signing after signing of documents and lawyer consultations ate study time I did not have.

Ruhua reminds me so much of Neffa.

She turns and leaves. I find myself exhaling, my body unstiffening from a rigor I had not even realized I had fallen into.

"She is not a nice woman," I tell Teo. He sneezes and shakes his head. "I won't let her hurt you," I promise him, and I mean it. I think. I waver. I would do anything to avoid returning to that cell; that is the key to controlling me. Does she realize that? I suspect that she does, but if she doesn't, it is imperative that she never find out. I could not bear for her to have even more control over me than she does already.

She has tipped her hand by acknowleging that she does not like me.

That was the most startling thing about the events that led me to that cell. While I knew that people did not like me—resented me, sometimes because they desired my place, or because they wanted Spring to come sooner—I had never felt that anyone was hiding such feelings while working against me.

Now it all seems so obvious. I think of the ill luck charms the boy Teo, the dog's namesake, found in the weekly bouquets that had been sent me. When he found those, I should have known. Should have looked to see what was happening in the shadows …

Should have, would have, could have … all left behind and what has happened, has happened. There is no use regretting such things. That is something Jolietta taught me, in her time. I do not remember anything of my parents, but I remember her and her lessons well.

Jolietta, for all her faults, was at least always open about disliking me. I knew to expect her blows and deprivations ...

Almost all of them. She'd stilled Phillip, the Centaur who had been my only friend and ally. Not killed him, but slid a wire into his brain and then sold him away.

And then Jolietta died the next day, leaving only anger and confusion that settled, like ash in the wake of some great fire, to settle and reveal clear intent: my path to the Brides of Steel, the knife edge of tension as I fought over and over again to prove myself, and then argued my way in.

Myrila told me much later it was that determination that made her finally argue in my favor, made her push through despite the objections of many of the faculty, angry at this precedent. Some went so far as to hint that I'd killed Jolietta in order to make my way there.

No, I did not.

But I would have.

CHAPTER 12

THE FANCY BLISS (LUCY)

*S*cowl poked his head in twice more before she was bundled back into the captain's cabin, while Maz was taken somewhere else. Another black candle guttered in the corner. She couldn't tell much difference between the air outside and the candle smoke, but she was so weary by now that everything seemed unreal and brighter than life to her, like a hallucinatory fever-dream.

"Well?" the captain demanded.

"What did you want with me?"

"Are you the Pot King's son?"

"Maybe ..." she stammered.

He leaned forward to stare into her eyes.

"Yes or no?!"

She flinched back from his shout. Her mouth worked noise-lessly, terror taking her tongue.

"Bring the other in and cut his throat to show this one we mean business," he said to the pirate holding her.

"Aye, sir."

Mary, she thought, I'm Mary. If I reached out to touch this man, he would be dead in an instant. "No!" she managed to squeak. Her voice was barely audible.

He slouched back in his chair, smiling, but did not speak.

She gasped, fighting to shape the words. "Please, you mustn't!"

The door opened again, and the pirate stood there, holding Maz against his chest, a wicked silver line against the boy's throat.

"I am, I'll do it, please don't!" she shrieked. The captain held up a forefinger to the pirate holding Maz. The knife stayed where it was.

"I'm his son, I am, I'll help you however you like," she babbled.

"Clearly the canary is of more use here than stowed away elsewhere," the captain said. He stroked his beard, eying them. "Do you intend to take your true form?"

Her bowels felt like they would turn to water and run out of her. Her heart pounded and the walls of the room pressed in on her.

She pulled herself up out of her panic, clinging to the thought of Mary. What was the story Maz had provided? "I can't. The magic went awry. I need another mage to lift it. A Master Mage."

His eyes narrowed. "I see. Pity we didn't keep the Sorcerer around longer. I congratulate you on your ingenuity. Who would think such a trifling form would mask a budding mage?"

"Trifling?"

"We have no use for you until we reach the Coral Tower. But I'm presuming you would rather see the sky and sun than spend the entire journey in the hold?"

Lucy frowned at him.

"All that I require," he said, "is your word on your name. The vow that no wizard can break without losing his or her magic."

The frown stayed on her face, knitting her translucent brows together.

"And you," he said to Maz, who still dangled, chin stretched upward to avoid the blade. "You'll swear to make no attempts at escape either."

"How could I escape?" Maz said. "Jump overboard and walk away on the water?"

"Just do it!"

They repeated the words after the captain.

"When do we set sail?" Lucy asked. Perhaps there might be way to get word to her family if she was allowed on deck.

The captain laughed.

"When?" he said. "Two hours ago, that's when. We're far out to sea by now."

"Where are we headed?" Maz asked.

The captain pointed at Lucy. "Her ... I mean his father's spawning grounds, in the Lesser Southern Isles. The island they call Fireah and the Coral Tower there."

He looked to the other pirates. "Take them away for now."

LUCY AND MAZ were fed together on deck, although it was a dried fish, some hard biscuit, and a half mug of sour beer apiece. Their watcher left them alone, telling them to eat hearty.

Lucy wondered how she had not understood the departure while in the echoing hold: the sway and lurch, the shouts and clatter of footsteps. Now, there was banging and clattering from below, where the cell room was being divided in order to keep them apart, a whim of the captain's that did not seem popular with the sailors.

"The Lesser Southern Isles will take us two weeks to reach," Maz said.

"How do you know?"

"They teach us geography—that's maps and how to read them— in the College." He stared forward, thinking. All around them was the creak of the ship, the wash of water, the smell of damp and the pepper coating the desiccated fish.

Maz went on. "Magic is unpredictable in the Lesser Southern Isles. There are artifacts there from other ages, like the Coral Tower on Fireah and the Speaking Skull. They say anything can happen in the Lesser Southern Isles, that Gods are born and remade there. I guess we'll see."

Lucy sighed. "Two weeks."

"Will your family miss you?" Maz asked.

"Two weeks," she repeated. "No, they won't. Well, yes, they'll miss me, though probably not, but they'll have no idea where to look."

"I am sure that the College will set seeking spells after me," he said. "It's just a matter of holding out until this ship stops and the spells have a chance to catch up."

"You're a wizard—can you send word back about where we're headed?"

"Not without violating my oath and jeopardizing my magic's source."

"What would happen if you broke your word?"

He looked away.

Kindly came up on deck. "All right," he grumbled. "Yer accommodations are ready, my little lord and lady."

AFTER THAT THEY were kept separate in theory, although they could whisper back and forth through the flimsy wall. In the mornings, they were allowed to stroll the deck together. Lucy would have liked to lean on Maz's arm but as the supposed Pot King's son she felt it necessary to exhibit a masculine swagger. She hoped it was more convincing than it felt.

She asked Maz about the Pot King. She knew little except that he was one of the Sorcerers who had survived the battles that had made most of the Old Continent ash and devastation.

"Everyone says they know the secret of his power and everyone says something different," he said. "But he's a match for any three Sorcerers on the Old Continent."

"Then why isn't his son a powerful wizard?" Lucy said.

"Mages don't manifest power until they start to come of age," he said. "You know, when they start getting beards." He blushed and left the rest unsaid: his squeaky voice and downy cheek showed no trace of manhood.

Lucy told him about being the youngest, an unexpected and unwanted child trailing after her louder, bolder, braver siblings.

"Mouse," she said. "And Meepling, and Slink, and Little Miss Silent, that's what they call me."

"I have no brothers and sisters to call me anything," Maz said. "I envy you."

Their friendship had changed. Before they had seen each other once in a while, at the mercy of circumstance and Press errands near the College. Now they could whisper through the wall to each other and so they filled the long hours with stories.

Maz talked about his classes, and what he'd learned, and the historical figures he admired. Lucy told him about her sisters and all the injustices dealt against her, which he agreed were dire and many.

But still every once in a while, he repeated that he had no brothers and sisters, until finally she said, "I will be your sister, if you like." They pressed their hands together, on either side of the wall, and vowed it to each other.

She liked him almost as much as Eloquence. Sisters were worthless. Only a brother could understand. Only a brother could see how special she was.

ADELINA'S SECOND LETTER

Dear Bella—

You've been gone a week and a half now. The city is much duller without you, but I manage to keep busy enough. The insurance over the press is still proving difficult, mainly because they charge that I had every reason to set fire to the building myself. And it's true, that would've been an excellent plan. However, it's not what happened, and I find myself quite irritated that something that should be as basic as Diahmo's page has become so exceedingly complicated.

There seems to be a riot every day now. Often it's between one political party and the next, and they've even taken to staging debates that usually end with some sort of struggle. Being out of all of that is one of the best benefits of the estrangement with my mother.

She does remain quite adamant about having me removed from the house and I must say, as you can understand, I do have mixed feelings about that. I don't mind being out from under all the obligations that it meant, but at the same time it leaves me very sad to think that I am no longer part of that house.

Do you remember the portrait that I used to point you at, the brown-haired Merchant from three generations before mine? I always wanted a sister, and she was my imaginary one. I used to have conversations with her in my head, because she was one of the few people who could be hoped to understand everything that there was about my life, being a Nittlescent herself.

I used to think of her as a friend and ally. Nowadays I'm not sure she'd approve of me anymore. She wouldn't be allowed to. Since my mother is head of the house, her word is law and so I have not seen any relative, not even a distant cousin or two, since her edict casting me from the house went out.

I could tell you that was an interesting thing in and of itself, because historically the last time the Nittlescent household, which has not been prone to the sort of drama some of the upper Merchant and Noble houses seem to draw like marsh flies, did such a thing, it was over fifty years ago. My mother would have known about it, but been a child herself, and not involved in any of the proceedings: it was a cousin who had given way to the enticements of Embezzlement.

At least I know my character is unimpeachable, at least in the ways Scholars account for such things. I have never lied in a book and presented it as the truth, and in writing history I have never changed the facts in order to make them read more pleasantly or better or for any other reason of propaganda.

Let's see, what else? The weather is warm and pleasant. Sebastiano and I took a picnic to the Sea Garden a few days ago. Yes, before you arch a brow, that does mean that he and I have become more than friends. I'm entertaining thoughts of marrying him.

He'd be an excellent alliance and he makes me laugh, Bella, like I don't think anyone else ever has, even you, and most of all, he cherishes me. I am the center of his world, as he's become the center of mine. Or rather it's that our worlds have merged together and become each other's, so we share them and they become richer, deeper, and altogether more enjoyable and wonderful as a result.

I hope I am making you laugh, to see me, once so very sensible, engaging in words like this. But can I tell you something, Bel? I can tell you this now, and I don't think I ever could before, because they would have made you feel uncomfortable, as though I expected something from you in return for them. I would have spoken so to you once.

I don't believe in soul mates, and everything the Trade Gods tell us underscores that belief for me. It is a matter of making accommodations, it is a matter of communicating expectations and beliefs. It is a matter of knowing that you can trust the other.

And it is a matter of friendship, of course, there must be friendship because how else would you get through all the hard times together?

But sometimes, when you have all of that, there is something more to it as well and you feel as though this is indeed the person that you were born to be with. Not all the time. Certainly there are always petty irritations, and many of them don't even have to do with the person at all, but rather the outside world.

So yes, I am more than contemplating marriage. It is, I think, a given at this point and just a question of working out all the arrangements. But now I am no longer a Merchant and so I do not know yet whether his family will agree to the marriage since I am disgraced, and his mother has been ill, so I have not been able to meet with them.

That is my greatest fear. Sebastiano pooh-poohs it. He says that he was more than ready to disobey his father by not marrying, and that if it comes to disobeying him by marrying, he is quite prepared to do so. But while I do not mind renouncing my own family, I find that I am far less ready for him to do so, that I worry much more about what it will cost him, to the point where sometimes I think it would be best if I went away altogether and did not tempt him to this alliance.

But if I disappeared now, he would follow me. He would track me down somehow, through magic or whatever means he could, in order to make sure no harm had come to me. So if I wish to break things off with him, then I must actually do so. I must have a conversation in which I renounce him and give him some good reason for doing it.

I just don't know about that part. I don't know that I could lie to him about the reason and so I would have to present the very one that he keeps rejecting.

That's the worst sorrow of having you gone. I wish that you and I could go out for chat and talk about all this, and while you probably would not solve any of my problems, you would undoubtedly make me feel better about them.

I do feel better for having written all this, Bella. Thank you.

I don't know where you will be on your journey by now, and the Duke has been quite secretive about things. I hope that it is proving pleasant and that you are having glorious adventures of the sort that only Bella Kanto can have. But you and I both know that Alberic is not the sort of man who sends people on pleasant trips, Bell, and I know how many of your stories about the journeys he had you undertake gloss over the discomforts and the dangers. I hope that you are well.

Your friend ever,
Adelina Nittlescent

CHAPTER 13

FROM BELLA KANTO AND THE LONG SLOW CITY: AN ACCOUNT OF AN AMBASSADORIAL JOURNEY BY TABAT'S MOST FAMOUS GLADIATOR.

*T*he Long Slow City lies many days west of Tabat, and most ships go along the coast and then strike southward towards the city when they reach the edges of Billow Bay. The Duke dispatched Bella Kanto on a trade mission of grave importance. Little did she know that she would uncover monstrous crimes and avenge a terrible wrong in the course of her journey.

I REMEMBER THIS ONE. She made up every word and wrote it without me, because that was the summer I was tangled up with that pair of twins that had just come to court and wanted to be shown all over Tabat.

Then, when it was ready, she brought me the manuscript and dumped it in my lap and walked away, and it was such a farrago of lies that I resolved to be better about telling her things. Which is, I am sure, what she intended.

It occurs to me that I never actually told Adelina about any of my time on the Long Slow City, and now I wonder if she read something into the omission.

I never said a word to her about Scylla.

WHEN I TRAVELED on Alberic's behalf, he kept me busy, going here and there all around the world. Negotiating treaties, making agreements and arrangements. Easing trade. Finding the things he wanted: sometimes rarities or luxuries, other times Beasts or magical wonders, and still other times, some negotiation to be held without anyone else knowing.

He is a Duke; he is used to ruling. And Tabat is more than a city now; it is all the surrounding lands, the ones that it looks after, and which pay it taxes—and plenty of them—in return.

That was one reason the Nobles of the Old Continent came here—it was a rich land and there was nothing and no one here that they considered Human, other than up north, where settlements from long ago had spread. Some go so far as to claim that the physical differences between the two—the dark skin of the Old Continent, the paler of the New, shows that they both came from some other, older group. (As always, Adelina had a scholar who was more than ready to wax at length upon the subject.) But this is rejected among most polite folk, by which I mean the people primarily descended from that Old Continent blood, with its desire to be thought the wellspring of the world.

I had been much at Court with the twins, where I was up to my knees in such discussions. There were no Abolitionists in those days, so whether or not Beasts played a part in any of this did not come into the conversations, but the fineness with which they defined Old versus New blood, even coming up with words to designate the gradations! That was something I was glad enough to see pass away in my lifetime. Too many Gladiators fell victim to those prejudices and they only split us.

So I was sick to death of such talk and when Alberic asked me to go and help with the most recent Cataloging of the raft city, I said yes, despite how tedious such things can be.

Every place that pays tribute or taxes is subject to Cataloging, not more than once a decade. It involves a host of Scribes and Scholars and Accountants, and it is both a listing of everything the place (or person, or business, or whatever) holds as well as what business it has performed over the preceding decade and what it can be expected to do over the course of the next. Thank the Moons that I was never required to do anything of that work, simply smooth over any important local feathers ruffled in the process as well as ensuring that things did not get dropped—perhaps accidentally, perhaps not, who knows, such things happen—from the inventory.

Adelina got a few things right. One was that I traveled there on one of the Ducal ships. They had no magic engines at that point, so it was one specially fitted out and rowed by Minotaurs. It took us eight days to cross the Silent Sea.

As we drew closer and closer, it filled the water below us, and everyone not devoted to the oars spent their time hanging over the railings, gazing downward at the mountain slopes under the sea.

I never went as far as the mountain's foot, but Scylla described for me what it is like down there. She says the water pressed so tightly on her skin that she felt compressed and as though it was difficult to make out sounds, and that each time she must come back slowly, or else find herself riddled with pain—a Mer can even die of it, she said, if the ascent was too quick, but they learn at an early age how it feels and when to slow themselves and wait.

The only light in those deeps used to be what the Mers brought themselves, and the small illuminations of the creatures floating in the water. That was one of the many things the Mage Ellora turned her talents to, back in her days, and she is worshipped there, in a way we do not back in Tabat, although her apples feed so many in that city. She created the long glowing vines, living ropes, that the Mers use to create guideways, ones which grow denser and denser over the years until the oldest glow like the white moon and it looks like a shining net spread down and outward at the city's bottom.

Beds of sea worms grow there to be harvested for their medicinal powers, and vast, slow-moving anemones. Sometimes, after a great fish has been taken from outside the netted boundaries, they bring the carcass down to the depths in order to let it bloom, slicing open the sides and letting water wash through the ribs. Scylla said you can see the results of past corpses, great sculptures of cold corals vaguely shaped like the creature on whose body they fed.

She told me that when you go far enough away from the mountain, there are canyons down there that only the boldest explore, full of vast kraken and eels and worse, tiny parasites that will latch onto a body and drain it bit by bit. A single or a handful is no danger, but they move in swarms, and can strip a body to a husk within a minute.

Much of what the city grows is not down in those depths, but higher up: kelp beds and rope baskets that hold shellfish, letting the water circulate around them as they fatten: globular oysters and succulent white scallops and the slow-moving, orange-fleshed conch, whose shells are used for so many purposes, including building.

Just a layer on the water's surface, so shallow compared to those glowing, jeweled depths.

When we hung over those railings, looking down, it was the most beautiful thing I had ever seen, and I could not help but think of Leonoa. For years afterwards, I kept trying to persuade her to venture there, but she has always feared to leave Tabat—or rather the doctor that has tended her for years—behind and finally I stopped speaking of it, because it only pained her.

It makes me think now that perhaps it is an option to stay, somehow persuade Ruhua that this is a sufficient place to keep me. It is not as though I would pose any threat to Alberic here, and it is a good place, a place of leisure and sunlight and good food, and perhaps I could even learn to city-dance this place, despite its lack of staircases and terraces.

But that is just a pipe dream, I know even without discussing it that she will be opposed to the notion, that it lies outside the bounds of whatever orders she has been given. It would be too easy for me to take a boat to some other place from here, far too easy for me to slip away and out of his grasp.

Still, I toy with the notion. Some small house on the raft's edges.

Get up in the morning and drink chal and then go for a swim. A leisurely existence. Perhaps I could even take on students—

That thought summons Skye, my student, who I killed, like a punch to my gut, so sudden that it's a wonder I don't double over.

More than one life can claim I have touched it and made it worse. There is more than one life that can hold a grudge against me without my thinking that unfair. That gnaws at me—it is not something I like thinking of myself. It does not fit with the Bella Kanto that was, and yet it is part of her. She did not care if she hurt the occasional life.

I think about Marta and all her plotting against me. She may have colluded with Alberic, perhaps not. It is certain that she did not wish me well. Teo found the spellwork that she had put in the weekly bouquets she sent me, spellwork that I did not bother to have deconstructed to find out its intent. I had been stupid and put the flowers in my chamber every week, thinking that she had forgotten the order that she had placed when we were lovers, before I turned away and she became obsessed with that rejection.

It amused me that she did so. I even joked with Adelina more than once about what an unmerchantly thing it was, to neglect one's bookkeeping to the point where an expense like that got overlooked.

And I should have known better than that, because she was a decent Merchant, and knew her Trade Gods, and even kept her journal the way Adelina had left behind. I looked at it once, but the truth is such things are as boring as accounts of people's dreams.

I did not do her justice, and it bit me. How much of what she did to me was something that I drew upon myself, caused by my thoughtlessness? Bella Kanto harbored an edge of smugness about how many hearts she left in her wake. I prided myself on being able to let people down without too much drama or trouble on either side, but even when someone did not let me do that, did not allow me to quietly slip away and out of their life, it still fed my vanity— look how alluring I am, that I drive some to such lengths, despite my best efforts, which I am known for!

Oh, I used to flatter myself in so many ways that it disgusts me now.

The first time I ever saw Scylla, she was in training, and sat to the left and back of her father so she could listen. I saw him speak in hand talk to her more than once over the course of the proceedings, which were primarily introductions and an overview of what all would be done. The old ruler had undergone others of the same before; this was the sixth for him and the sixth for me, and we made some jokes about that.

I have always been observant, always been one of those people who look around themselves rather than study my hands or the floor or some inoffensive spot on the ceiling.

So Scylla and I crossed looks more than once that day. I was treating only with her kind of Mer and the tribe they call Wetwalkers. There is a third type that is acknowledged Human, the Deepchangers. They are reclusive and scarcely seen, but the only one of the three that has produced Mages, and even there only one, whom Alberic sent south to establish a new branch of the college in Margolees.

They are the most inhuman in appearance, and the ones I would be the most hesitant to fight in an arena. Their scales are very tough, and they are fast and can breathe both water and air. I have fought them in the past and won—I do not think I could ever do such a thing again.

It was a long session and a hot day, even though the enormous chamber hosting us held archways open to the sea breeze. They brought us wine and fruit from under the sea, which managed to be sour and salty and yet refreshing.

We washed it down with fresh water that tasted faintly of salt and cucumber. I learned later that taste signaled that it was newly harvested from the great living lungs that are used to make the seawater fresh enough to drink.

A dozen inspectors had been dispatched to go through things and record them, and three Scribes accompanied them, who would collate and amass their information as well as audit the records of the past ten years' trade. Most of our company had brought servants, who had already been dispatched to the embassy to receive their orders. There were too many of us to house at the embassy itself and so many were placed in conch shell walled houses or hostels in the area kept to be used at such times by visitors.

I had opted to stay aboard the ship; I had a cabin there, after all, and my belongings, and a better degree of privacy than would have been afforded me in the city itself. Moreover, the chance that my belongings would be riffled through so I could be spied upon or stolen from while I was out conducting my business were significantly less.

It took a half hour and then some to make all the introductions, and I learned Scylla's name in the process.

Afterwards, while everyone was gathering up their papers, I went to one of the archways. It let out directly onto a balcony, woven of a wicker-like material that was translucent and steamed damply in the sunlight. The balcony's shelf extended out some ten feet and ran the length of the building; this was not the only archway that let out onto it.

Scylla stepped out and beckoned to me. I followed her. The material underfoot gave to the step, but not in a way that felt treacherous, rather that one could leap on it. I could not help but give a little bounce. Scylla turned and laughed at me. Like most Mers, she was lipless, and the laughter was an almost-throaty hiss, a sound of sensual enjoyment that made me wonder what she would be like in bed.

"When I was very small," she said, "my cousins and I used to come out here just to bounce. The goal was to manage to bounce high enough that you could go over the railing and into the water."

I raised an eyebrow. "And did you?"

"More than once!" she said. "Would you like to try, Bella Kanto?"

I cast a regretful look back over my shoulder. "I fear it would injure my dignity as a diplomat."

"That is a pity," she said. "For I would like to swim with you, Bella Kanto. Will you come swim with me tomorrow, in the early morning, before it is time for either of us to go about our boring business?"

Jolietta never dealt with Mers, but she had plenty of opinions about them. They are not native to the waters around Tabat, but there are some schools of the ones that are reckoned Beasts. The ones that are called Human have been denied a chance to build and settle there, the excuses usually phrased as being for their own protection.

The truth is that it makes many people uneasy to contemplate the knife blade edge, made of words only, not of flesh no matter how much anyone pretends to the opposite, by which Beasts and Humans are separated.

None of that was in my mind. All I knew was that I wanted her, and that she had made it clear she wanted me too.

Even so, this day had been my first exposure to Mers. I was still not quite sure what to think of them, or of the ease with which the Humans around them interacted, on the terms of equals.

It was at odds with all my experiences and also with the way that Alberic spoke of them, as though they were primitives, barely capable of building shelter for themselves, rather than the cultured and elegant folk I saw before me now. Scylla wore nothing but chains of beads that fell around her form. She had breasts like any woman, but they were slight, suggestions rather than statements.

She was very beautiful, and I wanted to kiss her, but felt strangely about that urge. For one thing, I was here as a diplomat. What if, for my kisses, she expected favors in return?

And what were the protocols? I had been told that Mers and other Humans cohabited upon occasion, that it was not unknown and not considered particularly scandalous here, while in Tabat there would have been different things said, for all the words of Human being used.

In Tabat, some people lie with Beasts. Some brothels cater to such tastes. They are in the seedier parts of town, and doing something like that is considered wrong, but understandable, somehow. But the children of such unions are rare, and they are always killed.

It was not as though I could have a child with another woman, not without costly and difficult magic. But I did not know what an alliance with this woman would mean to the people here.

But perhaps I was overthinking it all, I decided. A chance to swim in the early morning and explore this strange new place … It was not something that I could resist, in the end, and so I nodded, and said, "When and where shall we meet?"

Her startled look told me that she hadn't thought I would actually take her up on it. But her chin lifted an inch, and she said, a suppressed smile tugging at the corner of her mouth, "I will come to your ship at second bell."

As with Tabat, there is first bell, which happens an hour before sunrise, and second bell, which marks that sunrise, and then bells through the rest of the day, up until last bell, and the quieter callings of the night watch while most of the city slumbers. I roused at first bell, which sounded differently here. In Tabat it begins with the Duke's bell, one great-throated, rolling gong, followed by all the other bells of the city, as though they had been waiting for permission to speak out.

Here it was a clacking and clinking from chimes at spots across the city, each operated by a different acolyte, all delegates of Yarilnobo, the Trade God of Timekeeping. I roused when I heard it, and ate a handful of oatcake for breakfast, enough to keep myself from growing over hungry, and went out and sat on the prow of the ship to watch the sunrise.

Before I had left Tabat, Leonoa had been doing a series of portraits in the Sea Garden, all at sunrise in order to take advantage of the light at that hour. The sky this morning reminded me of those paintings: clear, glowing dark blue stippled with little cloudlets, like minnows in deep water, submerged so deep that they can barely be glimpsed.

I expected Scylla to come along the dock, which was foolish of me, but showed how little I thought about such things in those days.

Instead her head popped up out of the water below me and she shouted upward, "Good trade to you, Bella Kanto!"

"And to you!" I called and could not resist standing up upon the railing in order to make my dive. I had divested myself to nothing but my smallclothes and was barefoot.

I remember the feel of the railing under my feet, the clammy wood touching my soles and steadying them. I dove as I had learned: straight and true as an arrow and shaped like one, my palms held to each other and stretched above my head so they would touch the water first, my feet arched out behind my body in a straight line, the toes pointed.

I am sure it amused Scylla, who could have outswum me any day, and did more than once. Later I saw her and other Mers diving and it put any effort that I might have assembled to shame. But she said nothing about that as I surfaced beside her, only said, "This way," and bade me follow her.

She did not test me too much, but she did show me the underwater tunnels that stretch below the raft city's surface and which the Mers themselves use. There are air chambers there under the city, but they are not marked in the way that the other pathways are, and you must know which way to go in order to find them if you cannot breathe water like a Mer and do not want to drown.

She took me to one of the inner pools, a place where the city gives way to water inside its boundaries, the edges lined with greenery, the surface covered with great flat-water lilies and lotuses, their roots stretching down through the water thirty feet to find purchase in the netting strung there. The flowers were immense, the roots as thick as my hand, and you could swim among them and dip your head under the water to contemplate the undersides of the enormous leaves, most of them wider in diameter than two or three times my body length.

We were not the only people in that place. There were some children playing, and an older Mer with a net, gathering minnows, while another was trimming away dead foliage and trimming overvigorous living growth from where it threatened to encroach on the openings in the net that served as entrance and exit ways to the city below the surface.

Of course I kissed her there among the long yellowy-green vines as the sunlight began to illuminate the water. I remember the sinewy, wet, sleek feel of her, as though she was skin wrapped around lightning.

She told me later that her father had scolded her over and over for flirting with me, and that he'd warned her I was acquiring a reputation for bedding people. Which wasn't entirely fair—I had yet to meet up with Adelina and have her start writing the books that would actually be worth such a warning (so much sensationalism in the name of selling books!).

Of course, that had made her want me all the more, she confessed.

We had many more such swims—almost every morning I was there, and evenings and afternoons too. She never slept beside me in my bed—back in her own home, she had a nest of weed and wet sea wrack, in a shallow pool of water, that was her preference, although some members of her family slept entirely underwater.

She taught me so many customs of the raft city that I sometimes felt as though I could have stayed and been at home, eventually, with their existence, which was so much slower than Tabat's.

There is a saying that the Mers have, "the life of the Sea." It means that they move outside of time, that they do not worry about reckoning it in the way we do. The clicking and clacking of time-keeping is something that is provided for the benefit of visitors, and if Scylla had not understood enough about my people to know that it would have been a slight, she would have been just as likely to show up an hour or two after the appointed time.

It is a habit that Adelina would remind me of, much later. Why am I drawn to women who are habitually late, when I am never that myself?

A Cataloging is long and laborious, but even the largest must come to an end, and I was startled when the Scribes came and told me we had only another week, perhaps less. I got the feeling they were ready enough to be back in Tabat themselves; by then we had been in the city a full three white moons, a quarter of a year.

Scylla and I had never spoken of when I would leave, perhaps some mutual agreement or cowardliness, I am not sure which. Sometimes I caught her looking at me in a way that made me think that the conversation was about to begin, but then she would shake her head and break off whatever words had been coming to her lips and kiss me.

But I had to tell her, I knew. I kept bouncing the decision to do so just a little farther away.

And so she found out from one of the Scribes, and I wonder if a part of me had not known that would happen all along, if I waited long enough. I do not know what the circumstances of the telling were; the Scribe mentioned it at breakfast when we were together.

"Seemed a bit upset," he said, pulling a dish towards himself and sniffing the steam from it before nodding and ladling himself several large spoonfuls. He'd come to report the previous day's progress and had insisted all along on delivering these reports, including details of their methods, going by category of business first, and then another sweep moving a precise geometrical path across the city's surface. The great difficulty had been, apparently, the wealth that lay underwater, and he was worried that much of it simply had not been catalogued because of the difficulties it presented.

I was much less concerned about such things than he was. Alberic had more than enough money. If the Mers had a way to keep some of it back for themselves, good for them. I would have felt this way even had I not been sleeping with Scylla. I was never Alberic's best representative, only his most showy one.

The thing that worried me was breaking things off with Scylla, or rather, the fact that she had discovered that I would be doing so. It was not that she did not understand that the process of the Cataloging would not come to an end sooner or later. However, in the few conversations that we had had involving that end, I may have been a little vague and perhaps even overestimated the amount. I do not think the latter was deliberate; still, she would not have been expecting it. She would have thought it to be months still.

Although if she had put her mind to it, she would have realized that I had to be back in Tabat in time for the Winter games, in time to fight Spring's representative and determine once again whether or not the winter lingered in Tabat or we had an early spring. I had been Winter's Champion for six years then. The Merchants were only starting to grumble about six years of long winters.

The Scribe was a man noted for his lack of tact, else I would have thought that he had perhaps told her out of malice. But no, his face was placid as he methodically worked his way through his breakfast.

I took my time with my own, which was smoked fish softened and spread on flatbread, and great purple and green sea-grapes with their tangy, briny taste, and chal, the best chal I've ever had. Tabat claims that drink as their own, but the truth is that it had its birth here, where they live on fish and seaweed, and there are kettles here that have boiled longer than the ones in any other city.

So I knew beforehand that she knew, but she probably didn't know that I knew it. It was one of those conundrums that diplomats often engaged in, but I still was not sure how exactly to play my hand. I decided that I would let her bring the matter to me.

Still, I did not expect her to do it where she did. I had thought that she would find someplace private. Someplace where she could weep or try to seduce me out of my decision. To do me justice, those were the only tactics I had encountered at that point.

I agreed to meet her at the building marked with an octopus entangled with a Mer, the establishment that Antiope owned in those days.

It was a very pleasant place to visit. I had enjoyed being there before and letting them tend my fingernails. The attendant I usually had, Tersa, was unused to working with Human hair, and approached it as a delightful mystery, threatening to do all sorts of things with it in her experimentations, and yet always ending up simply combing it for a while in order to satiate her fingers with its texture and perhaps trimming away a few frayed ends.

She brought out her comb when she saw me. I settled into a chair near the table across which Scylla lay while her own attendant, whose name I cannot remember, a pale little Mer half her age, worked on the scales along her spine, massaging an oily substance into them that smelled of peppermint. It was strong—the Mers like their scents strong—and was all that I could smell.

We chatted about what we intended to do afterward, which was to swim out to one of the northern raft settlements, the little city-rafts that are unattached and move around in order to take advantage of fishing and the great kelp beds that lay out in that area.

As I said, I had thought that she would pick someplace private for the discussion and it seemed to me that was where it would take place. Here I could relax and enjoy the atmosphere, which I'd always found soothing. They burned lemongrass to hide the smell of burning chitin from the inlaying; no one was doing any that morning and there was just the faintest whiff of the old burning every once in a while over the peppermint.

Perhaps a dozen Mers in the room: I was the only Human. But I had gotten used to that by then. I would never have compared it to my time at Piper Hill, but the truth was that there were plenty of similarities and this was one. There I had been the only representative of my kind most of the time, surrounded by Beasts.

Here I was the only one of my kind again, and the truth, which would have appalled anyone back in the city from which I'd come, was that here they really didn't pay any attention to the distinction between Beast and Human and simply treated everyone alike.

I sat with my eyes closed, enjoying the feeling of the comb passing through my hair, and thinking about what exactly I would say, what sort of pleas she might make.

I was half-worried that she would not want to come back to the city with me, and just as worried that she would. It would not have been a friendly place for her, and I didn't want to have to explain to her why, how even though people here treated her as any other, it would be different in Tabat, where she would have stood out and many people would have automatically assumed that she was a Beast and treated her as such.

Even if she could avoid that, the upper crust still would not have accepted her and she would have found herself with few to socialize with, other than me. I didn't know what Leonoa would make of her, and she was my closest friend at that time. I did know what Myrila would make of her, which was nothing good; she thought the Mers of the Salt Market were sly cheats who hated all

Humans in their hearts, no matter what words they outwardly professed.

I was running through all this in my head, trying to assemble arguments, when Scylla said, "So I understand you'll be leaving next week."

Tersa's hand twitched at the words, despite the neutrality of the tone, and I knew I had fallen into deep water.

"Mmm," I said, which was not a word calculated to improve the situation, but only to buy me time to think. "Is that what they are saying now? They have given me many different estimates over the course of things."

"It does not seem to match with the estimate that you provided me."

The comb kept moving through my hair, but I was no longer lulled, only intensely aware of the listening attendants. "Do we really need to have this discussion here?" I asked.

"Does this discussion make you uncomfortable?"

Such deep water.

I decided to go on the offensive. I said, "It is only that it makes me very sad and I had hoped to speak with you of this in private. I found it out only this morning myself."

Her voice shifted and I deduced that she had changed position. I opened my own eyes and saw that she had raised herself on an elbow and was staring at me. By now I had learned to read her expressions with some facility. She was very angry.

She kept careful control of her tone in a way that underscored just how angry she was feeling. "Oh, does it make you sad? That is surprising."

I tried to infuse sincerity in my own tone, to show that I *was* genuinely sorry at the circumstances. That they were not what I would have chosen.

And they were not. But the truth was that it was also convenient that I was being taken away because it was around the time for me to break things off, according to the pattern I had established back in my own city.

There is no better way to vanish than to simply get in a boat and sail away. It is a convenience that I have used more than once in my time. It is one reason that I agreed to undertake this work for Alberic, even though I claimed it was the chance to travel and meet new people and see new things.

But I said, "I don't know why it would surprise you. These days together have been so wonderful." I looked her straight in the eye. "You knew that I was only visiting as well as I did. You knew that I had not come here to make a home for myself."

"You would not be welcome to make a home for yourself!" she snapped. "This city requires that its immigrants have useful skills, things beyond theatrical fighting and performances carried out in bed."

I refrained from pointing out that she had found my skills in bed more than useful at times. I said, and kept my tone reasonable all the while, "I cannot stay here, either way. I must go back to Tabat and perform its rituals."

"Did you plan to say goodbye at some point or just to disappear?!" she demanded.

That hit closer to the target than anything that she had said so far. I paused.

Her eyes widened at my reaction. "By the moons on the waters, you did mean to vanish so! What sort of person are you? You cannot be the woman I bedded. She would scarce be so heartless."

"I cannot help but be heartless," I tried to explain. "I have responsibilities to Tabat. That's what sent me here in the first place, those responsibilities."

But she would not listen to me. She lay back down on her table and turned her head away, speaking to her attendant in cool, firm tones as she directed her to finish up the burnishing. I kept trying to get her attention, but she would not relent, and the truth is that this nettled me enough that I stopped trying very quickly.

Tersa left off combing as soon as she was gracefully able. She did not meet my eyes as I thanked her and gave her ten times the amount of coins that I should have. I did not doubt that the story would be all over the city soon.

The rest of that week passed with excruciating slowness. No

matter how many messengers or messages I sent, Scylla would not relent and talk to me again. So I stayed aboard the boat and played cards with the sailors that were there to watch it and ate altogether too much and even read through an entire book, which is the detail that Adelina would find the hardest to believe.

I tried to find some word of Scylla, but no one would say anything and it occurred to me that perhaps she had gone back down under the city where there were so many others of her kind.

We could have cast off on the afternoon that the Scribes came to tell me that they had completed all their duties. The ship was ready and provisioned, freshly stocked with everything that we would need for the trip back. But I had us linger one more night, and I spent most of it sitting on the railing where I had first spotted her, watching the water and hoping to see her smile come out of it.

It did not, and in the morning, I was bleary and red eyed, but sat in the same spot all the time that we were casting off and the drummer beginning the cadence that would carry us back across the sea.

She never came, and I never wrote to her, although I could have. Although I should have, in all probability. As I said, it took Adelina to civilize me in such things, and even then she didn't tame me entirely. Witness Marta, who I was clumsy with, and all her hatred of me. Witness Skye...

That is the only memento of Tabat that I treasure. Everything else is replaceable, but not the little portrait of Skye. She had it drawn at some penny fair, and gave it to me as a love token, in those days when everything was first love and delight, when everything was sweet.

Gods, it feels like years ago and yet only a few white moons have rolled their way across the sky since then.

CHAPTER 14

THE FANCY BLISS (LUCY)

*T*wo days later, the captain sent for Lucy again.

He was dressed in blue velvet today, its lace stiff with newness. The smell of the anise seeds he was chewing wafted to her across the table as he unrolled a map and gestured at her to look.

What she presumed were the Lesser Southern Isles spread across the parchment in coin-shaped irregularities. One blob that aspired to hand-sized sat towards the map's upper edge. The captain tapped the space beside it.

"This," he said, "is where we are now."

He pointed to a circle halfway down the map. "And here is the Coral Tower, on Fireah."

"Which is?" Lucy asked.

He snorted. "Your daddy keeps it all close, eh, son?" He stroked his moustache, eying Lucy. "Or are you playing it coy so I'll underestimate you?" He smiled. "I presume you know the perils of a young girl caught on a pirate ship. They may be all charm and fishing lore while you're under my wing, but should that ... protection be withdrawn, you would find your form more disadvantageous."

"I told you, I can't lift the spell," Lucy said.

He studied her before returning his attention to the map. "Very well. The Coral Tower is an ancient artifact, discovered when the Isles were first settled. It sits in the water, surrounded by coral reefs. Inside, a staircase leads down. Some say to the Earth's center, others to chambers filled with treasure."

He shrugged. "Who knows for sure? What I *do* know is that your father went down there and returned with immense power, and that he had to use his own blood to pay for that bargain. Now the tower is sealed to all but those of that blood. You'll lead the way and take me down to where I can make my own deal."

"Oh," Lucy said blankly. "All right."

He smiled tightly at her and moved around the table. This close in the cabin, she could smell him, anise now mingling with sweat and the sweet amber fragrance that came from the clothes chest at the foot of the uncomfortably close and lavish bed. She felt hyper-aware of his presence, the way his moustache curled, the fine wrinkles at the corners of his electric green eyes.

"All right," he said. He sighed, sniffing at the air like a dog seeking a scent. "What use are you, little mage?" His hand took her shoulder; it was warm through her shirt's worn linen. She shivered. Something coiled and uncoiled in her core.

"What are you like under this disguise?" Captain Miryam's voice was husky and soft. "Is this the form you yearn for, the form of your soul itself? Are you a demure little maiden, eyelashes so blonde and fine I can barely see them in the lamplight?"

His breath stirred the hairs on her neck. She gasped for air, a sudden shocked sound that made him withdraw.

Her face burned as she was taken back to the hold.

Slumped back against the side of the wall, her wet cheek pressed to it, she gave way completely to tears.

Maz whispered through the wall, "Are you all right?" but she ignored him and after a few more whispers, he gave up.

How had she come to all of this? What had she done to deserve such things happening to her? And what would happen next?

She felt totally adrift, a chip tossed in the middle of the ocean to be washed this way and that.

The story of her life, that lack of control. Her sisters and her mother had had power over her, and her brother even more, enough to condemn her to an apprenticeship at the tannery at first, and later on having the power to say whether or not she worked at the press, without even consulting her to find out what she wanted to do, even though Adelina had asked *her*, not Eloquence!

And the press was no better, despite the fact that it had seemed to promise escape at first. No, Adelina had been proved as false as all of the other institutions that had let Lucy down in her life, starting with her family and her sisters, who would surely not care that she had gone. If anything, they would be happy that they would never have to contend with her for their brother Eloquence's attention again.

And now the pirates had control of her and there was no doubt in her mind that they had no intention of letting her take control back anytime soon.

In a story, the hero would figure a way out. But how? She looked around in silent misery at the inward-pressing walls of the tiny cabin, at the grimy wood and the thin cracks in it, at the worn planks underfoot, still splintery in a few jagged places that she had learned to avoid.

Her boots had been almost bare of sole at the time that they had taken her and now one sole was half-severed. She pulled it loose carefully, then gave up and removed both boots, folding them and putting them in the opposite corner from the slops bucket, which stood as isolated as she could possibly make it.

Maz must have gone to sleep, because he didn't speak even when he would have heard her stirring. She refolded the thin blanket they had given her, folding it into a long narrow strip and lying down on it. It was a choice between putting a layer of softness —such as it was—over the hardness of the wood or being warm.

Later on, when she was drowsier, she'd wake enough to unfold it and tuck it around her. She'd slept in worse places when she'd been living on the streets in Tabat. At least this one had no rain dripping in on it, and the food, while small and inadequate, was at least certain to appear at intervals, a dependability that was some-what comforting.

Sometimes when she thought about Maz, there was a haze over her thoughts, a peculiar greyness, particularly if she tried to remember him speaking with the sailors or the captain.

It was so odd. As though there was a Maz-shaped absence in those conversations, and the harder she tried to figure out what that was, to put it into words that she could speak aloud to herself, the slipperier it all became, the thoughts oozing out of her hand like trying to grasp sand under water, or sugar, that dissolved all the faster the harder you tried to hold onto it.

She wanted to ask him about this, but somehow, she never thought of it when she was around him. She thought she dreamed about it and roused long enough to get to the wall, meaning to press herself to it and whisper him awake so she could ask him, but then she found herself up against the wall and not remembering why she was there, only that she had wanted—what? Had she dreamed it?

Then she thought about something else and forgot to wonder anymore.

CHAPTER 15

ON THE RAFT CITY (BELLA)

*T*omorrow evening, we arrive at the Long Slow City. Surely Ruhua cannot keep me from the deck during the arrival. I will see the city by evening, at least. One of the most beautiful times to see it, with lanterns bobbing over the rafts, and the channel markers made of floating lanterns as well.

The day dawns bright and clear. The sailors rush around the ship, cleaning it, making it shipshape, readying it for arrival. By noon, every piece of brass shines, the deck is smooth and stainless, freshly holystoned, and everything is in order: ropes coiled as neatly as a Merchant's braids, sails furled, barrels in perfect alignment, even turned so the bungs are all at the same place in the row.

Alberic encourages rivalry between his ships. This is a result that would please him and I have to admit it is impressive to see how much fierce pride they take in their vessel. They love the ship as though it were a member of their family.

The day wears on and finally there comes a call from far above —the lookout has spotted the city. Everyone not otherwise occupied goes to the rail and strains their eyes, trying to see it.

Even in this my body betrays me as it never would have when the magic ran through me. My eyes water uncontrollably at the dazzle of late afternoon sunlight on water, and even after several people have spotted the smudge that signals it, it is moments still later that I can finally make it out.

WHEN I FIRST HEARD OF it, the Long Slow City, the raft city, I thought it was all one raft, one great platform floating on the waves.

It's true that the center is made of such a structure, but all around it are smaller rafts and barges and re-purposed ships, or sometimes just nests of logs, assembled by the merfolk to mark a portal or piece of territory. Plenty of gaps between them, alleyways of water that remind me with a pang of Tabat's canals.

Little boats—the basket boats that Adelina says were a result of the Duke's taxes, decades ago—skitter and skutter over the water like beetles, mixed with canoes and pirogues and some rowboats. The boat tax no longer holds here; Alberic's grasp has loosened with the coming of Tabat's changes, andthere are implications outside Tabat for everything that happens inside the city. The city's holdings extend across the continent, swathes claimed by the old explorers whose journals lie on my cabin table, unopened.

The city started with pirates, who'd found the thing that floats beneath that main structure: an underwater reef to which their raft could be moored, kept from the mercy of the wind and tide. Once they used ropes, but nowadays vast iron chains lead down to the rocks.

I'd seen them with my own eyes.

That makes me wonder if Scylla is still here. Surely not. Her family was prone to wandering. To spend a decade in the same place would go against her very nature.

Not that Ruhua would permit me any chance to see her.

Not that Scylla would want to, after she'd heard what I had done.

No, it is for the best, keeping me aboard ship. I can imagine how it might be, otherwise. At first people would be glad to see me. Then the word of my shame would travel at my heels, perhaps catch up and surpass me—that is the nature of gossip after all, whether spoken by Uhviodommu or their sibling, Ahviodommu, the Gods of such talk.

One by one, eyes would refuse to meet mine. People would look away as though I was not just invisible but something that would burn their eyes if they looked at it too long.

Ruhua hovers nearby as the smudge grows larger. I can tell she's waiting for the moment when she feels justified in ordering me inside. I take a petty satisfaction in thwarting her by watching her eyes, waiting until she draws the breath that will launch her directive, and say, before she can get her own words out, "My head aches. I am going to my cabin."

I turn and make my way inside, keeping a hand on the stairway railing for balance. I still don't feel as though I've entirely gained my sea legs—perhaps, no, probably because I've spent so much time abed.

I have let myself grow weak, cooperated in my own ebbing.

I am still irritated with Ruhua as I enter the cabin. Irritated that she feels she can give me prohibitions, as well as at the prohibition itself. I could have walked through the marketplace at least, picked up some fresh treat for the dog, perhaps something for myself or a present or two to send back home to Adelina.

I do not want her to forget me. But I worry that she will.

Could I coax her, somehow, to the frontier? She has always been devoted to our friendship. I could promise her history, a chance to the frontier being made, customs being established, things still finding their names. There are dangers, certainly—look at last winter's events, even, at Fort Plentitude—but Adelina is tough and surely, I am still enough myself to protect her.

Shouts and other noises from outside, the bump of docking. I refuse to go to the window and look out. Teo paces the cabin, twitching at every new sound, drinking in every new smell that creeps in under the door. He whines, not a sound of fear, but eagerness, perhaps smelling other dogs. There must be some in the city, there are always dogs, were dogs on every expedition that went forth and settled, Adelina told me once.

I lie down on the bed and pretend I am sleeping. But I am utterly awake, alert to every noise. There are so many of them: market shouts, and distant music, people talking on the docks, and the lap of water against the hull, the cries of sea birds searching the skies.

Teo paces for a little longer, then huffs out a great doggy sigh and flops onto the bed beside me, sticking his muzzle under my hand so I will pet him. We lie there together listening and waiting.

A whole day of this, I think, or more—they give people a full day to assemble their mail to pass on when a mail-boat arrives. I think irritably that it would not be unreasonable to expect people to have it ready, but who am I to decide such things? I bury my head under the pillow and try again to sleep.

THIS IS A MISTAKE. By the time the sunlight outside has shaded into darkness, I am as awake as I ever was. When the third night bell sounds, I give up. I will sneak up and at least see the city from afar. Everything is the same at sea, and it will be good to see some other shapes.

Teo springs up from the bed as soon as I rise, prances impatiently about the cabin while I pull out my socks and boots. It makes me smile. I wish I were more like a dog, taking delight in every moment, every chance wonder that presents itself. It would certainly be a happier existence.

He scrambles up the stairway ahead of me, nails clicking on the wooden stairs. We emerge into nightfall on the deck, the ship mostly deserted except for those few sailors unlucky enough to draw a watch this night while their fellows are in the city, enjoying themselves. Ruhua is nowhere in sight, no doubt off on her own errands. Teo and I walk the deck on the side closest to the city.

It is a clear night, and balmier than most, so I shrug off my cloak and lay it on a barrel beside the forward hatch. Teo whines and whimpers, staring at the city; he rears onto his hind legs and rests the forelimbs on the railing, throwing his head up to drink in every trace of smell on the wind that comes towards us from the city.

I can see little other than the lines of lights everywhere. The city is a thousand things strung together, a living hive of houses and structures, all built of woven reed and plaited kelp, or at least most of it. There are a few wooden buildings, assembled at great expense and very fine in their making, but not many can pay the cost of a ship to bring it out here.

The city reaches upward in a way few would expect: airy basket woven of sea-reeds supported by sky-globes, floating in midair with ladders and ropeways reaching up to tether the globes. Temporary structures easily disassembled or even cut away when a storm threatened.

Teo whines, low in his throat, then barks. He drops away from the railing to run around me in dizzy circles. He runs back to the railing.

"We are not going there," I tell him, and am surprised by the bitterness in my tone.

Sometimes I would swear the dog understands words, and this is one of them. His whole body droops, falters, expresses disappointment in every inch.

Then he barks at me, his tone defiant, and takes off running for the railing. At first, I'm amused. Then I realize his intent.

"No!" I shout, but he gathers himself up before he reaches the low railing, tucks front paws in while his hind legs drive him upward, so he clears the railing high enough to be showing off, a fine young creature in his prime challenging me.

I run to the railing and see his head, swimming determinedly towards the city. He is lucky they keep sharks off with wards and mazes, but who knows what will happen to him in the city, a dumb animal by itself, ready to be captured by anyone who has a mind to? I took Alberic's collar off him when he first came onboard and now I regret that decision because at least with it, he would be marked in a way that might lead to his retrieval.

He is my responsibility. I look around, but the sailors are not watching, but gathered around a dice game in the aft. I roll my boots in my cloak and thrust them down behind a barrel where they will not be easily seen. One more glance to check the oblivious sailors. And then I am over the side myself, slipping like a knife into the water.

It's warmer than it looked. The first few moments are pure joy of movement in the saltwater, buoyed and weighing so much less than I ever do on land. I turn towards the city. I don't see Teo, but I know the general direction in which he was headed, so I strike that way myself: a cluster of blue lanterns marks it. But of course, I think, where else would anyone head right now but the Night Market? I'll have to be careful to avoid running into any of my shipmates.

The lanes around the city are full of fellow swimmers and tiny boats at this time of night. When the day's heat is past, that is when the city comes alive and when it is at its most beautiful. Its most seductive.

Why did I never tell Adelina about Scylla? I hadn't refrained from telling her about other loves, either when we were intimate or when we were friends, even though I knew she did not like to hear about such things. But I did not want to pretend, because if you pretended such things, people believed them and started to think they were your only true love.

The closest I ever came to feeling anything like that was with Skye. And perhaps that was only because I did not have enough time to grow tired of her in the way I did every other lover in my life.

Merchants are making their evening rounds of the moored boats, taking advantage of the sailors that are unable to accompany their fellows into the city. Some sellers will be in boats, others swimming, usually the Mer Humans. The sailors will know they are other than Beasts; the new ones will have been instructed by their comrades.

Still, there is little mixing between land Humans and Mer Humans. My affair with Scylla was scandalous; that was much of its charm for her, I think. And for me, truth be told. I loved being thought the daring and unashamed Bella Kanto, always pushing boundaries, going past lines no one had gone past before.

Well, others had gone before me, if we were talking of Mer and Human mixing. Just that it was kept quiet. Because from Mer to Beast was a different slide, some thought, than Human to Beast.

Maybe that was why I had said nothing to Adelina. Because she would be unable to resist a lengthy analysis of how the situation had arisen out of economic interests—everything boils down to money, she insisted, which made following the Trade Gods not a matter of spiritual practice but pragmatic acts.

Where were lines drawn? And who drew them? Generations ago, it made the Duke at the time more money to declare Mers Human than to call them Beasts, and she or he had paid the College of Mages to make it so. The College was the ultimate authority on what was Beast and what was not.

Why did I never wonder about the implications of that before? I had always taken such things as a given. It is as though, hollowed out, the old Bella removed, there is space enough for new thoughts, seditious ones. What if the College declared something moved from Beast to Human, like Centaurs? They were the closest to Human thoughts I knew, at least Phillip was such, though I did not permit myself any other friendships with Centaurs after that.

As I pull myself through the dark water, I think about the dulled Centaur boy Myrila showed me so long ago. Whoever did that to him thought no more of it than castrating a horse or trimming a curly dog's tail. But they had robbed a creature—a thinking creature, no matter how one put it—of their will. Of their thought.

Not of their capacity to enjoy life, perhaps. I wish now that I'd paid to have the boy taken somewhere that he would be made comfortable, kept well fed and reasonably entertained. Why didn't I think of that? Or of the Fairy trapped in my bedroom? Abernia hated them, she'd let it starve to death before she'd touch the cage.

How many lives have I hurt with my carelessness?

At the raft's edge I pull myself up a knotted rope ladder and warm myself by one of the steam water collectors. Once my clothes are a little dryer, I set off, savoring the feel of the lifting raft below the soles of my feet. It has been a while since I walked barefoot, even longer since I ran a city, and for a second I itch to run this one, wondering what it would be like. Then the thought of Tabat, and what it was like to run there, overtakes me and drags me back into despair, slowing my steps.

The raft city is always changing, and now that I am onboard and unable to see the distant lanterns, I have to ask for directions twice before I find the Night Market. It envelops me in its swirl of noise and stink immediately, swallows me into sizzling grease and chalky-smelling incense, the reek of uncured hides and the cow-dung stench from a trough of fresh ambergris, dark waxy lumps stacked atop each other.

Battling voices as vendors outshout each other, a clang of hand-bells from two dancers trying to lure people into their tent. I brush through a stall of silks, fluttering across my still-damp skin, smelling of roses and musk, and pass an open-air bar where they are drinking fennis and playing drop-net counters, clicking and clacking on the wooden tables.

Was that flash of tawny fur Teo? I shoulder through the crowd, ignoring the jostle and bustle, speaking to no one, even though vendors keep trying to snag my attention, holding out trays of toys and jewelry. I do stop for a handful of sea-grapes and walk on, savoring each briny pop as I tongue and deflate the small, bitter-sweet fruit.

I have nowhere to go here and already regret, an unfamiliar emotion, nudges up against the edges of my mind. Ruhua will send sailors searching for me when she realizes I am gone, and I have no idea how she will react.

It is not realistic to fear that she will send me back to the place where I was tortured. It is not realistic to think she would turn the boat around, take me back to those walls. But it is something that I do fear, and it is an unreasonably sized fear—it swallows me whole, wraps me up like a package, holds me paralyzed in the heart of this crowd jostling and grumbling as they make their way around my frozen body.

I cannot breathe for fear and I will die of it.

Something touches my hand, warm and wet. The dog, who I thought to chase, has sought me out. He bumps my hand again with his nose, then licks it, wrapping his tongue around it in that way that dogs have.

As though by magic, it frees me. Ignoring the crowd, I drop to my knees and clutch his furry, although still somewhat damp, form to me. He licks my cheek.

After that, we wander. I have no leash, but Teo sticks close, perhaps unnerved a little by all the new smells, although his wagging tail and doggie grin make me think not. He watches over me, in the way of dogs, and it makes me think of Tabat and Scholar Reinart, who lived downstairs and whom I rarely saw without his own dog Cavall at his heels. He was writing something he hoped Adelina would publish and kept asking after her.

I wonder how her press is doing. I wonder if she misses me. I wonder if the city misses me. But I push all of this aside and instead we explore.

When last I was here, twenty years ago, it was smaller, and you could walk from one edge of the city to the other in less than an hour. Now it goes on and on, the rafts lashed together, the access holes to the underwater portion as regular here as streetlights in Tabat. There are even gardens now, rafts covered with dirt, plants and grass growing along them.

A smell catches me as we skirt the edge of the Night Market, savory and briny.

I follow it.

In a little stall, a squid is serving up dumplings, flakes of shredded fish wrapped in seaweed, flavored with hot peppers from the Southern Isles. Scylla's favorite.

The squid's arms dexterously move: gathering, folding, sliding each neat green packet into the tray sitting before it. As soon as one is full, the vendor snatches it, begins to dole the dumplings out to the waiting customers. I step up and signal for two. Lucky for me there are spare coins in my belt; where would I have spent them aboard ship?

I take my food to the booth's corner, out of the way of the

passers-by, and not coincidentally a place where I can watch the crowd and perhaps spot pursuit before it comes to me.

I lick spicy shreds of fish off my fingers and lean an elbow on the unsteady, well-worn plank that functions as counter along one side of this market booth, half-turning to watch the passing late-evening crowds in the crowded lane outside this space. Teo settles at my feet, at first hopeful of food, then propping his chin on his forepaws in resignation and going to sleep.

This crowd is mostly Mers, only an occasional Human or Beast. The tonk and flute music, musicians two stalls over, calls during an ebb in the murmur of conversation and creaking footing. The wind shifts and brings with it the tang of salt, as clear and sweet as the starry sky overhead, the slivered purple moon leading its fuller white counterpart in a climb, the upward half of the red moon like a smoldering bowl on the horizon.

A troupe of dancers passes, dressed in shifts sewn with clicking fish scales, more strung around their ankles. They are bone-dry, on their way to a wetter space to celebrate. One pauses to teasingly snake a hand towards my shot of sea-venom, and I let them snatch it up and tip it down, winking at me, red and white moonlight cradled in the curves of their scales. They stand for a moment in flirtatious trawl, but I do not stretch the encounter out, and they swirl back into the crowd with their fellows, the pack of them diving into the access point a few steps onward, a stretch of water leading down into the city below the surface, rippled in red and white and purple.

In their wake drifts a watchful city guard in their shark-skin gear, a tangle-net lined with stingray barbs and cruel bone hooks slung over one shoulder, a trident in their hand, three-set tines to pin a foe or more likely ward off one of the big fish that haunt the city's edges at nighttime, searching for the bait fish that take shelter there.

They pass, more Mers swallowing up the figures. Clusters of barely clad laborers on their way home from something after work in the kelp or shellfish beds, or on the other docks.

"Hello."

It startles me, how this woman has crept up on me somehow. She dazzles in this light; she would dazzle in any light. Her hair is white as new milk, her skin darker than my own by a multiplicity of shades. Perhaps a handful of years my elder, I think, and then amend that figure upward as I look into her thoughtful eyes.

She smiles like a woman with a secret.

She smiles like a woman who is *herself* a secret, who eats and drinks and sleeps with it, beautiful and deadly as a drawn knife. The sort of beauty I used to have.

I realize that is where I saw her last, long ago in Tabat, across the vast reach of the room, the parquet floor of Bernarda's gallery, just before the riot, and what seems even vaster, the intervening span of days—can it really not be years since that time? But every hour in the Duke's torture chambers was a day, a month, a decade's worth of pain.

What was her name, back at the gallery, this silver-haired woman, so straight and beautiful as the moon itself? *Selene.* Named for the white moon. That was it. She is dressed more simply than she was on that long-ago day, a grey robe, plain cut, with red and purple markings at the edge, her thin feet bare like my own.

I say, "Your name was Selene."

"And still is," she says, that smile like a sugar trinket dancing on her lips.

"How did you come here?" There is a suspicious part of my mind, still trying to figure out all of the Duke's conspiracies and machinations. Is she part of that? No, her eyes seem sincere, and they reflect the sky so clearly, with her namesake moon drowning in those midnight pools.

"I travel," she says easily. I remember her accent: strange, almost archaic, but well educated. A dilettante perhaps, a Noble playing at a trade, like Explorer or Merchant, before moving to some other pastime. Nobles often do such things. Some are even good at their chosen callings; others less so, particularly when it requires labor or hard practice, I have found.

She says now, "I had to come far to meet you here, Bella Kanto."

I don't know what to say. She *must* know of my disgrace. How is she here? She could not have come on the same boat that I traveled on. Her presence seems improbable, if not downright impossible.

She says into my silence, "You have nothing to fear from me."

"I do not fear you."

"No, perhaps not. But you fear what I might say, is that not the truth?" She tilts her head, smirks at me. Her eyes are as silver as her hair, her skin as dark and soft as any high-bred Noble's. Who is she? *What* is she?

Fear strikes me. I have been driven mad by the memory of the cells and this is what happens: I imagine encounters that could not possibly take place. At least this is a benign hallucination; who knows what will occur to me next?

"I do not mean to interrupt your quest," she says. "We'll see each again, trust in that." She steps backward into the crowd that has been ignoring our conversation, and she is gone.

I stare after her, or at least in the direction that I think she has vanished in. This night feels somehow *tangled*, as though the laws of luck itself have twisted and gone awry. My heart beats hard and fast in my throat and the cloudless sky overhead presses down on me, menacing.

Teo wakes, whines at me in question. I snap my fingers at him and move on. He yawns and follows.

CHAPTER 16

ON THE RAFT CITY (TEO)

*H*e could not help it. There were so many new smells that he had to get off the ship and get at all of them, had to investigate.

So off he went through the air and then the water. He swam through the water and some of it got up his nose, but that was all right. He would have liked to bark, but it was hard enough to make his way.

First he was in clear water, and then, as he neared the rafts, he was forced to avoid smaller boats, and those in them, most of whom shouted at him angrily.

Finally he was there at the side of the raft and climbing up the netting made of thick rope, knotted there for the benefit of the Mers, who climbed like him straight out of the water. A few paused to watch his progress and call out commentary, but most of the crowd ignored him.

He emerged onto the raft and immediately shook himself free of the water, showering everything in his vicinity indiscriminately, which led to his being chased away by the dock workers standing there loading a small schooner.

After so many days on the ship, this world of new smells was almost bewildering. He'd forgotten how there could be so many people that the smells buffeted you, and how each one was more enticing than the last: old fish and rotting meat, a scattering of dung and the tang of spilled beer. And the people here, most of them, smelled different from the Humans in Tabat. These smelled as though they had been soaking in saltwater for so long that they'd taken on its scent.

He didn't worry about Bella. She would have to come to the raft, and then how far could she go? He'd smell her eventually. And in the meantime, he had so much here to explore.

He spent a good quarter hour being petted by a trio of street children, but when they brought out a bit of rope and tried to make him a collar and leash of it, he nipped (careful not to draw blood) at the restraining hand of the oldest and raced away through the crowds, low and under stalls, so they could not follow.

He had enjoyed being petted, but there were limits, after all, and the children had shown no sign of being prepared to feed him.

He found a cat sitting on a doorstep and chased it along a fence, barking happily, until someone else came out and shouted at him. This was all very exciting, he thought, but the people here certainly seemed to shout a great deal.

But throughout it all, there was something lacking, something that itched at him. A need. A particular … what?

Then he caught the smell and knew. Bella was here somewhere. That was all that mattered. He set off down an alleyway, trotting eagerly. She was here somewhere, and he would find her, wherever she was.

He cast through the crowds. There were other animals here and there, but few other dogs. Many cats arched and hissed at him as he passed, but there were other things, like the great black eel that rose from a tub of salt water and confronted him with a round maw edged with teeth, or the bank of cages holding birds that all started screaming the minute he paused to sniff at them.

He hurriedly moved on, the vendor's curses nipping at his heels. Someone else kicked at him in passing, and he ran under one of the market tables and stood there long enough to catch his breath. Nameless longings moved through him. He wanted something but he didn't know what. To be something other than what he was, but he couldn't say what.

Then he remembered *I was a boy, a Human boy*, with a suddenness that dazed him, and a sad lurch to his heart. He was losing himself, forgetting who he had been. One day he wouldn't remember, wouldn't come back to himself.

Then he caught that familiar and welcome scent again. Bella. He cast around, checking it, and trailed her through the crowds.

He dodged from hands that reached down to grab at him, slunk along walls in order to elude a particularly ardent child, then back in through a crowd and under several tables, whose patrons objected, kicking at him as he moved onward.

There! Another whiff of Bella, strong and clear enough to show that she had been there only moments before. His tail wagged in spite of himself and he was no longer Human enough to find it in the least embarrassing. She was standing by herself and smelled sad again. He pushed his nose into the hand that hung at her side.

She wheeled, startled. He leaped at her, putting his paws on her chest in order to lick her face, something he had been too small to do at the beginning of their journey, back in Tabat.

"There you are!" she said and grabbed him gently by the fur at the back of his head to shake him affectionately. "You ruffian, where have you been?"

He had thought, in a resigned manner, that once he found her, they would probably go back to the ship, but as they moved along together, he found himself increasingly possessed of the delighted opinion that she didn't care whether or not they went back to the ship, and that she intended to continue wandering around this place and all its delightful and distracting and amazing smells that kept grabbing his attention. She stopped to buy a stick of little octopi grilled on a skewer and gave him one. He gulped it down, licking his chops, and followed her, hopeful for more.

He was happy to have found her, happier that she didn't seem angry at his escape, happiest yet that they seemed to be lingering in this place rather than going back to the stuffiness of the boat.

They lingered by the side of one of the big pools that seemed to serve as entrance and exit to the water for the Mer. Teo could smell so many different people, but here the smell of the Mers was the most prevalent, a dank and musty smell that smelled like water that had been sitting undisturbed for several days, but not unpleasantly so. There were so many fish smells that he had never realized, ones that were different from anything he had ever smelled before and yet which said unerringly in his head, this is fish. He'd learned many of them on the boat with Bella, but now here were dozens more, each new one a stick poking at his nose's internalities. He sneezed, then sneezed again.

Something caught his attention; he wasn't sure what. He sniffed and looked around. It seemed to him three of the Mers were paying particular attention to Bella. No, they definitely were. He could read it in their body language, and the way their eyes flickered across her from time to time, always as though moving to look at something else and just happening to encounter her.

Then he smelled the other woman, the one from the boat. He growled.

Bella tapped him on the muzzle. "Be good," she said.

He wished desperately she could understand him, and the desperation leaked out in a whimper.

They turned down an alleyway. Then everything dissolved into confusion. People rushed at them and he snarled and bit and snapped, but the woman had a collar, she grabbed him as the sailors with her closed on Bella, and then suddenly Bella stepped backward and vanished and was gone, and all he could do was howl as he was pulled along and away and back to the boat without Bella.

CHAPTER 17

ON THE RAFT CITY (BELLA)

*E*very city has its quarters, more than four of them, each devoted to a specific industry, or related industry, just as in Tabat, down near the docks, there are the warehouses in which cloth is stored, and there are the tailors, so close by, and all of their shops together, rather than spread out. Adelina has explained it to me more than once, how cities fall into patterns, and many of those patterns are the same city to city.

The place I go is not one that most visitors know or care to know. It is of little use to them, this place, because it is where the Mers trade their skills at ornamentation.

Mer skin varies—a very few have something close to Human skin, but even those have patches where it becomes something else, scales or the horny cartilage that they carry as natural armor. Others have much less Human about them. Here in this quarter, they specialize in ornamentation of a kind no Human would wear: jewels inset into carapace, scales carved and scored and made brilliant. I pass a few who wear witch wood inset into their arms, a substance that glows when it comes in contact with saltwater. An expensive indulgence, it is consumed by the very action that sets it alight, lasting no more than a season.

This is the quarter where you come for all the little body rituals

of grooming, the tending of nails and hair and skin. The bonding
moments, the reassuring little touches that are so necessary.

Did magic fill this need for me before? It seems petty, somehow,
to think that it had tended to things like rogue hairs or the occasional blemish, but that was one reason I threw the mirror out the
window. That, and the fine lines around my eyes.

The crowd is entirely Mer now, and I have not seen any
Humans for a while. Those that pass me look at me strangely; they
do not understand what I am doing here.

This place seems more familiar to me than the outer neighborhoods, which are transformed by all the visitors of the years,
grown bigger and grander in order to accommodate more people.
Here I find myself going along a path that I remember. Most of
the buildings are changed but a few are still the same. I go
through winding alleyways and then a path between buildings
and then a courtyard and then I am at a place that I remember
well.

I remember the smell of the incense that they burned to disguise
the under-smell of burning chitin, and the scent of baskets of
oranges that they kept there to refresh their guests, brought up
from the Southern Isles, baskets of woven seaweed holding the
huge fruit, each as big as my hand, the rind thick and plushy and
fragrant.

The sign above the entrance bears the sigil that it used to: an
octopus tangled around a Mer. I believe there was some bawdy joke
to it, but try as I might, I could never coax Scylla into telling it
to me.

I push at the light door, woven from wicker and weed, and go
into the entrance chamber just inside. There are several attendants,
and two Mers that they are tending to, buffing the carved tortoise-
shell textures of one's back while polishing the scales of another,
buffing away the little encrustations that collect if a Mer is not
careful.

Everyone is as still as though at an invasion, and I feel a clumsy
interloper as I never have before. I say, as apologetically as I can, "I
am sorry to disturb, but is Tersa around?"

Their faces do not clear at my mention of that name. One says, "She died three years ago."

I look around to see if there is anyone I recognize. Or more importantly, someone who might recognize me. But I see no one, no familiar faces.

I say, "I beg your pardon then, I was looking for a friend, who I know was a frequent patron here."

"Who is your friend?" the Mer says. She is small and fierce looking, her scales a beautiful, dappled purple and green that I am not sure is natural.

"Scylla," I tell her.

I had thought there was a hush over the room before, but at the mention of this name, there is absolute stillness. I look around, trying to read their faces, but I cannot. I do not know any of these women or men and I have not learned to understand their expressions. There is only one Mer that I have ever been able to decipher, and while these people seem to know her name, it is clear that they will not speak to me of her.

I bow, feeling awkward. I have made a mistake in coming here. "Excuse me," I say, and back out of the door.

I KEEP on through the crowds, ignoring the vendors and prostitutes who call or wave to me. I keep thinking I see Ruhua or familiar sailors and know I must take to smaller streets. A passage leads between buildings. At its opening, I look along it and see only darkness, here and there a trickle of light seeping out from a building.

I take a step down the alley, despite the fact that something is niggling at me, something is out of place. I cannot identify what it is as I venture a few steps farther in.

Then a rush of footsteps behind me tells me someone—several someones—have followed me into the darkness. Their speed and silence does not make me think they wish me well.

They pull me out, Ruhua and her men. And spin me round to face her, standing by one of the access holes. In the watching crowd, I see Selene's face. Her eyes meet mine. What is she promising?

"Come now," Ruhua says, her voice low and relentless.

What can I do but what happens next? Eyes fixed on Ruhua, I take a deep breath and step backward, into empty air. Then I plunge into the access hole, hearing shouts and a frantic bark from Teo just before with a splash and shock of cold water, I hit the surface.

I jack-knife in the water, kicking off my entangling cloak and fighting myself free, then swim fast—no time for thought, if I want to survive. Otherwise I will drown.

Below the raft city, the access passages let the Mers move from one place to another swiftly, in the water that they prefer to the air. The tunnels are not made for Humans, but a strong enough, fast enough swimmer can traverse them—or most of them. There are passages that wind too far for Human lungs to carry them.

Sometimes Human youths bet each other on how far they can swim, using the tunnels. Sometimes they drown.

All of the passages are marked with colored glow globes that hang on ropes suspended in the water. The colors tell you which way they lead, but I do not remember the codes and so I pick a globe that glows like the white moon, because it reminds me of Selene, wavering in the sea water that stings my eyes.

Air is already burning in my lungs. Moving hard and fast drains me as I swim past another white globe, then another. The urge to take a breath is so strong that I clench my teeth, and I see the ghostly forms of little fish moving away from my path.

There may be pursuit, Mers sent by Ruhua, but I know these people. They have no reason to love the Duke and his rule. They will not disobey overtly, but they will not obey swiftly or accurately, pretending to be simple and misunderstand commands.

My heart beats and my head throbs with each beat. Another globe ahead, only an arm's length, but I feel my limbs faltering. My old body could have swum this easily, filled with Tabat's magic even this far away. Despair nips at my toes, then climbs its way up my body as I swim towards the next globe.

A faint oval of light beyond it, the next access point. Adrenaline surges and somehow, I manage another burst of speed, arms pulling me through the water in the way that Scylla taught me.

My head breaks the surface, and the air is the sweetest thing I have ever tasted, but then a torch flares and someone shouts, "Here!" from above me and so I gulp as much air as I can, pulling it down into my stomach and lungs, and dive again.

It is a nightmarish hunt in the dark water, but I move from access point to access point. I think they are trying to track me on the surface, but I keep following the white globes, the underwater moons, leading me somewhere, I do not know where.

And then I hit the surface again and this time someone is waiting for me there, and I am seized.

CHAPTER 18

*B*efore I can fall back into the water, they grab me, rough hands around my upper arms, yanking me upward.

I know what I should do, exactly how to twist and snap back an arm, free myself while tangling them together, a sweeping kick to bring the other down. That's not what I do.

Something happens that has never happened before in my life: I freeze.

I imagine all sorts of things as they pull me up. Imagine my palm strike snapping a head back so it breaks like a straw. Imagine my kick snapping out to cripple a kneecap so another falls. Imagine gathering my breath and screaming, even, and bringing help that way.

But none of this happens. Instead fear paralyzes me, robs me of all will, all motion. A hood comes down over my head, and I panic, knowing what that fish-bladder smell means, but still I cannot resist as hands grasp my arms, another pair at my back shoving me along to urge me down a stairway. The smell and lap of water and then I'm shoved off balance and fall pinwheeling with a splash through what must have been a hatchway, one of the many here permeating the boundary between water and air.

At least I know enough not to panic as I go under. The hood is airtight; I'll have three or four breaths at least, maybe more, depending on how I use it. So I breathe shallowly as they pull me down, reassuring myself that they would not have put the hood on if they meant to drown me.

The water gets colder fast. They drag me along below the water's surface with speed, and I do not resist, let myself go limp so as not to impede them, and make that passage any slower.

As it is, there are spots hovering in the hood's blackness before I'm drawn up into the air and it's pulled away from my face. I gasp for breath, smelling saltwater and kelp's bitter bite and the wood rot that means this is an older place.

I'm in one of the Mer chambers, a hollow bubble somewhere below the waterline. Green plants, lifideca, line the basketwork; they give off air and eat the stale part of it. One of Scylla's cousins explained it in excruciatingly lengthy detail at one point. All I retain from her lectures is that a single plant puts out enough good air for a child that is no more than three years old, and that the basketwork must be loose to enable moisture to drip through.

And the basketwork is old, so old there must be magic reinforcing it, because here and there I can see the dark gleam of water through chinks and holes. All around this pool in the chamber's center is a lip of wicker shelving, perhaps twenty feet in width, ladders set at intervals to allow access. I expect them to loose my hands to let me climb up, but two take me and leap out of the water without effort, hauling me upward.

The structure is sturdier than it appears but shakes with every motion. They barely let me catch my footing before they pull me over to the shelf set a little higher, leading to the rocky ledge where Scylla sits atop her throne.

Her throne, a vast chair, as though made for some much larger creature, an accumulation of fish scales and pearl and luminous strands of weed. A nestlike thing that clearly is made, not grown, but has a sense about it of something other than Human. I wonder if many non-Mer have seen it, have seen this place. I have a feeling it may be very few indeed. Maybe I am even the first.

The thought does not make me feel so much privileged as wary. What does she want of me?

It was not until a week after we'd first fallen into each other's arms that I learned what Scylla actually was: the oldest child of not a lord, but something close, the leader of Thieftown. Which is a misnomer: Thieftown is the great market that trades in everything, the commerce on which this city depends, and the bloodline overseeing it has wealth in abundance, and all the power that brings.

She confided later that she'd come down to the proceedings to assess the visitors arriving on my ship. "You learn more from a person when they are speaking with someone they think does not matter than when they speak with someone who they think they can profit from," she told me, repeating a Trade God maxim I'd later hear more than once from Adelina.

"What did you learn from me?" I teased.

"That you go where your heart leads," she said, more seriously than my tone merited. "That is a quality that not all Humans have."

She was ruthlessly honest with me, and yet I never told her Alberic had sent me to spy, to figure out how to get more taxes from her people. Nor did I ever tell her what I did: give him absurdities and impracticalities and blame them all on my inexperience.

She never wrote to me in Tabat; and I never wrote to her, but I thought of her, more than once.

Now, in this time and place, she does not look older. Her scales still gleam on her supple form, and the great frilled crest on her head hangs down like damp hair. I have lost my touch at reading her face. I cannot tell what she thinks, to see me now.

I wish that I had written her.

She gestures at the two that stand on either side of me. "Go," she says.

"My lady, surely that is not safe," the left-hand one protests. She is young, so young that she reminds me of my Skye, and something in the look she gives her leader, ardent and full of worship, ready to fling herself in front of any danger, brave any peril in order to prove herself to her leader, reminds me even more so.

But I killed Skye, even if it was a death that she courted to the point where some might say she had brought it on herself.

Scylla gestures again, this time more impatiently. The guard releases my wrist and steps away, reluctance manifest in the motion. Both of them slip under the water, the angry guard still giving me an "I'll have my eye on you" glare that is only eclipsed when her head goes below the surface.

Scylla rolls her eyes once they are all gone. "Were you and I ever that young?" she demands. She rises from the throne in order to approach me.

"We were," I say. "You still look that young."

"You do not," she says. She inclines her head, examining me. "Rumors are flying through the city," she says. "They came on your ship, but they are spreading uncommonly fast, via one of the passengers."

"Ruhua," I say.

"That is the name she gives," Scylla says. "She says you are exiled in disgrace for unspeakable crimes."

"That last is not true," I say. "But I am indeed charged with a crime and I am exiled. I am traveling to one of the frontier cities."

"She said you would not leave the ship, and yet here you are."

"She might have forbidden it," I say, and leave it at that. It is sufficient, I can tell, from Scylla's lifted brow. She appreciates rebellion as she ever did.

"She said that were you to somehow leave, you were to be returned to her immediately." Light from a glow basket slides along her face as it tilts, studying my features. "She said that you had dealings with Sorcerers. Is that true?"

"No," I say.

"I wish that you could say yes," Scylla says.

"To what?"

"That you dealt with Sorcerers. I need help, and the kind that one of them might be able to give."

The enormity of her willingness to make such a deal startles me more suddenly than any punch or slap ever could, freezes me for a moment before I can speak again. "Why would you deal with such a thing?"

"The Duke sees his power waning in Tabat," she says. "He thinks he will grasp more here."

"How so?"

"He has his eye on a very large prize indeed."

"What prize is that?"

"Everything my people hold," she says.

The realization hits me. "He means to declare you all Beasts." I remember the Mer I saw so long ago on the ship that sprang the trap for me. I hadn't wondered, at the time, what brought a Mer so far, forcing them to resort to extremes like a watersuit in order to walk on land. Now I understood. Come to plead their case before the Duke, perhaps. Or somehow call themselves exempt.

"He does. There are Mages here, studying us. They say because they want to learn some of the magics we use to keep the city afloat, but if you happen to overhear what they say when they think no one is listening, the speech is very different. They seek to establish that the magic is part of us, not an outside force that we wield. That is the defining line the College of Mages has set, and they mean to change the way we meet it in order to slide us over it."

"But there would be riots," I say. "Your folk would not allow it."

"They will splinter us off, a group at a time," she says. "One family by one, declared Beast, their holdings to be taken and split between the city and the Duke. That practice, if allowed, will speed rather than slow it. When money is involved, common sense goes out the window for some, and they will not see the danger lurking under the surface of all their newfound wealth. They will not realize that the Duke does not mean to let them hold it for long."

"And what do you expect me to do about it?" I demand. She has brought me here for a reason, thinks I can solve this problem somehow.

"I do not know," she says. "But if ever someone could do something in the name of justice, surely it is the infamous Bella Kanto."

Plink, plink says the water dripping from the roof to the surface of the pool.

"Tell me more," I say, even though I don't want to.

INSTEAD OF ANSWERING ME DIRECTLY, she takes me through soggy passageways to another structure. I am well aware of the water pressing down on me. I don't know if I would be able to reach the surface if there was some disaster, and the thought of that makes flimsy walls seem even flimsier.

But the great underwater city that the Mers have built has seen its share of those from the surface, and I will hardly be the last to walk through these hallways that give uncannily beneath the foot, as though one were walking over the roof of a tent, sinking into the folds.

I have never been this deep before, even in the years long ago. I have to swallow every few minutes to clear the throbbing from my ears. Tight pain builds in the space between my eyes, echoes back and forth with every step, and breathing is harder than it should be.

We come out into a vast open space, and this time I gasp, because this is unexpected.

Imagine an egg, set on its top, and lined with greenery. Shelves and shelves of it, interlocking. In the middle of the great chamber hangs a point of light, so bright that it casts everything in shadow, and the center is white, so white, and then fades into green, colored by curtains of hanging weed.

But here and there among the green—blank spots, missing shelves, and in one spot a cluster of blackened foliage. The greenery has been cleared away in a circle around it, isolating it.

Scylla sees me looking at it. "That is what I have brought you to witness," she says.

We climb up to the spot, along hanging pathways between the shelves. Scylla leads me upward. Now is when I notice that age has not left her untouched, has thickened her form, but also made it slower. Not much. Perhaps only a Gladiator—or former lover— might notice such a thing.

I wonder what she thinks of how I have aged. I had been

untouched by it so long, protected by Tabat's magic, and now every morning is stiffness, soreness, creakiness.

The walls are clear, made of green-lit water; every few feet a glow-globefish puffs its way through the water on its tether. Along the rope, silvery shells cluster, growing large, hand-sized, before they are harvested. In other spots are the tendrils of sea grape and the spiral-leaved, snaking tendrils of Ellora's lettuce, vividly and unnaturally green.

But now much of it is blackened. The shellfish hang in limp clusters, shells choked with smutty black growth like accumulated soot, and the sea grapes are shriveled, the lettuce faded and blotchy.

"It started a few months ago," Scylla tells me. "These are crops we depend on to keep the city fed. Fish and weed rack is insufficient."

Ellora, the Mage whose caverns feed Tabat, came here once too, and showed the Mers how to cultivate these things, as well as oysters, and the great green lobsters that are so prized as a delicacy back in Tabat and which are common fare here.

These farms are the heart of the city. Ellora invented ways of storing sunlight and taking it underwater to augment the light fluttering down to the depths.

Magic as plentiful as sunlight, that was what Ellora wanted. Magic that did not adorn the rich or make them richer. Magic that fed and clothed and housed everyone. She did accomplish the first in Tabat but died without her work fulfilled beyond that.

At least she had a goal. What was mine? I'd achieved what I sought. First admission into the Brides of Steel, then rising in its ranks, then playing Spring in order to assume Winter's armor the next year.

And after that? Nothing, just existing. Being Bella Kanto, as though that were a sufficiency, rather than a void. As though it was not, in truth, existence of a compelling shell, a hollow thing without a core. Staring around me at the chamber, I feel it all pressing in on me.

"Stop it," Scylla says sharply. "I know that look. I have never seen it before on you, Bella, and it is not a becoming one. Where is the brave and bold Gladiator that seduced me so many years ago?"

I rally to answer her. "Are you sure it was I that seduced you? That is not how I remember it, and my memory is usually accounted quite good."

She looks at me suspiciously, worried that the despair still lingers, but I have put on a very brave face. She says, "I need your help to fix this."

"What can I do?" I ask. "I am here under guard, and the guard can kill me at any moment should she choose to."

Scylla's eyes widen. "By what means?"

I shrug. "Magic of some sort."

She chews her lip with a thoughtful gaze. She says, "There are things that dampen magic and prevent spells from coming to their conclusion. But they are not cheap."

"I have nothing," I say, frankly. For all of the trunks that they let me pack, there are few small, valuable things of the sort that could be easily pawned.

She waves off the thought with a flick of her fingers, "I have plenty, but it's a question of whether the investment is worth it."

"I'd like to think so," I say, but there's a trace of uncertainty in it and she rounds on me.

"What has happened to you, Bella Kanto, to hollow out the heart that I once knew? There was no timidity, no half-naturedness about my friend, that Bella. Now you are someone else, and I ask you again, is this new person someone worth my investment? If I can get you out of reach of this magic, will you help me find how to solve this conundrum?"

"What do you propose?" I ask, buying myself time to think although I am already sure that I am going to say yes.

Being out from under Ruhua's hand, off the leash, would be worth any risk, and a few last moments of freedom would be worth escaping a life of confinement.

Because I've realized over my time with her that such is her purpose, to see me confined within wherever I am bound to, not at large within it. There are plans within plans entrusted to Ruhua. I do not want to find out what they consist of by falling into their trap.

"I want to go to the Southern Isles. I have a little ship, a fast one, that the two of us can crew."

"The Southern Isles?" I am surprised. But the notion is appealing—I enjoyed my time in the Southern Isles when I was down there. The clear blue water and the chances for swimming, the fruit and spices and meal after meal of pork roast from the swine roaming the hillside. Peppers and bright fabric and pretty people showing flesh under it.

"It's where they took Ellora's papers, after she died. The Duke founded a University down there a few years ago and they took all those papers and her books as the start of a library, something to build the institution around."

"The College of Mages let him do that with them? I would think they wouldn't let such things out of their grasp."

"He promised them a branch of the College there, and they have taken advantage of it. But those papers may hold the secret of keeping the fruit of her labors healthy."

"That makes sense," I say. I am thinking, putting things together. "And someone who had access to those papers might have put together the disease that is plaguing yours right now."

"That thought had occurred to me as well. And there is a thought beyond that."

"Which is?"

"The rafts are dependent on the bounty that Ellora gave them. They would not have enough food to sustain so many people without her gifts."

"True enough."

"What other city has grown dependent on her gifts?"

The answer is immediately obvious. "Tabat," I say slowly. "Tabat, where the caverns grow the mushrooms that everyone depends on. That the Temples give out to the indigent and in need, those who could not find food of their own otherwise."

"That is exactly right," she says. "And so, you may have more at stake in all of this than you think, my friend."

I shake my head. "I have been exiled. I am never to return to the city, under pain of death."

"Circumstances change sometimes. Even now the elections are happening. Deep changes are moving throughout your city, at least if all the news that I have heard is accurate. It may well be that the council that is elected will choose to pardon someone who is such a past hero."

"That is a pretty thought, but one that will never come to pass. The taint of those charges can never be washed away;. You know that as well as I do."

"I still think that you will be surprised by what can happen when governments change."

"I will help you, no matter what," I tell her, "but to lose Ruhua, we will have to plan very carefully indeed."

Her look is coy. "It will be good," she says, "to collaborate with you again."

CHAPTER 19

THE FANCY BLISS (LUCY)

*I*t was cold in the morning when they took Lucy out to walk on the deck the fifth day, by herself because Maz had a headache. Was that why? Sometimes it was hard to remember things about him. She thought about wondering why that was, but the question slipped away from her mind even as it occurred to her.

Mist lay on the water like a blanket, muffling sound. She was allowed to walk back and forth, from prow to stern and then back and forth again, for a finger's worth of sand by the great hourglass that marked time in the ship's middle, perhaps half an hour by her reckoning. She could not hear gulls overhead, just the lapping of the waves against the hull and the sigh of the wind, rippling and unrippling the full-bellied sails.

She walked quickly, stretching her legs as much as she could without actually running. She would have liked to run, or at least to run the way she could back in Tabat, where it would have been part of a game of tag or catch-me-if-you-can. But she was afraid that the sailors would laugh at her, or say something unkind, and so she maintained a more sedate pace.

When she came to the prow, she paused. What were those lumps floating in the water? She hung over the railing, looking down into the curling mist.

Turtles, dozens of them, enormous and sad-eyed, all swimming in the same direction as the ship, which was passing among them. They moved slowly, ponderously, like boulders floating somehow on the mist-laden surface.

"What do you see, eh?" Kindly paused beside her and looked down. "Ah now, that's a stroke of luck!" He turned and shouted back over his shoulder. "Got turtles, an' plenty of 'em! Ready nets!"

He pulled Lucy back from the railing. "Time for you to go back down," he said.

"Please, can't I stay just a little longer and watch?" she begged. "It's so stuffy down there."

He looked at her shrewdly. "You won't get up to any mischief, won't do something like jumping overboard?"

"What would be the point?" she asked and gestured at the expanse of fog and ocean surrounding them.

He barked out a laugh. "Very well. Stand ye here and watch if you've a mind. Though if the captain comes looking for you, I'll say you gave me the slip and I thought you was already downstairs."

"Deal," she said, and almost put out a hand to spit and seal the pact, as she would have with her sisters, then saw him looking oddly at the hand and put it back down.

She stayed and watched, saw the early morning sun burning away the thin mist to reveal more turtles floating on the water. She wanted to shout at them to dive, to escape, but she held still, not wanting to jeopardize this rare chance at sunlight and a survey of the ship from a different angle than she usually saw it from, so close to the railing.

They lowered nets and drew them back up almost immediately, each time with several of the vast turtles caught in them, flippers waving piteously, their silent troubled eyes questioning the sailors hauling them aboard.

Lucy had wondered before what the big racks along the cabin side were meant to house. Now she realized their purpose as the turtles were stacked into them, unable to move forward, their flippers still waving, and their huge beaks clacking now and again, a startled but muted noise.

She hoped some of them had escaped. There had been so many of them, that surely at least a few had been able to get away, had been able to dive down into the water beyond the reach of the nets as they sank to the length of the ropes that held them. She was crying; she wiped away the tears with the sleeve of her dress.

A presence paused beside her. Reached over and took her chin between thumb and two fingers, turned it slightly so he could consider the shine of her tears. Captain Jusuf.

"You will feel kinder tonight, when we have soup from one," he said. "The flavor is unimaginable: rich and savory and tasting like the heart of the sea."

"Won't they die out of the water like that?" She nodded over at the racks of turtles.

He shook his head. "It is not as cruel as all that. They are used to going for weeks without food or water, and so they will stay there nicely until they are needed."

"Needed for you to eat," she said. "But we could fish instead."

"Are the fish somehow less worthy of life than the turtles?" he asked. "And either way, we will eat plenty of fish. Fish, fish, and more fish, until the turtle soup will seem like manna. It is a long journey to the Southern Isles and even when we are there, it will take longer yet to get to the place where we are going."

"Fireah," she said. "What does it mean, that name?"

He said, "In the old language, it means 'birthed from nowhere'. An island that appeared one day where one had never been. But so long ago, that nowadays we have lost any sense of wonder at it. Still, it holds plenty of surprises yet, and you are the key to unlocking those, I think."

He released her chin in order to touch a fingertip to her tear and then raise it to his lips. His tongue flickered out, tasting the salty drop.

"I had expected it to be sweeter, somehow," he said enigmatically and signaled the sailor to take her back downstairs.

CHAPTER 20

RETURNED TO THE STOOPING HAWK
(BELLA)

I cannot imagine how I am to tell Ruhua what all has happened. I will simply tell her I was looking for the dog. I ask Scylla to send her people searching for him, but they cannot manage to find him.

"Do you have anything more to ask me?" Scylla says at the end of our planning. I shake my head. Something about the way she is asking it comes too close to the affection we used to hold for each other.

I do not know why every iota of my body resists that urge, one that used to be so strong. The old Bella would have bedded her by now somehow, would have found a private place and explored all those intersections between skin and scale anew, found all those familiar dips and divots that made her gasp, that made her move and arch. By the end of our time together, I had learned to play Scylla's body more surely than any musician held their instrument.

Scylla did want old Bella to stay, but I knew—I knew even then, even when I did not want to admit it—that the desire was more than the pleasure. She loved me, and I made light of it in a way that she could not take offense at, told her stories of wandering and made it clear that I was what I was, and that she had no hope of changing me for what she would have thought the better.

I catch her looking at me more than once. I know what sort of thoughts are going through her head. I've seen them more than once; I saw them time after time before I learned to set expectations early. The eyes of someone who thought I filled some broken parts of their soul, as though I were a lodestar that could guide them.

I was nothing of the sort, nor did I want to be. I was simply Bella Kanto, in those days.

I am simply myself, nowadays, as well. That remains true. It's just that I don't know what it means anymore.

This time I am not dragged through the water, wondering if I will die. They take me up through air-filled tubes, and I swim only a few times from one to another, each time with Mer hovering nearby to make sure that I make the transition.

From this vantage, the moments between tunnels when I hang in the water for a few precious seconds to look before following a glowing strand to the next tunnel, I see the city by night as the Mers see it, and it is almost as splendid as Tabat, because it is made of light right now, luminescent ropes and guidelines stretching between the softer radiance of buildings.

I am reluctant to leave it, reluctant to go back to the close and hate-filled air of the ship. But Teo is there by now, I am sure.

Scylla's people are gentle enough until we get close to the ship, and then, in my opinion, they oversell it a bit, the way they shove me around.

I am tempted to fight back, but I resign myself to a few bruises, even though I know my body will not heal from this roughness the way it once would have. I fear that they may break one of my limbs, something that has never happened to me in all this time, and I'm careful to keep my arms tucked in as they push me one way and then another.

"Enough!" Ruhua, standing there, incandescent with rage. "Bring her to my cabin."

She turns on her heel and two sailors grab me. They shove me into the room behind her. At her gesture, they step outside.

She has no fear of me. She wears a gauntlet woven of steel and she points a finger of it at me. "Do you know what this is?"

"A fire-glove," I say cautiously.

"I suspected you would be familiar with such. Did Jolietta ever use them?"

"She did not," I say, as politely as though we were making after-dinner conversation and not how and why my aunt tortured the Beasts under her care. "She did not approve of magic used in training. She said it was too easy to go wrong."

"And yet it is effective."

She continues pointing a finger at me. Is it my imagination that heat is beginning to creep along my limbs, that I can feel it building? I can smell it now somehow, the fire it is lighting inside my body. But before the heat can turn to pain, she stops, puts her hand down.

"I told you that you were not allowed on the city," she says. "Did you think you would find allies there? Old friends?"

Her eyes are narrow with suspicion. I try to think back on my old reports to Alberic of my activities here, which she may have had access to. Did I ever mention Scylla?

No, caution ruled me then, as ever. I had some sense even then that there were qualities that Jolietta and Alberic shared, things that made them all too similar. Alberic showered me with favors in a way that Jolietta never had, but that was because he wanted me in his bed, with no chase or challenge about it.

I knew full well that not to submit was to provoke his anger, and so I might have been cowardly about it now that I admit these things to myself. I reckoned up the costs as carefully as any Merchant, and in the end decided that the price of not yielding to him far outweighed my pride.

I was much less sure of myself in those early days, back before I thought of myself as the Champion of Tabat and loved by the Gods. Back then I still expected bad fortune to catch up with me. Why was it so slow? By the time that it arrived, I had forgotten all such caution.

I say, "I found it very changed. None of the places that I once knew are there." I let my eyes fall. Should I blame the dog for my absence? It is true, but I think that her reprisal for such a thing might be much to the dog's detriment and so I bite back any excuses involving him and his errant ways.

I miss the old Bella, who never cared when anyone was angry. She was unflappable in the face of fury, no matter how loud or sharp. This new Bella flinches at Ruhua's anger. She is not loud, but she is sharp, and I can feel the anger grinding away in her like gritty gears forced together.

"I should kill the dog," she says. "The only thing saving him right now is that I have no orders to do it and he is from the Duke's kennel and therefore untouchable otherwise. But accidents happen. Sometimes dogs eat things they are not meant to. Or on a ship like this, one might fall overboard when no one noticed. Imagine how sad that would be, the poor dog, paddling and paddling, believing you would come back for him if he just waited long enough."

She knows my weak points, drilling in with uncanny ease to make my eyes sting with tears. I say, "He's done you no harm."

"The sailors say you used him as an excuse to go chasing away!"

"He is a dog; he knows no better!" I shift my stance, try to make it less combative, more appealing. This is what I have come to, trying to coax someone where once I would have commanded. I say, "It was an aberration. Nothing more like this will happen."

She snarls at me. "That is already decided, for you will be confined to your cabin for the rest of the days here," she says. "That is only two, but even after that, you will stay in this cabin, and no longer have the freedom of the ship."

I do not want to seem unmoved by this, even though the escape that Scylla and I have planned means it will have no effect. I let my head droop, as though tired and dispirited.

"I beg pardon," I murmur, staring at my feet. "I am sorry to have displeased you, Huntswoman. It will not happen again. Thank you for sparing the dog."

"There is nothing that prohibits me from leaving him behind, to be shipped back to the Duke," she says.

I keep my eyes downcast, my hands folded in front, trying to project humility and acceptance. "If that is what you deem necessary, Huntswoman."

She says, "You think you will have an easy life in a frontier town, living on your own estate and entertaining yourself as you please, no doubt."

"I have no coin with which to buy an estate."

"You think friends or family will send you the money to do it, once you have settled, perhaps. Or that the town will be so glamoured, having the famous Bella Kanto there, that they will build you a living place."

The lamp sways back and forth in the hot, stuffy air. The porthole is closed, and no breeze has stirred in this room in my absence. She is dressed as neatly as though she were going to work at the palace, and I find it hard to believe that my absence has put her out all that much.

No, she would have thought already of how to account for my death to the point where anytime she truly wanted me dead, she could have me so.

Lucky for me that, even with the interest that Scylla has stirred in me with this mystery of the sea farms, I am still dazed inside, unable to stir up a great deal of worry about this woman killing me. If she decides to invoke the powers that Alberic has given her, if she snaps the coin, then I will be dead and there is nothing to be said about that other than I hope it will be more peaceful, that estate, than my past few months.

I try to say all of this with my stance. If she wants to get a reaction out of me, good luck to her, because I do not care all that much. It would be sad for her to kill the dog, but it would not be me doing it, no matter how much she blamed the action on me. It would have been her choice to do such a thing, and all the blood of that would be on her hands, not mine.

Why does it feel as though it would stain mine more?

"I do not think anything like that," I say. "I know that I am under interdict, and they are forbidden from sending me anything but the smallest of gifts. And I have no doubt that you will make sure that everyone knows full well of the charges against me and has every reason to believe them."

She takes a step closer. "That's right," she hisses. "Alberic thinks there is some resonance still between you and the city, and that is the only thing that has kept you alive so far. But I have no reason to believe that true, and even if it is, Tabat is in chaos now anyhow, and more pepper will not make that brew too spicy yet. But it is more satisfying to see you settled in Fort Plentitude."

Her grin is feral. "It is very newly established. Six buildings, I believe, the report my lord gave me says. One is very large and holds an unexpected number. You will be joining them."

I try to parse the meaning out of this, try to extract what it is she is trying to say, but the malice in her tone is too distracting, keeps making me wonder what it is that I've done to make her hate me so. I say, "What do you mean, an unexpected number that I'll be joining?"

Like a fox picking berries from a thorn bush, her lips curl back from her teeth. "Near it is a penal colony. Newly established. That's why you haven't heard of it."

"I am to be imprisoned?"

"I think of it as caged," she whispers, leaning close, and the menace in her voice sends a trickle of sweat down my spine.

She stares at me. If eyes alone could light a fire, I would be ablaze.

"What have I done to you?" I whisper.

"You got in my way," she says, but does not elaborate. "I will hurt you now, you understand that," she says and points the glove again. "I will punish you for causing me trouble, for making me send my sailors all over, searching for you. For the way the officials here laughed at me for not being able to hold onto a prisoner."

Again the fire creeps over my limbs, and this time it kindles faster, much faster, and this time she does not relent.

She lets me go when my voice is raw from screaming and falters. The sailors come and take me to my cabin, drag me as though I were an insensible mass, and the truth is that I feel like one, like a sack of collected pain. All I can think about is what if this escape fails and she captures me and does it again? Because I do not think that I can bear it.

I think that I would rather die.

ADELINA'S THIRD LETTER

Dear Bella,

I know in my last letter I was going back-and-forth about what to do about Sebastiano. I finally decided, and it has been a bitter pill, but I couldn't justify breaking all his bonds.

I should probably back up and tell you what happened when I finally had dinner there. It certainly was a pretty table, and the sort of food I hadn't been used to for a while. Lately I have been buying meat-rolls from a bakery cart and eating them in my room—that lets me read and dine at the same time, and they are quite cheap and filling.

His mother was feeling better. Her name is Letha; I think you know her because she's bought a number of Leonoa's paintings and is often at her showings. She had a persistent fever this spring, one that has been going around, particularly in the Slumps and the lower Terraces, but while not entirely recovered, had said that she would like to meet me.

I do not know if they sprang me on his father as a surprise or not. I would hate to think they did, or at least would think that they would have warned me first if that were the case. But there was a great deal of surprise in his demeanor when he first saw me at the table.

Sebastiano made the introductions and we all sat down and started civilly enough. But after the soup had been brought, and everyone was raising the first spoonful to their lips (it was an excellent consommé), his father said, "She's the one that got thrown out of her family, isn't she? Don't tell me she's the one you decided on!"

Sebastiano shares a failing that so many of us come to adulthood with (I will be the first to say I'm just the same). His parent can make him more irritated faster than anyone else in the world. Still, his tone was very mild as he said, "Adelina was on the list of candidates that you gave me. She and I find that we suit each other very well. I hope that we may even get along as well someday as you and mother do."

"That's your way of reminding me that I married for love," the old man said. "But that's why I know better."

His mother made a sound at that, a sound that I'll always remember. A quiet little choke. The father's eyes went to her.

"Letha, love, don't get me wrong," he said to her. "What we have had is excellent. But a grandchild, one that will become a leader of the house, needs every advantage, including having sway in another powerful house by virtue of shared blood."

"It depends on how one defines need," she said, and her voice was neutral.

He thumped a fist on the table and shouted, "Don't act as though I don't do this out of love myself! I want the child to have the chance to be anything that it wants to be!"

"Indeed you do not," Sebastiano argued. "You want it to come out of such circumscribed circumstances that it will have no choice but to become head of a Merchant house. And in doing so, you are setting all of us up for disappointment. What if the child turned out to have a talent for magic?"

His father glared at him. "Then we would not indulge it in such foolishness the way that we indulged you."

Sebastiano did not make the noise that his mother had made, but there was the echo of it in his eyes nonetheless.

I could go further into the argument and tell you all the ins and outs of it, but I will sum it all up as this: if he chooses to marry me, then he will be removed from the family in the same way that I have been removed from mine.

And where would that leave us? I don't know. It seems unimaginable to me to ask him to make that sacrifice. He says that he is more than willing to do so, but it would mean more than sundering ties with his father. It would mean giving up time with his mother, whom he loves so dearly. It would mean giving up money and, much as I love Sebastiano, I am not sure he could make his own way in the world if he had to.

Yes, he has skills. He knows more about Beasts and magic and the combinations of the two than anyone else I know. But how much call is there for that sort of thing, and how much will there be if what I think comes true and Tabat's nobility, its upper class, find themselves lowered a few notches and do not have as much money to spend on frivolities like sponsoring scholarship?

And if the Beasts are freed – as the Abolitionists insist they must – where does that leave him?

I don't know what to do. I went to see Leonoa and seek her advice, but her friend Glyndia would not leave us alone, stayed in the room even when I tried to signal that I had come to speak to her alone. She is a pushy woman, that one. I do not trust her.

And she reminds me so of someone I know, but I cannot figure out who.

We still have not found my old apprentice, Lucy—or Obedience, depending on who you're speaking to. Her brother, who did not approve of the name change, still sticks to the old one. We'd thought she was stealing, but it turned out to have been some confusion. She'd been scavenging in the ruins of Bernarda's gallery after it burned—remember that night, at Leonoa's showing, with the riot?—and came across my little pocket mirror. She'd shown it to her brother as a treasure, and then weeks later when I found her with it, I thought she'd stolen it and threw her out because not only that, but she was the one who told my mother who really ran the press and started all this off.

I am sure she would say that none of this was her fault. She was a sweet girl, but too prone to blaming other people for her misfortunes.

Who knows why things happen as they do? The Moon Temples tell us the Moons move among us, pushing and pulling, and the Trade Gods tell us that there is another world that reflects our own, and the Mages will not tell anyone what they believe.

Perhaps Sebastiano will; I will ask him sometime, purely in the name of recording such things for history.

I remain your friend, and wish you were here.

Adelina

CHAPTER 21

THE STOOPING HAWK (BELLA)

*I*f I am to escape, Scylla and I have decided, I must disable the *Stooping Hawk*, so Ruhua cannot pursue us. It would not be hard for her to track me using magic. But if I can move faster than her, that does not matter, because she cannot catch up. Scylla's confederates here will make getting a replacement ship slow and laborious.

The Dragon eggs in the hold are the key. Any of them could power this ship; any of them could drive it long enough to overtake us. So I must take them.

Not to destroy them. I will not do that. I do not know everything that has been done to them in order to preserve them, but Dragon eggs can last for decades before hatching out, some say centuries. But to smash them would be killing them, and so we will take them with us, despite all the faces that Scylla makes when I tell her this.

We made the plan before I came back to the boat. There were only so many things that Ruhua could do to me, after all, and all of them involved confining me in some way there.

We have chosen a classic plot. Drug the wine of the sailors aboard, and have Ruhua summoned elsewhere, to talk to the bureaucrats that run this port and go over her cargo manifest once more.

Scylla has taken care of that. She is perched much higher in society than Ruhua realizes, or she might guess that she is being lured out. But the invitation comes from the highest Merchant here, Tabaki himself, and so she will not turn it down, from curiosity as well as the need to represent Tabat.

I know Scylla has bought a sailor aboard this ship, but I do not know who. A few minutes after the midnight bell, there are furtive steps in the hallway. Something slides under the door, a lock pick and a shim, tied together with a bit of thread.

Picking a tumbler lock is not a matter of just jamming a lock-pick in the hole and turning it as though it were a key.

Instead you must use your pick to feel along the tumblers, easing them downward, while you push at the same time with the shim, keeping pressure on the lock's barrel so that as the tumblers yield, one by one, they are kept as you want them and do not spring back into place.

It is an art I learned at the Brides of Steel—one that many of us picked up, actually, because among other things, the pantry had a tumbler lock on it, and girls are ever hungry, particularly late at night when all the keys have been put away.

The obvious comparison occurs to me as I delicately probe it, but the lock yields faster than any woman ever did and clicks open.

I have prepared a pack and gone through my belongings to skim off what I'll need, while still leaving enough scattered about that it may not be obvious at first what is missing. The more confusion I can sow in my wake the better, and if it seems as though I did not prepare for the opportunity—or had anyone else help me in that preparation—then the better.

Let Ruhua play detective trying to figure out what has happened. Better yet, let her summon the mystic that Scylla has planted, who will claim that we are bound in the direction of Tabat. But that is a slim hope; surely she will double-check.

You can never plan too much, you can never lay out too many contingencies, or so Jolietta would have had me believe.

For the first time in my life, it occurs to me to wonder what my aunt would have thought of what I have become. I do not know that she thought of me as her apprentice, but I am as close to that as anyone has ever come. Sometimes it did seem to me that she was trying to encode her knowledge, trying to give me rules by which to live.

But at the same time, she was not a stupid woman. She would have realized how much I hated her. She would have realized that there was no chance that I would continue along the same path that she had chosen.

I would like to say I do not understand why she took me in, but the truth of it is that it was cheaper than hiring someone and there were times when she needed another Human around. If not for such moments, I think, she would have passed on my care.

It is a dark hour on the ship but not one of the darkest. We chose to enact this while Ruhua was off ship and there was only so much time that we can keep her away. I move as quickly as I can, down to the chamber that the captain showed us when we first embarked.

This lock is harder to pick, but not too much so. It takes me longer than I want it to, though, and my heart is hammering in my throat by the time I have clicked it open and slipped inside.

There is no light in here, but I manage as best I can by feel alone, taking each egg down from its padded shelf and wrapping it well before I secure it in the sack I have brought. That is tied tightly and put inside another, and then that in turn inside the pack I have brought.

Will they survive this desperate attempt? But surely this gamble for a better fate is preferable to staying here to be consumed.

They need fire to hatch, these eggs, not cold seawater. But I hope that I have preserved them from the worst of that icy touch.

Out in the hallway, I catch my bearings again, breathing in caution as I pause under the swaying of the hall's hanging lamp. My confederate here on the boat, whoever it is that Scylla has paid off, has left me a clear path, and this is where I deviate for the first time, because I go to retrieve Teo.

Scylla would have told me not to, would have told me that too much lay in the balance for me to risk it all on the life of a puppy.

But he trusts me, this puppy, and he has come to me, and he is mine and I will act to protect him. If I leave him here, Ruhua might well kill him out of pique, or she might simply let him pine away.

His whining leads me along the corridor to the right place. This time the door is unlocked. He is tied in the hold, with a rope around his jaws to keep him from howling. He dances in place when he sees me.

"You have to be quiet," I tell him. "If they catch us, I don't know what will happen but there is no doubt that it will not be good."

This is what I had doubted, that the puppy would be able to control himself, that I'd have to carry both him and the heavy pack. But it is as though he understands every word I say. He stays ghost silent as I unbind his jaws, then follows at my heels as we go up the stairs.

I kneel in the shadow of the opening and listen, the dog a silhouette beside me, not moving a hair.

Another clear night, and so much moonlight, which is not a lucky thing. All three moons are high in the sky, pouring down their light as though in some competition to see who can shine the brightest.

After endless moments, I hear the night watch's feet approach and pass, see the flicker of their lantern as they walk towards the prow. We move then, heading towards the back of the boat.

This time I do have to carry Teo, and climbing down a rope ladder with both a puppy and a heavy, unwieldy pack is not easy. But he has the grace to lie quiet and not squirm too much, and finally my foot finds the rowboat that waits there for us, its oar locks muffled.

Teo takes up position in the front of the boat as I row, nose working, testing every scrap of wind that comes within its reach. He stays dead quiet. I might think it uncanny if it was not so necessary.

We do not have far to go, but I am tense, my shoulders stiff to the point of ache, until we pass under the shadow of a long, fat-bellied grain ship, out of the sight of the *Stooping Hawk*.

Ruhua will eventually be able to hire oarsmen, and a small boat to chase me, but that will take time to arrange, and we will gain hours. And there will be a surprise or two waiting for her when she does hire a boat.

Scylla meets me at the lesser docks. She has a good little boat named *Tiny Pearl*, and several Mers to help row it to the edge of the current. There, we can let ourselves be carried by that; once it takes us out of the Silent Sea, we will be able to keep to the current but also to perhaps use the boat's sails from time to time to augment our speed.

So much depends on how well Ruhua can track me. The trick with such magic—or so it has been explained to me—is distance, because it grows more and more unreliable the further the distance. That unreliability can lead to the magic detecting things that bear less resemblance to the target but are close enough that they seem to resemble that distant target.

I don't know how much time any of this will buy us. And luck has turned so badly against me of late—dare I think this moment will be any better?

I try to avoid thinking of Ruhua's reprisals, but they cannot help but creep into my head. The echo of her words, her tone, all the things that she had threatened, in my head sends a shiver down my spine. *You got in my way*, she'd said, and now I have thwarted her again.

Teo senses my mood. He stays pressed close to me, an insistent presence along my calf where I kneel near the prow, listening to the dip of oars and the sibilant breathing of the Mers. I offer to take a hand rowing, but they wave me off, accustomed to working as a team. I would only slow them down.

Instead I crouch with my cloak drawn around me, watching behind us, worrying that I may see some sign that my absence has been detected already and know that pursuit is hopelessly close.

But the raft city behind us remains the same, and I see no burst of lights or activity. Teo licks my hand to remind me he is there, and I pet him.

Scylla rises from her seat and comes forward to me.

"Your boat then was the *Coral*," I say.

She chuckles. "A pretty boat but such a whale to steer." She caresses the railing beside her. "I built *Tiny Pearl* a decade ago and have been adding on to her ever since. She's my masterwork."

"You have no desire to build something newer, more up-to-date?" I tease. "There have been many advances in engines, back in Tabat. Sail is outmoded."

She only snorts in answer.

For the first time since leaving Tabat—for the first time since the time in the torturer's cells—I feel happy. A small, shy happiness, as though my soul had gotten so unacquainted with such a thing that it has to creep up on it, must not startle it away. I lift my face to the air's touch, lick away the tinge of salt that has accumulated on my lips.

Scylla nudges my shoulder and hands me a hunk of Mer-tack. She was the one that introduced me to that treat, a mass of seaweed and smoked fish, tough and salty and satisfying in the mouth.

I break off a chunk and chew it, feeling the dry fish slowly soften as I work at it. The thought that she has remembered that like, all this time, is another satisfaction.

Who knows what will happen next? We are bound for the Southern Isles, and we may or may not get there—everything is uncertain, but here and now I am with someone who cares whether or not I am hungry or unhappy—two of them, really, if I count Teo as I should.

It is not a bad thing to be loved. It is a compensation for anything else.

THE NEXT MORNING DAWNS CLEAR, the sunlight dazzling bright as it bounces on the waves. I ache from sleeping on the hard bunk; another way age is creeping up on me. It makes me wonder. At one point the magic of Tabat moved through me and made me its own creation. Sometimes it seems as though I don't remember those days at all, what it felt like.

Is that what creatures of magic experience, their bodies constantly infused with that energy? It seems as though they would act differently if that were the case. And what does it mean, that the Gods have chosen to bestow such gifts on *them*, while denying them to the Humans who supposedly have dominion over everything?

Such thoughts are heresy, but who has not wondered them, from time to time?

We reach the edges of the current. The Mers make their good-byes to Scylla, nodding at me as well. I do not recognize any of them—she's told me she recruited them from among cousins that did not know me, in order to throw less suspicion on the circumstances of my flight.

I wish that I had something to give them. When I traveled on Tabat's business, I used to have all manner of honor gifts for those who had been kind to me: blue and gold feather cockades fastened with a gilt coin worked with the seal of Tabat, and miniature silver swords with snowflakes on the hilt, and of course, books, which people particularly loved if I had signed my name in them.

It always seemed a great shame to me that they did not care whether or not Adelina—the author of them all—did the same. I wish that they understood that the Bella Kanto of the books was a hollow and false thing, inflated by magic, and that the person that Adelina created was a story that she and she alone told. If there was anything in those books to inspire—and people tell me that there is, insist on that time and time again—then it is the thing that Adelina created, the Bella that she made.

My Bella was a petty thing, made of practiced grace and vanity.

Adelina's was more noble than I could ever hope to be. She took the best of me and made it shine so bright that it obscured all the darker parts.

One by one the Mers slip into the water. The last two help us row out to be caught by the current, a gentle tug at first and then an insistent pull. I sit in the aft and watch the tiller as Scylla says good-bye. They wave to her and fall back over the side of the boat to make for the side of the current.

They will take their time returning. They knew the longer they waited, the longer their swim home, but they do not mind it too much. Mers love water, and here around the Long Slow City, the waters are relatively safe, particularly when they travel in a group. The others will be waiting for those two, and then they will swim back, hunting for fish along the way, enough to buoy up their claims to have gone on a fishing expedition.

Tiny Pearl's tiller shudders and bucks under my hand as the current seizes us in its full grip. The wind has picked up and is going southward as well. I help Scylla wrestle the sails into place; even before they are in place, the wind bellies them out, snaps them taut. She secures the halyard and I go back to the tiller where Teo sits, wisely keeping out of the way of our labor.

At first there are traces of mist on the water, but the sun burns those away almost as soon as it has fully stretched over the horizon. The waves are vast and green. The sunlight fills them so I can see the small fish hanging in the water near us. A gull takes its rest on the top of the mast for a while and then, with a companionable dip of its wings, is on its way.

I take a breath and feel weight slip away. I had not realized how much of it my shoulders held.

CHAPTER 22

THE TINY PEARL (BELLA)

*W*hen I first went to the Southern Isles, I was in my early twenties, full of arrogance and desire. I'd practically set off sparks when I crossed a room, that was what I was like.

I never allowed myself to be bedded but did the pursuing myself. The more timorous, the rarer, the more coaxable the better. Adelina played down the list of broken hearts in her accounting of that time, but, thinking back, I can't help but wonder if it had been then, the time I told her all those tales so they might be put down into yet another book, that her own heart cooled towards me and any trace of infatuation faded.

It wasn't that I hadn't broken off the sexual side of things by then already. But the person-who-wants-to-fuck-you-yet-is-aware-that-the-closest-they-will-ever-come-again-is-friendship was by now a familiar one to me and I could tell that there was a point where friendship had attracted Adelina more than my body.

The realization had even piqued my interest in a contradictory way, making Adelina seem worth revisiting for the sake of the new conquest. I refrained, though. That surely showed that I'd grown somewhat over the years. Young Bella wouldn't have thought twice about breaking Adelina's heart multiple times and erasing the friendship entirely. It wasn't that she didn't value the friendship highly. Just that my younger self had been so brash and unaware of consequences.

When did that change?

As recently as the Duke's cells?

My mind shies away from those dark memories like a panicked horse. I pull it in another direction, wrestling it into control even as my fingers tighten on the ship's wooden railing to the point of pain.

"I will not share your bed during the trip," I tell Scylla. "I am past all that sort of thing."

Her lips twitch and I wish I had not chosen that phrasing. "How so?" she asked.

I refuse to smile. "Because," I say flatly, "they tortured me in the Duke's prison, and when I think of having my flesh touched, of certain … intimacies, that is all I can remember."

I do not care if I shock her. I do not want her pity. I want her to understand that this is not a flirtation, not coyness for the sake of some game. This is the truth I am laying before her.

Teo whines and noses at my hand. I rub the warm hollows just behind his furry ears, still keeping my eyes on Scylla's face. It is important that we get this straight, now before the trip truly begins.

I have put my bag of Dragon's eggs downstairs. Are they still viable? Could I hatch them if I wish? And would there be any way I would possibly want to do so? Dragons are dangerous.

I remember that one we saw flying overhead. I remember the slide of its scales past me in the air, so close that if I had reached out and stretched a little, I could've touched it, perhaps. How beautiful a world, that contains such a thing.

Moons and Gods, what I would not give to be back in Tabat and not here and this uncomfortable but necessary conversation.

Scylla's smile falls away, drops as I think of this. I brace myself for pity. But "Oh, Bella," is all that she says. She starts to touch my arm, then pulls her hand away and awkwardly finds a new place to put it.

I shrug at her. "I am saying this now so there will be no misunderstandings."

Scylla's chin lifts to point at me before she nods. "It is good to be careful of such things," she says in a neutral tone, then adds, "and I will not take it as a rejection and understand you have forsworn such."

Teo whines deep in his throat, looking between the two of us, not sure what to do with all this tension. I keep petting him, feeling the bone of his skull beneath the soft, loose, warm skin.

"I will go take inventory and make sure of the supplies we have to get us down to the islands," Scylla says, and goes back inside.

I turn my attention back to the tiller. The two of us can make it, spelling each other, but it would be much more pleasant if we had a third set of hands. I grimace at Teo. "I wish you were the real one," I tell him fondly.

He barks and wags his tail, as ever delighted to have my full attention. I kneel fully and embrace his comforting, doggy weight, feeling the damp salt crust over his coat, smelling the doggy reek of him.

Scylla thinks I will be able to solve her problems for her, defeat whatever force is sending its contagion to taint the food that the raft city depends on. She thinks I am her savior. I am less convinced of that, less convinced that I can be that for anyone, even myself.

But Alberic has a hand in all of this somehow, and I am wondering if he had a hand in what happened to me. It is a thought I have avoided, but it is quite possible that he knew I was in those cells. That he knew what was happening to me, what was being done. That he thought to himself, *Well, I'll have it all magically secured, and she'll be none the worse for it, perhaps even the better, and then her spirit will be ...*

My thoughts skitter around whatever would follow. I cannot believe he truly wished me broken. Only more compliant to his will, not realizing that the two were the same thing.

But am I giving him too much credit in thinking that? He has always wanted his own way in everything, been one of those men who kept the argument going and going, until you didn't just give in, but had to say that he had been right in whatever it was all along.

Petty and grudge-hoarding. And cheap, moons, how cheese-sparingly cheap! That is what has flummoxed me about all the money he mounted for this expedition. To spend that kind of coin, there has to be something that he is getting back, and it has to be something that he considers worthwhile, which means power.

Why not just have me killed, if I was a hindrance? He is not such a sentimental man that he would keep me alive simply because we have shared a bed more than once. At least, I think reflectively, unless he thought he would be able to do so again?

Does he plan to join me in exile? Surely not, that is a destination I cannot imagine for him. If he lost in the elections, he would still linger in Tabat, the city that his ancestors founded and augmented, where every third statue on Salt Way bears the features of someone related to him.

No, he would never settle for exile. But I am more use to him in a city far away than either close at hand in some form, which could be loose or in a cell, or dead. No, alive means I am a game token that he intends to play again at some point.

How deep do his schemes run? I wish that I had Adelina here to talk this through with me. She understands patterns, has read so deep in history that she can see where events resemble those of the past. She is canny at predicting things, and I would suspect, whatever way she thinks the elections in Tabat will blow, that is the case.

Fondness and sadness swim through my thoughts, chasing each other's tails. Will I ever see her again? It is quite possible that there is a great deal to regret about the way that I've treated Adelina, that I did not treasure her friendship as I should have, did not see that she is as unique as Bella Kanto, perhaps even more so, because what she was did not depend on the city's magic.

The Trade Gods tell us we cannot regret. The Merchants each keep their journey books, at least the dedicated ones do, where they follow what the Gods say that canny Merchants should do: write down the particulars of every decision that they make, and what Trade Gods they considered in making it, and later what the outcome was and what they learn from it. Therefore, you never regret anything because you learn from it. You gain by adding to the store of your knowledge.

Adelina does not follow the practice. She is a scholar, first and foremost, and a publisher after that, and a Merchant third of all. She says that she records the circumstances of other people's decisions and learns from those instead.

Teo leans solidly into my leg as I tend the tiller, keeping the boat pointed towards the constellation of the tilted scale where it straddles the southern horizon. We have a compass for the days, but at night the stars are so much easier, and they are so clear, hanging in the velvet black sky, sometimes so low that I think I might reach out and touch them, their glittering, icy fire.

THE NEXT EVENING Scylla comes down from her watch. She's gone for a quick dip beforehand, and she'll sleep in a nest of moistened weed and old blankets.

She lies down there, and I climb the ladder and make my way up to the deck. Teo does not climb it after me, even though he cracks an eye to watch me and yawns before resettling his nose below his flank and returning to sleep. We are on the ocean, his posture seems to suggest, so what possible danger could there be?

The salt air is moving with the breeze; light clouds shroud the red and purple moons. Only the white one is unobscured, pouring over the deck's planking like liquid silver, gleaming wherever there is moisture—and there is plenty, so everything is silvered, like a sculpture made of metal.

How do I know she'll be standing there in her namesake's light? Selene, with her hair flowing. Selene, almost glowing with reflected light.

How can a woman, an impossible woman, be poised like a pillar, be looking at me with eyes deeper than the sky?

For a long moment I think I may be dreaming, that Selene's descent is one of those dreams in which one is woken over and over, long before the appointed time.

But no. I can smell the water and feel the wind's cold bite on the skin of my face and bare forearms. I smell the fishy spot where Teo first ate garbage and then threw it up, despite the fact that I've sluiced it down repeatedly with sea water in the two days since then.

It's this final detail that convinces me, that forces me to accept this as reality rather than vision. I still feel as though I've stepped into the pages of one of Adelina's novels about me, almost all embroidery and only a scraping of truth when you root around in order to find the heart of things.

Selene smiles at me as though there is nothing that could make her happier than to see me. Maybe that's the moment I fall in love or maybe it's already happened. No matter what, I feel that giddy dip of delight only an infatuated heart is capable of executing, and it takes my breath away.

I pull myself up on the planking and walk over to her. She doesn't speak as I approach, but keeps on smiling, and the white moon is reflected in her eyes. She wears something loose and draping, made of the soft fabric they weave in the Rose Kingdom.

She lifts her hand as I approach. I take those cool fingers and bring them to brush against my lips in the promise of a kiss.

A practiced move, one I've executed a thousand times or more, but now it is entirely new and so sweet it makes my heart leap again. A heat builds in me, in my core, one that I have not felt in so long that it startles, almost frightens, me. Nonetheless I let my lips linger on that candied skin, smelling of lotion and moonlight.

Does she feel this pull as strongly as I do, a pull almost dizzying and inhuman in its depths? But there is nothing of that in her smile, and that clenches at me.

I say, "How are you here?"

She pouts. "So practical." Her eyes are sly with laughter.

I should find out how this impossibility is possible, how she came to this place, but in her look … I only lean forward to kiss her, and that kiss lasts for centuries and seconds and parts of me will live inside it always.

MORNING COMES TOO SOON. Teo, roused when Scylla is, follows her up the ladder. My visitor is gone. I still don't know whether I dreamed her or not.

Surely I must have.

"Why isn't chal ready?" Scylla snaps at me as she produces the round of bread she's brought with her.

"I was distracted," I say.

"By what?"

"Thoughts of Tabat," I say.

Her face softens. "Do you think you'll ever return?"

Here in the sunlight of the morning, with the wind continuing to move us along so happily and brightly, it seems more possible than it would have a few days ago.

"I would like to," I admit.

She pauses. Thoughts work behind her eyes. "Is there anyone there …"

She flounders and I let her before I finally fling a lifeline. "A lover, you mean? No, there is no one like that. My friends and a handful of cousins. Most of the Kantos are gone, though. My cousin Leonoa is the only worthwhile one of them, anyhow."

She says, "I never knew what to think of your life back there, and so I never wrote, because I was not sure of my place in it. In the books, there are so many lovers, here and there, and it never seems as though they are part of your life, afterwards."

Shame slams into me at those words. It is true, it was a deliberate strategy on my part, in order to avoid complication and drama. And it did not work, all of the time, and sometimes when it did not work, it hurt and scarred people. I think of Marta and her angry face, the last time I'd seen her.

You would think she would have come to see me off.

Were her bad luck charms, sent week after week in her bouquets, what brought about my downfall, moving me towards the tipping point that sent me plunging from the pinnacle to the abyss?

I say, "It was wrong of me not to write. I remember our time together fondly, very fondly, and I thought of you often."

She catches on a particular word. "Thought. Not think."

"I have had a great deal on my mind lately," I point out. My dry tone makes her grimace.

She says, "I am sorry that you had to endure all that. It was not what you deserved, Bel. I may have hated you for leaving me behind, but I never wished anything like that on you."

I shrug. "I would like to think I did not deserve it—and I know that I did not consort with Sorcerers," I add hastily, because of all the charges that came my way, that one rankles the most.

I remember the courtroom, when they opened the satchel I had been given to deliver—and foolish me, not to have looked, to have believed the lover who sent me down there on his errand! The satchel held jars, each as big as my hand, a dozen of them, packed and padded cunningly so they would not clink or clatter against each other, and each of those held something unspeakable. I thrust the thought away.

I tell Scylla, "I did not treat you well. I cannot say that I have treated any lover well. There is only one, back in the city, who I have stayed friends with and that is much more her doing than mine."

"How did she do it?" Scylla asks. There is more curiosity than wistfulness in her tone, and it reminds me for a moment of Adelina herself.

"She just kept patiently being there and reminding me she wanted to be my friend," I say. "It was never obtrusive, never one of those people who follow you from place to place, going wherever they know you will go. But sometimes she was there, and she always made a point of coming to speak with me, but it was never demanding. Do you know what I mean?"

Scylla nods. "It does seem the best way of handling you," she drawls dryly.

Again, I'm reminded of Adelina. She was a significant part of my life back in Tabat, and now that I am not there, one of the many holes in my life is shaped like her.

I push the thought away and say to Scylla, "The elections are just around the corner in Tabat and no one knows what to think of what will happen."

"Do you have guesses?"

"The Merchants have money behind them, and they have spent plenty of it. I think they will hold the day and have the majority of seats on this council they're creating. But there will be some odd cards here and there, I think, before all the hands are played out."

Adelina has escaped that fate, at least, when her mother thrust her from the house. I worry again that she will not be doing well— or Leonoa, who has no money sense, and a lover who I am suspicious of. I sigh.

"You will power the sails with such gusts of wind," Scylla says. "Come, I will mind the tiller and you will tell me stories of Tabat to keep me company."

We eat bread and drink chal. The day is clear and bright and high by the time I yawn. I keep thinking of Selene and that kiss. Keep feeling it on my mouth. It makes me watch Scylla and remember entanglements with her, kisses almost as deep and burning, explorations and experiments—sex underwater, for one, is not anywhere as exciting as any story about it.

There is not much labor to be done here, all in all. The current is steady and so is the wind. Scylla relates gossip of her cousins— she has dozens of them, and each more dramatic than the last—and I give her some of my stories in return.

I find myself telling her about Skye.

"She was my student, and I shouldn't have, I know," I say as I stare off over the water. "But moons, Scylla, she chased me as ardently as ever one person has chased after another, far past the point where an older one would have taken no for an answer and moved along, perhaps."

"It's hard not to love someone who loves you wholeheartedly," she says. "That's the appeal of dogs like yours." She points her finger at where Teo sits, gnawing at a coil of knots I've made him. He looks up at the sound of his name, thumps his tail on the floor-boards, gives us both a doggy grin.

Scylla and I argue as well.

"You pride yourself on breaking free of all your aunt's teachings, but the truth of it is that you have fallen into step, heel and toe, with her and all her views on Beasts," Scylla tells me. "The very fact that some Mers are accounted Humans and others Beasts speaks of how arbitrary this is, and so do the rules that say any offspring of such matches is counted Beast. There is no sense to it!"

"There has to be an order to things," I say. "There have to be rules. Or else how is everyone to exist together? How is society to run?"

"But who is to decide these rules? When it is a single person—and you will admit that Alberic is an example of such a single person, put into place to rule when he is far from capable of doing so with justice or with wisdom—then what checks, what reins are there to keep them from destroying those around them, out of spite or whim or even just stupidity?"

"You will welcome the outcome of the elections then," I say. "For everyone in Tabat will vote and thus choose their leader."

"Not the Beasts," she says, her tone challenging.

"Not the Beasts," I say, "but there are candidates who might lead the city down such a path."

"And by all accounts, Alberic has outlawed such Abolitionist thoughts!"

I think of my cousin Leonoa's paintings, deemed sedition for daring to show Beasts as though they were Human, dressed in cere-monial regalia, conducting Merchantly activities, engaging in the trade that was forbidden to them. Was it right that she should have suffered fire and riot, simply because she was moved to paint something? What harm did such things of paint and fabric and wood do to anyone?

I say, sullenly, "All of this is far beyond me. I am only a Gladiator. I fight with blade, not words."

Outrageously, she laughs at me. "Pretend that you are not a hero of Tabat if you will," she says. "Whoever writes the books of your adventures knows better than that. They know that people read the books and see themselves in your actions. What you do and say today is what they will do and say tomorrow, and the days beyond that."

"That was true once," I say, "but no longer."

"Who did write those books?" Her eyes are bright with curiosity. "They loved you very well, whoever they are. Do they still?"

"Her name is Adelina," I say, "and she is the one I spoke of. We are no longer lovers, but we have stayed friends."

"That takes extraordinary patience, I suspect," she tells me. "Being your friend has ever been a difficult business."

"But worth it, surely," I say, and when she pretends to think, I poke her in the ribs so she laughs, and, for a while, it is like old times as we laugh together in the sun with only the water watching.

CHAPTER 23

THE TINY PEARL (TEO)

This boat was so much smaller than the other one, but nonetheless Teo thought it a vast improvement. No cats, for one thing, not a single one! And the angry woman who made Bella unhappy whenever she was near was gone, not a trace of her, not even her lingering smell, because she had never been on this boat.

He couldn't run properly the way he could on the other, but that was all right. He dashed in circles around Bella whenever she was up on deck, particularly when she was at the tiller. He ran then, because it amused her and she laughed at him, a deep fond sound, that reminded him of Bella as she had been, back when he had first known her.

Back when he had been Human.

He thought about that sometimes, but less and less nowadays. When he had first followed her onto the boat, he had thought that he would somehow be able to tell her what had happened, so she would know and free him, because surely she would know a way. She was Bella Kanto. Surely she'd guess what was happening.

If not, it would take only a small hint to clue her in, make her guess his secret, the one he wanted her to guess, so then she could turn her mind to freeing him.

But every time he tried, he felt the magic binding him, felt it hindering him, confusing him, befuddling him like a head full of sparks and bees and lye. He stopped being able to understand *her* words at such times. The haze of erratic pain made them jumbled and unintelligible.

Would he ever be Human again?

Not that he had truly been Human. Back in his village at home they shifted from Human to animal and back without thinking about it. That was his village's secret, the one they kept from travelers. He hadn't been able to shift, and so when it came time to pledge someone to the Moon Temples in exchange for their curing his sister, he had been the logical choice.

He had come to Tabat knowing that he held Shifter blood but thinking that it would never manifest because it hadn't yet. That it didn't matter at all, despite how much the Humans hated his kind.

On the docks, when he'd arrived, there'd been a fight that had allowed him to slip away from the Moon Temple Priest and into the city itself. He'd lost himself there because he didn't want to be sworn to the Temples, didn't want his life dedicated to and circumscribed by its dictates.

He'd lived on the streets of Tabat for a while. That was where he'd stared down at his shadow, cast by the magical aetheric lights that illuminated its major streets, commissioned by the Duke of Tabat and created by its College of Mages, and seen it not a boy's, but a great cat's, the low-slung form of a cougar.

That had been bad enough. That had kept him from certain streets at night, knowing that his shadow would betray what he was. He'd worried that the Duke would install more and more of the lights, but with all the election campaigns going on, the Duke had chosen to reserve his money for other, less prominent projects.

Nonetheless, it was a given that sooner or later the College would create more and then more again and then more on the heels of that, until the whole city was lit by them at night and he would have to never go outdoors at all after the sun had set.

But none of that really mattered, because in Tabat, he'd changed for the first time, had run the streets in cougar form and even killed things in the little park called the Piskie Wood, near where he'd been given shelter by the woman Jilly Clearsight, the photographer.

She'd turned him out after he'd left the door open and her pet, the tiny ancient Gryphon he'd heard speaking with her, had gone outside and died in the cold.

That was fair enough. The death still haunted Teo. It was something of a relief to have his Human side slipping away and no longer have that memory pop up now and again, making him guilty and ashamed.

So much had happened! It whirled in a jumble through his mind and sometimes it got blurry when he looked at it.

He'd been safe when Bella had taken him in, had given him food and a bath and fresh clothes and then a job! He had been so frightened when she'd disappeared and then he'd been caught himself, and turned into a dog, this shape, the shape that was starting to be more him than that old Human form.

At least now he was with Bella, and even when he was no longer Human, when all of that had slipped away and he was only a dog, one without thoughts of being anything else, he would still be with her. Now he knew her even better than before, had smelled her emotions, and felt her touch, and even slept beside her in the great bed, and he knew that she would never let harm come to him, and that as long as he lived, he would never let harm come to her.

And here there was sunlight, and the boat was full of interesting old smells, including one corner that smelled of old piss that was particularly intriguing. He lay his head down and slept, and was a dog dreaming of being a Human dreaming of being a dog ...

CHAPTER 24

*J*n the morning, he set himself to hunting. All the time Teo had smelled it, the tiny interloper, but had not been able to track it, even when he waited patiently outside the crack in which it had secreted itself.

"Do you have a rat?" the other woman said with interest. He whined, deep in his throat, but could not tell her it was something worse, something with wings, something that smelled *wrong* but smelled like Tabat, all at once.

Even up on deck in the sunlight, he could feel the presence. This time, while the women were chatting, he crept down the stairs silently. He smelled the creature again and this time, he resolved, he would catch it. He hunkered down in the corner and set himself into silence.

He could hear the women on the deck above, one talking to the other, and the sound of the gulls.

There was silence, a long silence that tugged at the edges of his patience. But he waited.

Long after his nose started itching and he had suppressed several sneezes, he saw a flutter of motion. Then it went still again, waiting to determine if its movement had drawn any attention. A whine built in his throat, but he kept it down, kept himself breathing evenly.

A Fairy. He had not seen them before while he was in dog form and the smell was new to him. But he remembered them from being a boy. Remembered the horde of them descending on the Moon Priest, Grave, that he'd traveled with, and the egg Teo had been forced to cut from Grave's flesh afterward.

But also the Fairies that Bella had entrusted him with. What would have become of them, the cage of them, when he had been turned into a dog by Murga? It had not occurred to him to wonder or worry about them before and somehow this realization, so unlike him, made him feel even more doglike.

Very well then. He would be a dog, and a good one. And dogs hunted. He watched the Fairy creeping near the stairs, wings buzzing. Its head cocked as a noise came from above, stilled and then relaxed and began to move again.

He sprang. It tried to dart one way, then another, then dashed straight at him, as though meaning to go under him. For a terrible moment he thought he had failed but then his teeth went through its back and it shrieked, a shrill buzz of agony, and died with a burst of heat and sweetness in his mouth.

"What was that?" Bella said from above, startled.

When the women came down the stairs to investigate, Bella examined the corpse with interest. "A hive Fairy, I'd bet," she said. "They are a little larger than their solitary counterparts. But you do not have such things aboard the Long Slow City."

"Indeed we do not," the other woman said. "It must have come with your ship."

"And followed me, all this time. It is unlike anything I have ever heard of Fairies."

She patted Teo's head. "Good dog," she said. "Good dog." That was enough for him.

CHAPTER 25

THE TINY PEARL (BELLA)

*A*nother day here at sea, this time a storm smoldering on the horizon. Scylla tells me we will skirt it.

Teo rests against my leg, and I stand with the tiller at hand as we move forward over the waves. All I can do is stand and watch, and let the thoughts roll around and around in my head.

What do I owe Tabat? Many would tell me that I owe the city nothing, that it is the place that falsely accused and rejected me. In whose cells I faced tortures of a kind no one should ever be asked to face. They would say the city was fickle and deserved its fate.

But it's the love that I remember, more than anything, the love of the people for me, the way I used to walk anywhere in the city and have people eager to talk to me, vendors giving me gifts and food, children following me, emulating me, asking me questions ...

Fame was very sweet, all that attention. I had not realized how sweet and seductive until I lost it.

No, Alberic is at the heart of all of this, and the city is blameless. It is a city, after all, so how can I hold it to account? It is nothing like a person.

I do not know how to account for Selene. She sets all my thinking wrong with her presence. Is she an actual goddess? The thought seems absolutely ridiculous, like something a child would arrive at.

And yet.

When I think of her kisses, they fill my senses, and I would swear that I could smell her at those times, the fragrance of her perfume, the sweet musk of her mouth.

There is something healing about these days at sea. They are not languid days—this little boat does take some minding, and with a sparseness of supply, I am always scanning the waters for signs of fish.

I rise one morning to find Scylla on deck, watching the waves. Are we coming through some mass of drowned logs, I wonder for a panicked second, as I see sunlight glint on something in the water, many somethings. Then I realize that we are in the middle of a great host of turtles, hundreds of them. They are not moving with the current as we are, but at an angle, headed somewhere else.

Teo stares down at the water and whines happily, tail wagging. I don't know what goes through a dog's head, but I suspect that this is something new and therefore to be greeted as a source of potential joy, which is the puppy approach to life. It was tiring at first, but as time has gone by, it has become more endearing and increasingly a reminder of the boy that was the dog's namesake.

"There's plenty of meat swimming by, if we want it," I point out. But I know before the words leave my lips what Scylla's reaction will be: a swift shake of her head. The turtles are sacred to the Mer-People, and the Human habit of eating them, particularly the oracular ones, has been a bone of contention between us in the past.

But nowadays I am old enough that I have learned better than to argue with people about such things. I've given up any sense that I should need to convince anyone but myself of anything. Life will roll on, no matter what absurd notions anyone holds around me, and who's to say that I don't hold a few of my own, from time to time?

So I just shrug and nod at the head shake. She's as hungry as I am, and better at fishing. We stand in the sunlight, enjoying it.

Moments like this, moments where I simply exist, have been so scarce in my life since my fall. I've felt as though someone were peering over my shoulder all the time and that was justified, given the Duke, and then Ruhua, who had been appointed to do that very thing.

Now I am free. I can see under the starlight or the sunlight and think my own thoughts, and Scylla does not press me for attention or conversation except when I am ready for it.

She has changed in the years intervening as well. One time she would have chattered at me all day long, regardless of how I felt about talking, and that would not have been a terrible thing, because the old Bella was a social creature, almost as though she could not exist except if she were being seen.

That thought gives me pause because something about it ... it's true. I was sustained by the magic of Tabat, and the reason that magic infused me was because I had been the city's Champion, someone seen every year defeating Spring. Witnessed. The thing that I had been, depended on being seen, and being seen in a particular way beyond that. And now here I am, and what defines me now?

"Are you getting sun-addled?" Scylla says beside me. "You will hurt your eyes, staring at the light on the water as you are."

"I was thinking," I say.

Her smile is sideways and tentative. "Dare I ask after the subject?"

"That we have both changed in the years since we first met."

She snorts. "That is natural. That is what we call aging, and despite you saying that you have changed, I see less of that in you than in me."

I hesitate before I say, "There is some magic behind that."

"I thought as much," she says. "There is a look to someone touched by magic, and you have it."

That startles me, the thought that the magic's touch has left some mark that I cannot alter. "What sort of look?"

She shrugs. "It is ..." She searches for the right word for so long that I think she will never find it, but finally she says, "A hollowness, somehow. As though something rested on your soul for a long time and left its impression, a space that it fit, like a head that has slept on a pillow, and so changed its shape until that trace is fluffed away."

"How do I fluff it away?" I say with bitterness.

She considers me. "It is not an unbecoming mark," she says. "It gives you a certain trace of poetry instead of raw animal vigor."

That makes me snort. "What sort of poetry?"

"Tragic, elegant poetry."

I glance down at my sun-reddened arms, then flick hair out of my face. "Hardly elegant."

She starts to say something, then stops and says instead, "You are wandering into a realm of flirtation, Bella, where I pay you compliments. Is that what you want? Because it is contrary to what you told me earlier."

Blood rises to my cheeks in a way that I am sure is visibly not sunburn, and I am at a loss how to reply.

Do I want to flirt? The thought of intimacy with her makes me flinch. When I do, I see Scylla's face change, become tinged with pity in a way that somehow hurts more than anything has yet on this pleasant day.

I stoop down and occupy myself with rubbing Teo's ears, an affection to which he gratefully submits. "Not yet," I say to the top of his head, although I am addressing Scylla. "Maybe? But not yet."

"I understand," she says, then hesitates before she adds, "but I will tell you now, not for sake of pressure but so you do not have that wondering to worry over, that if—if not when—you should, I am here and willing."

There is a grace to how she says it, a trust in opening herself to me that somehow is more healing than anything else she could say. We stand in the sun and watch the turtles' slow progress all around us, until the last of them is gone.

I GO UP for my watch. Teo follows at my heels but settles by the tiller near my feet, pushes his nose into his side, and falls asleep almost immediately.

It is like every other night, only a few scattered clouds more wisps than solidity, and beautiful with low-hanging stars. The air smells of cold brine.

The red and purple moons roll on the horizon as though they were swimming or perhaps dancing on top of the water. The white moonlight pours from high in the sky, washing down to once again turn everything silver so I know that I will see her again, even before I turn to find her at the railing, her white hair unbound and falling around her, her gown loose and tousled as though she were freshly come from bed, or perhaps contemplating going to it.

I say, "Selene."

"Bella." She takes a few steps forward until we are so close that if I take one more step forward myself, I could gather her to me. But I refrain, savoring the moment. Right now, I do not need to wonder about the how and why of her presence once again here. Her impossible, delightful presence.

She does not step forward either. She is poised there like a dancer, but it is not a practiced, posed grace. It is something that comes out of her, as though she were incapable of making a clumsy move. She smiles at me and points at the sleeping Teo.

"Bella," she says. "Why haven't you figured it out yet?"

That makes me blink. "Figured out what?" I say stupidly.

"Why did you give the dog that name?"

"Because he reminded me of the boy."

"Where is that boy right now? Why have you lost track of him?"

"I don't know where he is. It is one of the things that worries me from time to time. Adelina has money for him, should he come to her at the press, and there is no reason why he should not have done so, but she has not mentioned seeing him and that is something she would surely tell me."

"Perhaps he is closer than you think." She points again at the dog. "Think about it. You have seen him behave uncannily more than once. Do you truly think that he is simply a very smart animal?"

I am utterly taken aback, in the way I would be if an object in my hand suddenly came to life and bit me. "What?" But my mind is racing through everything and one thing it comes to, over and over again, is that moment that started our journey.

The small furry form, the leash trailing it in a line kept straight by the speed of its passage, racing along the dock, towards the ship, despite the fact that it was pulling away, and that the gap was widening with every passing second.

I remember that jump. How could I not when every person there was watching and holding their breath to see whether or not he made it? An impossible jump, and yet he did it.

And then once on board, came straight to *me*, as though he knew me already.

And refused to leave my side, no matter how anyone tried to coax him away.

And growled at Ruhua whenever she made me sad or angry.

And tried to coax me into laughter whenever I was either of those things.

I look down at the sleeping dog, then at Selene. "How would such a thing be possible?"

"You have heard of such transformations before. You've even met someone claiming to be caught halfway between."

I think of Leonoa's lover Glyndia, of the great golden wings in place of arms. "But how?"

"That part is much longer and more difficult to explain, which is why I have no intention of doing so." She points again at Teo. "The time is coming when you may have a chance to do something about the curse that binds him. Believe me, it is a curse. The things that make him who he is when he isn't Human are not being used, and so they slip away, bit by bit. Every day he becomes a little more the dog Teo rather than the Human Teo in dog form."

This dazzle of revelations stuns me. "But surely he would have done something to draw my attention to it?"

"A clever curse keeps its victim from playing any part in its undoing."

"What do I need to do in order to break the curse?"

"You need to find that out for yourself." She takes a step backward. I can see the silver light dimming as a cloud nibbles at the edge of the silver moon, like a lacy scarf slowly settling on it.

Then she is gone. Without my even looking away, just blinks out of sight, so I am forced to acknowledge something else that she has not bothered to tell me: she is here supernaturally, somehow. Or else she is a supernatural creature herself.

I cannot help it. My eyes flicker upward to contemplate the white moon's face.

The Moon Temples tell us that each of the three moons sometimes walks this world in Human form. That they observe and judge and teach.

To believe that I have drawn the attention of the white moon is to be as egotistical as I was in Tabat. Tabat, where I thought myself worthy for something that was only a product of circumstance.

Or was that true? Before my time, the Winter games had gone on for centuries without anyone putting them out of balance. So there was something about me that had done so.

What was that factor? Maybe if I could figure that out, I could become myself again, or at least something close to that old Bella Kanto.

I toe at Teo's sleeping form. He rouses. Licks his chops and regards me with sleepy eyes.

I say, "Teo?"

It is the same name that I have hailed him by hundreds of times, so there is no reason for him to understand the question that I am asking. But he does. There is a different light in his eyes as he regards me.

The tiller is set. We will not go astray if I do not tend it for a few minutes. I kneel beside him as he sits up fully, cocks his head to regard me as though to say silently, *So what now?*

But I need to make sure. I say to him, "Were you the Human boy Teo?"

He nods twice, quick sharp motions of definite assent, then goes into a chorus of sneezes in rapid succession. He lies down and puts his paws over his nose before it stops.

I think of Selene saying, "A clever curse keeps its victim from playing any part in its undoing." Magic has been laid on him, active magic, so that when he thinks about his freedom something happens.

I reach out and rub his ears. He uncovers his nose and sits up again, twists around in order to lick my hand, then switches his attentions to my face.

"It'll be all right," I tell him. "We'll figure a way out of this for you."

I don't tell him how it is that I came to my realization of his true nature. I don't tell him that she said the opportunity to free him would be coming up. I still do not trust any of this. There have been so many odd circumstances, so many things going awry, so many small betrayals. I debate whether or not to tell Scylla.

In the end, I do, though I do not tell her how I came to the knowledge. I let her think I puzzled it out myself.

"He's what?" she says incredulously. We are drinking chal and eating flatbread. She has already swum back and forth around the prow this morning, leaping out of the water once or twice as adeptly as any dolphin. After starting breakfast, she'd put several lines over the side and is watching them now out of the corner of her eye.

"He's Human," I say.

"Who happens to be in dog form at the moment," she says dubiously. At my nod, she throws up her hands. "That makes as much sense as anything that has happened to me in the past few months, so I will not object about impossibilities. But what are we to do about it?"

"Once we are down in the islands, perhaps we can find some cure down there," I say.

Admittedly my tone is vague, but there is no need for her to bristle quite as fiercely as she does. She says, "And I will repeat *again*, what are we to do about it?"

"Think on it," I tell her. "We are looking for the source of a magical plague. Someone who knows how to twist magic, subvert it to evil ends."

"A Sorcerer," she breathes out, her eyes round.

I nod. "Someone who deals with magic will know who the practitioners are in the area. And someone who deals with cures is not likely to look kindly on someone who creates the things that corrupt. If we are looking for a person to lift the curse on Teo, then it seems certain we will find someone who will also be able to point us in the direction of our primary quest."

She still looks dubious, so I add, "Think as well how useful it would have been to have a third set of hands aboard the boat and another person to take watches. The boy is a good one, and I hired him myself in his Human form."

"But I still do not understand how he came to be a dog."

"That is something I would like to know as well," I admit. "Although the reason to see him back to his original form, so that you may ask questions about how he came to be in something other than it."

She looks at me. "You think that this is somehow connected with everything that has happened to you."

I nod down at Teo. "Whose hand was holding the leash when he slipped it and came to me? Alberic has shown himself unscrupulous. Perhaps the boy knew something that he should not have and was put in this form so he could not betray anything of what he knew."

Scylla crosses her arms. "When I think of how many times that dog has been around when I was changing clothing," she says. I can tell she is thinking of discussions we've had, ones she would not have had in front of a stranger.

Teo lowers his head as though he is reading her thoughts as well as I am. Perhaps he is. Dogs can smell emotions; he may know both of us better than we know each other.

The thought is an uncanny one and yet I find it intriguing. What is it like to be in another form? It is not a question anyone has asked of a Shapeshifter, at least that I know of, because they are so feared that any of them are killed as soon as they are discovered.

Teo's head goes lower yet. Is he worried that I will think the less of him because he has been so transfigured and thus edges up on the borders of being a Shifter? His tail is absolutely still, and he is flattened to the decking in a way that I cannot understand. It is the sort of behavior I would expect of a dog that has done something terribly wrong.

Have I misunderstood his situation? Did he bring it upon himself somehow? But if that had been the case, then would Selene —whatever she was, god or creature or hallucination—have spoken up on his behalf and revealed his situation to me?

"We will find a way to free you," I tell him, but he stays pressed to the decking until I finally manage to coax him into better spirits by offering him bits of my flatbread, which he takes gratefully enough.

I keep forgetting that he is something other than a dog, and he does too, licking my fingers to extract every bit of flavor and then looking abashed as though he had suddenly remembered how odd that behavior would have been in his true form.

Scylla keeps frowning at him as though he were somehow responsible for all this and had presented himself under false pretenses.

"I do not think he brought this on himself," I finally say to her.

She gestures dismissively. "I don't believe he did, no, but it is one thing to know a creature as just a creature and then suddenly have it presented in the light as a fellow person."

She breaks off and grimaces, "I sound as bad as an anti-Abolitionist, preaching the division between Human and Beast, and yet it is more permeable than that, we both know it."

Her assertion surprises me. "We do?"

Her head swivels to regard me, narrow-eyed. "Bella, you know as well as I do that Mers are the same, no matter that a few have managed to get themselves redefined in a way different than the others. The Mers that are acknowledged Human are done so because of ancient treaties and bribes, not from any innate thing. It is only a matter of words, and I do not believe that words reflect reality, particularly in cases like this."

Only a matter of words. Jolietta would have disagreed. And I would have once.

Do I believe in the nature of Beasts any longer? Did I ever?

THE TINY PEARL (TEO)

She knew, she finally knew who he was, and this was good, so good.

So good. Bella is good.

Something about the thought roused the old him, the boy Teo. He realized with a shock of fear how close he had come to losing himself. How close he was right now.

The point of no return, the point where he could not be reclaimed, was very close and nipping at his heels.

ADELINA'S FOURTH LETTER

Dear Bel—

I told you that Sebastiano was faced with the choice of whether to renounce me or be put away from his house. He chose what I could have told you he would choose. Even though I think his common sense completely suspect, he has in fact chosen me.

How silly to find something so foolish so endearing! He is a dunderhead and has betrayed all the maxims of the Trade Gods in this alliance, and I could not but love him more for it.

Where shall we live, what shall we do? I do not know, and truth be told, Bella, times are so tumultuous here in Tabat, so full of riot and crime and upset, that I cannot help but think that we might as well seize these moments while we can. The world is falling apart around us, and everything is changing, but we have each other.

You, of all people, will find this ridiculous and absurdly romantic.

Three days ago, the Duke's troops slaughtered dozens in the Plaza, those who had come to hear the political speeches. He has gone mad. He had some plan to stay in power, and it came to naught, and now he does not know how to deal with that failure.

The Mages are helping him, or at least most of them are, but some groups within the college resist and will not let their magics be used against the citizenry of Tabat. Sebastiano was one such and said so overly loudly. Now his name is on one of the lists of the people to be taken in for questioning.

Luckily he knows this city well, too well for soldiers to ever find him, as long as he has a little warning. He has befriended the Beasts, and many of them trust him, but, overall, their position in the city is tenuous and they are assumed rebellious and killed out of hand, without any asking after their sympathies and how they feel about the Duke.

The cousin who has taken over my mother's house has been selling away all the furniture and despoiling the estate. There are no legal niceties in these days, and I think she means to have all her work over and done before order is restored.

I do not miss my mother much. She was always thinking of things I should be doing, or ways in which whatever I was doing for the house was inadequate. Not a relationship calculated to create fondness. But I admired her, admired all her sharp wit even while I was praying that it never got turned on me. She was clever and pragmatic, my mother, and those are not bad qualities to chase after.

I only wish that approval of me and my doings had been another part of the mix. But you know how Emiliana was. You may think I reckon her too harshly, even.

It is so odd to be with a man who counts me cleverer than himself, who thinks the sun and moons set and rise in my eyes. I do not mean that as a reproach, Bella, nor do I think you will take it as such, really, because you never promised that sort of love to anyone —and I never saw it in you.

Every day things seem more dire, Bel. Scant food comes into the city, even though we are nearing the harvest season. Many fields have been set aflame, torched. One side says it is the Beasts doing it, and others say it is profiteers who have stocked up on provisions and now will fleece us all.

Other rumors hold the Duke's troops responsible, saying that he means to starve the city into submission. I would not like to believe such a thing of him, Bell, but you and I both know that he is unscrupulous when it comes to things of power. Still, would he starve all the people he is supposed to be overseeing, in the name of doing so?

Now I start to worry and wonder whether I should commit any of this to paper. I do not think there is a sufficiency of labor to examine all the letters going out of Tabat, but if you were Alberic, would you not keep watch over some people, those with the eloquence to perhaps shape things and persuade people? Or am I overthinking all of this and giving myself too much credit?

I never thought myself important in that sort of way until recent years, when people started to say it to me, Bel. When someone would gush on and on about how one of your stories had inspired them through a difficult time—yes, I can hear you objecting now, that they were inspired by you, not me, but the truth of it, the real heart of it, Bel, is that it was me, my words, and that I could have told such stories of all sorts of figures.

I don't think you've ever read a single one of my historical works, but if you did, you would recognize plenty of carryovers, because I draw on those stories as much as on the vainglorious almost-lies you tell me about your own adventures.

I can tell when you leave things out, Bella. Sometimes I've chosen to describe an edge of those, just enough to haunt someone and let them know that you were really there. But you've never picked up any of the books that I've written about you, even to proofread. It is maddening and unreasonable of you—I know you say that living the stories once is all that you can bear, and yet I have heard you tell some of them to students, over and over again.

I don't mean to whine. I have always tried to take you as you are.

What am I trying to say in all of this? I don't know. I've given up on any thought that you will answer—I'm not even sure that you're still alive and, no matter what, Alberic has sent you far, far away to a place that you will never come back from. Oh, Bel, prove me wrong and write back whenever, wherever you get this. Please.

Anyhow. It's morning, and I think past the ninth hour, but they blew up the Duke's Tower a few days ago—a whole set of explosions, including the great Tram—so part of the senselessness of our days now is that we cannot reckon times other than roughly, use dawn and noon and dusk, speak in meals sometimes.

Sebastiano has brought pastries from his mother. The Figgis carts still rumble along the streets, but they reflect the cost of wheat now, and so they mainly keep to the safer upper terraces, the rich neighborhoods sheltered by the Duke's castle and the College of the Mages, set off by the canal that runs through the Twelfth Terrace.

Down here things are more precarious, but I have leased a warehouse and sell paper for the moment, and we live in the apartment that someone built into the rafters for the night watch. Sebastiano has brought in a pair of little Gryphonlings, tiny cousins of the great Gryphons, and they keep the premises free of rats or mice and look a good deal plumper on that diet than any of the Humans around here do.

I do not know if you would recognize some aspects of the city nowadays, Bel. The Beast market is closed down—they think it might be a center for a rebellious attack and moreover who wants to buy an unproven Beast, one that might turn on a household, now? Many businesses that depended on Beast labor have closed, and others will soon, I think.

A steady stream of Beasts escapes, and there are plenty that assist them in getting out. They say that Verranzo's New City has swollen almost double in taking in all the Beast and Human refugees. Sebastiano and I have spoken again and again of following that pathway, but he does not want to leave his parents behind.

Letha will not leave, she says, till the city has resolved itself and come to an accommodation with the Beasts. She is ardent in speaking of this cause, the same ardency that Leonoa shows, and so

I introduced them last week and found, to my delight, that they hit it off as perfectly as I thought they would.

I do not think that Glyndia appreciated it as much as I did—I get the sense sometimes that she would just as soon have Leonoa all to herself, regardless of what might be best for Leonoa. That makes me uneasy, that jealousy—it's like the way that Marta regarded you and refused to give you over when you told her that things were done. You remember how well that worked.

There's one more thing I want to speak of, Bel, before I seal this letter and consign it to the post and hopefully not the wartime censors. Someone did everything that they did in order to use your magic, the magic you have gained through being Tabat's Champion, in order to destroy the city. That's at the heart of what's going on now, I think—your magic is being used to fuel this unrest and daily rioting. You must find a way to take it back.

How, you are asking, and making faces at me when I tell you this: I don't know. You're going to have to figure that one out yourself. But just thinking of you, of you being yourself, has cheered me to the point where I cannot believe you dead. Where I think that you will find a way, and I will see you again, in Tabat.

With love,
Adelina

CHAPTER 26

THE FANCY BLISS (LUCY)

*N*one of this was Lucy's fault. She had been swept along by things, as though the Gods intended to carry her onward, whether she resisted or not. And so it was on the day they saw the Dragon.

She was above the deck when they first spotted it. Just an odd little marking, like a little curlicue in the sky, inscribed near the rising sun, a curve of a line that, at first, she couldn't see moving.

The woman who'd spotted it was at the railing, waving over the others, and even the sailor who was supposed to mind Lucy at these times went over to stare with the rest. Lucy couldn't see over their tall forms, but she went off to the side and spotted it then.

This was a rare chance to be on deck and unsupervised, but she didn't know how to make the most of the opportunity. If Mary Silverhands had been there, she would have done something to win her freedom, something clever and reckless and undeniably heroic.

But Lucy was Lucy—and at least that instead of Obedience, which was her old name, and Lucy was not a hero like Mary Silverhands, even if sometimes she had been thrust into a story like that.

She stood by the rack of remaining turtles and gazed into their dark eyes. Their shells shone glossy in the sunlight; two still waved their flippers slowly, as though thinking they might crawl through the air and into freedom. Others had stilled and no longer acted as though they might escape somehow. They did not move their flippers; the only motion was their heads, turning to watch Lucy as she walked among them.

She still felt sorry for them, but she felt sorrier for herself, headed to some unknown destination, kidnapped for purposes that had yet to be revealed to her, and—it was clear—once they figured out the mistake, they would do something to her—perhaps horrible, perhaps not, but in all probability ending with either her death or sale as a slave to someone.

While she had lived in Tabat, the city had seemed unremarkable to her. Now it seemed all her heart's desire: to see the cobbled streets or sniff the aromatic trail of one of Figgis' bakery carts. At night she sometimes woke and thought herself at home for a few, brief, and precious moments. Then reality would reassert itself with the ship's sway and creak, and she would know she was still here, and would wake with tears running down her face.

Surely they were sorry, back home, that they had treated her so harshly.

But knowing her sisters, she thought that might not be their first thought. Rather it might be that her absence meant more of everything to go around in a household where things rarely stretched to encompass them all.

She watched the sailors craning over the rail and stepped closer to hear their conversation.

"Dragon, sure as spittle," one said.

"That's certain," another retorted. "Question is, is it heading this way?"

They all stood in silence, watching.

"I think so," one said. "But not making straight for us."

"Planning on circling?"

"Possibly? Thought they don't hunt ships, though."

The first mate was a stocky, squalid man with scars on his face and a blue gem ring through his nose, perpetually crusted with some noisome substance. He said, "They do if they think they got cause."

Another scoffed. "What sort of cause might a Dragon have?"

"Eggs," he said. "Duke was paying a lot of money for them; still does. Dragon whose nest been robbed, that's one that will be out for vengeance."

A sailor, who had been watching and listening in silence, spoke up for the first time. "It be coming this way."

They argued briefly, but Lucy could see as well as the rest of them that indeed the curlicue—which writhed in the air as it moved along—was larger now and presumably closer.

"Send for the captain," the word went around and a few moments later the captain appeared.

Lucy had been trying to stay out of the way of the sailor appointed to guard her, and she did the same with Jusuf, but to little avail. She caught his sardonic eye on her and shivered, but he said nothing about her presence, simply went to the railing. The sailors parted for him as smoothly as curtains, and just as smoothly he pulled out a little telescope and set it to his eye, looking out across the water.

They all kept quiet as he looked through the brass tube. After a long breath's silence, he lowered it and closed it between his hands, reducing it to the small cylinder it had previously been. He said, briefly, "Reef the sails."

Someone objected, "But that will stop us dead."

The captain pointed. "That Dragon means to intercept us, and it will do so soon, whether we pause for it or not. If we pause, we show it that we mean no harm and are not trying to escape. Try to run, and we will meet with a fate like a 'scaping mouse, for Dragons are like cats, and nothing rouses their hunt lust more than something trying to elude them." He squinted at the sailor that had spoken, and said softly, "Though we will prepare by reversing the cannons. These Beasts do not understand such things, and in a pinch, they may serve us well."

Lucy saw now that the cannons had been made so they might swivel in their mountings, to the point where they could be aimed in almost three quarters of a circle. The sailors went and pointed them inward, while others pulled in the sails.

Captain Jusuf stopped by Lucy. "I will let you stay on deck, little bird, if you will be good," he said quietly. "If this encounter goes awry, it will be better for you to be up here than below decks, where you will drown if we go down. Will you serve to stand and be quiet?"

She nodded, afraid to trust her voice.

He studied her for a few seconds. "I mean what I said," he added. "Should the Dragon land on our decks, stand your ground. Run, and you will set off a fate of the sort you do not wish to court."

They waited perhaps half an hour as the Dragon approached. Bit by bit, Lucy could perceive more of it, could see the long, elegant head, the sinuous coil of its body in the air, reminding her of nothing so much as the scarf dancers she'd seen at a fair once, dancing with the long tails of fabric that gave them their names, tied at their belts and wrists. Its color was a deep aquamarine, its scaly mane a pale orange that shaded into rose gold at the tips. Its eyes were black as night. Two long whiskers, colored the same shade as its mane, grew from its chin and flowed outward like thin tentacles.

She didn't know much about Dragons. They were the fiercest kind of Beast, she knew, and the most dangerous, because they could breathe fire or lightning, depending on their kind. They were also the most intelligent. Some people said they were more intelligent than Humans, but the Moon Temples said that was impossible, because Humans had been given dominion over all the Beasts.

She remembered the Sphinx she had seen more than once back in Tabat, the one that had chased her at one point. That creature had seemed as intelligent as any Human. She wondered—as she had before—if perhaps there were things that the Moon Temples maintained in error. It was a new and very strange thought that had only recently come to her, only within the last year.

It was not that she had gone among those who did not follow the Temples and thus been corrupted, or so she would like to think. It was more a matter of noticing the holes in the stories that were told, and still, every time, she considered the possibility that everything she had been taught about the Moons was wrong. Was it this way with everything—did the Trade Gods that the Merchants followed also not exist? Did anything?

The sailors murmured among themselves as the Dragon neared, and gradually the space around the captain, where he stood on the foredeck, cleared away. Lucy still stood close; her minder started towards her, as though suddenly recalled to her existence, but the captain waved him away with an impatient hand.

Closer and closer. Lucy saw when the Dragon started descending towards them, but it did not land on the deck immediately.

Instead it nosed curiously at the barren masts as it flowed through the rigging, seeming to move through spaces and nets far too small to confine it, all without harm to either it or the ropework.

Finally, it reversed its movement, coiling back in on itself, and flowed downward.

As it began to land, she realized how large it was. If it had sat on her old house, back in Tabat, it would have crushed it, surely. But perhaps Dragons did not weigh as much as they looked, for while the boards groaned beneath the weight as it landed, they did not buckle or break. Each scale was the size of a dinner plate, and they gleamed in the sunlight as though made of freshly washed glass, so clean that water droplets still stood on it.

The captain looked so tiny where he stood, but he held himself erect and poised, as though utterly calm in the face of the monster.

Lucy held her breath as the Dragon lowered its head towards him. If its jaws had been open, she would have feared that it was about to eat him, because he would surely have made nothing more than a mouthful to the vast Beast. But its jaws were closed, though its nostrils flared as it sniffed him, and she saw the soft red flesh, frilled and folded, that lined them, stretch and wave as though trying to catch every scrap of scent.

It spoke as it came to his level, and the noise was loud enough that everyone on the boat heard it. It must have been very loud, almost deafening, at close range, but the captain showed no reaction.

Its voice was melodious and sweet, the sound unexpectedly like singing, but with the faintest buzz of menace underlying it like canvas beneath an ornate painting.

It said, "What do you hunt, Humans?" and it drew out that final "s" until it was as much a hiss as a word.

"We hunt nothing, but journey to the Coral Tower," the captain said.

"Yes?" the Dragon said. Its head roved restlessly, surveying the crew. "You look much like the hunters who have been taking eggs."

"We do not have such a thing on board," the captain said. "If you have some means of checking to see whether or not what I say is true, I invite you to do so."

In answer the vast head inspected him again, almost butting him over as it traced its snout over the fine cloth of his waistcoat, this one embroidered with moths and snails, a fine grey and brown pattern scattered over pale blue cloth.

"You do not have eggs on this ship, or I would have crushed it already and retaken them," the Dragon said, its melodious voice matter-of-fact.

"We wish to show you that we mean no harm," the captain said. "We have stopped in the water so you might not have to exert yourself in pursuit."

"That," said the Dragon, "is the act of a very wise or a very foolish man. Which one are you?"

"Very foolish, I suspect," he said.

The Dragon's eyes roved back and forth, taking in everything on deck. It looked at each of the sailors, one by one, and Lucy could see how uneasy and frightened that stare made them. Several turned white; one, after the Dragon's gaze had moved on, leaned over the rail and vomited.

When it looked at Lucy, she thought she could see interest in its stare. It said to her, "Come closer."

The captain said, smoothly, "The child is under my care."

The enormous head swiveled to face him again. "Is she a child?" it said mildly. "It seems as though she is as much adult as child. By the end of this journey, she may be something entirely different.

But I will leave her under your care rather than take her into mine, if you wish."

Jusuf smiled as though happy to be vindicated that there was some reason that he had taken Lucy, that he did have an intelligible plan, although a faint perplexed line rode his forehead, reminding Lucy that the Dragon was referring to her as *she* when Jusuf was convinced she was a boy in magical disguise.

"I will take a tribute," the Dragon said, "before you move on."

Jusuf's eyes narrowed but his pleasant smile did not change. "What sort of tribute?"

The Dragon's head swiveled, its eyes midnight and unreadable as the stare passed over the group of sailors. "Two of your crew."

At that, pandemonium broke loose and a sailor darted towards the railing, intending to jump overboard. But as she climbed onto the railing, the Dragon's massive foreclaw flashed out, moving so quickly that Lucy completely changed her evaluation of the creature, and seized the hapless sailor where she stood. Without hesitation, the forepaw rose, clutching the shrieking sailor, whose cries were cut off when the Dragon's jaws closed around her form.

Everyone else stood frozen with horror and dread.

"That is one," the Dragon remarked.

"I will go and confer with my crew," the captain said softly.

The Dragon rested on the deck, waiting, as the crew and captain gathered towards the back of the boat. The huge creature pretended not to be listening, but Lucy suspected that it could hear everything that was said.

The sailors wanted the captain to give her to the Dragon, they kept insisting, but Jusuf and his second managed to keep order in the chaos. Lucy felt a chill deep down inside herself at the thought and she pressed herself a little deeper into the shadows beside the rack of sea turtles.

Sometimes there were oracular turtles or pigs. They were special animals, who could see the future, but people killed them and ate them anyway, because if you did, then you could see the future, for a little while at least.

Lucy had never eaten such a thing. She looked at the turtles, wondering if any of them were oracular. If they were, then they would be magical and able to talk and, so far, none of them had spoken to her, but would they actually have any cause to?

Or would they have foreseen any interaction with her? She tried to fold the idea up tightly enough that it could fit into her head, but pieces of it kept spilling out, setting her thoughts awry. She didn't know how such a thing could be—she tried again and again to puzzle it out, because thinking about that was so much easier than thinking about the discussion taking place so close to her, and the voices arguing that if anyone should be fed to the Dragon, it should be her.

It occurred to her that no one was saying Maz's name.

The realization was like cold water, as though thoughts of him had been muddled and mixed to the point where they simply had not occurred to her, the way that they were not occurring to the captain and the arguing sailors.

She wondered what would happen if she mentioned his name to them.

"Don't," said the turtle next to her elbow, its voice dragged out like a slowly turning, creaking iron wheel. "Don't, Human child, or you will regret it."

Despite the fact that she had been contemplating such a thing, the manifestation of those thoughts, right beside her, bewildered her. She stared wide-eyed at the turtle and its round black eyes stared back at her. Like all of its fellows, it moved its legs slowly in the air, as though it thought it might fly out of the rack, if it simply found the knack of it.

"Be quiet and listen," it creaked when she said nothing more. "They are almost done."

It was true. The small group of sailors was choosing from the handful of straws the second-in-command held out.

She could tell the moment someone drew the short straw. They slumped their shoulders while around them, their fellows stepped away, as though afraid that they might be contaminated by their fate and follow them into the Dragon's maw.

The captain clapped the man on the shoulder and murmured

something in his ear. The man did not seem to be listening; his gaze searched the deck and the other faces around him feverishly, looking for some escape.

When his eyes lit on where Lucy crouched, his entire face changed. He pulled away from the two beside him even as they reached out, came pelting at her over the floorboards, grabbed at her, pulling her up, as he shouted, "No, I didn't sign on for anything like this! Not while we got prisoners ready and here to go down its gullet!"

He was yanking her towards the Dragon, pulling her arm almost out of the socket, the muscles screaming pain at her as she tried to resist, tried to plant her feet, but kept lurching forward. She could see the Dragon's head just before, the enormous whirling multifaceted eyes.

"STOP," said the Dragon, and everything did. The other sailors running toward them—she wasn't sure whether in rescue or in assistance of their fellow—halted, but more importantly the hands on her fell away, and she stumbled backward, falling on her tail-bone hard but, even as she did so, pushing away with her feet, trying to put distance between herself and the Dragon.

With no need. It paid her no attention at all, but rather fixed those whirling eyes on the man, who stood slack-jawed, open-mouthed, his own unblinking eyes fixed on the Beast before him.

"COME CLOSER," said the Dragon.

Its voice was not loud now, did not hurt the ears or leave them ringing, but it still had a quality that made it the only thing that was audible, made all other sounds, like the lap of the waves or the whistle of the winds through the ropes overhead, all drop away, become inconsequential and insignificant. The only thing in all the world was what the Dragon said, and every word fell into her soul as though fitted for it, so she wanted to step forward, even though she knew she was not the person that it was addressing.

The man moved forward, step by step. She could tell that some part of him was still resisting; the set of his shoulders showed the muscles were angled against the dreadful pull, as though he fought the compulsion. But it was undeniable, and so he kept moving forward while the Dragon waited.

When he was a few steps closer, it opened its mouth.

The inside of its mouth was scarlet, and its teeth were ivory slashes, dagger-pointed but enormous. Its tongue was surprisingly thin in such an enormous maw; it flickered in the air, and the man flinched every time it came near him, but it never touched him, simply sampled the air around him and in his wake.

Step by step. When his foot first stepped on Dragon flesh rather than earth, a shudder worked through him, as though his body fought one last time to resist, as though it were trying to pull him back. But he was helpless to stop the advance, and the tongue flickered around him as the jaws slowly closed.

She heard the crunch and splinter of the bones, but he did not make any sound other than that.

The Dragon swallowed, then breathed out. The smell of its breath was like fetid, swampy sulphur, and it was unpleasantly warm and humid, feeling as though it clung to the little hairs of Lucy's bare arms. By now she had managed to backward crabwalk to the turtle rack, watching the dreadful ingestion while escaping. The whirling eyes passed over her and she felt the weight of the Dragon's attention, just for a second, before it moved on.

Everything else was silent. She collided with the turtle rack and crawled beside it, putting her hand on the reassuring solidity of the nearest turtle's shell. It was the one that had spoken to her before, but it did not speak now.

The Dragon swallowed again, and its thin tongue writhed out, slithered along its lips. Then the boat rocked as it leaped upward, pushing off with its back legs and snapping its wings open as it launched into the air. The first downward flap buffeted them, and the sails billowed and swung on their masts as the Dragon climbed into the sky and was gone.

For the first time, Lucy realized how her heart pounded in her chest. It had been doing so all along, but fear had prevented her from noticing it before.

Jusuf pointed at her. "Take her downstairs," he said, and two sailors did so.

SUPPER WAS late in coming that night, and less ample than it had been in the past. She wondered if the cook had been friends with the sailor that had been eaten, and if so, if the cook were exacting their own revenge. She sniffed at the food to make sure there was no contamination but could detect none. It was heavily spiced and made her thirsty; she drank all of the carafe of water that had been provided and only then thought to wonder about it as well.

No matter. She had to eat, had to drink, she thought. And Jusuf had shown that she was valuable to him for some reason and that he wanted to keep her alive, to the point where he would sacrifice a sailor rather than use her to placate the Dragon. What did it all mean?

The food burned in her stomach in acidic worry. If she was valuable to him, then surely he would not hurt her in any way. But also, if she was valuable to them, then there was the chance of disappointing him, as she had so many people—despite the fact that still none of it had been her fault. They had had too many expectations of her without telling her what it was they really wanted.

She wondered what her sisters and brother were thinking, and whether or not they regretted how they had treated her. She hoped they did. She hoped it burned at them, drove them mad with guilt. She didn't care if she ever returned to Tabat, really. One city had to be as good as any other city. But she wanted the people she'd left behind to miss her, to be full of misery whenever they thought of her, and that they would do so often.

These thoughts of anger and revenge were more palatable than her fear of the Dragon. She let herself linger on them, thinking of each sister, and what would be a particular torment for each of them, and particularly Eloquence, who should have taken better care of her. Should have watched over her so she didn't get kidnapped, should have found an apprenticeship for her where she could have flourished. Could have flowered and become whoever it was that she wanted to be, even if she wasn't sure exactly who that was.

Even as she lay down, she could see the moment still. The blank-faced crewmember, walking forward, into the Dragon's mouth. The crunch and snap of bone when the Dragon closed its jaw. The way the ship juddered underfoot when it leaped into the air. She kept thinking that she felt it landing, come back to demand more tribute.

"Lucy!" the hiss came through the wall. She rolled over to face it. He'd been taken below before she'd been taken up; all he would have felt was the Dragon landing and taking off, and he would not have known what it was.

"It was a Dragon," she told the crack. "A big one. It landed on the ship and the captain let it eat one of the sailors. They drew straws for it."

Even as she said it, she thought, "Why did he have a crew member eaten when he could have fed Maz to it?" How was it that at the moment when the crisis had occurred, that somehow everyone forgot about Maz's existence? Her brows furrowed, but he whispered back, and she forgot her question in order to listen.

"A Dragon? That must mean we are getting close to the Southern Isles. There's supposedly a place down there where lots of them nest."

"So you think we'll see more of them?"

"I don't know," he said. "I hope not; we don't have that many sailors."

Her mind jumped back to its earlier question. "Why do you think they didn't feed you to it?"

His reply was slow to come, his tone careful. "I'm not sure. Why do you think they didn't?"

"Because everyone forgot about you," she whispered. "Because when it landed, then all of a sudden no one remembered about you, even me."

"You were all very scared and I wasn't there. Out of sight is out of thought in moments of great peril."

"Mmmm."

He sighed. "You doubt me," he said.

"It's odd, as though they forgot you. Like magic. It doesn't add up."

"Does it have to add up?" His voice was wistful.

"It's hard not to ask why it doesn't."

"You ask so many questions, Lucy," he whispered. "Listen, I'll tell you part of it, but lean close. I can't risk the guard overhearing us."

She pressed her ear to the wall, so close she could feel his breath on the inner folds of it as he spoke, "Listen now, because this is the truth of the story..."

His voice was soft, so soft she had to strain to hear it, so soft that she could pay attention to nothing else, that she ignored everything else around her until she thought *oh, I'm falling asleep* and almost roused but not quite and then the next morning she woke and couldn't remember what they had been talking about, which nagged at her a little in the first hours after waking, but then faded away, lost in the other small moments of the day.

The next afternoon, as she walked the deck, her bored guards talking to each other—where could she go, after all?—she thought she heard a turtle whisper her name, like an echo in her head. What had it said to her?

She paused by the rack where they were stacked. Their flippers no longer waved as wildly as they had at first, but they still moved, slowly, as though swimming through sand.

She leaned her head near the turtle she thought had spoken. It clacked its bill, three slow clacks, and its flippers waved to and fro as though they were their own creatures, looking for each other, but forever separated by the hilly curve of the shell. She said, "Did you call my name?"

"Lucy, who is sometimes and will be Mary Silverhands," the turtle said. "Free me, little goddess in the shell." She smelled the sea-brine tang on its breath, which was unexpectedly warm on her skin.

"You are too heavy," she said. "They will see me and stop me."

"Not if you do exactly as I tell you, if you wait for the right moment."

"Why should I?"

The glassy eyes regarded her. "If you do, I will get you help. I will swim to a spot where a great Champion sails, one who will come and be waiting ere you arrive on Fireah, there to fight all the pirates and take you home safe, to another fate."

She scoffed. "A Champion is sailing?"

"If I tell her you are waiting, she will not wait as long as she does to come."

Lucy tried to parse this out in her head. It was annoyingly like all the sorts of things that they said at the College of Mages, all the clouds of words that they threw out, like an octopus flinging out ink, to hide the fact that they intended to do nothing.

Nettled, she said, "You are lying to me because it costs you nothing. You mean to trick me, and then they will be angry with me."

"They will still treat you fair enough," the reasonable voice of the turtle said.

"I will think on it."

"You have only tonight to act, Lucy," it said sadly.

She was tired of people trying to manipulate her. "That's not true," she said. "You're just trying to make me feel sorry for you. The cook said he wasn't going to make turtle soup till tomorrow and even then, I doubt he's selecting you. Not to offend, but you are skinnier than most of your fellows.

"Only tonight," the turtle repeated.

But she turned away.

"Human child, the moons are frowning at you," it whispered, and she went down the steps.

Later, she told Maz through the wall about the turtle hailing her. He asked, "What did the turtle say to you? Did it make sense? They are irrational creatures, oracular turtles."

"It said that I should free it," she said.

"It made you no promises?"

"It said it would go and fetch someone who would get to Fireah before us and ambush the pirates."

He chuckled. "Does a turtle have many friends, then? Would it bring us a clam to help us, perhaps? Or seagulls to fly overhead and squawk in a discouraging manner?"

"A Champion," she said. "That was the word they used."

There was a little silence and then he said, in a very different voice, "It is time for you to sleep, Lucy."

"It is early yet," she started to say, then found herself yawning. It had been a long day. It was reasonable to sleep now.

Hours later, she heard shouting on deck. When Kindly brought her breakfast, she said, "What's happened?"

He tsked. "Some mischief-maker was among the stores, killed some of the turtles. Slashed their throats. They're salting most of the meat and cook's working on the rest, but he's as mad as an upside-down taper and no one dares ask him for anything, even the captain, for fear of how he might spice their soup for the rest of the journey."

The turtle had said she only had that night. Had it known the fate that had been waiting for it?

She thought of the sadness in its tone, the gentle wave of its forelimbs where it hung helpless in the rack. Tears pricked at the back of her throat. She could have done something.

She tried to tell herself that it didn't matter. That the turtles had been captured to be chosen, that their fate was assured, and that turtles being eaten on journeys was the way that things always had been and always would be.

Aiding her in these thoughts was the way the conversation was fading in her mind with what an outside eye might have labeled unnatural swiftness.

Had she dreamed the conversation with the turtle? Maybe that was what had happened. What had they been talking about? She couldn't remember, only that it had been sad, so very sad.

No, she must have dreamed it, must have heard the sailors talking about oracular turtles and then created the encounter in her head.

Yes, that was surely it.

CHAPTER 27

THE TINY PEARL (BELLA)

I have faced a Dragon once and never want to again, which is why when I see that distant speck far up above in the otherwise vacant sky—not even a wisp of cloud, only blue and the boiling white of the sun and the glimmer echo of the white moon, half-masked and hanging near the horizon—I want to deny it.

But it is unmistakable. A Dragon flies like no other creature, the way it snake-swims through the air, as though its wing were there more to shape its flight than to propel it. No bird or insect flies like that, nor any of the larger Beasts, Griffons or Hippogriffs or Sphinx.

Teo whines at my side, his body taut and unhappy, nose pointed at the thing that's drawn my notice, confirming any doubts if I'd had any left.

"What's amiss, Bella?" Scylla there in the hatchway.

She pauses in response to my upraised hand's signal. I can hope it hasn't spotted her, so I try to keep my body's language as though focused on the spot far above even while I hiss, "Get below and near the emergency scape and stay there. You'll know when it's time to get out."

If it tears the boat apart, she can swim downward, elude its notice. After that, it'll be a long swim back for her, but she may be able to catch a passing ship.

I wish that I could send the dog with her, but it's too late for him. The Dragon will have spotted the both of us from far above where it circles, keener-eyed than any eagle.

It lurches downward in the air, playing at falling, then executes an amused upward loop that still manages to bring it farther down, closer to us. Scylla has gone below.

Teo whines again and I reach down to pet him in reassurance, wind my fingers through the folds of skin on his neck. The Dragon loops again, writes something I cannot read against the sky. Closer now.

Warm wet as Teo licks my hand in a waft of doggy breath. The wind is full of salt and the smell of sun-warmed tar from the railing close at hand.

I use my free hand to loose my sword in its scabbard, thumbing away the safe-strap. Sometimes they like a formal challenge, Dragons. They fancy themselves the most rational Beasts, more civilized than any Human. If you've ever heard two talk together, you will have heard an amount of pretentious boasting that puts any Merchant or Noble I've ever heard to shame, and I've heard my share of such.

Closer yet. They are beautiful in flight, Dragons. Long ago when I was a child, apprenticed to my hated aunt and living in strict misery at Piper Hill, I'd had the care of feeding their cousins, the little Dragonlings used for hunting. A cousin that no Dragon would care to acknowledge but one nonetheless.

Jolietta taught me that you could extrapolate one Beast's behaviors sometimes, by knowing what creatures they were kin to. Centaurs were often as panicky and ill-reasoned as horses could prove, disliking fluttering ribbons or odd shadows as capriciously as cats.

Dragons are curious as cats, driven by that and the need for warmth and food. There is plenty of warmth here, so a great deal will depend on how recently this Dragon has eaten. We are close to the Southern Isles, and those usually abound in game in the form of the tiny island deer as well as wild pigs fattened on fruit and game, not to mention sea turtles, sharks, and immense rays.

The odds are reasonable—I reckon them at one in three, and if I can make myself seem intriguing enough, exciting enough, puzzlesome enough, I might nudge that up to one in two, if I do not overflatter myself.

The Dragon is taking its time. I find my mind wandering as it flutters downward.

At least I no longer think that it might suddenly swoop, barrel into a devastatingly fast and strong dive designed to shake the boat to boards at impact. That would leave the Dragon momentarily at a disadvantage, itself floundering among the wreckage, but I've seen others recover and launch themselves back into the air with startling speed.

No, this one intends to have a conversation before it decides what to do with us, and that means the odds are good it won't decide to eat us immediately.

The question remains of all the other things that it might decide to do instead.

Dragons are truly beautiful things. Watching this one, an enormous length of black scales and leathery ebony wings, coiling its way down to us is a moment where I feel myself drinking in the beauty of the sight, feeling privileged to have witnessed such a thing in my lifetime.

Perhaps I am bewitched by the rune spells that it had written against the sky, I cannot attest that I am not. How else can I account for the fascination with which I watch it?

I cannot say the same for Teo. He presses hard against my leg. His breath comes in gulps, taking in the air as though each lungful might be his last.

He growls. The sound breaks my trance. I could have sworn that the Dragon was still far off, hanging out of reach in the sky, but when I hear that sound and blink, I see it is there, in the air before us, in all its size and glory.

It is far too large to land on the boat, but it does not need to, because it continues to flow through the air like a snake swimming through water, as though the air around it has thickened enough to hold it up despite the slowness of its flight. Its wings have abandoned all pretense of utility; they are folded and pleated like paper fans, moving with the sinuous coiling and uncoiling of its body, looking like metallic paper on the point of melting, just about to shimmer away.

But its head remains fixed relative to me. Its eyes are fiery emeralds, set in the black scales of its face, a black so dark it drinks in the light until it looks more like a shadow hanging in the air, the undulating outline of a Dragon, so big that it can take up the boat between its claws and carry it far away and above us into the sky and then devour the contents or drop them screaming one by one.

It says, "You are Bella Kanto, once the Heart of Tabat."

CHAPTER 28

THE FANCY BLISS (LUCY)

*S*he asked Maz what he knew about Fireah. They were in the unlit hold again, each propped against their side of the wall, hearing the creak and lap of the ship through the water, and the occasional footsteps in the hallway outside. An amber line of light marked the doorway, and the light it cast glowed across the room and touched Lucy's bare toes.

"Fireah?" Maz said, pronouncing it a little differently than Captain Jusuf had. "That is to the west of the Southern Isles, Dragon-haunted waters where very few sailors go. It is an island that is itself an artifact. They call it the Coral Tower sometimes. It stretches far up into the sky and just as far, even farther, into the ground. An ancient Sorcerer made it and used it to draw magic out of the heart of the earth itself."

She frowned. "How did they do that?"

"There's a tunnel that goes down and down," he said. "Haven't you ever wondered what it looks like, down below the earth's surface?"

"It's caves," she said. Every schoolchild knew that below Tabat there were caves, and more caves below that. Sometimes people tried to explore them, but they were very dangerous, not just because there was dark and rocks and tunnels, but because things lived in those tunnels.

He grunted negation. "Tabat is a special case. When you go down far enough, it becomes warmer and warmer, and the magic is stronger and stronger. There are focal points where it gathers, that magic, and the stairs lead down to a chamber that holds such a point and collects it."

"Are there monsters, as with Tabat?" she asked.

"There are guardians," he said. "I don't know much about them, but accounts vary. One even said that they change 'in accordance with the challenger,' which means that when someone approaches, they draw on that person's fears and memories to shape themselves."

Lucy shuddered. What were her deepest fears, what forms would something like that take? Probably her sisters, she thought, remembering how they had tormented her in the days after their mother's death.

"Why are they taking us down there?"

"They think that the Pot King's son will be adept with magic and able to channel it," he said. "Once he does, they will harvest it."

"Harvest it?" She wasn't sure she liked the sound of that.

"They will kill the son and take the magic as he dies. It is a known process. We covered it this year in Basic Concepts."

"That's horrible!" she said.

"Most magic is. Even if it doesn't depend on something like that, it often uses parts of Beasts. Sebastiano showed me the furnaces under Tabat that burn Dryad logs. So many of them, dozens and dozens. He said that the Duke and College send out expeditions to find them and fell them."

"But they don't have the Pot King's son. I mean, I'm not him."

"It's true. You won't be able to withstand the magic." His tone was matter-of-fact.

"You don't care!" she said.

"I would care if I had the luxury," he said. "Believe me. But they're going to kill you either way, and if I'm fond of you, it'll just hurt more."

She strained her ears, trying to decipher his tone. "You're serious!"

"I'm just being sensible," he said. "You have to be pragmatic about these sorts of things, at least that's what my father always says."

LUCY WAS DREAMING, dreaming of a day when she felt very Lucy, brave and serious and self-determined. She could imagine all sorts of things on those days—could imagine escaping, even, going off to live her own existence in the Southern Isles, becoming a trader or Explorer or even a pirate herself!

Then when she was wealthy and powerful, she'd return to Tabat and show them all. She'd found a press ten times bigger than Adelina's and drive her out of business! She'd hire the College of Mages, but demand that they oust Sebastiano! She'd find very special apprenticeships for all her sisters, horrible ones, but she wouldn't leave them at it too long, just long enough that when she took them out, they'd be grateful—*so* grateful—and maybe they'd know all the time that she could put them back and never dare cross her again. That was good.

Eloquence would finally see how very special she was and step down as head of the family, cede to her. She knew better than he did how to handle everyone—he'd been away so long that he didn't understand everything.

Would she send him out exploring for her when she ruled Tabat? She thought not. It would be nice to have him around all the time, and if he wanted a spouse, she would find a nice one for him, much nicer than Adelina.

And she'd do away with the Temples. They did nothing for anyone. They claimed to feed the poor, but they did that with children stolen from the poor. No, the Temples were nothing but priests trying to justify their existence. She'd heard her mama repeat that one after Canumbra said it, and she'd filed it away for herself, that sentence full of fine words and condemnation.

These dreams though, had a way of falling apart whenever she became Obedience again. Obedience was frightened of everything. Obedience didn't know what to do in the face of new things, and so she feared them most of all.

The next day was unremarkable, but, as she was falling asleep, she half-dreamed that Lucy and Obedience both came to her and knelt down beside her.

You have to listen, they said together, and they began whispering, saying, *Something about Maz is wrong.*

Who is Maz? she wondered? Then the answer came to her.

Lying on her back, she opened her eyes and stared at the ceiling. *Something about Maz is wrong.*

The image of the Dragon came to her, the sight of the crewmember walking forward, into its jaws. Something to do with that ...

They had drawn straws to figure out who would be eaten by it. And no one had said, *Have the boy be the one who's eaten,* even though they'd spoken before of him as expendable. It was as though they had not thought of him, as though he had been hidden from their memories for a time, and from Lucy's too, because she had not thought of him either.

Were there other times that he wasn't there like that? Did he accompany her on every trip around the deck? Now that she thought about it, she wasn't sure. It seemed as though sometimes she had walked around the deck talking with him and other times she had been alone, only her thoughts for company, while the sailors chattered with each other and ignored her except to call her back when they thought her too close to the railing.

As she thought of these things, unease crawled through her, as though her bowels were being packed with loose sand, as though her bones would give way.

If she stopped thinking about Maz, she felt better. The sickness just made her think the harder, though. He was using magic, that was clear. Something that they'd taught him at the College of Mages, perhaps. And his magic didn't discriminate between her and the crew, that was just as plain to see.

Her stomach twisted but she persevered. He didn't seem to be able to cast his magic all the time, or he would not be imprisoned as she was. No, it was as though he had a little store of it, and used it only when he felt it judicious, like her mother sprinkling salt across a dish of beans. That was useful to know. He did not move constantly in a haze of magic.

If he were truly her friend, would he cast magic like this on her? And if he could not help himself—if magic was something that could not pick one person from another aboard this ship—still, shouldn't he have spoken of it to her, let her know what lay in the wind, what to expect? Warned her so the effect was minimized, perhaps. But he had not, had treated her the same as he had all the sailors, all the folk that had taken him captive.

No, he was not a friend of hers.

It might have saddened her, to lose an ally, but instead it only made her angry. How dare he deceive her like this? He had magic, and so he had the upper hand for now. But Lucy was capable of waiting, and watching, and using whatever she could to achieve her revenge.

He was not her friend? Well, then, she would be more than not his friend.

She would be his enemy.

CHAPTER 29

THE TINY PEARL (BELLA)

*E*ven I do not expect all of the world to know Bella Kanto by name.

I am notorious in Tabat, and that has always been sufficient. Even when I was wandering at the Duke's behest, in lands that did not know my name (though some of them have come to know it in the interim), it was enough to know that at home I was loved and cherished, and that these foreign lands were simply foolish.

Still, to find a wild Dragon knowing one's name means all sorts of unsettling things, not the least of which is the idea that such Beasts communicate with each other enough to impart such information. Jolietta always insisted that Dragons were by nature solitary and that the female Dragons mated once and stored up enough vital essence from the males through that one act of coitus to quicken all the rest of their eggs, through all the years of their remaining lives, which could number centuries, perhaps millennia, if the legends were all true.

The only way that made sense for a Dragon to know my name was if one that had been captured had been freed and communicated its thoughts to all the rest. And of all the Dragons I had ever spoken with, there was only one that had escaped.

"How is Longthought?" I say. "Does he prosper?"

There is no immediate reaction to my question, only those eyes, so large that my arms would scarcely have met around one, hanging in the air contemplating me. By the size of it, this is a female. She it huffs out a dry little laugh, tiny for a Dragon, but sizable enough to buffet the sails, making them snap in the gust of sulfurous outbreath.

"He does, and he has told stories of you," she says. "And I know more than one of your old friends, Gladiator."

I raise my eyebrow. Who else might this Dragon know? I scour my brain and the Dragon lets me, clearly savors my confusion.

"Who?" I say, rather than let this game play out any longer.

"A Centaur, who knew you long ago at your aunt's establishment."

Phillip. The thought of him hits me harder, faster, more unexpectedly than any blow, landing with an impact that sucks all the breath out of me, leaves me gasping, as though the world were pushing in on me harder than it should, harder than anybody should ever have to withstand.

The Dragon's eyes whirl as she continues to sip at this reaction.

"When did you see him?" I demand. "And where?"

It could not be in Tabat, and yet ... if there were Beast minds behind the revolution, then surely his would be one of them, full of eloquence and anger.

But he was not capable of such. Jolietta had gentled him, stripped away his ability to think.

I'd seen it done.

I'd seen the aftermath, the way his head hung, bloody tears on his face.

Was it possible that he had recovered from her savage act? There was magic, after all. But something like that ... if a Healer had been at hand, ready to reverse the damage before it took hold ... but I could swear with assurance that there had been nothing such at Piper Hill.

He had been taken away after that. I had never been able to find out where he had gone, even all the times I searched through Jolietta's things after her death.

I went through her papers and notebooks over and over, but there was so much that she had never put down. I suspected it was just as well that many of her cruelties had not been passed on, because that was her method of training and the thing that she had a genius for.

I knew many of her secrets, but I would never write them down, would never leave them in this world for another person like her to practice. I would take those things to the grave with me, and never let them go.

The Dragon is silent, not answering, as all of these thoughts whirl through my mind. "In Tabat? Did Longthought see him in Tabat?"

"Not there," the Dragon says. "What, do you think he goes walking in the evenings in Tabat, in order to go buy himself sweet rolls and feed the gulls?"

"Some said the Duke freed him."

The Dragon snorts. "You know Alberic," she says. "Would you believe it of him, that he did a kindly act by freeing a creature that had cost him so much expenditure in expeditions?"

"That is why I never gave the rumor credit," I say, "but I find myself at a loss to explain it otherwise, a Dragon escaped from such a secure pen."

"You find yourself at a loss to explain how a Dragon picked its way free of a puzzle?" she asks with a sly menace that slides like a centipede along my spine.

"Not that at all," I say, stepping out from underneath that subtle pressure with a grace learned from Tabatian courtiers. "Only that no accounts celebrating the cleverness escaped as easily."

Her eyes spin, contemplating mine. I find myself sliding into thoughts of how incalculably old this Dragon must be, how tiny and fleeting the lives of such as I, how our moments of magic would be like flowers blooming day to day, just as transient and unremarkable, even when pretty.

I shudder and pull myself out of the eddies of thought like a swimmer pulling themselves up out of deep water, not lingering lest I drown again in those thoughts and never speak again.

Dragon-dumb, they call it, a peril that is why Beast Keepers are wary of speaking to Dragons, why they arm themselves with charms and cantrips before dealing with them, even to the point of stopping their ears up with clay.

"Why do you speak to me of Phillip?" I ask, and my voice seems harsh to me, accented by anger, in a way that the Dragon cannot misread.

"Because he will not speak of you. In his account of his time with Jolietta Kanto, he never writes of her apprentice. A book has spread across Tabat, telling of his struggles, and it is complete in some regards, but utterly lacking in that one particular thing: there is not a word in all its pages of Bella Kanto, and when she is mentioned in conversation with him, he turns his face away and will not speak of her. Of you. And that is a riddle to me, and I would understand it, because I have no little investment in seeing the cause of the Beasts prosper to the point of freedom in Tabat, and the reason behind his silence is perhaps a weapon to be used for—or against—that cause. So I will master it."

The great head is close to me now, so close that I can see myself reflected in the fluid, velvety depths of her slit cat-pupils, where threads of metallic gold and silver roil along the surface of its irises, meshed like netting, like patterns of chains sliding over each other.

I say, "I tell you once, that I do not know why he will not speak of me."

As I utter the ritual words, the Dragon shutters her eyes in a slow blink before she replies, "Will you tell me twice?"

"I tell you twice, I do not know why he will not speak of me."

The head dips in a considered nod. These are sacred words, and if I speak them wrongly, my good word is forfeit. To this creature it does not matter that my good word is already shredded back in Tabat. As she reckons things, my word is still worth something, because it is worth something to me, and I find that heartwarming.

She says the third time, "Will you tell me three times?"

"I tell you three times I do not know why he will not speak of me."

With that the moment is sealed. I feel magic rippling around me, seeking out weak points, ready to crush me with consequences if I am forsworn. But there is no give to what I have said—I cannot think why he will not speak of me.

When all of this is done—when I have found my magical relic, restored myself—then I will seek him out and we will have this conversation. Because surely if I am there face to face, he will not be able to turn away in silence. I try to think what that conversation will be like.

I know that I can play upon the Dragon's curiosity. "Will you help me find him?"

"I will try," the Dragon says, with a readiness that leads me to believe thatshe expected this question. There is weight to the words as though it is pronouncing prophecy—although no Dragon has such gifts, only common sense to the point of being able to guess the future well.

"We are bound first for Margolees," I say.

"Perhaps you will be lucky enough to find word of him there," the Dragon says, "but I doubt it. I will take you to a place where you can speak with others of my kind, and we will speak with you, and then I will take you to the port city."

"Take us how?" Scylla says, folding her arms. I had not noticed her come out from her hiding place, so deep was I in the Dragon's sway. Teo is still flattened to the boards.

The Dragon holds out a vast claw and flexes it. "I will pick the boat up and carry it."

"We could just sail after you," she says.

"No, because the place to which I will bear you is landlocked, and you cannot sail there."

"How long will you be carrying the ship?" She looks the Dragon over. I want to nudge her to say that perhaps it is a trifle impolitic to anger a Dragon, but luckily enough this one seems to be more amused than irritated by her presumption.

The Dragon bares her teeth in what is surely an attempt at a smile. "Not far. I am quite capable." The lips twitch apart to reveal even more tooth. "I will not allow you to fall."

SCYLLA INSISTS that we stay in the hatchway, sheltered by its roof, while the Dragon picks up the boat and springs into the air, a single smooth motion that should feel jarring and yet feels like sliding upwards, a stomach-flipping change in orientation that just as quickly reverses itself. Only then will she allow us to venture on deck, which holds remarkably level as the Dragon flies, swaying only slightly in the onrushing wind.

Teo sits in the entranceway of the hatch and refuses to go near the railing, ears and tail clamped tight to his body by terror, and then lies down to close his eyes, looking determined to ignore his plight. I am quicker to the railing.

"Mind the balance," Scylla says and moves to the other side to compensate. It's definitely a different feeling underfoot than when we were on the water, and one that feels more precarious. I wrap my fingers around the railing as I stare over the side. Across from me, Scylla is doing much the same.

We rise into the air. Underneath us is only the glitter of water.

Very soon we see an island rising from the water in front of us, volcanic rock heaped high, its surface black and glassy, a beachhead on the side nearest us heaped with glittering black sand. The Dragon ignores the beach and ascends, higher and higher, a swoop that carries us perilously close to the side of the mountain, so close that I can see tiny plants clinging to the planes of the rock wherever they can find a foothold.

Suddenly we are up and over the ridge. Then descending into the hollow center of this valley, which is filled with more Dragons than I have ever seen in all my life.

They are basking in the sun, which gleams dully on their scales, some of them in a giant sand pit. As I watch, I see one in the sand pit yawn and writhe, like a tabby cat possessed of the sun. An almost comical sight, were it not for the fact that this tribe of over-grown housecats is actually some of the most dangerous creatures I know, and that I have never seen them before in such numbers. It is unprecedented. It is against all lore, which accounts them solitary creatures unable to coexist except in the brief period that marks the flight.

These are all large female Dragons, bigger than any I have ever seen anywhere. Not that many are capable of keeping such—Jolietta never dared, for example, or at least never wanted to put herself to the trouble of it.

I do not see Longthought, who was small and stunted from the beginning, and had shriveled further under the callous care of Alberic.

"You have gone quiet," Scylla says. "Are you rethinking what we have agreed to? Dealing with Dragons leads to no good end in all the stories. Indeed, there is not a single story involving a Dragon that I can think of that involves a happy ending that is not confined to the Dragon alone."

"I think that we will see what happens," I say. "Certainly Dragons have no reason to love Humans of any stripe."

"They have no quarrel with the Mers," she says. "Their territory is far away, and none has ever come raiding the One-Story City."

"Yet," I say, and she flinches.

"That would be overmuch irony, to have my trip to save the city be the one that draws attention to it," she says ruefully.

We do not speak of the sack of Dragon eggs.

We are almost to the ground now. I look over at Teo and make sure that he is still braced in the hatchway. I lace my own hands against the railing, but the Dragon sets us down without a bump, on a grassy verge near the immense sand pit.

Dragons are rousing, some of them strolling our way. You would think that they move in an ungainly fashion on the ground, but the truth is that they are as graceful there as they are in the air. These are all sorts of colors, from a pale moonlight white that makes me think of pearly hair to a brilliant blue and green more preen-worthy than any parrot.

Our carrier is the darkest, its hide a deep black that gleams in the sunlight and shows our shadowy forms reflected in miniature on its smoothness.

The Dragons reach us and circle around. Teo whines where he

lies, his eyes still firmly closed. It is apparent that he does not approve of this situation. Scylla and I stand at the railing, some unspoken accord keeping either of us from flinching back. The immense heads move to consider us from multiple angles; their breath smells of brimstone.

"What is this, Bruna?" the blue and green one says. Like the other, its voice is high and clear, but still resonant to sound through our bodies as though the creature were plucking us, harp strings beneath its invisible touch. It has long whiskers like a catfish's, and up close I can see they are striped blue and green, as carefully as though someone had done it with a paintbrush.

"This is Bella Kanto of Tabat," the black Dragon says. Its voice is deliberately casual, but with an edge of mockery, a little well-now-how-will-you-handle-this tone that I remember from a student or two.

All of the Dragons rouse at this, even the ones that have been continuing to sleep (or perhaps pretending to be asleep while listening, given the speed with which they move upon hearing the name.). The number of heads peering at us doubles; I can see up the nostrils of one that is yellow as a lemon; the skin inside is shaded a deep orange that matches the flicker in its silvery eyes. They are exquisite as butterflies, written a thousand times larger and an incalculable deal more deadly.

"The once Champion," lemon yellow says. "Thrown down!" Its huff is amused.

"Still tied to Tabat," Bruna says. "Still linked, even magicless."

This is the first I've heard the Dragon say of anything like this. I perk. Who knows what else will be revealed over the course of this conversation? Perhaps the Dragons will turn out to know a way to bring back my magic, so I won't need to go chasing off to the University.

A jade green snout jostles along my skin, snorting and snuffling like a pug dog, almost staggering me, and says in confirmation, "Still linked."

"Still Tabat!" A silver one almost spits the words, as though indignant at the idea. I have the sense that part of the conversation is being carried on in a space far beyond where I am, a vast unknown region full of words that explain so much.

How are they involved in all of this? What part have they played? Oh, past Bella, sometimes I have to admit that you have done stupid things out of vanity or obliviousness. Scylla was more accurate than I would care to remark when she accused me of that. But I have the feeling that these Dragons hold part of the mystery that has exiled me.

I listen to the rumble of the Dragons talking, and spare Scylla a look, to make sure that she is all right. She has a look of awe on her face as she gazes up at the huge shapes all around us. It's true, even though we are in more danger than either of us have ever been in our lives, I suspect, this is a wondrous sight.

"She wants to find Phillip, but first she wants to go to Margolees," Bruna says.

"Why should we do her any favors? She lived with Jolietta Kanto and saw her methods close at hand. She, of anyone, should have become a fighter for the Beasts. She, of anyone, should have understood their plight, let alone identify with it. She, of anyone, should have fought to correct this injustice."

"The Gods gave her power," the blue and green one says, "and she used the power to fight only for a few, not the all. She is no Champion. She's only a pawn, used to keep that power turned to the service of the unjust."

That stings. More than stings, strikes home like a well-delivered blade. Of all that I have been proud of in my life, being the city's Champion is the pinnacle If anything, I valued it *too* highly, let it convince me that I was more than worthy of the magic that was sustaining me, that it was my natural right, the privilege that was somehow innately mine. Should I have fought for the Beasts?

But it always seemed to me that was the natural order of things. That it was how things were. And I had been taught that, unlike Humans, Beasts were slaves to their natures, could only act in predictable and venial ways. And now I stood in the midst of some of their most powerful representatives and if it were true that they could only act in such a way, then I would have been dead already.

"Look at her," says a Dragon whose brown scales hold hints of violet and crimson along their edges, its eyes like liquid bronze. "Even now she questions the worthiness of the cause."

Enough is enough. I take a step forward. I say, "It's not so much the worthiness of the cause. It's that its champions so far do it no service by killing people and destroying the city."

"Killing Humans, you mean," another Dragon says. "Were any of the Beasts housed with you at Piper Hill to be trained by Jolietta Kanto unworthy of life?"

"There were some I hated," I say steadily, "because they joined in Jolietta's abuse of me."

"But you say that is their nature, and that they could not choose otherwise," the Dragon says, echoing my thoughts.

Is that part of this conversation, the unspoken part, that they can read my thoughts, while I can only guess at theirs?

"Even so," the Dragon says in answer to what I have not said aloud, "but it is not our fault that you cannot hear us in return."

Scylla glances at me in question.

"You don't have to strain your voice unless you want me to hear," I tell her. "They can hear anything you think."

There is a rumble of laughter from a Dragon beside me in reaction to whatever she says in her mind. I'm not sure I want to be in on the joke.

"If you can read my thoughts, then you can confirm my intentions if I tell you that I will go back and help the Beasts, if you will help me in this thing now. That is to your advantage, because if I have magic working for me, then I am a more effective agent in that help. I have no reason to love the Duke. I have no reason to work to keep him in power, nor any Human group. I will be your agent if you will have me.

"But more than this," I say. I reach for the pack I wear, bring it around. Take out the rough sacking, unwrap the first of what lies within.

They sigh, all of them in unison, at the sight of the egg.

"I do not return these as a favor, to buy Trade God power. I give them back because they are *yours*."

Relief comes to me as I speak these words, laying the sack carefully at Bruna's feet. A feeling of purpose seeps into me. Not magical in nature, but more the assurance and strength that has been lacking ever since my day at the hands of the torturers.

Around me there is an utter silence. I can only presume they are all debating what I have proposed before they pose me any more questions.

I move away, shouldering past two Dragons that don't seem to notice my passage, to sit down upon one of the nearby rocks. Scylla comes and sits beside me, leaning into my shoulder. Our weight settles against each other, unspoken promise to prop each other up in this unexpected place.

"Do you think they're going to eat us?" Scylla whispers.

"I think they would kill us first now, at least," I reply. "I believe they would think it rude to eat us alive."

Bruna gives me an amused look over her shoulder before her long neck snakes back in the direction of the conversation.

After an hour or so, the tenor of the conversation changes, and then the Dragons fall silent. I wait a few breaths and then a few breaths more, but before I can stand, Bruna is there. She says, "We have sent for the males, for they should be part of this talk. I have sent two of the young ones to catch a pig for you. A fat and tasty one." She bares her teeth in a silent laugh.

"Tell me something," I say. "Why concern yourselves with doings in Tabat? You seem very well informed."

"We follow affairs in Tabat because if it changes, eventually all will change. New Verranzo's City is seen as an aberration—but let Tabat join it and the world will follow suit."

We see a few Dragons descending. If these are all their males, then each must share a dozen or so females, but I do not ask of this. I see Longthought being carried by two great females.

"At the same time," Bruna continues, "all the world is currently unsettled. The meddling in Tabat has led to portals beneath the earth being rediscovered in the hunt for power. There are strange times coming, and if people do not act to seize and steer those times, disasters will ensue. All of the continents will be destroyed in the way that the Old Continent was. The size of the New Continent has made people complacent, but it can be rendered down to only ash and storms in the same way that the Old was—perhaps even faster nowadays that science has lent itself to magic."

"What do you want from me?" I ask. "Why have you taken us from our journey?"

"There were ships chasing you and so we will put you out of their reach. And tell you another thing. If you want to save Tabat, you need to reconnect with your magic."

If I recover the magic, I will also recover the physical health and prowess that being Tabat's Champion gave me.

But before I can answer, Scylla says, "Meddling with ancient magic has never been a recipe for good luck."

The great head, big as a sculpture in the Duke's garden, swivels to regard her. "Such a weapon would allow you to defend your raft city from Tabat's depredations. You know that conquest is the way of Humankind. If you are not careful, the Humans will further narrow down the definition of Human and use it as a justification to enslave all of the Mer folk."

Before Scylla can answer, Longthought waddles over. He does not greet me, as though I were beneath notice, just noses at Bruna's side.

"We must finish this conversation later," she says, and turns back to the draconic discussion.

DRAGONS ARE, I learn, given to longwinded mental conversations, and the talk raging around us shows no sign of dying down. As promised, a Dragon appears with a wild pig for us. I butcher it while Scylla builds a fire to roast it over.

Teo chooses to devour his raw. Scylla and I thread long slivers of pork onto sticks and set them over the coals to drip sizzling fat. Teo insists on a portion of this as well. Afterwards he sits cracking bones methodically in his jaws, looking content.

When the sun sets, we curl up in the sand next to the fire. There is no need to set a watch; paradoxically we are safer from dangers of a non-draconic nature than we would be almost anywhere else in the world. Teo lolls on his side to display his belly, distended from his gorging, to the fire's warmth and closes his eyes. Scylla and I wrap ourselves in our cloaks and cuddle together, the awareness of the surrounding Dragons one of the best anti-aphrodisiacs I have ever encountered.

She says, "You lead an interesting life, Bella Kanto."

And it is true, and for now that seems sufficient. Perhaps I will survive outside of Tabat.

CHAPTER 30

AN ISLAND (TEO)

The fire was warm, and the meat smelled good, so good that Teo's mouth kept watering, making him drool and almost singe his nose, trying to get close enough for just a taste. It smelled overwhelmingly tasty, that fresh meat after days and days and days of fish, and he couldn't help but whine.

Bella told him to hush. She and the other woman were talking about what to do about the Dragons, and he didn't understand all of the words. They kept patting at the sand while they talked and sometimes the tone of what they said wasn't like the words. They were both worried and fearful, an acrid smell that clung like smoke.

He nosed Bella's hand, trying to get her to take more meat from the fire and give it to him, just a little, just a taste now, but she pushed his snout away, then relented and rubbed behind his ears until he gave up on trying to coax food out of her and instead closed his eyes.

CHAPTER 31

THE FANCY BLISS (LUCY)

*S*ometimes Lucy thought about how Adelina would have written about the journey, how she would have described the high white clouds overhead, or the way the horizon and the sky merged in a silvery line sometimes, or how a gull's cry could sound beyond lonesome, sound as though there were no friends left in the world.

She and Maz rarely spoke to each other anymore. That seemed to suit him. More than once, Lucy herself found her mouth opening and herself about to say something, some conversational gambit or observation. Then she'd remember and close it again. If he didn't want to be friends, then there was no point in trying to be pleasant.

Instead, she talked to Adelina in her head, but this was a more pleasant version of Adelina, one that had already apologized for all the terrible things she had said to Lucy. This version of Adelina thought that Lucy was very clever and appreciated all her insights and her descriptions and observations. This version of Adelina was quite preferable to the original, aside from the issue of not being real.

But there was no other way to entertain herself than sleeping or thinking or the treasured moments when she was allowed to go on deck and feel what the weather was like.

Despite what Maz had said about them being close, it was another week before they came to land. They saw no more Dragons, not even at a distance. The days and nights grew warmer yet, and there were three fewer turtles waving their flippers on the racks near the railing. On a sky-blue afternoon, gulls wheeling above like lookouts, they glimpsed Fireah, the Coral Tower. The captain sent for both Lucy and Maz and had them join him at the railing as the tower neared.

It was much larger than Lucy had imagined. In her head it had been the size of her home, three rooms, grown up and downward into a long thin stalk.

In reality, it seemed as wide around as a small city, and she understood now the awed undertone with which both Maz and the captain had named it. It was round and windows spanned its circumference, each large enough for their ship to pass through. The lines of windows continued upward, upward, towards a top that was far above in the blueness. Its color was a rosy, warm shade, but bird droppings encrusted the lower levels, thick mottled gray and white layers.

"It's at its best right after a storm," Maz said. "Then everything is washed clean, and you can see all the details." He stared forward at the tower, eyes wide.

The captain patted her hand. "We'll be pulling in tonight," he said. "You'll do your part, lad, or else your young friend here will die."

They forced the captives down below while the ship approached Fireah. Lucy pressed her ear to the outer wall and heard the sounds of water crashing on rocks, felt the lurch and sway of the ship as it used its sails to adjust its passage through the reefs around the island. Then the rumble of the great anchor-chain's wheel turning, sending the anchor down, and the feel of its drag when it hit bottom, earlier than she expected.

She went to the hallway door, to determine if she could hear anything there, but the minute she leaned to it, she heard footsteps coming down the hallway and scrambled back.

The door opened and Kindly stood there with another sailor. "Captain says ready yourself," he said.

"Ready what?" Lucy said scathingly.

His eyes flicked over to the bundled blanket, the comb and change of clothes she'd been allowed. "Be happy you have something," he said. "Some folk will be sleeping in the cold sand tonight."

She stared at him blankly. He grimaced at her, drawing his lips back, and slashed his index finger across his throat.

"Who?" she said in terror, suddenly wondering where Maz was. Had they discovered the magics he'd been casting? Despite her decision that he was her enemy, he still thought she believed him friend and ally, and if the pirates had killed him, he would be of no use against them.

She thought he'd been biding his time all this while, that he wanted something on the island and would not move directly against Jusuf and his crew until that was achieved. When he did, and if he was successful but weakened by the encounter—as he would have to be—Lucy intended to take advantage of that. He'd think she'd be grateful for the rescue, if he thought of her at all. He'd believe her still spell-wrapped, still trusting.

Did he have something intended for her fate as well, or was she just an unremarkable side note to him? People had underestimated her before. Everyone had, including Maz. And the moment she struck against him was the moment she'd start striking back at all of them.

She grimly assembled the blanket, using it to make a crude pack with everything she had. The sailors stood watching her. When she was ready, they took her along the hallway but paused to take Maz from his cell, directing him to follow Lucy's example. So he wasn't invisible to them right now, she supposed. She thought he would be saving his magic very carefully now, ready to spend it when it was time.

They came out of the cramped stairway into the sea air and were hit by the stench of coppery blood and spent musket powder.

On the island's beach, the sailors were dragging bodies, a dozen altogether perhaps, into a heap near what looked like a campsite, made just a little ways above the water line, near the stairway that led up into the tower.

A little sloop bobbed beside the much larger pirate vessel, its flag that of the College of Mages. Lucy heard Maz make a sound at the sight of that flag, an indrawn breath, but he did not speak, and failed to retreat into obscurity.

The sky was relentlessly blue overhead. The sun blazed, reflected off the white sand, and making the scarlet blood trails as vivid as though freshly dyed. Two sailors were going through the tents, pulling out crates and bags and dumping their contents out onto the sand in order to rummage through them.

The sailor pointed and they descended the rope ladder to the tiny dock. Jusuf was overseeing the labor. He glanced up as they approached, and indicated the piles scattered on the sand.

"You will need gear, as though you will be going camping," he said. "There is an abundance of it there. Outfit yourself with whatever you need, but remember you will be carrying it, and some of our food as well."

Lucy was not looking at him but at the pile of corpses. Their eyes stared back at her. They were mostly young, perhaps a few years older than she, but a handful were older. All were dressed informally, as though ready for labor. Sshe could see where they had been digging in the sand near the stairs, uncovering the eroded lines of carving there, almost indistinguishable among the worm tracks and thickly clustered barnacles.

Jusuf reached out and took her chin between thumb and forefinger, pulling her gaze back to him. "Do not look at those, little bird," he said, far too gently for a man who had just overseen the killing of others. "Go and find what you need. Remember a waterskin." His dark eyes were shiny with an emotion she could not read.

The captain wheeled to face the pirates. "It's time, my squaddies. A few to stay up here, those as has difficulties with deep places. They'll watch over things and get an equal share, same's the rest of you. He pointed at the three. "You, Matty. And Karel and Thien.

You'll be the watch." The two men and woman he'd indicated nodded and went below to gather their supplies.

"According to the Sorcerer, it'll take a while for the Tower to know you," the captain said to Lucy. "We'll stay here tonight."

They climbed the slippery stairs, overgrown with wet yellow weed ribbed with shadowy purple. At the entrance they paused, gazing inward. There was no interior to the Tower, just a vast upward stretch. A narrow, unrailed staircase spiraled along the inside, leading upwards. They headed into the middle, where a black pit marked where a similar staircase led down into the earth.

Lucy and Maz were dumped unceremoniously to one side like unwanted baggage while the rest went about setting up camp. A few seemed to know what they were doing, but it seemed as though for many of them, life on dry land was something unexpected and a little unnatural.

Two of the sailors built a fire of scavenged driftwood beside the pit. They set a small pot amid the flames, which boiled with merry abandon, smelling of steeping double-fin and onions.

A crew worked methodically, setting a growing series of packs beside the hole in the center. The packs were canvas, straps holding useful extras such as ropes, bandoliers of torches, and small rock picks. Under different circumstances Lucy would have admired the neat efficiency and ingenuity with which they had been put together.

Another sailor came from the ship, bringing a narrow wooden chest to the captain. Opening it, he took out silken bands, each mounted with a slippery gray soapstone disk. He passed them out to everyone except Maz and Lucy but tied one on her. Like the rest, he wore his fastened around his head, the stone disk resting flat against his forehead.

"I have been exploring and researching this Tower for over a decade," he said. "While many chambers will not open except to the Pot King's blood, since he was the last person to bind energies here, there are others that can be explored. Many hold sorcerous energies that play upon one's spirit—these disks absorb the effulgences but can hold only so much. So to find these pools of invisible, noxious influences, we use captives, just as miners use canaries in mines to signal deadly gas. Should you," he nodded towards Maz, "fall prey to the energies and seek to destroy yourself, we will know we are in the presence of such, and hurry on."

"That is the usual sign?" Maz asked.

"A few have managed to hurl themselves into the pit that lies at the center and fall for we do not know how long."

Lucy shivered. She could feel a cold serpent of fear coiling at her belly. She had thought things were bad enough before, but here they were getting even worse, and in a way that was clearly leading to her death. Her eyes welled with uncontrollable tears; her own body was betraying her, refusing to let her be spared the wracking of her emotions.

"There is no need to expose her to all this," Maz said.

"Who?"

He pointed at Lucy with his chin. "I'm the Pot King's son. She's an innocent who got swept up in your plot unawares."

The captain frowned, looking between them. "You're just trying to make yourself less expendable, at her benefit."

"Your men got confused," Maz insisted. "They took the two of us instead of one, because our auras overlapped."

Jusuf stared at him, then shook his head. "We'll take both and see who falls prey to the energies first," he said, removing Lucy's disk. "A Sorcerer will have enough training to overcome the worst effects. But in the morning. We'll sleep here overnight before going down at dawn, in order to use the daylight as long as we can."

He looked around at the sailors. "Set up my tent, and another for a set of guards." His glance fell on Lucy. "The prisoners can sleep out here as well, rather than stay on the ship. It's not like they will be going anywhere, after all."

Another turtle was brought and butchered on the sand, and they cut it into chunks and used the vast shell to cook the broth in, and they had biscuits made by winding strips of dough in circles on flat rocks among the ashes as they began to accumulate.

They drank watered wine, but neither of the prisoners were allowed any. Afterwards several of the pirates sang and another played a cittern, and they all sang a couple more songs and then the evening was done and everyone retired.

Lucy did not feel that she slept at all through that long night, though whenever she looked through one of the high arched windows, she could see that the stars had assumed new patterns, showing her a different slice of the glittering night sky that stretched outside.

The inside of the tower roared with the waves' murmur, magnifying it into a steady throbbing at the back of her head. She had been given an actual bedroll this time, rather than the worn blanket she'd previously used, and by contrast it felt as luxurious as a goose down mattress underneath her, but she was too tired and tightly coiled deep inside to even think of sleeping, nor did she feel like she ever would.

She strained her ears, listening for noises from the depths of the hole. Maz was restless too. In the early hours she was roused from what she would have sworn was a wakeful state by clamor. His restless thrashings had knocked a supply pack over the side. The captain swore at him but kept his voice down.

I can't do this anymore, Lucy thought, filled with despair at the anger in his words. *I can't get up in the morning and go down into that pit.*

Tears leaked from her eyes, and a shudder passed through her as the waves cried out again.

There's no choice, she realized. *They won't listen to my refusals. It's not like escaping a school day by claiming stomachache.*

She thought of the people she'd known and what they would have done in the face of all of this, but, in the end, they were simply too real to her for her to predict what they would do and so she retreated into Mary Silverhands. SLike Lucy, Mary had no choice; she simply endured and did the best she could.

There was something calming about that thought, as though resignation to her fate plucked away all its terror. The others would be with her; they would have lights. It would have been an entirely different thing if they planned on sending her down by herself, or even if they had planned to hook her and Maz together and send them both down at once.

She had wanted—well, maybe not adventure on this level, but something other than Tabat. Something that set her apart from her sisters, showed that she was better than them, no matter how much they had picked on her, how much they had acted out their hatred and blame for their mother's death.

Which was unfair! The riot had killed her, not Lucy. At the time it had happened, she'd been at the Gladiator match with the man who had rescued her when she had been lost, Sebastiano Silver-cloth. In retrospect, she realized now that she could have—and should have—asked Sebastiano to send a messenger to her home, but the truth was that such a thing had never occurred to her.

There were all these things you were supposed to know, without anyone telling you. And that was also utterly unfair.

If she were in charge of things, the world would be very different. Very different indeed. All the people that had been so unfair—her brother Eloquence, and her six sisters, and Adelina Nittlescent, who had released her from service, thinking that she had stolen from her, when she hadn't! And Seraphina, Adelina's secretary, who could have spoken on her behalf and hadn't.

And Sebastiano Silvercloth, who hadn't thought to send a messenger himself, and he was an adult and should've known better. All of them would've gotten what was coming to them. All of this city, the unfair city, full of people who didn't care what happened to her, who stood by while she was kidnapped!

She turned over in the bedroll. There was a layer of sand over the rock, but it was hardly soft. She'd thought the flooring aboard the ship was bad enough, but this was worse, and she didn't know how anyone was managing to sleep. She opened her eyes and gazed at the fire that crackled only a handful of feet away. Captain Jusuf was awake and sitting up beside it, talking with one of the sailors. As she watched, he leaned over to poke another log into the center of the fire's circle, and she watched how the light played along his skin.

He was so beautiful. He was perhaps the most beautiful man she had ever seen. Her sisters would have agreed, would have run around giggling and flirting and trying to catch his attention. That was never anything that had interested Lucy. In fact it had even repelled her when sometimes visitors, like Canumbra and Legio, seemed to be looking at her that way.

Was this what being in love was? She didn't trust the captain and she wasn't even sure that she liked him, but she liked to look at him. Liked to listen to his voice. She didn't know what his accent was. She had never heard anything like it before, the little sing-a-song twist he put on the ends of words. As though you were speaking songs, songs that she had never heard before.

As she thought all this, he looked up and caught her eye. She felt the blood rush to her cheeks as he smiled at her.

"Go to sleep, little bird," he said. "Morning will come soon enough." The sailor beside him muttered something and he cuffed the man, then spoke again to Lucy. "Go to sleep."

And so she did.

CHAPTER 32

*I*n the morning, they started down: Lucy, Maz, the captain, and five of the sailors. The ones left behind waved farewell. They had been left with supplies by the captain, including flasks of wine, "to drink health to the success of the journey," he had said.

The party were all roped together as they proceeded down the stairway: a sailor, then Maz, another sailor, Lucy, then yet another sailor, then the captain, then two more sailors bringing up the rear. The walls were unadorned and slick with salty moisture.

The nightmarish, narrow part seemed to continue for hours but eventually they came to a place where tunnels led off in every direction, allowing them to make camp and sleep. The captain told Maz that he might explore. The boy took a torch and headed into the darkness. His pace was quick and eager, untired where the rest ached with weariness.

A rope trailed after the captain and back up towards the top. It led to a small windlass that had been set up beside the hole with sailors to watch over it.

"We may be a while down here," he explained to Lucy. She sat a few feet away from the pit's edge, watching the darkness while the sailors built a fire and set water boiling for tea. "And it will be easier to have them lower supplies than have someone go fetching and carrying along the staircase."

"We might be down here for days?" Lucy asked, dismayed. The oppressive darkness dampened her spirits.

"In two more circles of the rim, we will have come as deep as I ever have. There is a closed doorway that I think will open to the Pot King's blood. But who knows what lies beyond it, or how long it will take to wrestle the magic free?" He laughed. "Perhaps when all is said and done, we'll come flying up out of the pit, hovering on great wings like falcons before we burst out across the Isles in glory and splendor."

Lucy continued to watch the darkness.

"So you are not the Pot King's son?" he asked.

She shook her head. "Just a girl," she said.

"Ah," he said. "Just a girl."

The silence stretched out between them.

"Do you know why going into the earth's heart is so perilous?" he asked.

"Why?"

"Down there, we are closer to the bones of sorcery. Emotions go awry and thoughts can damage you. So it is best to be calm down here, to avoid emotional extremes." His voice was strained. "Satisfying lust, for one."

"Oh," she said. And then, "Oh!"

He stooped to whisper, "But when we are back on the surface, just a girl, we will speak of this again." He turned and went to oversee the sailors as they prepared the meal.

I am not invisible to him, she thought. Back home she was used to her sisters drawing men's stares, used to their gaze passing over her absently. But Jusuf Miryam's green eyes saw her, every inch of her. She smiled to herself.

CHAPTER 33

AN ISLAND (BELLA)

*B*runa comes to us near midnight with their decision. She will take us to Margolees because they will not force us.

"But there you will find it only leads you to where we would have sent you," she tells me. "You will regret this choice."

Trust a Dragon? I count myself simply lucky that they have not chosen to enforce their will.

IT WOULD HAVE BEEN splendid to arrive via Dragon back, the sort of entrance you can make once in a lifetime. I have made many, but never one like that. It is cheering to think about all the entrances I have made, in fact, and that there will probably be some still to come.

But we do not wish to draw attention to ourselves, and so Bruna flies out in the darkest hours of the night, and puts us near the port, out of sight of it, but only a few hours' travel east and north.

I trust the Dragon not to put us down near any late-night fishing boats, of the sort that we see as we fly over the port's edge, little boats each holding a lantern at the top of their highest mast, little globes of light floating among the answering waves, so every light is surrounded by watery trails.

It is cold high in the air, and it would be smartest to go below deck while the Dragon is carrying our boat, but instead, we dress in several layers, Scylla and I, and Teo huddles between the two of us with a blanket I have draped around his form.

The two of us peer over the railing to see the world as few Humans are privileged to see it: the maze of lantern lanes that marks the port, and the lights of a few farms around that. Other than that, everything is in shadow and you can only tell farmland from jungle by texture in the intermittent islands. The white moon is high in the sky and its light lies on my skin like a caress, like soothing water after sunburn, like the promise of comfort to come. Its light dances on the water.

Scylla points out a thing or two, but mostly we are silent, watching the water flit by, as fast as though we were galloping full tilt, maybe faster, driven by the Dragon's speed. It is not impatient, but it is efficient, and it has other things to do. We took on fresh water and fruit at the island, and I smoked a little of the pig meat, so we are full stomached as well, down to drinking the last bottle of wine aboard.

Soon, far too soon, the Dragon swoops, lets us down into the water as gently as she can, although we cling to the railing none-theless for the shudder of impact, and I brace Teo against it with my leg to keep him from skidding away.

The water receives us, though not without some rocking at first, the water and the boat establishing their mutual accord. Without another word, the Dragon's dark shadow flits away from us and rockets upward into the vast and shimmering starry sky.

Here in the Isles, those stars are like nowhere else, so close against the sky's velvety depths, the white moon rolling in those shimmering waters as though pleasuring herself in a pool … ah, it has been far too long since I have lain in someone's bed, that I am having lascivious thoughts about the moon!

If this were not such an urgent time, I'd draw Scylla downstairs and act on these achings, fresh in a way I had not thought would come again, as though the Duke's prison was what it should be by now—a memory, and one lacking the iron grip it had once held. But there is plenty to do, and so we work together to set the sails and head in towards the port.

The wind is carrying us towards our destination for the first two hours. But when we are almost there, it shifts back, the fickle thing. Suddenly we're awash in the harbor smells of fish and smoke and people-stink, so sudden and thick that Teo barks as though he's smelled cats.

Then, just as quickly, the wind shifts again. Now we are sailing towards the masses of lights that mark the harbor. Some are fading now as the horizon lightens, the first sign of the sun stirring. The white moon is pale, washed out. She rests near the horizon as though keeping a proprietary eye on us, while Toj peers from high above.

The music of the dawn bells and their lilting calls to prayer call out, shouting, "Come celebrate the day to come, that which begins," as we swing in between the two high ridges that guard either side of the bay.

Each is surmounted by a sky-pointing tower of solid masonry, limestone quarried from further inland, each crowned with a battery of cannons. Margolees is a trade port, and it boasts some of Tabat's armaments as well as the soldiers to back that up. Despite the sometimes-deadly summer fevers that make port life miserable, most reckon this a desirable posting, particularly since the forts are usually above the line where such fevers breed and seethe.

There is trade aplenty here in the Isles. Many young Merchants posted here will later serve as advisors and consultants to the houses that make their living through the trade that flows through island ports: fabric and dyes, spices and sweeteners, liqueurs and fruits. Not to mention the trade that we have come to sample, the trade that very few will admit to, the trade in ancient magic.

Adelina explained it to me thus: once there were people who came before us, so long ago that all record of them has been lost, other than sometimes accounts of legends already ancient at the time they were inscribed. Those people were powerful, they did beautiful and terrible things, and they split the world open for their amusement, and then they flew away on wings that built themselves of the last fires at the earth's heart.

And when they were gone, some people came out of the wreckage and the sorrow and the ashes, and they were the Humans who were left behind and who rebuilt the lands so they were all fresh and green again.

"Except the Old Continent," I said, but she shook her head at me.

"Even the Old Continent," she insisted, "because this was from a time before the Sorcerers despoiled it, when the world was green and new a second time."

"How can something be new a second time?" I ask.

"Things are new again all the time," she says. "Every spring—that's something you of all people should know well."

That truth hits me now like a stone, even though one she hadn't meant to throw. One whose irony I didn't realize at the time.

Yes, I had been Champion of Tabat, and every spring I acted out the ritual battle that let me take its magic. I didn't know it. No one knew it. No one had been Champion enough years in succession to begin to accrue such magic, to take on the armor that had made me unbeatable.

At least—until someone attacked me on that very thing, the magic that made me invincible, and stripped away the circumstances that let me draw on it.

I feel that lack every morning, feel it when I move, when I sit down and feel a snap and sizzle in my back, a twinge that doesn't bode well unless I go stand and stretch and move around the deck. I avoided aging for all those years and now it is sidling up again.

Can an ancient magic force it to step away once more just as the Dragons promise?

I glimpse a tower whose roof is green glazed tiles, imported from Tabat.

I point it out to Scylla. "That is where we are bound for."

"The University?" she says with interest. "I'd always meant to come down to see it. It seems more accessible than going to scurry about being called a Beast in Tabat. We should try a tavern first and listen to what the students say about its recent doings."

"A good notion," I say. "And a chance to drink."

Her look is canny. "But not to flirt too much, because that would draw attention to yourself."

"It might be the best way to find out things," I say.

"The most enjoyable for you."

"Actually, I was thinking you would flirt, and I would catch the broken hearts strewn in your wake," I say with the smoothness I have ever been known for. For a moment I am back to myself, the old Bella Kanto. She sees it too. She bites her lip to avoid smiling, but still only grumbles something.

We tie up to one side, a dock reserved for smaller ships like ourselves, and pay a sleepy dockmistress for a ticket entitling us to two days' stay before we must pay again. Scylla names the ship the *Dizzy Bee* and ourselves as Galatina Corklick and Elba Spumewit, business partners come to speculate in medicinal herbs.

Despite my thoughts on the silliness of the names, it is a well-thought out and plausible accounting. She even holds papers to back it, carried in the fish-skin pouch at her belt. All I do is stay back, as she's directed me. While it's been years since I have been in these isles, I am still the notorious Bella Kanto, still the hero of so many books across the Known World, including the libraries and bookstalls of the Southern Isles.

But this dockmistress shows no sign of recognizing me, and the business is done soon, and the port stamp affixed in the counterfeit logbook that Scylla presents.

"What now?" I ask as we step outside. Dawn is fully broken now, washing over Margolees, and the last of the night fishers are coming in, handfuls of them, while their day companions in their larger vessels are setting out, as are three Merchant galleons, companied by two small, fiercer ships bristling with cannon.

"We should find an inn and sleep for now," Scylla says. "And then go to the student tavern where the news is thick, in order to learn as much as we can." She frowns at me.

"What?" I say.

"You are too distinctive," she says.

I cannot help but smirk at that. "I am as the Gods have shaped me," I say.

She rolls her eyes. "And as you have been portrayed in penny-wide after penny-wide, it is a shape with which many are acquainted." She makes a face. "Though you are broader in the hip than you used to be and more long-nosed."

"I beg your pardon!" I say. At some point during the evening, I will have to purchase new travel kit, including a little mirror, in order to find out what changes might have resulted in such words. I have been aging, I know that, but surely it is not too echoed in my outer form yet.

She chooses not to argue the point, although not in a way that promises that the argument is closed. "No matter what," she says, "Your hair—even grown out as it is now—is distinctive." She fishes around in her pouch and hands me a kerchief. "Tie it up in that."

I cede her point by using the fabric to tie my hair away from my face, obscuring it. She has me keep my face ducked until we pass a stall of straw hats, where she insists on purchasing one with an enormous shadowy brim that curtains my face effectively although it also hampers my vision. I let her pull me along through the streets of Margolees as morning brings everyone to life and they become increasingly crowded and noisy.

At the crossing of two streets, vendors are setting up food carts, but Scylla presses on, despite my slowing to look significantly at the food. It is less that I need it—the Dragons fed us well enough—but this is city food, full of fat and sizzle and crunch of the kind one does not encounter on a boat or at a Dragon's fire.

Does any Beast respect food as we do? Jolietta kept old Bebe to serve as cook, but Jolietta also had not cared about food, except as it could be used as punishment or motivation. That might be what lay at the heart of this urge—ever since I finally came to Tabat, I've associated certain tastes with freedom and having left the rigors and misery of Piper Hill behind, and these vendors both promise such food.

Still I sigh and follow Scylla's straight-backed form through the waxing crowds, Teo in turn at my heels. I was last in this port over a decade ago. It is amusing to see how it has grown, a swelling fed entirely by the trade served by the port.

Or perhaps not entirely. I catch a glimpse of the tower again through the crowds.

The University had no southern outpost here until Alberic sponsored this endeavor, around the time that he last sent me down here. I carried with me the plans for this set of buildings, that tile-roofed tower.

Scylla is looking at it. "But how tiny it looks from this angle!" she exclaims, ignoring the scowl of an old man passing by who chooses to take this as a personal criticism.

"That is for their stargazing, and there's another for their devices of the air, on the other side," I tell her.

The streets wind back and forth, though, and sometimes we are forced to turn down alleys, something I might have feared more in Tabat. Winters are not a thing here. There is no cold or rain, and fruit enough to eat, fish enough to cook, can be pulled from the trees and waters close at hand, so many end up here in this hospitable place.

Sometimes the ships come hunting sailors, and it does not do to be unwary in their path, but most of the town's unhoused inhabitants know enough to go to ground on such nights and escape the man-catchers that patrol for drunks in the morning's early hours.

Down near the docks is Prophets' Row, and the catchers never come there, because they know slaves taken from those ranks are usually more trouble than they are worth. We go along that roadway now, and Scylla says, "If I had more coins, I'd stop and have them read our fortune."

"No one can know what is to come," I say automatically. It is the heresy most argued by those who follow the Trade Gods as well as the moons. If someone can know the future, then their fate is immovable, unchangeable.

We're in the right place to discuss it. Philosophy students can argue for days on such things. Every university has its hangers-on, its people who live on its outskirts, and this place is no different, full of chal shops and stores full of books and parchments.

She shrugs and takes us to engage a room at a Mer tavern, a place that overhangs a dock, with a sturdy rope laddering that enables some clientele to come and go from beneath. She pays for a room overlooking the water and elbows me when I would have protested the extravagance of the cost.

I roll my eyes, playing the part of a Merchant partner concerned about an expedition's purse. I hope this is what she meant me to do; if it was to stand back and let her beggar us, then she has chosen wrongly.

We leave our duffels in the room and go out into the streets. It is full daylight now and my stomach rumbles. She will not let me approach the meat-pie cart with her but insists on leaving me loitering in the shade of my hat beneath an awning, like some flower doubly afraid of the sun, an unspoken assertion that makes me itch with impatience.

The pie that she returns with does assuage some of my indignation, makes me feel better about things overall in a way that makes me realize that at least half my temper before was caused by hunger.

This pie is flaky and rich—while there is not much meat in it, what there is oily and full of flavor, soaked in a spicy sauce that makes my lips tingle, and the chunks of tuber that are the rest of the filling are soft and tasty, the flesh fragrant with amberspice, which does not last more than a day or two, so you never taste it anywhere but here.

I take the first few bites quickly, almost ferociously, but slow after those, letting myself taste the spice. It's been a long time, but I've remembered this spice in my dreams, or not so much the spice itself but the sensation of missing it, wanting it, without being able to remember exactly what it had tasted like. There is nothing else like it in the world, like meat and honey and sky sewn together with pepper.

Scylla meets my eye with a grin, and I am reminded why I

stayed so long with her, why I thought about staying longer, because she is so unafraid to show her pleasure in this simple thing.

In Tabat people are sophisticated in their palates. No one is more conscious of such things than the Merchants, who always fear they will be found vulgar.

Even Adelina, who was better about it by far than most of them, had her self-conscious moments, the moments that felt as though they had been borrowed from someone she had seen and been impressed by as a child or teen. They were moments I disliked because I remembered being part of them myself at one point. Before I had become Bella Kanto, *the* Bella Kanto, and had no need of such things anymore.

Scylla is herself and unworried about being anything else. Maybe it is just the result of the fact that she is far from home, that she knows that no one here will report her doings, her demeanor, to her family, that she cannot be penalized or thought outrageous or injudicious. She would have to return to the Long Slow City at some point, but she could enjoy anonymity till then, which was why she was hoping for mine. We could be free together for a day or two before moving on, and I found myself wanting those hours as much as she did, maybe even more so.

It had been so long. Even the last few happy years in Tabat had felt fraught, had been full of those folks who were unhappy that Spring stayed away so many extra weeks each year, kept at bay by the fight that I fought with Spring's Champion each year, in which Spring always, inevitably lost.

Until now.

CHAPTER 34

FIREAH (LUCY)

The darkness waited all around them, and whenever a lantern flickered, it pressed inward, insistent as an unanswered question. They climbed in silence, the sailors' chatter washed away. Two burly sailors went first, then Captain Jusuf, with Lucy walking beside him, then another sailor yanking along a silent and sullen Maz, and then another two sailors after that, laden with the bulk of the supplies.

Even with their stalwart labor, the rest of them carried packs as well, all except the captain and the two lead sailors, although Lucy's pack was not too heavy, and she thought it perhaps more for show and to keep the others from grumbling.

Because they did grumble sometimes, when they looked at her. She wasn't sure exactly what they were saying to each other in low whispers, whispers always cut short by Jusuf's glare.

"They think you're unlucky," Maz said that night as they crouched together, eating the bread and dried meat that had been allotted them.

Lucy was savoring her waterskin, swallow by swallow, using it to force down the dry food, knowing that if she didn't, she'd feel the worse for it the next day. She felt grim and grownup as she tore away a thread of salty and unidentifiable meat with her teeth, then took a half mouthful of water, holding the tepid liquid in her mouth and pretending that there was more of it.

She didn't reply to Maz. He'd lost her trust and she was no longer going to pretend otherwise.

"Unlucky," he repeated into the face of her silence. "Because you're a child. The Trade Gods don't approve of risking children."

Lucy reflected that this would seem to be an advantage that the Trade Gods had over the Moon Temples, who seemed much more unconcerned with the welfare of the children in its care, but it was a different part of the assertion that snagged her irritation enough to tug words out of her. "I'm not a child."

"A mere girl," he said with enough relish to make her regret rising to the bait. "The Trade Gods will punish them, and Profit turn her face away from the venture."

"Don't pretend that you believe in them yourself," she snapped.

"Of course not," he said, and lowered his voice. "There are no Gods other than what we make of ourselves, my father says, and he …" He broke off, swallowing the words.

"He …?" she tried to prompt him, but he shook his head.

"It's what the sailors believe that matters. Maybe they will throw you and the fine captain down the pit and insist on returning to the surface."

"They will not!" she said hotly.

They had been speaking too quietly for the others, some distance away and holding their own conversation, to hear, or so Lucy judged. But her exclamation caught Jusuf's attention.

"Be quiet over there," he said, "or we will separate you to keep you from plotting." He sat facing her, his hands resting on his knees, the fine leather boots crossed at the ankles. The tiny fire that crackled and whispered in the center of his group lit his face from below, made it unrecognizable for a moment.

Her lips dry, she took another swallow out of sequence, before gnawing again at the gritty bread.

"Unlucky," Maz whispered. "Better stay awake. They might come for you in your sleep otherwise."

DESPITE HIS WARNING, sleep took her immediately, dragged her down into a pit darker than the world surrounding them, and it seemed like only minutes later that a sailor's toe against her ribs nudged her back into weary wakefulness. She'd taken her boots off to sleep and putting them back on felt raw and painful and swollen. She arranged them as best she could and shrugged on the rest of her gear.

She still felt grim and grown up. And alone. So very alone.

CHAPTER 35

MARGOLEES (BELLA)

*W*hen I was last here, this bar had a different name, but otherwise it is much the same. Its scope is constrained by the building whose lowest floor it occupies. Short of stretching out to claim rooms in nearby buildings, it cannot grow any further. They have managed to cram more furniture within its confines, of a certainty. Nowadays those at one table rub elbow to elbow with the occupants of the next, and the servers are adept at stepping around and hovering, contorting themselves in awkward angles to keep from colliding with diners or other servers.

You are meant to order spirits here, and even the current name reflects that, The Parched Cockatrice. There is a minimum of food, mostly skewers of roasted meats, but a variety of liquids to suit the throats of those who have sharpened their palates across the world, at other islands, other continents.

We maneuver around two tables, following the server's finger, then sit where he indicates. Teo slithers under the table to avoid all the crisscrossing feet, slumps down over my boots with a huff of relief. The servitor asks our pleasure and Scylla says something complicated, while I simply say, "red wine, recent pressing." He scurries off.

We're conveniently in a corner, able to case the room. There are several tables in earshot, and I can see Scylla appraising them one by one: the table of female Merchants nearest me, arguing about bulk pricing; the large table of what looks like a family crew, all aunts and uncles and cousins, the youngest boys and one of the girls flirting with the server at their table until an older man snaps something. They all fix their attention on the dishes in front of them, although the boldest, the girl, still winks once before dropping her attention to her meal.

Three military captains, all older—a woman and two men—near us but not talking much, their attention devoted primarily to the meal in front of them. It takes me a moment to cipher out their uniforms until I see the sigil for teacher and realize that all must be instructors at the University there in town. Alberic had always planned to make the Universities the places where his officers came from, back before he had known about the prophecy that would eventually depose me.

A pair from the Rose Kingdom, their robes marked clearly as law requires, but sitting by themselves, unobtrusive. I shift myself back into the shadows rather than let them see me—the Rose Kingdom still has an interest in my whereabouts, and if I am ever found on their soil again, there are certain things they deemed criminal in nature that have yet to be answered for.

"This was a bad idea," I murmur to Scylla, and flick my eyes towards them.

She shrugs. "It is hopeless that no one will recognize you. Instead we will work on rumor spreading. Talk pleasantly to me of the expedition on which the Duke has sent you, in order to escort some valuable cargo."

I raise my voice. "... The medicinal teas, you mean? Truly, they are a thing for which his Grace holds high hopes, for the doctor who has assembled them swears that they are efficacious against the summer fevers, to the point where she has brought the entirety of her family, including a child of less than three summers, to live down here, so confident is she in the strength of it."

She makes her eyes go wide. It makes me want to smack her,

this degree of overacting, but I dare not stop now that we have set things in motion.

"That must truly be a valuable thing!" she warbles, every note an insincerity. "No doubt all sorts of dangerous folk would like to waylay such an innovation in order to use it for their own."

In actuality, the people down here are sensible enough that they would have done whatever was needed in order to make sure that the innovation survived enough that it could be perpetuated. Island folk are sensible, after all. It was in Tabat that people got overly greedy and thought that because fortunes came out of the islands, they must be scraped to the bone, despite everything that the Trade Gods said about such parsimonious and shortsighted practices.

But I play along. "No doubt, and so they have sent me to guide the packages, which are very small, to require such warding." I add the last before she is tempted to make it so I am carting around decoy crates as part of this addle-brained scheme of hers.

"I look forward to working with you," she says inanely, and raises the glass that the server has brought, tipping it to clink against mine.

We both drink. Mine is serviceable, more than serviceable after the sour wine of the raft city. I take another gulp and another, savoring the tang of it against my tongue.

"Don't set yourself reeling," Scylla warns. I scoff at her.

"Teach your mother to give suck," I say, quite rudely. For a second I don't know whether or not she will take offense at that, but in the end, she simply laughs at me.

"Another drink here," she says, "and then I will go and find a student who may teach us."

The second drink goes down quickly, along with several little skewers of roasted meat and peppers, bright and spicy enough to make me lick my lips and drink even faster. We have not been drinking much on the boat, and moreover my body is probably losing its facility with alcohol, as it has lost so much of its ability over the past few months.

Tables of students are scattered through the room. Were she and I ever that young? There are plenty of older students and those who serve the University here, but there are also so many so young that they look like children in a way they never have before. They seem such feckless, foolish things, chattering like sparrows, preening like peacocks.

Scylla winnows through the crowd, and I see her asking a question here and there, following a pointed finger to one table, and a gesture from there to another. She returns with someone in tow.

I'm relieved to see it's not one of the beardless children, but a youth with a decade on those, at least. He has the look of a northerner, once-pale skin now ruddied and toughened by the fierce sun down here. Give him another decade and he'll be wrinkled into brown leather.

"This is Stalkal," Scylla says. "He studies here at the College, focuses on magical artifacts."

"Are you treasure hunters then?" he says with cheerful curiosity as he sits down. Scylla puts down a clay pitcher of ale and mugs to match that she has taken from a passing server.

"Never you mind what we are," she says with equal cheer. "We're the two as is buying you drinks."

I don't recognize the reference, but the two of them laugh.

He's studying me with that same curiosity. "I've seen you before," he says, but it takes him a long moment before he places me. His eyes widen. Some exclamation springs to his lips, but he bites it back, making me respect him more, that he knows how to keep his silence.

"Tell us why the University has such a division," Scylla says. "I was told it's because there's many sites within the Isles that have such things."

"Not as many as there once was, but, overall, you have been told rightly," he says, picking up his mug for a gulp before leaning forward. "There are a good two dozen within a few days' sail, mostly to the south and east of us. Most of those are very small, but they find new ones all the time."

"What sort of artifacts do they discover?"

"Mostly things that do nothing but impart some knowledge of the ancient days, scroll gems or story-scraps."

"But sometimes more."

"Rarely more, and always heavily guarded, perilous. They explore them with great expeditions. They are working on one right now, to explore an area recently mapped where it had been only rumored, Fireah. They have already got folks working there, while they prepare the bulk of the expedition."

"Will you be on that expedition?"

He shakes his head. With a little bitterness, he says, "I can't afford it. That sort of expedition will give one credentials and so only those who can buy a share in it will go."

"That seems a system that does not work well," Scylla observes.

He spits. "Merchant children, the more dunderheaded the better, are sent down here to laze about and pretend to learn until it's time for them to return home."

Scylla and I exchange glances. I find myself calculating. That sort of anger, that sort of bitterness, can be used, but it's also a knife that can turn in the hand. Soul-deep hatreds are chancy, and the holder will always listen to those hatreds over the importunings of reason or logic.

Still. You use the tools that come to you, as they come to you, or else you are ill-prepared for existence in this universe. For now, we need to be as practical and pragmatic as ever Jolietta was.

"When is the expedition due to leave?" I ask.

"Two weeks from now. They are waiting for scientific equipment to come down from Tabat, special machines that will help them read the air and the levels of magic."

"What do they expect to find down there?"

He shrugs. "It could be all manner of things. Machines constructed millennia ago or raw magic, waiting to be shaped. Equally likely, or unlikely would be more preferable. Ancient magic holds all sorts of curses simmering in its surface."

"What do you mean?" Scylla asks. "Are there legends of cursed weapons?"

"There are things that one does not think are weapons, but which turn out to be," he says. "Rods that turn in the hand and shoot missiles, armor that takes over the wearer's mind and gives them uncanny powers."

I scoff. "Fairy tales."

Scylla gives me a look. I have to concede that I should not be scoffing at thoughts of magic, not I who have ridden a wave created for me by magic for decades now.

"All right," I begrudge. "How can you tell when something is cursed to turn on its user?"

"That's the point," he says. "It seems as though all of it is created in order to turn in such a manner, as though every dagger were shaped to collapse back to cut the hand that holds it."

"That is overly flowery," Scylla says in a severe tone, and he blushes. "What chapter of your dissertation is it from?"

"The third," he mumbles, his cheeks blushing a red that had not yet been evoked by the avid sun. "I am talking specifically about cursed weapons, rather than cursed things, but the truth be told, it is more accurate to say that *everything* that comes out of the ruins is cursed than to say weapons that come out of it are cursed."

"Mmmm," Scylla says. The look she gives me grants full permission to tease the pompous little toad, but, at the same time, I find myself reluctant to act on her permission. It will only alienate him.

But he says something before I can summon up the sort of language that I need.

"Look," he says, and leans forward even closer, so close that I can smell the garlic and cumin on his breath from that afternoon's dinner. "You want to go on a dig beforehand, yeah? That's your only real chance to find anything before the University expedition catalogues every inch, packs up every treasure. I'm sympathetic to that desire. And I know some of the people already there. They're, well, bribable. And once I'm there, they won't turn me away. I'll be part of things. You help get me on the expedition and I'll slip you enough ancient loot that you'll be able to buy an estate back home. It won't be that hard, and, once it's done, you'll be comfortably well off and never have to worry about money again."

"What do we need to do?" I ask.

"Tomorrow morning I'll introduce you to a friend of mine in

the engineering department. She can get us to Fireah. But once we're there, it's to you and your resources to talk them out of turning us away. Think you can do that?"

"I can try," I tell him. Scylla smirks.

The evening is growing old by the time that Scylla and I walk back to the inn. She goes up before me, and I say, "I am walking off a little booze yet, but I will be up soon." She is drunken herself, and too sleepy to protest, and so I go back out into the street.

All three moons have risen. It is one of those rare nights when they make things almost as bright as daylight, but a different color altogether, one born of the purple and red and white light mingling.

I walk along slowly, and when I come to a little park, I stand there listening to the night. Finally the footstep that I have been listening for grates behind me, and I turn to face her.

Questions spring to my lips, demands for information burn in my throat. But when I see her, all of this dies away and there is only a beautiful, icy stillness, an answer to a question I have been asking all my life, one that drove me ever onward even though I did not realize I was saying it with all my being, until now when she is here.

As before she is beautiful and slender as the white moon, and she wears red and purple ribbons in her hair, winding through it like the moonlight braiding itself.

She says, "You want to ask me how it is that I have come here."

I say, "How is it that you have come here?"

She says, "You want to ask me if I have been following you." Her dimple is deep, teasing me.

I say, teasing back, "Have you been following me?"

"Always," she breathes out. "You know who I am."

"You are Selene," I say.

"I am."

"You are the white moon come down from the sky to kiss me," I say. I do not know if I am flirting and do not mean it, or whether a terrible and glorious realization has come upon me that either this is full madness or none of this has been a dream, and the moon herself has come down from the sky in order to flatter me and tease me and distract me from everything else with the lushness of her lips, with the black glimmer of her eyes, with the smell of her, like the earliest flowers of the spring, the ones that you must hunt for, that you cannot smell unless you find them and pluck them and bring them to your nose, and then they smell like winter saying goodbye to spring.

"I am the white moon," she agrees, "Come down from the sky."

She leans forward and there I am, standing on a dark street in a port, and the moon is kissing me and all I can think of is that Adelina would never believe it. That she would never agree to write this tale. Because who in the world would credit such a thing?

CHAPTER 36

FIREAH (LUCY)

The deeper they went, the angrier Lucy grew. It was a slow smoldering heat that seemed to gather in her eyes, making them hot and watery. It was a feeling that slowly grew around the seed of self-pity that Maz had planted in her soul.

The walls of the cavern did not seem natural; as they went deeper and deeper into the earth, though, the lines grew more subtly curved, as though they were becoming the lines of living flesh, corners diminishing, shrinking, smoothing, until there were no more corners to anything.

Jusuf did not look at her. No one did. It was unfair. It was unjust.

If only she could, she'd make them all pay.

CHAPTER 37

MARGOLEES (BELLA)

*T*he University is a pleasant enough place, made of clean limestone bricks, still rough-edged and feeling freshly cut. A little stung by Scylla's accusations that I am not observant except on rarefied occasions, I am paying attention to everything we are passing. The halls are all of them named after Alberic, a pomposity someone has justified by naming them things like "Alberic's Clear Eye," "Alberic's Beneficent Hand," "Alberic's Tireless Feet."

Scylla catches my eye as I read the last, and mouths, very clearly, "Alberic's Ever-ready Cock." I snort, audibly, so that Stalkal turns and says, "What?"

"Where are we going?" Scylla says. "Alberic's Impeccable Spleen? His Inexhaustible Buttocks?"

Stalkal grins outright. "You would fit right in at the next drinking and puns contest," he says with admiration. "Pity that we won't have time for that. No, we're going to the workshops. They got added on a couple of years ago and no one got around to naming them, because they got built by a bunch of students pooling their money and no one could agree on a good name. So everyone just calls them the workshops."

The workshops prove to be built onto the back of the building labeled, "Alberic's Vigilant Ear." They are a series of wood and mostly bamboo structures, housing a wide variety of machines. Many are clearly agricultural in their intent: planters, tillers, harvesters. Others seem more idiosyncratic, like the huge bamboo and foil winged pig that sags in one corner.

Stalkal leads us through the corridors and through a few more doorways until we stand in the largest of the workshops, a good two stories tall, all of it open space.

This is not a classroom. This is a machinist's shop, full of the smell of heating metal and the fuel that stokes the vast furnaces, red heat glowing out through the glory holes.

Several large balloons are draped on racks, baskets swaying below them. In a corner is an enormous structure made of blue silk stretched over a framework, a wickerwork casing holding it up from underneath.

There is an immense thing down at one side. At first, I think that it is a boat, because of its shape, but as we get closer, I realize that's not right.

Much of it is swathed by great canvas sheets to keep dust and metal grit away, but despite that, I can tell it is not just a boat, but a boat with wings. Vast metal ones, each feather made of stamped foil, the pattern intricate as a real feather, gleaming like a coin newly minted and ready to spend, and a balloon framework over-top, its silk colored blue and white like a summer sky where it has not been splotched black with oil or sealing tar.

Someone is working at its side, a small, squat woman in sensible, grease-stained coveralls is working on the copper and brass machinery affixed to the casing's back end, hammering at one of the leg-wheels.

"Oi, Wilda," Stalkal shouts, and she looks up from staring into the machinery to nod to us.

"This," Stalkal says proudly, "is the noted scientist Wildalenaja of the Southern Isles, which we always append, because she is one of our own, and we cannot ever acknowledge that enough. Some day she will bring fame to us all, but probably not fortune. This creature that she is working on she calls her Iron Beetle, and it flies as badly as one, buzzing from one point to another without much finesse in between."

Scylla is faster by far than I. She immediately says, "You mean for us to fly to the site, so no one under the water will know that we have come."

I am looking over the thing again with this in mind and I do not like it. It is one thing to fly while being carried by a Dragon. No one could contest a Dragon in the air. This thing, though, looks to be an entirely different matter. It is too bulky, too large, too unnatural.

The little woman has put down the large hammer with which she has been belaboring the wheel and comes over to us. Her face sparks when she looks at our guide, as though she likes him and wants to impress him. By the way he straightens at her glance, and the fact that he has brought us to her, the feeling is mutual.

That would be sweet, this little conspiracy to work together, if it did not involve having us fly through the air.

I say, "Has it been tested?

This is entirely the wrong thing to ask, because they both launch into exhaustive accounts of the testing that has occurred already, and none of it is particularly intelligible or interesting.

"It doesn't matter either way," Scylla says firmly, "because we cannot afford the cost of employing such a machine."

The two of them exchange glances, our guide and the mechanic, and one pulls the other over to the side in order to converse in whispers and fierce hisses, like two tea kettles arguing which gets to steep the longest.

Apparently at some point he introduces my name, for she shoots him a shrewd glance, then looks harder at me. This time her eyes widen and when she looks back at him, he nods in solemn confirmation. I am so exasperated I could kick him, but I refrain.

There's a great deal of admiration in the woman's look all of a sudden. I recognize that expression. There are always a few of them at the large events, people who have been reading about my adventures since they were children, who want to attribute all the victories of their existence to their uncanny shrewdness in claiming me as a role model.

They always want to talk. Sometimes they are unnerving in the amount of detail they have preserved from Adelina's books. I suppose if I'd ever read one of them through to its entirety, I'd be better prepared for such events, but the truth be told, often I cannot stand to read of myself, and to hear my adventures retold, so differently from the form in which I would tell them.

They are always eager to do me favors, to help me in any way, and that is something I have never hesitated to take advantage of, because I give them good value for it, I am full of charm and entertainment, so they will remember the interaction all their lives.

I hear Adelina in my head, sardonically saying she's heard good actors claim the same, and the truth is, there's no shame in sharing words with an actor. I say, "Lady, we would ask a great favor of you. I'm in desperate need of a way to get to Fireah unseen and unprevented."

It's as I thought. Her breath catches at the idea that I'm asking her for help. She says, instantly, "Of course. How soon do you need to go?"

Her eyes are wide with wonder in a way that I have not seen in a long time. You would think that word of my disgrace would have made its way down here already, but it seems that it has not. That thought gives me pause because I would not want that look to fade into disappointment.

I don't know how to say that gracefully, but Scylla saves me it. "Kanto has had all sorts of conspiracies against her," she says, "and you will hear all sorts of inaccuracies in months to come, ones that may make you regret any decision to help us."

But the little woman shakes her head. "I will not change my mind," she says. "It was reading of Bella Kanto that made me run away from home in order to come to the University." She drops her eyes after saying this, as though she fears she has said too much.

"Very well," Scylla says.

"Wait," I protest. "Have I no say in the matter?"

They all look a little surprised that I am speaking. "It is untested!" I say indignantly.

"It has been tested somewhat," our guide says earnestly. "Just never carrying living Humans."

Somehow despite all my protests, I am overruled, and we agree that we will set out that night, again traveling by night till I swear I will become nocturnal with the strain of it all.

"So we will never get a chance to enjoy our clean beds, after days at sea," Scylla says regretfully, then, "Don't laugh at me, Bel! I've seen you rubbing your back in the mornings as much as I've done with mine."

"It would have been nice," I admit, "but what's done is done, and this way we get there sooner rather than later, and I reclaim my magic or find something else to restore it."

"And then you go back to Tabat and set everything aright?"

"There were problems before I left. Someone was working against the city, and I think it was the same person that was working against me. They wanted my magic, to use it against the city. I can only presume that they've been working towards that end ever since and that with me out of the way, they've stepped up the pace."

"Why defend the city that exiled you? They could have stood by you, could have insisted that they knew you were incapable of such an act."

"Alberic never gave them the chance."

"So you will return and work in a way that helps depose him?"

"If that is how the elections dictate, yes. But there are ways that things are done. Tabat is built on ritual and without it, it will fail."

"You have been a Gladiator too long," Scylla says. "You have absorbed all the pomposities, all the self-important beliefs and mannerisms."

I flick a finger at her in a marketplace gesture that makes her laugh. "That is a bad example to set, Bella Kanto," she says. "Do you think they will ever return you to teaching youth if you are so full of lewd gestures and social corruption?"

The words are flip, but they catch me by surprise. What will I do, when everything is said and done, and order has been restored to the city? Will I be allowed to go back to teaching, or will rumor hold such sway that no one will be willing to commit their child to my care?

And if I were a parent, would I commit my child to my care? I betrayed their trust when I gave in to Skye's advances. She argued it round and round, that she was but a year from self-governance, that she knew it true love, that she would not have persisted if she had not known it to be true, but the only thing true in all of that was that I was the older, and the wiser, and I should have told her no and turned her away until she was no longer under my care.

"I have touched on something painful without meaning to," Scylla says gently.

"Life is full of painful moments, and we can scarcely exist without developing some armor," I say.

"Still, I am loath to be the one battering you in order to produce that armor."

"Why?" I say to her. "I disappeared on you, as though I became a ghost, went back to Tabat and never sent you a single message. Why should you care enough to have brought me halfway across the world?"

"Because you are Bella Kanto, and while you are—or have been so in the past, for I must admit I find you somewhat improved in this regard—one of the most arrogant and sometimes insufferable people I have ever known, at the same time, you bring an enchantment to life. As though great events were always happening around you, as though you were playing on some great stage to some audience other than myself or any of your other admirers."

"Bah," I say, although I find myself smiling. "Do not take up poetry, Scylla, for your metaphors are strained."

She cocks an eyebrow at me. "And you are such a great judge of literature?"

"I can appreciate it," I say. "And I myself am the subject of such a thing, do not forget that."

"Stories meant to be exciting, so servants can neglect their work," she snorts.

"Say rather stories of universal appeal!" How has she cheered me up so in just a few short words? I am lucky in my friends, very lucky.

We leave in the early dusk hours, through thick fog that muffles all sound from below, so all we hear are the harsh sounds of our breathing, the thrum of the engine driving us upward.

The movement of the fog is the only thing that makes me feel as though we are moving. We all stand on the little platform that hangs below the bag of gas pulling us upward—something Wilda has explained in length worthy of Adelina at her most tedious. I do not care how it moves, only that it does, and that it does so consistently and reliably, in a way that never falters and drops us into the ocean far below.

"This will burn off at dawn," Wilda declares. "But by then we will be well out of sight of the boats monitoring the channel that leads to the island."

"A channel seems an odd thing, in an island cluster," Scylla says.

"There are underwater reefs and other dangers," Wilda says. "There are waters that are by compact untraveled, where no Humans come and therefore are suffered to live there."

I scoff. "Island tales," I say loftily.

She looks at me with her button eyes and her tone is still cheerful enough. "Indeed? I've lived here long enough to think that it is best to lend some credence to at least a few. Legends are seeded in facts, often enough to make them worth heeding. At any rate, we bypass all that by approaching from the air."

I roll my eyes at Scylla when Wilda turns her gaze away, but Scylla chooses to ignore the gesture. She says, "How soon will we be there?"

"By midmorning, probably a little earlier, time enough to say that we have brought new supplies." This is the cover story we have decided on. There are bundles stacked in the hold: cots and tents, cooking supplies and a few lanterns. Some of them have an odd look, as though they are things she has improved on, to suit them to travel through the air.

I have never been on a journey like this one. There are so many firsts since I left Tabat, in a life where I thought such things might be few and far between.

You can say many things about my life in Tabat, but the truth is that it was also predictable, unchanging, a wheel that turned over and over again in the same street. Skye was a respite in that tedium; was that why losing her had hurt so badly?

But now here I am in exile, and every day seems to bring a new experience, whether it is flying in a boat far above the ocean, being carried by a Dragon, or whether it is now, floating among the clouds in a wicker basket. The Dragon's flight was noisier—there was the flap of wings, the huff of breath, and even sometimes the sound of its heart beating, and above all the sound of wind moving past.

Now we are carried along by that wind and so the air seems silent and unmoving all around us.

The Coral Tower is visible from far away, a slender pink tower that sticks up out of the fog. The sun is not yet up over the horizon, but the very topmost of the tower is touched with light that seems to come from nowhere.

"It is a pretty thing, is it not?" Wilda says from beside me. "Though everything is pretty from up here. It makes things miniature, lets you see the world in a new way. I'm sure you've seen this before, in Tabat, though."

"I've seen Tabat a time or two from above," I say, "but rarely. It's very different though. You can tell when different sections of the city were built by the color of the roof tiles. A friend of mine wrote a pamphlet on it."

"A scholar after my own heart," Wilda says. "What is it like in the city now? Down here we hear that there is a revolution brewing, that the Beasts wish to free themselves."

Her tone is approving, which startles me. "You are an Abolitionist, then."

"Most of the students down here are as well." Stalkal nods, leaning on the rail beside her.

"I find that hard to believe," I say, hearing myself pompous. "None of my students have said such things."

"Most of the students you teach come from the ranks of the rich, the Merchants and nobility, do they not?"

"Some. Not all."

"Not all," she says agreeably, "but the ones that are not, they wish to achieve affluence, to make their way among the Merchants and Nobles, do they not?"

"Yes," I agree, warily. I can think of Gladiator after Gladiator deeply involved in games of status and billing, who was catered to more respectfully, who the crowds cheered for.

I would like to say I had not been motivated by such things when it came my time. That is the story I have always told myself, that I did it solely to buy myself free of Jolietta, to have a thing that was not hers at all, had never been touched by her, because I had never confessed my dream to anyone, not even Phillip, even though I told him so much.

Jolietta would have mocked my ambitions. "Some again. Not all."

Wilda purses her lips. Stalkal maintains his silence, but she speaks. "Very well, the ones that do not, what do they want?"

"To be the best."

"But why?"

"Because it pleases the Gods."

"Do you really believe in all that? You don't like being Bella Kanto, the famous Gladiator, and all the deference it wins you?"

"It is not always good being Bella Kanto," I say.

"So it's true what they say? That you've been exiled?"

"Who said that?"

"There was a woman who came looking for you at the tavern. She told us that Tabat reckoned you a criminal and that the Duke would pay well for word of you. Everyone said they'd never seen you, of course, but it was a lot of money that she offered, to a group that doesn't have a lot most times."

"Where was she going after that?"

"Down to the docks."

Ruhua would probably have found Scylla's ship, but would she be able to identify it? It was small but nondescript, and the papers that she had furnished the harbormaster would surely stand up to scrutiny. After that she would have gone to inns, perhaps, so it was good that we did not use our rooms after all. At what point would she have circled back to the University? I suspected sooner rather than later; it was good that both Stalkal and Wilda were with us, but would anyone notice their absence?

"Do you have classes that you are postponing or cancelling for this?" I ask her.

"A study session that I lead. I sent word that we would meet next week."

"Is that unusual for you?"

The question surprises her, but she answers, "Somewhat, yes. But to help you …" She shrugs. "How often does one get to have the story of helping a dangerous criminal and once-Champion of Tabat?"

Said like that, it cheers me. I do still have some qualities of the mythic, the outrageous about me. I remain Bella Kanto, even in exile.

But unusual is what Ruhua will be looking for, and she will discover Wilda's absence, and then the absence of the Iron Beetle, and she will think to herself, "Where would they have needed to go by air, rather than boat?" which seemed like a question with a limited range of answers.

So figure her a day behind us, perhaps—she'll have to sleep, after all. So we will surely have enough time to find whatever it is that we are looking for.

We are overtaking a hawk, I see it ahead of us, as does Wilda. By mutual accord we all stop our conversation and wait and watch. It does not hear us, does not look around. Why should it? It knows that if there was some other bird or winged thing to contest it in the sky, it would know its approach by the flap of its wings. It does not reckon on such a thing as us appearing.

We pull abreast of it. Suddenly it notices us. It gives us a startled, panicked look that somehow is also entirely annoyed at the unreasonableness of our appearance. Then it lowers its head and dives downward, slanting away from us, its wings tucked in to make it move as fast as it can. Wilda and Stalkal start laughing, and I have to join in.

"Did … you … see … its expression?" she gasps.

"As frantic as a Merchant whose clerks have gone rogue and are selling off the warehouse," I solemnly agree.

That makes her laugh all the harder, and we keep laughing until Scylla emerges from the cabin where she has been trying to nap, looking more annoyed than the hawk, a comparison that occurs to both of us, so we exchange looks, which makes us laugh all the harder, and annoys Scylla even more.

Wilda heads back up the ladder. Scylla and Stalkal stay with me, watching the seething fog around us as we approach a clear spot.

"You are sure there will not be anyone from the University there?" I ask him.

"No one," he says. "They would not suffer anyone to remain there by themself, lest they learn something useful and refuse to share the fruit of their knowledge. There are only three Mages in the University, and they are very jealous of each other. All three will be coming along, in order to make sure neither of the others steals a march."

"Still, a watcher—a student or soldier perhaps?"

He shakes his head, plucking at the basketry rope work's mist-sodden knots. "None of them would trust anyone. You have never seen such a hubbub as when these ruins were first reported. All of them were worried they'd be left out of the planning of the expedition, and all of them have pet experiments that their students must bring along and execute along the path of the expedition."

"I thought you said that this was a hole in the ground, on a very small island," I say. "What do you mean, 'path of the expedition'?"

He gazes at me with limpid, solemn eyes. "I thought I explained all that. The hole goes deep down."

"How deep down?"

He shrugs. "Miles, perhaps? As deep as the caverns that underlie Tabat, perhaps farther."

There is a soft shuddering change in the sound of the engines, and Wilda comes clambering down from above. "We are almost there," she says. "See how the mist is parting, there up ahead? I have set us to rise a little, just to make sure no one is there watching for us, but then we will descend again."

CHAPTER 38

FIREAH (LUCY)

They wove through roseate stone tunnels, lighting their way with fish-oil lanterns that sent out a black, stink-laden smoke. By now, she thought, they were miles below the ocean's surface. Sometimes there were signs of earlier visitors—writing scratched or painted or in one case seared into the stone, nothing that Lucy could read.

Half a day later, they stood before the portal. The rope had been fastened beside their camp at the pit's edge and they had paused to eat and drink before entering the tunnels and coming to the small, boxy room, two doors set along its northern wall.

The tunnel ended in doors made of a different material, a pearly slab that reflected the lanterns' sullen glow. "See?" Captain Miryam said, looking pleased. "That door and that both were closed before. We'll try the right-hand side first."

He gestured to Maz, who jittered in place, impatient. "After you, lad."

Drawn in their wake and trailed by the sailors, Lucy entered the room. It had a seashell's inner glow and was far wider within than it had seemed from without. An immense ribbed ceiling stretched overhead, and white crystal veins laced like ivy across the pink surface.

"Captain Miryam," Maz said. "If you allow me to step forward and seize the same power as my father, I will take you to safety. Otherwise, I will watch as you, a novice untutored in these arts, are consumed by its energies and then step forward and take the same power as my father."

His voice was altered, taking on an older, more bitter cadence but still high and excited. Lucy stared at him.

"Who are you?" she said.

"It's his son still," Captain Miryam said. He sounded amused. "So the rumors are true—he keeps you barred from adolescence and has for decades, to prevent you from challenging him."

Maz's face worked angrily. "Yes!" he spat. "Decades I've been a boy, decades I've been in this form, a puny child not fit for adult company. But now I can have the power and mature my body after all."

Lucy paid them no attention. She stepped forward, seeking the glow's source. Here in this oddly shaped chamber, the acoustics were erratic. She heard whispers in her ears, half-heard tugs at her attention.

The captain turned to the sailors. "Hold him," he said.

The sailors stepped forward, only to vanish in showers of bloody sparks. Maz's thin lips crept up from his teeth to assume an eerie rictus.

You have to hurry, Mary's voice said to Lucy.

She paid them no attention. Surely she was close, so close to the source of the light. She managed somehow to turn a corner while standing still. She managed to step through a door while closing it. She managed to disappear and appear for the first time. The light was all around her now, her body spongy with it, seeping into her bones.

I'm Mary Silverhands now, she thought, distracted by the power washing through her.

Someone was shouting. Maz was shouting, shouting at her. She put out a hand and recoiled in horror as her energy and his met and she obliterated him.

He fell away into pieces, as he was unmade by the collision of the light. Sorrowfully, she kept her own edges from raveling by reweaving them as each strand dissolved.

The energy roiled through her, wore her like a wave, but she closed her eyes and focused, drew her awareness down into a single point, and relaxed and opened them. She stood in the chamber, alone except for Jusuf, who stood staring at her. Char marks were laid upon the wall to mark the sailors' passing. There was no sign of Maz.

Jusuf's eyes were wide with fear. "What have you done?" he demanded.

"I'm Mary Silverhands now," she said to him, smiling.

"I don't understand."

"Everything I touch will change now," she said. "Everyone will know who I am, and all my sisters will be sorry. You'll be sorry you scared me."

Her smile was like an icy silver knife. He felt it reaching inside him, she knew, could feel his thoughts echoed in her new perceptions, which somehow encompassed everything around her, felt all the currents of magic and life and luck, and even all three strands of moonlight, red and purple and white, she saw with fascination.

Those strands stretched out and out and out, many of them upward, towards the surface, but just as many down towards the heart of the world itself. She could feel now some of what lay down there, the red-hot fire that burned inside it. Even the creatures made of magic and thought and energy that moved there in the hot depths' pressure where no other living creatures could have survived.

It was a fascinating web—no, it was more like a tapestry, stretching out and out so far that she could have lost herself in its contemplation, could have disappeared forever in that contemplation, except that Jusuf made a noise of terror that pulled her abruptly and impatiently back to herself. Back to the moil of angers and grievances that was Lucy, all her sorrows and hurts and all the people who had done her wrongs.

She was tempted to take Jusuf apart then and now, as she had done with Maz. But he had also fascinated her, had been there at the first stirrings towards adulthood, and she had imprinted on him, just a little, till he was the shape of a desire that she found herself contemplating now much more dispassionately and outside herself, now able to see how he had played on it, just a little, adeptly.

She riffled through his memories, not caring that the heaviness of that mental tug sent him to his knees, grinding at his forehead with the heels of his hands in a vain attempt to relieve that relentless pressure, and found there everything she needed to corroborate. He knew what a charming and alluring figure he'd present to a young girl, particularly one thinking herself friendless and imperiled. He'd counted on that fascination to counteract any desire she might have to do him harm.

It was that, reckoning her harmless, that finally decided his fate, because it made her angry, to be thought that. It was being thought harmless that had let her sisters bully her, knowing that she couldn't fight back. It was being thought harmless, ineffectual, that had led the College of Mages to reject all her appeals, to not think her worthy of being a student.

She would show the world—and Tabat, and Jusuf, and everyone else, all of them, every single one—that she was anything but harmless.

CHAPTER 39

FIREAH (BELLA)

*W*e see the devastation from afar, the pile of bodies, the tents, one of them blown over by wind and allowed to lie uncorrected, so that it is half-buried by the blowing sand. We touch down, and Wilda and Stalkal immediately leap off, as quickly as they can make the balloon ship fast to its moorings, and running to the bodies with half-choked cries of horror.

Scylla and I descend more slowly, wanting to give them space in which to know their grief before we cast our shadows over it. These are not people we knew, but to the two of them they are friends and colleagues, and beyond that, they are not used to violence in the way that I am, or that Scylla is, who comes from a rougher land where the Mers must fight with the Beast counterparts sometimes to survive.

Wilda comes to us with tears on her face. "They were not hurting anyone," she says. "They were scholars, hunters after the truth. Who would do such a thing?"

The answer is there in the form of the corpses of two scimitar-bearing Humans that Stalkal pronounces to be pirates.

"I'm not as surprised as I could be, I guess," he says. "Rumors get around, and pirates know that magical artifacts can be sold for a great deal of money. Still, I would have thought that superstition would keep them off. This is supposed to be a source of great power but one that is cursed, one that the legends say was tucked away in order to keep both Beasts and Humans safe from it."

"This is the stuff of penny-wides," I say impatiently.

"Bella!" Scylla says in shock.

"Look, the magic of Tabat—there was some logic to it. And the ways the magic of Beasts works, the University has set itself to studying such, to proving that there are underlying principles. But magic artifacts from long-ago creatures, bearing curses, no less?"

"Those are the sorts of words that certainly, in a penny-wide, would predict what was happening within the next few chapters," Wilda says. "Are you sure, Bella Kanto, figure of legend, that you want to taunt the powers that decide such things?"

I bite my lip and shake my head, looking away. "These corpses look several days dead, if not longer," I say. "Can you tell what they died of?"

"I think poison," Stalkal says. He takes the wine flask that one corpse holds, its contents mostly spilled, only a dribble remaining, and sniffs it. He winces and holds it away from his nose, fanning it with his free hand. "Adder-milk. It's used in these islands for killing vermin, usually. Not a pleasant way to die, but they won't have noticed much taste to the wine it was mixed in, would have thought it a little bitter, that's all. A fancy flask—perhaps someone left them their special reserve. Whoever it was wasn't worried about anyone coming after them. Just wanted to make sure these fellows weren't going anywhere once they were no longer needed."

"So whoever it was went down the hole and came out?"

The guide shakes his head and points at the two ships. "No, they went down the hole and haven't come back out yet."

CHAPTER 40

FIREAH (LUCY)

*L*ucy led the way along the tunnel back to their last campsite. Jusuf followed her in silence. She walked feeling the energy leak from her, feeling it collide with the world. It was a constant struggle to keep from changing it, to keep from doing things like letting wildflowers spring up in her wake, or the air in her lungs be breathed out as lastflower perfume.

At the camp and the pit's edge, she paused.

He took her hand, level eyed. She leaned to touch her lips to his. This time she did give into the urge. With her kiss, he breathed in sweetness: the air in a pear orchard just as the first sunshine touches the blossoms open. He rocked back on his heels with the magic's passionate force, his green eyes wild and entreating.

She unfolded great falcon wings and leaped into the pit, flying upwards towards the dot of light so far above. He fell to his knees and watched, watched as a new goddess ascended towards the skies of the Lesser Southern Isles, then suddenly was yanked upward in her trail.

BELLA—LUCY APPEARS

We dig a grave and bury the bodies, which takes us the rest of the daylight. We sleep in their abandoned tents. Tomorrow we will investigate the stairs and the tower.

When the sky begins to lighten, a breeze kicks up over the water, chillier than the one that has lingered overnight, and wakes me. I lie there listening to the sound of the water against the rocks of the island's base and a cri-cri of gulls, far away and mournful.

I sit up. Has something in the night caught my attention in particular? I feel as though I have been awakened by a sound, but that I don't remember what that sound had been, have left that crucial detail behind me in sleep.

I strain my ears to hear the gulls, the water. What was that other noise? A distant, smothered screech, like a hawk's lost chick? It sends shivers down my spine, whatever it was. It did not come from the sky or across the waves.

No, it came from below.

Below, where that other expedition had gone.

I listen hard but hear nothing now. Nonetheless, I find myself scrambling to my feet, pulling on my outer clothes and nudging Teo with a foot. He comes awake almost immediately, whining and sniffing the air. So does Scylla.

The others are slower to rouse, shaking off sleep like the soft city-dwellers they are.

"What's amiss?" Scylla asks.

"I don't know," I say, my unease deepening with every passing minute. "But something is coming, and it will be upon us soon."

We see the glow, an angry red throb of light caught in the hole's throat, before we hear the rush of wind that accompanies her, the screaming of air in her wake.

She rises in a rush of crimson and purple energy, magic made manifest, dazzling. A small, foppishly dressed man dangles in her wake, his face dazed, hovering a few feet below her, almost touching the ground, while she hangs higher in the air, an awkward teen girl just on the verge of changes.

Her face is as calm as pudding, I find myself thinking, but it is colder than that. It is stone and logic and decisiveness. Don't I know this girl? Adelina's apprentice, I think, the one whose brother was sniffing about after Adelina.

She looks like any child of Tabat, her blood the mingled pale of North and the dark skin of the Old Continent. She says, "Who are you?" and her face is stern.

LUCY

Lucy was astonished to see Bella Kanto—surely *the* Bella Kanto, she'd seen her enough to know, even though this woman seemed ineffably older, a little more stooped by the years.

Adelina had sent Bella Kanto to find Lucy! That thought softened all her harsh anger towards Adelina, all her feelings of having been misjudged dying away as though by magic, assuaged by the tenderness of this gesture. Adelina cared deeply what happened to Lucy, else she would not have sent her best friend as far down as the Southern Isles to rescue her.

Still, there were others there as well—two women and a man that she did not recognize. And an airship! The sort you saw but rarely in Tabat, and smaller than any of the others she'd seen.

So she said, "Who are you?" and made her face cold, because she was a god now, or something like, or so the voices that echoed through her bones kept telling her. She had destroyed everyone responsible for bringing her here, except for Jusuf. She was still not sure what she meant to do with him. He'd pleaded with her all the way up from the caverns below, at least until she made it so he couldn't speak.

"I'm Bella and this is my friend Scylla," Bella said. "This is Stalkal and Wilda, whose ship that is. Did you come from the tunnels of Fireah?"

"I did," she said coldly, a suspicion growing that perhaps Bella Kanto was not actually here to retrieve her, a suspicion that was confirmed the next moment, when Bella said, "And what is your name?"

She pulled herself up straight in the air and let her energy flicker around her anew, reassuring her of the grandeur of the gesture. If she could overawe Bella Kanto, who could she not overcome?

It was not as though Bella was still the Champion of Tabat. No, she'd been disgraced, so who was she to act as though she had the right to demand answers from Lucy?

"My name is Lucy," she said, putting disdain into the reply, and even more into the next sentence. "I used to be Adelina Nittlescent's apprentice."

"I remember her mentioning you to me, back when she first hired you," Bella said.

Lucy wavered. Had Adelina sent rescue or not? Determining the truth of this matter seemed of the utmost importance, but she didn't want Bella to skew her answer and say whatever she thought Lucy wanted to hear. She said, "I was kidnapped. I thought she sent you after me ."

"Is there some reason she would have known to find you all the way down here?"

The quirk of Bella's eyebrow, the half-pulled lip made it easy for Lucy to laugh at herself. "It would be a long way to come," she said, then felt obliged to add, "Still I would have thought she would make some effort to find me."

"I am sure she did, knowing Adelina, but I suspect she would have confined her efforts to Tabat. Who was to know you would be halfway across the world? How did you come to this place?"

BELLA

My heart throbs in my throat. There is something dreadful about the way the girl hangs in the air, sometimes cold as ice, other times her voice and mannerisms as warm as those of an affectionate child.

Something inhuman crawls through her bones, not some Beastly energy, but something older, more certain and implacable.

It makes me feel as though my terrified guts are crawling up into themselves, trying to get deeper in order to escape this Lucy girl.

I force calm and cheerfulness into my voice, asking after her circumstances, trying to find the places where I can connect with her and remind her that she is Human.

She says, "Pirates took me. They thought I was someone else, someone who could unlock the secrets of Fireah."

"Who did they think you were?"

She hesitates, then says, "A student from the College of Mages. They didn't know what he looked like and so they took both of us together and then thought I was him."

"He didn't speak up to correct the mistake?"

"We thought it best to tell them as little as possible, he and I."

"Where is he now?" I ask.

Her eyes flick over to the hole, but her expression doesn't change. "Dead," she says.

"Dead how?"

She lifts her stare from contemplating the hole and puts it back on me. "Killed by ancient magic," she says. The flatness of her tone does not invite any question as to how that ancient magic worked.

"I see." I might as well ask and see what happens. "Do those ancient magics still work, down there?"

She smiles. "No," she says.

"They have died away?"

She shakes her head and points to herself, and says, "They have come to me, and I now hold them."

"What do you mean to do with them?"

"Return to Tabat."

For a moment I think to myself that this is not the worst of outcomes—a creature of magic headed up to Tabat, an idealistic young girl who will resist all of Alberic's machinations.

But she does not have the face of a savior. She has the face of a sulky child as she contemplates the man below her.

I point to him. "What will you do with him?"

"He is the one who engineered my abduction," she says quietly.

He looks up at her, shaking his head in protest.

She raises her voice. "He is the one who locked me in darkness and terror."

The head shakes again, denying it all. He holds up his hands towards her, pleading.

"He is the one who toyed with me, because he knew himself more experienced, wiser. Able to manipulate my confused affections."

These words come as an utter shock to him, the gestures grown so large now that they are almost comical. His shaking head moves without ceasing, denying her words. *No. No.*

"You've kept him alive for a reason," I say.

"I kept him alive so someone could witness his death," she says, and holds out a hand to make a fist. As her fingers close, he wraps in on himself, still screaming silently, contracting into a ball of broken flesh. She turns back to me and I can feel my bowels like water.

"I saw you in the ring," Lucy says. "I saw you kill Spring."

"That was an accident," I reply, but Lucy shakes her head.

"Everyone fought because of that. Everyone fought all over Tabat, and some of them killed my mother, because she had come out looking for me."

"You can't hold me responsible for that," I protest. "Blame the moons or the stars as easily."

"The stars did not cause riots, nor did the moons," Scylla says. "I think she has a little reason in her logic here, Bella. You sail through life without knowing how you hurt others, like a boat with devastation and fire in its wake."

That is a hurtful image, to think me someone capable of careless harm, but there is a certain amount of truth to it as well, enough to make it truly sting, enough to make it hurt in the way an observation from a friend can, more than anything a stranger or enemy could say.

"She is a child," I say coldly.

"You don't even know what is around you," that child says, just as coldly. She points at Teo. "How long will you keep him like that?"

How does she know what he is? I look at Teo, who seems the

same as always. But he is, like all of us, afraid. His ears are flattened, and his tail dips low. He whines deeply, urgently in his throat.

"Keep him like what?" I say.

"As a dog rather than a boy. He's more complicated than that. Much more complicated."

She gestures and the dog unfolds itself somehow, becomes the boy I knew, lanky and wild-eyed, naked in the dust.

I gasp. How easy for her to do this thing that we had been hunting for. How deep do her powers run?

"Who did this?" I say.

"The same one who drove you from Tabat," the child sneers, as though she knows all my doings and finds them invariably inadequate. "Murga."

"Murga the circus owner?" This all makes less and less sense the more I find out. "Teo, what is all this?"

But he is still gasping and wild-eyed, too used to being in the canine form for this one not to feel awkward.

The girl holds up her hand as though plucking something from the air. Now she holds the little portrait of Skye that I have kept safe all this journey. She smiles at me and it bursts into flames, and her smile grows even wider at the expression on my face.

The girl holds out her hand again and it's filled with a bundle of papers.

"I can do almost anything now," she says. "See these? Adelina has been writing to you all this time. Her letters, chasing you fruitlessly, growing more and more desperate as she hears not a word of you, as she reckons that the Duke has killed you."

She drops it and it thuds to the sand. How powerful is she, that she can reach across space and gather these things to her? She looks at the airship as though contemplating destroying it, and Wilda makes a pained noise in her throat and tries to step forward, but Stalkal prevents her.

The noise and motion draw Lucy's attention and she looks over at the interaction. "Let go of her," she says, and there is force enough in her voice to drive him to his knees. Wilda pulls away, rubbing the wrist he had grabbed, and straightens in order to face Lucy.

"That is your ship," the girl says. "You built it?"

"I did." Wilda's voice is small but determined. She ignores the tangle of flesh that had once been a man, lying on the sand between them.

"Was it hard to build?"

"Very hard."

"Did they tell you that you couldn't build it?"

Startled, Wilda says, "Yes, but I went ahead and did it."

"That's good," Lucy says. "When people say no, sometimes they don't know what they're talking about."

She turns back to me. The early morning sun is still mild, and I see its reflection in her wide eyes. She says, "Adelina was wrong. She said I'd stolen her little case, but I'd found it in the gallery where she dropped it."

"Bernarda's gallery?" I say, startled. How long ago that all seemed! "You were there when the fire broke out?"

She shakes her head. "Afterwards," she says, and then adds with defiance, "It is the law that the poor are allowed to glean. My sister made me do it. Anyway, that's where I found it."

How small things are that set other, much larger things in motion! Had Adelina not lost her case, she would not have discharged Lucy and sent her wandering the streets of Tabat to be kidnapped in a plot of confusion and chaos.

"Of course you did," I say, soothing her with my voice the way I might have soothed a Centaur colt or young Minotaur, the soft voice Jolietta used so often in her dealings with Beasts she wanted to coax into doing one thing or another.

Lucy is smarter than either would have been. "You're just humoring me," she says. "Adelina was wrong, and I'm going to go show her, and everyone at the press, and my family, and the people at the tannery, and all the Moon Temples taking advantage of people!" She looks at Teo, then points at him. "All the people that other people are making do things. It's wrong and I'm tired of it."

Schemes and thoughts are circling through my head,

surmounting the dull throb of impending disaster. This girl is too powerful, and she carries grudges like gold coins, ready to spend them on revenge, a revenge directed at my best friend.

I say, "May I take the letters?" and move forward without waiting for her reply. Sometimes when you act as though permission has already been given, people think they have given it. It's a matter of acting with enough self-confidence to carry it off. I pick them up, thick, good paper, with my name written clearly in Adelina's careful hand, legible but distinctive, a writing unlike anyone else's in all the world, and put them away.

"Very well," Lucy says ungraciously.

I act as though her tone has been more welcoming. "Perhaps we might accompany you back to Tabat?"

She smirks. "You're welcome to try," she says with an arch grimace. "But I will be flying, and I think my speed is much greater than that thing's."

Wilda, stung, says, "It's faster than it looks."

"Be careful," Lucy says to her. "If I thought you were any sort of threat to me, I'd kill you now. I could do so at any moment." Her voice is staggeringly casual as she speaks, as though the words she were speaking are commonplace. Wilda opens her mouth, then closes it, steps back and allows herself to be drawn into Stalkal's sheltering arm.

I beckon to Teo, but Lucy forestalls me. "He'll be coming with me." She looks around at the island scornfully. "I can take care of my good friends." This time her grin is ferocious. "What's to stop me from destroying your ship, keeping you from following me?"

"Nothing but hubris," I say.

"What?"

I shrug, keeping the gesture casual. "Overconfidence on your part, thinking you have everything under control, that you've figured all the odds and know all the factors."

As I'd hoped, the words sting her. She says, "I do have everything under control." She smirks again. "I see what you're doing, you know. You're trying to play on my pride. Very well, I'll take that challenge. I wager that I'll be in Tabat days before you, and that you can't do a thing to stop me, even when you arrive."

"Done," I say.

Teo yelps, startled, as an invisible tendril picks him up and draws him to her feet.

"I'm still taking him," she says coldly. Her eyes flicker over us. "I should kill one or two or maybe even three of you," she says. "Everyone but Bella Kanto. How much despair would that bring you, Bella Kanto?"

And with that she gestures, and the ground drops away and I find myself gone.

CHAPTER 41

FIREAH (BELLA)

*H*ow much later do I awake? I do not know.

I look around in dismay. Everything is gone, and the sandy surface of the island is now glass, melted as though by some vast heat. The Iron Beetle is gone, no sign of it, perhaps burned away in the fire. Needless to say, no tents. No bodies.

I know the last for certain because I spend hours hunting over it, looking for any trace of them. But Lucy has left me nothing, has simply obliterated them, erased them from existence with only a thought, and left this glassy monument to them. Did she know that I would climb out eventually? Did she think I might give way to dismay and stay down there in the pit?

The only thing left is the packet of letters she has left to taunt me, as though to say, *See how I could have preserved your friends?*

I tilt my chin and harden my eyes, even though there is no one there to see it. I am Bella Kanto, and I can win over any situation, no matter what.

There is soft clapping from behind, a gentle and appreciative applause that spins me around.

I should not be surprised to see her, but I am. Selene.

"You are a delusion," I say to her. "I have gone mad and now I see you everywhere."

Her face is amused. "Delusion or god," she says, "I have some-thing to tell you. Your Dragon is returning. Tell Bruna to take you to the port."

"Will I find my friends there?"

She shakes her head. "Not there."

I only mean Scylla, I think, but I will not say that. Taking her from her city was another in my long list of things I have done wrong. I had refrained long ago, and now I see that was wisest. I bring death and disaster to those around me, I kill them with my hubris. Is it really a wonder a god might be drawn to me, as I move through fate, changing it to destruction? More hubris. I sink to my knees in the sand. I do not know what to believe, do not know what to say. I am at a total loss.

She must be a god, for any other woman would have come to comfort me. Instead she stands there, arms crossed, as though waiting for a coughing or sneezing fit on my part to pass.

I say, my voice unsteady, "So what will I find there?"

"You will find a preview of what she will do to Tabat, if she is loosed upon it," she says. "And that is what you must do. Prevent that."

This pulls my look to her face, startled as I am by this assertion. "Me? What can I do? I am nothing now."

"Oh?" she says. "That is not true. You remain Bella Kanto. You only have to figure out who she is."

Then, outrageous and fickle, she fades away, and I am still unsure if she is a God or a hallucination. I have never seen her interact with anyone else, never seen anyone else note her presence.

I must be going mad. I hold my head in hands and sit there in the sand until I hear the flap of Dragon wings, far overhead, then approaching.

It is Bruna that lands, sniffing curiously at the lip of the hole in the ground. She says, "Ah, you were too late, Bella Kanto. As I told you that you would be."

"You failed to tell me what the consequences would be of not listening," I say with bitterness.

"There are always consequences to every decision. Some of them are better than others. This one? Mmm."

"Will you take me to the port?" I say.

"It is that, or leave you here to starve," she says. "Or I could eat you."

The last is almost appealing. At least it would be a connoisseur's death, a way to perish that very few people followed. But I do not invite her to do so. There is a rumble of anger to her words. "What has happened?" I ask.

"The child has killed one of my sisters," Bruna says. "All that we have done is to try to avert disaster, and still she killed her without thought. You are the last chance Tabat has."

"Me?" I say incredulously. "Tabat has exiled me, have you forgotten? The city turned its back on me!"

"And now it is your choice to accept that, or to reach out again," Bruna says. "Your fingers have been burned, and badly, Bella Kanto. Will you let that keep you from reaching out again? Are you so marked by what has happened to you that you have been crippled by it?"

"Do I have a choice in that?" I say. "I cannot think away a scar left by a blade. Is it not the same with scars left in the mind?"

"The mind heals differently," she says. "And you have seen how one person marked by a blade will heal quickly and another who does not expect to heal will do so more slowly."

I snort. "You are an expert in the minds of Humans?"

"Do you really think Humans and Beasts that unalike?" she says. "In all that you have seen, all that you have witnessed, that notion still sticks with you?"

It is an odd piece that does not seem to fit the puzzle in my head, but the more I worry at it, the more its edges yield and reform, begin to fill in holes. It is true. Thinking of Beasts as I would a Human, with all the fickle changeability and jealousies and irrational moments, makes sense now in a way that it had not before.

"She is eager to test her powers in the port, to see what she may or may not do in Tabat."

"Do you think the city has that much to fear?" I say curiously.

"With your removal, it has been stripped of the heart of its magic, so that very force could be used to destroy it," the Dragon says. "To be sure, those doing so intend to rebuild it afterward, but it is not a given that the city would survive the process and even if it should do, it will be a very different place, and not one where many Humans will want to come, I think." Her eyes gleam. "Perhaps not the most terrible of outcomes, one would think, but there are problems that accumulate in time with such a thing, and then there are deaths and killings, and siblings set against each other in the sky."

Her voice is a low hypnotic croon, whirling and multicolored.

"Stop that," I say crossly, and she only laughs at me.

"Look to the waters." her voice is amused. "And perhaps you will forgive me a little."

I turn in time to see Scylla climbing from the waves.

I almost rush at her, but she wards me off. She shakes her head. Her dispirited shoulders hunch up, her chin sinks forward, she huddles into herself. "Just give me a few moments, Bella. After that we'll get back to saving our cities. But I need to catch my breath."

My hand falls back, and I step backward. "All right," I say, and hesitate, but in the end add nothing, just turn back to look at the rest of what remains, and the smooth glass under which lie the bodies we buried.

She takes perhaps ten minutes, I don't know. I spend my time sitting in one of the wide-silled open windows, my legs dangling out over the water, wondering whether perhaps I should just jump in. Whatever magic was here seems to have taken up home in Lucy, which is a truly frightening thought.

Power is hard to resist. With it comes its sister, unspoken privilege, and then later another sister yet, unquestioning privilege. The Duke is firmly in that triumvirate's grasp.

Finally Scylla raises her head.

"How did you escape?" I ask.

"When she turned to us in rage—after you had fallen unconscious—I dove into the water and swam deep, as deep as I could.

Either the intervening water saved me, or the girl spared me for some reason of her own."

The strange child did not slay either of us, although she could have. That is what is terrifying about her, as though one of the thoughtless students I've suffered through over the years at the Brides of Steel, as though one of those had been gifted with incalculable power.

Gifted, not earned. My own power was earned, was carved out of tradition and ritual and custom, was something that assembled over time, not fell upon me like a crown falling out of the sky, simply because I had happened to go down a particular hole. That was absurd and unreasonable.

"What?" Scylla says, and I realize that I have said the last of this out loud.

"It is unreasonable," I insist to her, and irritatingly enough, she laughs despite all our misery, and Bruna joins in.

"Should the world behave only in a way that meets with your expectations, then, Bella Kanto?" Scylla teases me, then sobers. "I am sorry about the boy. The dog. I reckon there is more to that story than I know."

"He was a street boy that I took in and engaged in my service," I said. "How he became a dog is your guess as easily as mine; I have heard that Sorcerers can do such things."

"Perhaps the boy was a Shifter?" she asks.

I laugh. "Of course not. You think that I could live in a household with a Shifter and not know it? Give me some credit."

"Bella Kanto is known for her acumen in battle, but not her powers of deduction," she says.

"Are you saying that I am stupid?" I say with outrage.

"I am saying that you are not the most observant woman in the world when it comes to things outside fighting and flirting."

"I do not think that is entirely true."

"Oh?"

"Well perhaps," I say. "But the boy is not a Shifter. I would bet my life on that."

CHAPTER 42

AN ISLAND BEACH (LUCY)

The surprise took the form of a Dragon, the same Dragon Lucy had seen on the ship on the way down. At least, she thought that it was probably the same; she had not seen so many Dragons that she thought she would be particularly good at distinguishing one from another.

It lay on the sandy beach and by the way it undulated and rolled on the dunes, like a cat in sunlight, it was enjoying the warmth of the sand and the sensation of it against its scales. Lucy stepped towards it and she knew that it heard her, but it ignored her and continued to writhe against the dune.

Teo followed her at a distance, which she thought was touching, that he already trusted her to take care of him in the face of a Dragon. She stopped about twenty paces away from the Dragon and said, politely, "My name is Lucy."

The Dragon gave off its long sinuous wriggle and slithered around so its huge face confronted hers. It was so much larger than she was that it could have simply opened its mouth and swallowed her whole.

She found herself rehearsing mentally what she would do in such a case. The teeth would be locked, the skull a prison of bone, but down the throat and then out …

"There's no need to consider such incivilities." The Dragon's voice was honey and fire, its eyes great golden pinwheels, translucent wrinkles of light aligned with the pupils to create mesmerizing starbursts, full of wisdom and beauty ...

She caught herself leaning towards one of those eyes and pulled herself backward, shoving a barrier of magic between herself and the Dragon's lure.

"Huh. Well, you can't blame someone for trying." The Dragon's voice held a sulky note despite the overwhelming sweetness. "Where are you bound next?"

"Tabat," she said.

"Mmm, Tabat. To do what?"

"To destroy it," she said steadily. The great eyes whirled, but she found herself able to resist their pull this time. As though sensing her immunity, the Dragon left off trying to hypnotize her.

"Mmm," it repeated. "To destroy Tabat. That is a tall order, my mouseling."

"Still, one I intend to undertake." She found herself considering the Dragon's strength. She thought she had the advantage, overall, but Dragons were long-lived and cunning and there was always the possibility that a Dragon had run into a thing like her before, encountered a creature that was, she had been thinking with increasing complacency, something quite like a god, as powerful as the pretend moons or Trade Gods of Tabat, blind little porcelain faces that people thought should dictate when and where and what they did in life.

"You have enough power to destroy it, to be sure," the Dragon said. "But I do not wish you to destroy it all. I want you to leave the Beasts alive. In fact, to encourage them, to help them make the city something of their very own."

"A Beast city?" she said, incredulous. "Something like that will never fly."

"And if I told you that it would, that I knew it?"

But she shook her head again. "At best I would find it unbelievable, at worst I would think it overly gullible on your part, to have fallen for some trick tailor-made to your wants. This city will never accept Beasts as equals—intolerance is baked into its tiles, has been since day one."

"That doesn't mean that it has to continue."

Lucy said, "You can believe what you like, but if you went to Tabat right now, even if you proclaimed yourself uninvolved in politics, interested only in the city and its meager ways, you would still be struck down before you could do more than overfly the city once."

"And you will overfly it and destroy it. Will you let my fellow Beasts be?"

"I will take my foes as they come at me," Lucy said. "And I will spare no one that does so."

And with that, the Dragon raised its head, taking a deep breath.

Then it paused, and said, "Little godling—are you sure you will not listen to what I say? I ask you once."

"I have been waiting for you," Lucy said, for she had. "And I say no."

"I ask you twice."

"And I say no."

"Because you fear me," the Dragon said with complacency.

"Because I was curious about this," she said, and silver fire came directly from her left hand, blinding fire that made Teo shelter his face, that blasted directly at the Dragon's head.

For a few seconds, it quailed back, and then it opened its great jaws and breathed out black fire that fought her starlight clarity, clung to it like sticky smoke or black tar, overpowering it, forcing it back at her.

It quivered in the air. She swung her right arm up and forward, and with it a curtain of silvery blue lightning, crackling and sizzling like a newly birthed thunderstorm.

It slashed, leaving holes in the air where it struck, swathes of terrifying nothingness, and then it slashed again across the Dragon's throat and opened it up.

The scales parted as though an unparryable blade had leapt forward to do its work, and flaming blood poured out, vast gouts of it that steamed in the air.

Teo cried out and flung himself backward before the puddle could envelop his feet. Lucy simply levitated herself upward above it, so none of it could touch her. She could smell it, though, the raw bloody smell of it tinged with sulfur, so thick that it burned at the inside of her nostrils.

Teo was quiet, staring at the enormous corpse in the slowly spreading crimson pool. Two gulls swooped down. They stood in the sand as though considering, then one hopped away from the puddle's swelling edge and onto the Dragon's form. It flapped its wings awkwardly, balancing itself, as though ready for the Dragon to rebuke it, to snap or snarl in a deadly motion that never came.

Little crabs began to assemble and test one drying edge of the gore. Flies followed.

Lucy decided the beach was not so pleasant. She did not speak to Teo, but he was prepared this time and did not fall as she swept him upward.

No one would ever push her around again. No one would ever slap her. Or piss on her. Or make decisions about her life without consulting her. She found herself grinning. Or if they did, they'd be sorry—very, *very* sorry.

Her senses spread all out around her as though she was part of the landscape regarding herself. She didn't look like Lucy or Obedience any more at all. She looked like a creature made out of fire and light, not something of flesh and blood.

She couldn't actually remember what it had felt like, being flesh and blood. She thought it had probably been rather unpleasant or she would have remembered it better.

She cast it from her mind. There was no point in thinking about such things.

Behind them the Dragon's body cooled.

TEO

It was very odd not to be a dog anymore. His mind kept trying to insist that he was a dog, so he found himself doing doggish things, like trying to use a foot to scratch his ribs or licking his nose.

He knew what being in another form was like. He'd run as a cougar once.

But he'd awakened from that the next day, himself again. Being a dog—unable to change back into a boy—had been a prison at first and then faded, becoming more a way of existence. Murga had done this to him, had turned him into a dog back in Tabat, the same night he'd seen the Sorcerer turn the Dryad into a monstrous wooden golem. He had been able to remember himself better when he was a cougar—being a dog had been overwhelming, something that had wracked him down to his innermost core.

Lucy was sleeping now, and he was lying awake and staring up at what he could see of the stars through the branches. They hung bright and low and sweet, and the red moon hovered high in one spot, while the white moon winked at him from between two branches as they shifted in the wind.

The susurration of the water, the waves rolling in over and over again, filled him with a drowsy lassitude. He wondered what Bella and Scylla were doing. He thought Bella might be pursuing them, or have some sort of plan, at least. That was the sort of person that Bella was, the sort of person who did things rather than spending more time talking about them than doing them.

Something soared through the sky far above and he froze for a moment, not sure if it was a bird close at hand, or a Dragon much further off, moving silently. How many Dragons were there in the world? Would they know that Lucy had slain one of their number and come chasing her for vengeance? In all the stories of Dragons, that was the sort of thing they were prone to doing.

Then he heard the wings flap and relaxed. Just a bird.

Lucy was taking him back to Tabat. He thought the journey would be faster than the trip down, but those days on the boat all blurred together in doggy memory to the point where they could as easily have been three days as three weeks.

Tabat—what would the city be like now? What had Murga and his golem and all his circus done to the city, and what was his connection to the Duke? Now that he was no longer a dog, his mind was starting to whirl a bit, to make connections. How much of the riots, the restless Beasts, was something Murga had engineered?

How much power did Lucy have? Did she have something that helped her, or was the thing inside her? She'd told him the night before that it had come from going down to the center of the earth and taking it, but she had been vague about the process, saying only that it had been difficult.

He thought that maybe there had been more people with her when she went down, and that they had all died when she was on her way back up. He wasn't sure whether or not she had killed them, but he suspected she had.

So—a lot of power. Enough to defeat Murga, surely. But Murga and the Duke, and whatever else the Duke could bring to bear? He was less sure of that.

And what would she do with it if she won?

Tomorrow she had said they would go to Margolees before they set off for Tabat. He had asked why, and she said, "I'm curious about it. Aren't you? How often do you get a chance to travel?"

"Never," he'd said. It was true, it was like living an adventure from a penny-wide and Lucy was surely worthy of such a story. She was magic, after all, and had righted wrongs and rescued herself from pirates. He wasn't entirely sure what she intended to do when they got back to Tabat but surely she must want to right other wrongs.

There was certainly one wrong in Tabat, which was the way that they treated Beasts, just as the Dragon had said. Lucy could change that, and he would talk to her, so she wanted to do it, wanted to right that particular wrong.

And *then* maybe he could persuade her that not all Shifters meant harm, not all were treacherous or evil and bent on replacing people. That they should be allowed to walk freely in Tabat. Maybe even own a house or run some business. He wasn't sure exactly what sort of business he could run, but surely Lucy would need someone to handle things, a job more important than the sort of errands he'd run for Bella Kanto.

Dawn was starting to edge the sky and crowd out the stars on the eastern horizon. He rolled out of his hammock and moved quietly to gather fruit. Lucy should see that he didn't intend to take her for granted, that he would work for her and her aims. That was the safest thing, and possibly the one with the brightest future.

It was also one that let him wait and see what Bella Kanto did and whether or not she would come for him.

CHAPTER 43

AN ISLAND BEACH (LUCY)

*I*n the morning when she woke, she found that Teo had gathered fruit already, a big heap of it.

"You didn't need to bother," she said grumpily. She felt frowsy and fuzzled by sleep, and the sun was too bright, the air too hot and sticky already. One thing you could say about Tabat, it was only in the summer's very hottest days that it got anywhere even close to this southern misery.

His face fell, but he didn't say anything to reproach her, which only made her feel more grumpy, as though she were accommodating a sulky child. She announced, "After we eat, we are going to Margolees. I want new clothes and to see the sights and eat some delicious things."

"Do we have money for that?" Teo asked.

"We don't need money," she said. She smiled. "I can take what I want now, and no one can stop me. You saw what I did to the Dragon."

He looked uneasy, but nodded. He sat down beside the pile of fruit and started peeling one. She waited until he was done, then reached out and plucked it from his grasp. She put it to her mouth and took a juicy bite, watching him, waiting to see what he would say, if he would bristle out some challenge or roll over.

He picked up another and began to peel it. "Would you like another?" he asked.

After they had eaten, Lucy made them new clothes out of air, splendid clothes of the kind she'd seen back in Tabat, bright velvets and diamonds dripping from the hems. She looked like a play-acting child, Teo thought with dismay, looking at her bright eyes as she peered at herself in the mirror that she had summoned, but he said nothing.

"We don't need to go to the city. You could just as easily make us something," he said.

Her eyes gleamed brighter. "I can only make things that I've tasted before. I want to try new things so I can make them. I want to try everything." Her voice took on a resonance that made him flinch away, made his stomach twitch.

His face hurt from smiling, hurt from looking pleasant and unafraid. He wished that Bella was here to tell him what to do. He felt grateful to Lucy—the person who had, finally, rescued him from his dog state, had made sure he didn't keep being a dog all his life, falling farther and farther into its mind until he was entirely lost. She'd saved him from that fate, and it was terrifying to think that she might put him back.

She seemed fond of him in a way that she had not been of Bella. He thought that maybe she was a little lonely, that she regretted killing all of her pirate companions, of whom she never spoke.

"Let's go," she said, and they rose into the sky.

THEY CAME at Margolees from the east side, flying over the citrus groves. Teo smelled the waft of orange and lemon from below and thought it one of the pleasantest things he'd ever smelled. Fruit like that usually did not come to Tabat except weeks old, when it had already started to dry out, and this was lush and fresh in a way he had never experienced, almost as though the joys of his canine nose, which had smelled so many wonderful things during the time he was a dog, had been briefly restored.

But all too soon, it was interrupted by the odors of a poor quarter on the outskirts of town, where the fruit pickers lived. Sour food and sewage mingled with the stink of too many people living too close together. Lucy made a face.

"It smells like home, but not in a good way," she said.

He agreed. In Tabat, there would be the chemical tang of the smoke from the Slumpers, and the ozone and mist of the etheric lights that lined the main streets. He thought wistfully of Tabat—while he missed the village he had come from, it was mostly the people there, like his parents. Tabat had been his first taste of a city, and he loved it for that introduction, loved it down to his bones.

They landed in a courtyard filled with little apple trees growing in white ceramic pots. Someone came at them, shouting about trespassing.

Lucy waved a hand before Teo could even see the person who was shouting. They disappeared into a fine red mist that coated the surface of the fruit dangling around them, giving them an unappetizing, sticky gleam that made his stomach churn.

Lucy looked around complacently. She said, "This place is pretty enough, and I like all the birds and flowers. Perhaps I will make some of them appear, back in Tabat." She turned to him. "What do you think?"

He started to speak, and instead was heartily, noisily, wretchedly sick in the corner.

Her lip curled. "Poor boy. You're still suffering the aftereffects of all that enchantment. You said the man who did it owned a circus? That will be fun to visit."

He doubted from her tone, as well as what he had experienced by now, that Murga would enjoy the experience.

She strolled through the archway and onto the street. No one noticed her until they began exploding, one by one, as her gaze fell on them. She cleared the street and walked down it, looking at the houses. Teo followed in her wake when she beckoned to him. What else could he do?

"The houses are nicer in Tabat, but these colors are pretty. Perhaps we will make the houses in Tabat look like this." She smiled at him as they stepped over the sticky red street. He tried to ignore what lay beneath their feet. Unable to summon a smile, he simply nodded.

"Pretty place," she mused again as people continued to fall. "Such a pretty place."

BY NIGHTFALL, the city was gutted. Teo was sick of the smell of blood and smoke, and Lucy's smile was so bright it could have lit the night.

"I think I am entirely ready for Tabat now," she said when the last of the screaming died down. And she did not pause, simply scooped him up into the air and began to fly north.

CHAPTER 44

EN ROUTE TO MARGOLEES (BELLA)

*W*e see the smoke from Margolees long before we reach it.

THE SMOKE TURNS out to have been from unattended fires taking hold in the city, caused by the fact that whoever would have tended them was dead.

At first, I think that she has made people vanish and that is why so few crowd this devastated place, making it feel eerie and uninhabited. But then I look closer at what lies to hand, and why it is that fat carrion flies circle everywhere, so big and buzzing that you cannot ignore, and sometimes landing on one's flesh for an exploratory bite.

We find some neighborhoods harder hit than others. In a space near the docks, we're able to purchase food. I decide that a skin of wine will not go amiss, despite the fact that Scylla argues with me over it.

I have a handful of coins left, and we are about to travel in a way no Human ever has before. We shall have wine to accompany us.

The little shop is still grieving one of its clerks, who was unfortu-
nate enough to run into Lucy in the marketplace, and so they give
me a good price on the two skins I tuck into my belt. The bell of the
shop tinkles as I step out onto the street and find Ruhua standing
there.

CHAPTER 45

(LUCY)

The flight was nightmarishly cold. Lucy didn't pay him any attention, and the rush of the wind was too loud for her to hear him, even when he tried shouting. At length he gave up and simply watched the rush of water underneath him. Once or twice, he thought he saw great ocean fish, but they always passed far too quickly for him to decide what he was really seeing.

Once they passed a boat, seeing its lights down below them. Lucy paused, hovering in the sky, looking down.

"They haven't done anything," Teo said, feeling wretched. She could kill these people here and now or they could go ahead to Tabat, where she would kill many more people. All he wanted was a little rest from all the bloodshed. Perhaps killing them would slow her down, make it easier for Bella Kanto to catch up, but it seemed a poor bargain, particularly given the enthusiastic speed at which he had already witnessed her commit mass executions.

"Very well," she said agreeably. He thought that she might want to be at home in Tabat as badly as he did, but he also thought that their reasons were entirely different. She kept talking about her sisters and how much she hated them, how ready she was for vengeance on them.

"What about your brother?" he'd asked, and she'd given him a dark look.

"He can watch what I do to them," she said with wicked zest. "And then he'll know all the things I could do to him if he doesn't act the way I want him to. No more telling me what to do, no more sending me out on tasks. Everyone will bow to me, same as they did the Duke. But I'll be nicer than him. A better ruler. Everyone says he's shit as a ruler."

Teo had never heard anyone speak of Alberic with fondness, even Bella, who knew him as well as anyone could, by Teo's way of reckoning things. It wasn't that he'd snooped on Bella, but she was very frank about where she was going, and to do what, and with whom, because it saved on misunderstandings if she was utterly frank.

Abernia had just laughed at her, but Teo had always been a little shocked, particularly when he'd found out one of the "with whoms" was Alberic, who'd installed the etheric lights that could allow a mage to spot someone who was a Shifter like Teo.

The red and the purple moons rose and cast chains of laddered light across the dark ocean. The white moon was nowhere to be seen.

CHAPTER 46

MARGOLEES (BELLA)

*R*uhua looks thinner, more drawn, than when I saw her last, as though she has been traveling hard, as though she has come as quickly and unexpectedly as I have.

She says, "You might have thought your ruse successful."

I say, "I had hoped. It is clever of you to have seen through it."

She makes an impatient noise deep in her throat. The air here smells like copper and despair. She says, "Cleverness had nothing to do with it. The coin led me to you."

It glints as she holds it up and my heart freezes. She smiles as she sees the expression on my face.

"Ah," she says softly. "There is what I hoped to see. The ice has started to thaw, and you've begun to take joy in life again. Now you have something to lose. Now I can take something from you. Come, we will go and talk to your rebellious friend before I do anything."

"I am alone," I say. "No one else has survived."

Her smile widens. "I do appreciate your loyalty. The way you will not betray your friends. But it's too late for that."

I follow her through back streets to the mean little inn she is occupying, which has for the most part escaped Lucy's notice and still stands, intact and untouched but filthy beyond imagining, as though perhaps it was the extraordinary degree of the dirt that saved it. All the way, my thoughts race, chasing each other, trying to find a way out of this.

It isn't even that I hope to save myself. It's the city. Who will save the city from Lucy?

She has Scylla tied to a chair, wrists bound, mouth working furiously against the gag the moment I enter the room, trying to warn me but dying away as she sees the Huntswoman behind me and realizes that it is too late for warnings.

Ruhua contemplates her as she points me to a chair across the chamber. "Sit down there, Bella Kanto. I'd undo the gag, but she has proven herself tiresomely uncooperative so far."

She stares at me with greedy eyes, like a starving woman who has found a feast.

"You have led me quite a chase, Bella Kanto," she says. "The Duke did not mean for you to come to the Southern Isles, and I'd thought that if you did run, it would not be to a place like this."

"Tabat is in danger," I say.

Her face does not change. "Tabat is ever in danger," she says. "Right now, the elections endanger it, move it away from the strong leadership that it needs to keep it safe."

"You mistake me," I say. "The same danger that destroyed this port now flies toward Tabat. I have spoken to her. She is a child and a god, and she means to have revenge."

"Look here, Bella. Here is your death, still around my neck," Ruhua says, ignoring my words. She touches the medallion. "You've wondered why I have not killed you. Perhaps you even thought my power to do so was an ineffectual lie, a trick without teeth."

"That thought has crossed my mind," I admit, "but you have never been the sort to bluff, Huntswoman."

"Indeed I never have," she says. It strikes me that this is as happy as I have ever glimpsed her. How she must hate me, and how much she must love Alberic, to stir up such a deal of hatred on his behalf.

"Perhaps I wanted to see your face when I did it," she says, still holding the medallion out from her skin, between thumb and forefinger.

She holds it, staring at me, and I feel my death creeping up on me.

Then she shakes her head and lets it go.

She picks up the packet Lucy gave me. I have not thought to look at it in all of this, though I have held onto it.

"Here," she says softly, "is the only reason I have not to do so."

She tosses them to me.

I read through the letters, one by one, as slowly as I can. I can hear Adelina's voice speaking them, the cadences of her speech, that I would know anywhere, but I worry that the voice has been fading in my head. Now it is renewed.

I read with horror of events and wish that she had brought some pieces of news that are lacking. There is word of Leonoa, but nothing of the Brides of Steel and its students, which is typical thoughtlessness. If there were riot and unrest, the area that the school is in is not a good one—it will be as prey to attack as any other in the city. Like the neighborhood that Leonoa keeps her studio in, for that matter.

I look up from the letters I have been reading. The last sentence ends, "Where I think that you *will* find a way, and I will see you again, in Tabat." And it is signed with Adelina's name.

"Most of this is no matter," I say. "Tabat is in chaos, has been for some weeks now."

"I know that," Ruhua says. "I have had messenger birds that came before the port was destroyed. But now that ... that thing is on its way to Tabat, and the Duke does not know to react."

"If I knew a way up there, faster than any ship, and agreed to take you by that road as well, would it build some amity between us?" I say.

"You are exiled. It is illegal for you to go back to Tabat."

"The government that exiled me is tattered, if not torn apart entirely, and so such considerations are not foremost in my mind," I tell her. "You wish to warn the Duke, to prepare him? I can take you with me, but we must go, and go soon."

She is reluctant, I can tell. She does not trust me, and with good reason. And truth be told, I am not sure how the Dragon will react to her, for she has slain more than one of Bruna's kind over the years.

But now we have a common foe, all three of us, in the form of a Tabatian girl given unthinkable powers, and able to change the world in ways that none of us desire.

Some ancient magic, stirred from a place where it should have slept, now coupled with the pettiness of a wronged child. She is flying towards Tabat even now, and we do not have long to catch up.

"We have a chance," I say, watching Ruhua, "but not if you kill me now."

CHAPTER 47

(LUCY)

*L*ucy felt the city on the edges of her consciousness long before she saw it. Teo was lying on his back, watching the clouds float by. She nudged him in the ribs.

"We're almost there," she said. The late morning sun beat down on the ocean, making it a dazzling sheet of silver underneath them. The brightness forced Teo to keep his eyes shielded from it, but Lucy felt no such need. She wasn't sure her flesh was capable of being hurt by such small things anymore.

By now, she wasn't even really sure where the fleshly part of her left off and the magical part began. They had seeped together, until she was Lucy sometimes Obedience and also part of some larger, vaster thing that found her insignificant and annoying for the most part but was willing enough to go along with her desires, as long as they involved destroying things.

She liked destroying things. When you unmade them in a certain way, it tasted like cookies, like waking up after a delicious night's sleep, like water when you were so hot and thirsty that you thought you might die of it. If they were alive, they tasted better, but she still felt a little bad about the ones that were smarter than the others, so she had confined herself to fish and a few whales on their journey here.

She floated a hundred feet or so above the water, Teo at her side, a few inches back. By now he had lost all unease about dangling in nothingness, although he still had trouble with his limbs. He wasn't talking at the moment; they had exhausted all conversation. He looked to be still drowsing.

She slowed her pace. From here she could see Tabat more clearly: the terraces, interrupted by canals coming down the mountain side like an enormous staircase, wider than it was tall, the eastern side sliding away into one mouth of the Northstretch river, bordered on the other side by the purple marshes and beach lands. The western side hunching upward into the pinnacle where the Duke's castle perched, hanging above the waterfall that was the Northstretch's western outlet, overlooking the city.

The harbor was full of boats, big-bellied Merchant galleons swollen with cargo coming in and going back along with two big naval men-o-war as well as smaller ships ranging down to tiny pinnacles and rowboats going back and forth between some larger ships and the docks.

She could not see the people from here, but she could sense them, could feel the press of their minds, could feel their life force. So many of them.

Teo said, "What are you going to do?"

She considered the distant vista. She would not sneak in, pretending to be something milder than she was, although there was a certain appeal to that idea, to showing up to Adelina and her family and letting them welcome her back (surely they would, she told herself) and then enacting all her schemes. But that would be only a small part of her plans overall. She had this power now, and so she would rule Tabat. The Duke had had his time, after all, and whoever had been elected, well, they would just have to resign themselves to being unelected.

Still, she didn't know the limits of her power yet. She had consumed the Dragon almost effortlessly, but not entirely—there had definitely been some sort of expenditure in that action, and she was not sure yet whether or not it was one of the self-replenishing kind, the sort of thing that came back with enough rest.

Her opponents in the city would be the Duke's peacekeepers and whatever soldiers garrisoned inside the city. And there would be other groups, like the College of Mages, thoughts of whom kept plaguing her. She wondered what the only Mage she had known so far, Merchant Mage Sebastiano, would have thought of her transformation. She thought he might have approved—he seemed the sort to root for the underdog, despite his refusing to help her get admitted to the College of Mages, and she had definitely been an underdog.

A nasty little thought bubbled up from somewhere, *But you're not the underdog anymore.*

This was all taking too long. She'd start from the top and work her way down.

She decided to land atop the stone gate that guarded the castle's main courtyard, wide enough to hold three wagons abreast, topped with two stone towers and a walkway that accommodated two soldiers walking side by side, who stared up at her as she descended. Neither brandished their weapon. If anything, they looked amused by her presence.

She floated down to let her bare feet settle on the stone. They watched in silence as she landed. Teo said nothing; when she glanced sideways at him, she saw that his eyes were wide with fear. This was the place where he had first been the dog, been forced into that alternate form and filled with despair for his future.

One soldier, an older woman, said, "This is not the place for playing games, child. Are you two of the student mages? You should know better than to try out your flying here."

She flicked her hand and the soldier fell away into gray ash, sifting down onto the stones between them. The second soldier gasped and pulled his sword. Before she could say anything to warn him off, he rushed her, and she gestured again with the same result. Teo inhaled sharply.

There were shouts from down in the courtyard and she could hear the sound of people running up the stairs.

Well, that was answered easily enough. She floated herself and

Teo back up into the air, then downward in a long slant that landed them on the front steps of the castle. There were guards there, but she dissolved them all before they even had a chance to react.

The front doors of the castle slammed open.

The last days of Tabat began.

ACKNOWLEDGMENTS

Writing is solitary, but it's fueled by connections. Tabat would not exist without them. Here's some shout-outs to people who have stoked the fire with extra fuel.

My first readers—Terra LeMay, Aurelia Pitchstone, Sandy Swirsky, and Ziv Wittles, who read bravely in the face of incoherency.

My Chez Rambo co-working group but particularly Jennifer Brozek, Kris Dikeman, Margaret Dunlap, Mark Engleson, Terry Gene, Aynjel Kaye, Jane Pinckard, P.J. Manney, Xander Odell, Frances Rowat, Rosie Smith, and Joanna Weston.

All of the members of the Chez Rambo community, which keeps me sane and connected.

My editor, the inimitable Kevin J. Anderson, who always writes "yum!" in the margins of the food scenes.

My mother, who continues to push me on her book group as well as make helpful suggestions, both in the best possible way.

My spouse and partner in pandemic isolation, Wayne, who might know the world of Tabat as well as I do.

ABOUT THE AUTHOR

Cat Rambo lives, writes, and teaches somewhere in the Pacific Northwest. Their 200+ fiction publications include stories in *Asimov's Science Fiction*, *Clarkesworld Magazine*, and *The Magazine of Fantasy and Science Fiction*. Their most recent works are Nebula Award winner *Carpe Glitter* (Meerkat Press) and ongoing serial novella *Baby Driver*. Forthcoming are space opera *You Sexy Thing* (Tor Macmillan, 2021) and the conclu-

sion to the Tabat Quartet, *Gods of Tabat* (WordFire Press, 2022).

http://www.kittywumpus.net

facebook.com/catrambo
twitter.com/Catrambo

IF YOU LIKED ...

IF YOU LIKED *EXILES OF TABAT*, YOU MIGHT ALSO ENJOY:

Rise of the First World
by Christopher Katava

Oshenerth
by Alan Dean Foster

The Saga of Seven Suns, Veiled Alliances
by Kevin J. Anderson

OTHER WORDFIRE PRESS TITLES BY CAT RAMBO

Beasts of Tabat
Hearts of Tabat

Our list of other WordFire Press authors and titles is always growing. To find out more and to shop our selection of titles, visit us at:
wordfirepress.com

facebook.com/WordfireIncWordfirePress
twitter.com/WordFirePress
instagram.com/WordFirePress
bookbub.com/profile/4109784512

CPSIA information can be obtained
at www.ICGtesting.com
Printed in the USA
BVHW081757040521
606416BV00002B/140